Black Love, White Lies:

A BWWM Romance

Black Love, White Lies:

A BWWM Romance

Genesis Woods

www.urbanbooks.net

Urban Books, LLC
97 N 18th Street
Wyandanch, NY 11798

ISBN 13: 978-1-62286-794-3
ISBN 10: 1-62286-794-7

First Mass Market Printing December 2016
Printed in the United States of America

10 9 8 7 6 5 4 3 2 1

Distributed by Kensington Publishing Corp.
Submit Orders to:
Customer Service
400 Hahn Road
Westminster, MD 21157-4627
Phone: 1-800-733-3000
Fax: 1-800-659-2436

1

Audrielle

"Your total with tax is one fifty-seven eighty-five, ma'am. Will you be paying with cash, credit, or debit?"

I smiled at the young hostess and gave her my debit card. I had about an hour to get home and set up the romantic night I had planned for my boyfriend, Antonio. He loved the T-bone steak at Ruth's Chris Steak House, so I drove all the way to Beverly Hills to get our dinner. I went all out too. Along with his steak, I ordered potatoes lyonnaise and creamed spinach as his sides. For an appetizer, we'd eat the sizzling blue crab cakes and lobster bisque. For my entree, I went with the shrimp and grits, the same thing I had every time I went there. Then for dessert, I ordered crème brulée for him and the bread pudding with whiskey sauce for me.

Today was our two-year anniversary, and I wanted to make our night special. A smile spread across my face as I thought about the day our paths crossed.

I had met Antonio Smith about two and a half years earlier, when he came into one of the custom shoe and apparel stores my sister and I owned and operated. As soon as his tall, six foot three frame walked into the store, my breath caught in my throat. I'd never seen a man so gorgeous or perfect in my life. It was as if he had walked straight out of a magazine. His smooth, hazelnut-colored skin looked sexy as hell in the white V-neck T-shirt he wore. The wash on his Rock Revival jeans was the style I loved to see men wear. His all-white Forces looked as if they were fresh out of the box, while his neatly-trimmed lineup looked as if he'd just gotten out of the barber's chair.

I couldn't help but think, *If this man looks this damn good dressed down, I'd probably die and go to heaven if I ever see him dressed up.*

Once I got all of my ogling and fantasy sex scenes out of my mind, I finally approached him. "Hey, welcome to Kick Biz! I'm Audri. Did you need any help today?"

God, that's the wackest greeting ever.

He finally turned around after putting an exclusive pair of Air Jordans back on the stand.

"I actually do need some help . . ."

"Audri!" I told him with the biggest smile on my face. I pushed my hand out, and he took it.

Hmm, nice and firm. I love a man with a great handshake.

"Okay, Audri." He released our connection. "My man's having this big birthday party for his born day this weekend, and I wanted to lace him with something out of his norm. He's the clean cut preppy type, always wearing slacks and loafers." He laughed.

Oh my God! Are those dimples?

"I wanted to get him some fresh kicks for a change."

I was stuck for a moment, still mesmerized by the natural indentation in his cheeks. When I finally decided to respond, "Dimples" was what came out of my mouth. His eyebrow shot up, and a look of confusion registered on his face.

Oh Lord, I'm so embarrassed now! Where the hell is Ari so that I can go jump off of the bridge already?

I was just about to turn around to go and bury my head in something when he laughed, and the prettiest set of white teeth were put on display. "Uh, yeah, I have dimples." He stepped closer to me. "Is that a problem . . . Audri?" he asked with a raised eyebrow.

Gathering up all the strength I had left inside of me, I responded. "No! Not at all. Look, can we start all over? I'm sorry for being so unprofessional." I shook my head to get back into owner mode and extended my hand again. "Hi, I'm Audri, and welcome to Kick Biz! How can I help you today?"

He walked more into my personal space and lowered his mouth to my ear. "First, you can get me the new Jordans in a size eleven, no customization needed. Then you can accompany me to my man's party this weekend, followed by breakfast Sunday morning if you don't have any other plans."

When he stepped back and looked into my eyes, it was like I got fascinated all over again. I would be considered deaf, dumb, and blind if I hadn't noticed the attraction he had for me. Hell, if I didn't know it at first, I damn sure knew it now. The way his eyes roamed up and down my size twenty body made me shiver a little. When he licked his lips and smirked, I almost came on myself.

"So?" he asked. "Am I going to have the finest woman I've ever met on my arm this weekend, or do I have to go alone?"

He didn't have to ask me twice. Of course, I took him up on his offer, and we'd been together ever since.

"I'm sorry, ma'am, but your card was declined. Would you like to try another one?" the little waitress said, snapping me out of my thoughts.

Hmmm. That's weird. I just deposited money in our joint account a few days ago.

"Can you try this one?" I asked as I handed her my credit card. She slid the second option and waited. A minute later, a piece of paper started to print out from the register. I went to grab my to go bags but was halted.

"I'm sorry"—she looked at my card—"Audrielle, but this card has been declined as well."

What the hell!

"Maybe you wanna try another card or order something cheaper. . . ." she said as her voice trailed off.

I gave her a heated glance but kept my mouth shut. I was too upset to even check her on what she'd said. I had bigger things to worry about anyway. Damnit! I reached back into my purse for my wallet and pulled out my company credit card. I knew this one would not be declined. I handed the rude hostess the platinum card and took out my phone. I needed to log into my bank accounts and see what the fuck was going on.

2

Cairo

"Fuuuck! I swear I'ma kill this ho, Cai," Finesse screamed as he barged into my room.

"What happened now, bruh?"

"The crazy bitch slashed all of my tires and threw a brick through my windshield. I go to the manager and ask if I could see the footage from this morning because I knew it was her, and the motherfucker says I needed a police report or some shit." He plopped down in the chair next to me. "I promise when I catch up with her, I'ma knock fire from her ass, man!"

"How do you know she did it? You don't have any proof, and let's keep it real, man; you've fucked over a lot of chicks. There's no telling who it might be," I said, laughing.

"Oh, I know for sure it's her."

"How?"

"Because she's the only psycho bitch I've been dealing with for the last few months. That's why!"

I lay back in my chair and continued to flip through the channels on the TV as my brother went on and on about the crazy chick he met at some party months ago, had a one night stand with, and who is now possibly having his baby. All I could do was shake my head at this fool. I don't know how many times he'd been told to start thinking with his head and not with his dick. Finesse was the type of man who tooted and booted women constantly, but because of his carelessness, he was having to buy new sets of tires almost every month.

"Man, do you hear me talking to you?" he asked as he nudged my arm. "I need to use your AAA so that I can have my car towed to Kong's shop."

"Oh, hell naw. You've used my shit so much that I have to pay for towing now. You better call Kong and see if someone can come get it for you."

"You're supposed to be my keeper, Cai. You can't do this for me one last time?"

"You said that three times ago. Call Mama Faye and ask her if you can use hers."

He just shook his head and waved his hand. I knew after that statement, he'd get to calling Kong. Calling Mama Faye to ask for help in regards to his car was a no-no. He knew he'd have to listen to an hour-long lecture in her deep Jamaican accent before she even decided whether she would help him.

He hung up his phone and turned to me. "All right, wigga, I'm out."

"Ah, dude, what I tell you about calling me that dumb shit?" Just because I was a Caucasian man who was raised by a black woman and around black people did not make me a white nigga, or "wigga," as he would sometimes say. He knew I really hated that word. Yeah, sometimes "nigga" came out of my mouth. Somewhere, somehow, and some way, society changed the word from meaning ignorant to being used as a term of endearment. Finesse and the dudes we hung around didn't mind me saying it. I'm not going to front; I used the word in my daily vocabulary when I was growing up, and I still did. I just limited who I said it around. I'd been in a few fights because a black man didn't like the fact that a white man was saying it.

"My bad, Cairo. I apologize for calling you a wigga. I forgot how sensitive you can be." He gave me a pound then a brotherly hug. "I'm out, though. I'll call you in a few to come get me after I drop the car off."

"All right, bruh," I said as I closed my front door and went back to watching nothing on TV.

3

Audrielle

I had finally made it to my home after being embarrassed, insulted, and pissed off all at the same time. When I pulled up in my driveway, I noticed Antonio's car already parked. I wasn't shocked to see it there because he always got home a couple of hours before me. The fact that I left work two hours early and still managed to be late was why I was so upset.

I grabbed my purse, his gift, and the Ruth's Chris bags and hurried into the house. By now, the food was good and cold, so I knew I'd have to reheat it while I set the table.

I went straight to the kitchen to get started after making sure my car and front door were locked. When I took the food out of the bags, the containers were still a little warm, but not enough. I popped a few trays in the microwave and headed toward the dining room. After setting the table, I changed out the food in the microwave and warmed up my dinner. I didn't have time to hop in the shower, so I just went to the bathroom and refreshed my makeup and hair.

"Antonio!" I yelled as I placed our plates full of food on the table.

When he didn't answer after the second time, I decided to look for him. As I got closer to our room, I could hear the faint sound of "Let's Lay Together" by the Isley Brothers playing through my Bose speakers.

I opened the door and smiled at the scene before me. My baby had candles lit all around the room, making it glow. There was a tray of chocolate dipped strawberries, which were my favorite, sitting on the nightstand beside the bed. The champagne in the ice bucket had already been opened, with the glass he drank from sitting right beside it.

I guess he got thirsty waiting on me. I laughed to myself. When I stepped into the room, the soft feel of the rose petals caressed the bottom of my feet. *Pink roses are one of my favorites.*

I followed the love trail toward the bathroom. When I heard the water from the shower pouring down, I took off my clothes.

Damn, what about the food? I thought. *Oh, well. I'll just have to reheat it after I sex my man down. It's been a few weeks since we made love, and I need to feel him inside of me bad.*

Once I pinned my hair up and was completely naked, I walked into the bathroom. Antonio had the water so hot that the glass doors on the shower were damn near impossible to see through. It was so steamy in there; I could only see the outline of his muscular frame, and I instantly got heated. This man was sexy as hell and had the body of a god. Just thinking about his broad shoulders, impeccable pecs, defined abs, and muscular tone overall had me wet. I walked up to the door and put my hand on the handle, bracing myself for the glorious sight I would soon be looking upon. However, before I could even crack the door open, two small feminine palms pressed against the glass, smearing the fogginess.

What the fuck?

I swung the door open and was hit with the most horrifying scene I'd ever witnessed in my life. I slowly started to back out of the bathroom, knocking over any and everything in my path. I kept shaking my head, trying to will myself not to cry, but the hurt and betrayal was just too much for me. This was just like my previous relationship with my first love, Eli Blake, all over again. My body started to shake as the tears streamed down my face.

"Audri!" Antonio yelled as he hopped out of the shower and searched for a towel.

I turned around on my heels and ran as fast as I could to my closet to find something to throw on. I needed to get the fuck out of there.

When I entered my bedroom, everything I didn't notice the first time stuck out like a sore thumb this time. The candles were so low, which could only mean that they'd been burning for a while. The chocolate covered strawberries on the nightstand were half eaten. The other glass sitting next to the champagne bottle was empty, but the lipstick stains on the rim revealed someone other than me had drunk from it. I even recognized something was off with the music. When we had sex, we always set Pandora on the Mint Condition or Jodeci station. When I looked at the screen on the iPad, I saw that someone had switched it to Howard Hewitt.

"Audri, please. Let me explain," Antonio said as he reached for my shoulder.

I pulled away from his touch and backed away from him.

"For two years, Antonio—two fucking years!— I've given you my heart, body, mind, and soul"— my lips trembled—"just for you to pay me back like this!"

"Audri, please, it's not what you think. I was waiting for you to come home. I wanted to surprise you for our anniversary, but then she—"

I cut him off. "Well, happy anniversary to me, huh?" I put on the rest of my jumpsuit. "If this is how you love me, I surely wouldn't like to see how you hate me."

"Audrielle, stop being so damn dramatic. Antonio and I have been seeing each other for a while now."

I cut my eyes at this bitch who had the nerve to address me, and shook my head in disgust. What the fuck do you need friends for when family can do you worse than anyone else?

I looked at Antonio with tears in my eyes, waiting for some sort of explanation, but he just turned his head and looked at everything but me.

"It's about time you found out anyway. This little charade has gone on long enough," this bitch coolly said as she fully came out of the bathroom, tying my robe around her body.

"Did you really think that a man who looked like this could fall for a girl like you?" She sighed. "Be serious, honey. We hired him to get you back on track and to get your self-esteem back up. When that ex of yours packed up and left, you just let yourself go. Gaining weight, dropping out of school, and not taking care of business."

She shook her head. "We thought that if you got back into the dating world, you'd get yourself together. And after a year of being in this relationship, you did. Antonio here was supposed to come up with some way to break it off with you, but he didn't. Something about catching feelings and really liking you. Of course, I didn't believe that shit, because he faithfully cashed those checks we were giving him every month.

"Anyways, about six months ago, Antonio came to me for some financial help because it seems he has a big problem with gambling."

I shook my head because that explained the missing money from our joint and personal accounts, which caused my card to decline.

She continued. "Since we weren't paying him to date you anymore, he needed to get the money somehow, and having sex with me is what he did. Oh, and sweetie, I must say, you were right. He is a beast in those sheets."

I lunged at that bitch, but Antonio caught me before I got close to her. I was mad as fuck. This shit was so embarrassing. I needed to get out of there, and get out fast. I shrugged from his hold and started for the door. Before I left, though, I needed her to answer one question for me.

"When you say *we* paid, who are you referring to?"

She smirked. "Well, myself and my sister, of course. You know, your mother."

To say I was beyond hurt was an understatement. My mother and I didn't have the best relationship, but to hear that she paid someone to date me totally crushed my soul. I knew my mother always talked about my weight and how I needed to lose about seventy or eighty pounds, but damn, to totally humiliate me was crazy.

I rushed down the stairs, grabbed my keys and purse, and headed out the door. There was only one place I was headed, and she better pray I didn't totally lose it on her ass.

4

Cairo

"Mama Faye! Where you at?" I yelled as I walked through the front door of the home I grew up in. Everything was still the same as it was almost fifteen years ago, with the Jamaican flag hanging on the wall behind the couch and everything.

I walked through the living room and into the kitchen, hoping to find Mama Faye, but she wasn't there. I searched the rest of the house just to come up with the same results. When I called her name again, there was still no response.

Where can you be, lady? I asked myself as I dialed her cell phone number. I knew she was there because her car was out in the front, and the mail had already been placed on the dining room table.

The loud, generic ringtone that echoed throughout the kitchen caught my attention. I looked over near the cutting board and saw the screen lighting up. There were two chayotes lying on the cutting board, cut in half with the middles already scooped out. Just by looking at the rest of the ingredients lined on the counter, I knew Mama Faye was about to make her famous stuffed cho-cho. My mouth instantly started to water, just thinking about the goodness that would be ready in about thirty minutes.

"Don't just stand there, boi. Help an old lady with this," my mom said as she walked in through the back door with a basket full of herbs and more chayote from her garden.

I grabbed the basket from her hands and placed it in the sink. After I turned on the cold water, I went to the fridge and poured her a glass of pine juice.

"You staying for dinner, or are you just stopping by?"

"I'll stay for dinner, but I gotta go pick up Finesse when he gives me a call."

"Pick up Finesse? Oh, Lord. What done happened to mi boi now? I swear him just like his father. All these women and millions of problems," she said as she went back to chopping up stuff on the cutting board. I could tell she was starting to become mad, because whenever she did, her accent would become thick as hell.

My mother and I had a close relationship, and we talked about everything, so when I told her about Finesse's latest slashing, she just laughed at his misfortune.

"That boi der ain't neva gon' learn until them girl kill him dead. I don't know how many times mi got to tell him to stop playing with dem girls' hearts."

"Yeah, me too," I said as I rubbed my hand down my face. I looked up and saw my mother staring at me.

She shook her head. "So how are you?"

"I'm fine, Ma. I just gotta get my mind right for the game I have in a few days. I need to go buy some new shoes."

She looked down at my feet. "What's the matter with dem shoe you got on?"

"I can't play in these, Mama Faye!" I said as I looked down at the Nike Air Max I had on. "I'd break my ankles in these. I have to wear high tops playing basketball."

She lifted her chin. "What about that head? You need your locs twisted again."

I touched the roots of my hair and could feel the new growth that was coming in. Sometimes I liked being a white boy with dreads because of the attention I would get. Other times I thought about shaving them all off because I got tired of hearing how I "wanted to be black."

"Come on back to mi room so I can hook you up. 'Bout time mi finish, dinner should be ready."

An hour later, we were seated at the table enjoying a big bowl of oxtail stew and some stuffed cho-cho. Finesse, who showed up about twenty minutes before dinner, was chowing down on the food as well. When Mama Faye asked him how he got there, he said another one of his female friends picked him up instead and dropped him off.

"Ness, you need be more careful with dem girls. I don't want mi grandson to be found in a ditch somewhere."

"I know, Ma. It's just Rima's crazy ass. Who knew one night of pleasure could lead up to a lifetime of pain? I don't even know if I'm the baby daddy yet, and she's already making my life a living hell."

We all shared a laugh after he confessed that.

Changing the subject, I asked, "What you got going for tomorrow?"

"Shit, nothing right now besides work. After that I'm free. Why? What's up?"

"I wanna go check out that new custom shoe store in Fairfax. A lot of my teammates say they have a nice selection of kicks in there."

"I'm game," he said. "What time you wanna—"

Before he could finish what he was saying, a loud bang, followed by some glass shattering, caught all of our attention.

"What the hell?" Finesse and I both said at the same time.

When we walked to the front door, my blood immediately started to boil.

"You gotta be fucking kidding me, dude! For real, Finesse, you need to get this bitch under control. Now she fucking up my shit behind your stupid ass!" I shouted as I walked around my car, assessing the damage that was just done.

"Man, I'm sorry. I don't even know how she knew I was here. Better yet, I don't even know why she would damage your car." He looked like he was in deep thought for a moment. "Shit! I forgot I told her I had two cars. She seen me in your shit a few times, and must've assumed it was mine."

"Nigga, you don't have two cars! Look at my shit!" I screamed in his face.

"Man, I'm sorry. I'll pay for all the damages. We'll just call Kong in the morning to come and pick your car up." He turned to Mama Faye. "Is it okay if we use your car for a bit tomorrow, Ma?"

"Hell no!" she said before she started going off in her Jamaican tongue. I couldn't understand everything she was saying, but I'd been around her long enough to know that she said something about a stupid idiot and hurting this crazy bitch.

5

Audrielle

My tires came to a screeching halt as I pulled into my parents' driveway. The back and forth swaying of the blinds told me that my mother had already peeked out of the window.

As soon as I stepped on the porch, she opened the door with the biggest smile on her face. Her golden brown skin was flawless. The long flow of spiral curls in her hair accentuated her round face. With hardly any makeup on, my mother could easily pass for my sister, but the wrinkles that started to form around her face told that truth. Her amber-colored eyes dimmed a little when she finally noticed the upset expression I had on my face.

Sensing there was some sort of problem on the rise, she raised her French manicured nails, which she got done on a weekly basis, to the medium-sized pearl necklace around her neck and started to twist it. It was something she always seemed to do whenever she was nervous.

"Audrielle, darling, we weren't ex—"

"Is it true?" I asked, cutting her off. I didn't have time for that fake pleasantry bullshit.

She looked behind her, I guess trying to locate my father's whereabouts. Her face turned back to me with a nervous gaze.

"Audrielle, sweetie, what are you—"

"Is . . . it . . . true?" This time, I yelled a bit louder as I stepped through the foyer.

"Audri? What's wrong, baby?" My father's deep voice boomed from the top of the stairs.

"Ask your wife."

He looked at my mom as he proceeded down the stairs. "What's going on, baby? Why is Audrielle screaming at the top of her lungs?"

My mom looked at me with pleading eyes. I could tell she wanted to discuss the situation at hand without my father's involvement. She knew that once he heard what she'd been up to, he'd put her on punishment, which meant no weekly nail appointments, shopping trips, or going to the beauty salon. I didn't care or give a fuck about any of that shit, though. To keep it real, that was part of the problem now. My mother believed that in order to be accepted into today's society or certain circles, you had to look and act a certain way. Although I was pretty in the face, my voluptuous and curvy size twenty frame was a problem for her. A day never passed without her mentioning some sort of diet she'd heard about or some workout DVD she seen on TV.

My father finally reached the part of the foyer where we were standing. I looked up at my father and just admired the man before me. In my eyes, he was the epitome of black men everywhere. A great family man, highly educated, and a pillar in the community who just happened to love the hell out of me was the best way to quickly describe my father. A very handsome man indeed, his chocolate skin blended well with his coffee-colored eyes. My father didn't work out as much as he used to, but you could tell that he still had a nice body underneath his clothes. The low cut fade he sported was neatly trimmed, and the salt-and-pepper goatee around his lips was lined just right. I used to hate the way my friend's mother or the women at our church used to throw themselves at him whenever my mother was out of earshot. Although she and I weren't as close as we should have been, I still thought that they were the perfect couple.

"Is somebody gonna tell me what the hell is going on?" he asked, looking from me to my mother.

Since she didn't take it upon herself to enlighten my father with what she and her whore of a sister had done, I decided to make the pleasure all mine. I looked into my father's eyes and told him about everything my aunt and Antonio told me, not leaving out one single detail.

When I finished telling the story, I looked at my mother, who had her head down with tears in her eyes. My father's nose was flaring. He shook his head from side to side as he intently looked down at my mother.

"Honey Bee," he said, calling me by the nickname he'd given me as a child, "please know and believe that had I known what your mother and her trifling-ass sister were up to, I would have stopped it before it even started." He turned his attention toward me and his eyes softened. "Audrielle, you are very beautiful girl, and don't you let anyone, including the woman who gave birth to you, tell you any different."

My mom tried to say something, but he gave her the coldest look, making her snap her mouth shut.

"Do you remember what I told you the night of your junior prom when that knucklehead Andrew Fielder stood you up?"

I nodded my head as a tear escaped my eye.

"And what was that?" he asked, lifting my chin.

"Whether average, big, or small, I can and will have it all. And once I start to believe that, everyone else will too."

By this time, tears were steadily rolling down my cheeks, and my father grabbed me into his arms and hugged me.

"Now that we've got that out of the way, I want you to get back into your car, drive back over to the house that you bought, kick that nigga and his shit out, and then go on with your life. Don't let anyone, including family," he said, side-eyeing my mom, "take your joy away." He kissed me on my forehead and proceeded back up the stairs he'd just came down from a few minutes ago.

"Oh, and before I forget, your mother will be over there within the next hour to help you with cleaning your house out and to apologize." And with that, his six-foot-six frame disappeared into my parents' bedroom.

I was kind of surprised when my mom walked over and wrapped me in her arms. I wanted to hug her back, but the anger I had at that moment wouldn't allow me to. Before she could say anything, I retracted from her embrace and headed out the door.

I got into my car and put the keys into the ignition, but didn't start it. I let down all of the windows and let the warm night breeze brush against my face.

"Two months!" I heard my mother scream at the top of her lungs.

A small smile slowly crossed my face.

"That's right, Daddy, punish her ass!" I said as I finally started my car and drove off.

Two months of her allowance being cut off served her trifling ass right. What kind of mother does that to her daughter? Although the punishment my father gave my mother did little to mend my broken heart, it helped to heal it a little bit. Knowing that she wouldn't be getting pampered for sixty days was just enough for me. Since my mother was all about appearance, it was going to kill her to not be put together from head to toe. I made a mental note to call my father and thank him for having my back as always. Right now, however, I had a date with a gallon of pistachio ice cream and some Lorna Doone cookies before I started to get Antonio's shit out of my house.

6

Cairo

A couple of days had passed, and I was finally on my way to pick up my car. Not only did Finesse's crazy-ass baby mama bust out all of my windows, but she put some white powdery substance in my gas tank. Kong said it wasn't granulated sugar, but more like powdered sugar. Because we had run outside when we did, she wasn't able to put enough inside to damage anything, so all he had to do was drain the gas then clean out any residue that didn't mix with the oil.

Mama Faye was beyond pissed and wasn't talking to Finesse behind it either. He was trying to act as if her silence wasn't affecting him, but I knew better than that.

"So what did the police say when you made the report?" I asked Ness as we drove down the highway headed toward Kong's auto shop.

He blew out a frustrated breath. "Man, that bitch is going to be the death of me. When I got down to the station to make a report and get some type of restraining order on her, the officer told me there was already a restraining order in the system filed by her against me. Do you know how stupid I felt at that moment? I couldn't do anything but laugh. Muthafuckas were walking by and looking at me like I was crazy."

"So what did you do?"

"Shit, I still made the report and filed the restraining order against her. The officer informed me that it would really help my case if I were able to get her on video damaging my property or harassing me."

"Well, that won't be hard."

He shook his head. "Not at all. Rod hit me last night and told me that the case had been assigned to one of his partners, so I know his boy won't let me down. When that crazy bitch comes around the next time trying to fuck up my shit, I got something for that ass."

We pulled up in front of the auto shop and got out. One of Kong's employees had just finished detailing the inside of my car when we stepped into the lobby.

True to his word, Finesse paid for all of the damages. He even filled my tank up and splurged

on a few cans of that cherry car freshener I
liked. We sat around and chopped it up with our
childhood friend, Demetrian "Kong" Stewart, for
about an hour or two before we decided to head
over to the shoe store I was telling Finesse about
a couple of days ago.

"Ay, man, how did you hear about this spot
again?" Ness asked as we got out of our cars and
headed toward the store.

"A few dudes on the team were telling me
about this place. They said the shoes were dope,
and the clothing was off the chain."

Walking past the storefront, I could see that
my teammates weren't lying about this spot's
dopeness. I became more impressed by the
setup that was visible as we walked in front
of the establishment. One half of the window
display would be any baller's dream, while the
other half catered to men who were into fashion
and name brand shit like Tru Religion or Levi's.
On the side that had my attention, there was an
open black Jordan shoe storage box with almost
every pair of *J*s there ever was. Next to that was
the red Nike shoe storage box, which was lined
up with Kobes, Hyperdunks, LeBrons, and any
hot basketball shoe you could name. Different
colored basketball shorts and shirts hung loosely
over the mannequins in a stylish yet athletic way,

while basketballs were strategically hanging from the ceiling. The more I looked around, the more excited I became to go inside.

"Hello and welcome to Kick Biz," a pretty, brown-skinned chick said. "I'm Ariana. How can I help you today?"

I looked over at my brother, who had his tongue hanging out and that predator-stalking-its-prey look in his eye. From her long, dark hair to the shapely body in the Nike women's jumpsuit, this girl was Finesse's type hands down. She stood around five foot nine, which was kind of tall for a girl, but with Ness being six foot three, it wouldn't be a problem if she wore heels.

Clearing my throat, I extended my hand and greeted her. "Hey, Ariana, I'm Cairo, and this speechless dude staring at you like that is my brother, Finesse."

She looked from me then to him with a slight frown on her face.

"We have different dads," I said, causing her to laugh. I was used to people giving Finesse and me weird looks when we introduced each other as brothers. With me being white and him being black, we usually got that kind of response.

"My bad. I hope I didn't offend you," she offered up with a smile. "To be honest, I was trying to figure out what your race was, especially after you said that you two were brothers. You look white, but then again, you could just be a real bright black dude with neatly twisted dirty blond dreads."

It was my turn to laugh now. "Naw, you good. But to answer your question, I'm white. I was adopted into the family." I said, nodding my head toward Finesse, who was still sitting and staring at Ariana like a dog to a bone.

"That's cool. I don't think I've ever met a white boy with dreads. I like it, though. It fits your face." She looked me up and down then added, "And your style."

I subconsciously looked down at myself. I didn't know how she got what type of style I was into from what I was wearing. I mean, I had on some Abercrombie khaki shorts with a Varsity graphic shirt, my black Nike swoosh slides, and white socks. Half of my dreads were hanging in the back, while the other half was pulled into a bun. Maybe the word *frugal* popped in her head when she looked at me. Other than that, I was lost.

Before I could get a chance to ask her what she meant, my phone vibrated in my pocket. Looking at the screen, my head instantly started to pound when Alexandria's name and face flashed a few times. I wanted to decline the call, but I knew she'd keep calling until I answered. I didn't even know why she was still calling me. I had told her months ago that whatever we had or planned on having was over. For some reason, she figured that I'd eventually get over her betrayal and come running back to her because of who her family was, but she seriously had another thing coming if she thought that about me. Rich or poor, well off or just okay, I didn't know any man who would stay with a woman he couldn't trust as far as he could throw her. My phone started ringing for a second time, so I excused myself from the conversation Ness and Ariana were now having.

"Hello!" I answered my phone.

Silence. I shook my head. This was why I didn't like answering her calls.

"Hello!" I said again, a little more forcefully.

"Cai, it's me. Please don't hang up."

I pinched the bridge of my nose and blew out a breath. "What is it now, Alex?"

7

Audrielle

God, my life sucks right now.

Hell, who was I kidding? My life had sucked ever since the doctor told my mother that I was a girl.

I sat in my king size bed, wrapped up in my 3,000 thread count Egyptian cotton sheets, watching the *Twilight* saga for the umpteenth time within the last few days. I didn't know what it was about this movie, but it had me in my feelings every time. Maybe it was the undying love Bella and Edward, the teenage vampire, had for one another that I longed to have one day, or maybe it was the unconditional love Jacob, the werewolf, had for Bella before and after she became a vampire. Whatever it was, I wanted it and still believed that it would happen for me in the future.

My house phone ringing broke me from my train of thought. I knew it was my mother because she was the only one who called that phone before she called my cell. I really didn't want to talk to her, so I let the voice mail pick up. Ever since that day my father made her come over to my house to apologize for what she and her sister had done to me, she'd been trying to bond for some reason. Maybe if this were about fifteen years ago, I would've welcomed any affection or bonding from my mother with open arms, but now that I was older and understood what this sudden wanting to bond was about, I knew better.

I looked at the alarm clock on my nightstand and sighed at the time. It was only eleven o'clock on a Friday morning, and I didn't have shit to do. I had called out from work for the fifth day in a row and didn't give a shit. It wasn't like I could get fired anyway. I knew my sister could handle everything because she saw me do it a thousand times before. Besides, if she had any questions or needed some help, I was only a phone call away.

The picture Antonio and I had taken on our trip to the Temecula Wine Valley was still sitting on the nightstand on his side of the bed. I don't know how I'd missed it when I was burning all of our other pictures in the trash can the day before.

The smile on his face looked so genuine and real. Too bad it was all a load of crap. I rolled over to the other side of my bed and picked up the expensive-ass Tiffany frame he had picked out and hurled it at the wall. That shit made a loud bang then broke into a million pieces. Hopefully, that was the last reminder of him that I had in my house.

Finally deciding to get out of my bed, I headed to the bathroom to wash my face and brush my teeth. It had been three whole days since I had even been inside of my bathroom other than to pee, and I needed to get my hygiene back in order. When I looked at myself in the mirror, I almost didn't recognize the person staring back at me. My thick black hair that I usually kept flat-ironed and bone straight was in its natural curly and kinky state. My eyebrows and upper lip needed a serious waxing. My face was dry and ashy. Then to add more to that, I had bags the size of carry-on luggage under my eyes. I looked bad.

I turned to my side and examined my full-figured frame. If I didn't know any better, I'd say I had lost a few pounds. In the last couple of days, I'd been on a diet of Club House crackers and wine. It wasn't the healthiest way to go, but at least I was eating and drinking something.

I looked at the tortilla flap above my coochie. Although it seemed as if it had gotten a few inches smaller, it was still noticeable. I didn't really have a gut, but a few months of sit-ups would probably work wonders and make that little thing totally disappear.

After finishing my bathroom regimen, I headed toward the kitchen. I needed to make a list of the items to get when I went grocery shopping and to the bank later on. Because all of the food that was in the fridge was that healthy shit Antonio used to eat during the week, I threw all of that mess out. Now my poor fridge was just as bare as my heart.

The house phone rang again, and I rolled my eyes. My mother was not giving up on this bonding shit. I was about to ignore the call again, but then I remembered she would be out running errands and would probably stop by unannounced. I didn't have the time or the energy for her and her shenanigans, so I picked up my land line on the fourth ring.

"Audrielle, honey, I know you heard me calling you earlier. Why didn't you answer the phone? Are you still moping around watching movies, eating junk and gaining more weight by the minute?"

"Hey, Mother, how are you? Fine, that's good. Oh, me? I'm doing okay, especially for someone who just found out that her relationship of the last two years was all a lie thanks to her mother and aunt."

She blew out an exaggerated breath. "Oh Lord, Audrielle, stop being so dramatic. How many times do you want me to apologize? And I didn't feel the need to ask you how you were doing because I already know. I went by the store today to bring you and your sister a healthy lunch. Imagine my surprise when I saw Rima's pregnant ass prancing around and helping customers. When I asked your sister why Rima was there, she told me you haven't been to work in a week."

I swear I'ma kill my big-mouth little sister the next time I see her. It had only been five days since I'd been to work. Technically there were two more days to go before a full week ended, and being that the store was open six days a week, I still had one more day of calling out to do. I looked at my reflection through the shiny stainless steel door on my fridge. With the way I was feeling and looking, I might take two more weeks off. I didn't know how you got over catching your boyfriend balls deep in your 49-year-old aunt's pussy. I was emotionally distressed.

"Audri, you know Ariana can't handle the whole store by herself. You've had enough time to heal from this Antonio situation, don't you think? It's time to get back to the real world, honey. If I would have known you'd fall into the same type of depression stage you did when Eli left, I would've never hired—"

I hung up in my mother's face. See, this was another reason why my mother and I could never get along. She always thought she had the answers to everything and every aspect of my life.

You want a good man? Lose some weight!"

You want financial stability? Go to school and own your own successful business or lose some weight and marry a successful man.

You want a fine Greek brother? Lose some weight and pledge AKA like me.

According to her, all I needed to do was lose some weight and everything would be handed to me on a silver platter.

I shook my head as I walked back to my room. I didn't even feel like going shopping anymore. My mother always had a way of making me feel way worse than I had. The funny thing was, she didn't even know that she was doing it.

I had just popped the third installment of the *Twilight* saga into my DVD player when my cell phone rang. I looked down as Ariana's face flashed across my screen. I accepted the call because I needed to tell her ass off for telling Mom my business, but before I could even say one word, she started screaming at the top of her lungs. After I got her to calm down a bit, she was able to tell me that everything in the store had just gone off. There was some sort of blackout in the area. The lights, computer, cash register—nothing was working. To make matters worse, I could hear Rima's ass in the background, yelling and telling the customer to "get the hell out of the store!"

I hung up the phone after telling Ari that I would be there in twenty minutes. Going into my closet to find something to wear, I couldn't do anything but laugh at Rima's stupid ass. That girl was too much, and if I wanted to keep my customers coming, I needed to get down there as soon as possible to get control of her crazy ass.

Normally I'd dress a little sporty-chic when I went into work, but because I wasn't planning on staying that long, I threw on my red maxi dress, gold gladiator sandals, left my hair curly and loose, grabbed my purse and keys, then headed out the door.

8

Cairo

"Wait, wait, wait a minute, bruh. Are you sure you can believe anything Alex says? That bitch has always been a little on the crazy side. Her craziness is damn near up there with Rima's psycho ass."

I ran my hand over my face and let out a frustrated breath. It had been a few weeks since I got that call from Alex when Finesse and I were in the shoe store. I didn't even get a chance to look around like I wanted to. What she told me had me walking outside and getting into my car, while Ness stayed behind, flirting with the girl who had greeted us when we walked in.

"I hear everything you're saying, but I don't think Alex would lie about something like this. You know with her family having one of the top investment brokerage firms, they are always looking for potential clients," I said.

"But, nigga, you don't have the money to invest in anything. I mean, unless you are really thinking about marrying her to inherit that fifty mil." He shook his head. "It would be your white, nappy-headed ass to have a rich grandmother who left you fifty million in her will, but only if you are married by your thirtieth birthday." He came and sat next to me on the couch. "Being that today is July first, you have exactly six months to find you a bride and get hitched."

"Or I could take Alex up on her offer."

"What! Marry that psycho bitch just so she can file for divorce after that money is deposited in your account, and then take half of your shit?" he yelled.

"Naw, she said all I had to do was give her five percent and she'd be good. She just wants enough to start her own company and advertise it," I explained.

"You can believe that shit if you want to. I sure wish those dreads could make you think like a black man too. That is some straight white-boy shit you talking. No nigga in their right mind would believe that load of crap from any bitch's mouth. Especially in a state where divorced people split their property and assets fifty/fifty, regardless of you coming into the marriage broke. Did she tell you how she, out of all people, came upon this information?"

I went on and explained to Finesse what Alex had told me: the dude who was my biological father grew up with her father. She said that they were at my grandmother's wake when her only son came through the funeral home drunk as fuck. She said when her father took him to the back office away from everyone else and sobered him up a bit, he broke down and told her father everything about how I got here, what happened to me, and what my grandmother put in her will. Alex said she didn't know who I was when we first got together in college, but I kind of found that hard to believe. I didn't doubt that her father had hired someone to track me down, which resulted in Alex and I meeting, then dating for some years. Now that I thought about it, she was the only ex-girlfriend I had who constantly tried to get back together with me. She even pulled the pregnancy card before, but after I made her take four different tests in front of me, we cleared that right up. I had also changed my number and address a few times, although every time I did, she always seemed to find me. That behavior right there was why Finesse called her psycho. He seemed to think either she was that much in love with me, or she was on some real life stalker shit.

"Yo, if this ain't on some *Brewster's Millions* shit, I don't know what to say. Have you talked to Mama Faye yet?" he asked.

"Naw, why should I?"

"Um, because she adopted you. I'm pretty sure she may know a little about your biological fam. Especially if you had what they call an open adoption."

I looked at him quizzically. "Open adoption? Your ass been watching too much *Oprah*, bruh."

He laughed. "Maybe. But for real, though, it won't bother you to ask Mama Faye. I'm pretty sure she'll tell you something if there's anything to tell."

"I will," I said as I nodded my head up and down.

At that moment, Finesse's phone rang. He turned his nose up at the screen but answered it anyway. Two minutes later, he ended the call and grabbed his jacket.

"What's up, Ness?" I asked, looking at the twisted expression on his face.

"They finally caught that bitch Rima fucking up my shit on camera. Rod just called from his office phone and said that a couple of officers were on their way to pick her up. He's gonna text me the address they're heading to so I could meet them there."

I jumped up and grabbed my keys. "Well, I'm rolling with you. It's about time I meet the woman carrying my niece or nephew, although I wish it were under different circumstances."

We both laughed as we headed out of my office to his car.

9

Audrielle

"So he was that fine, huh?"

"Audri, I've never seen a man, let alone a white man—with dreadlocks, might I add—as fine as he was."

I watched my sister as she used her hand to fan away the invisible perspiration on her face. She was just catching me up on all of the new and old customers that had come into the store while I was at home watching *Twilight*. The white dude she was talking about must've been something to look at because I'd never seen her get this giddy over a man before.

It was a quiet Monday morning. We'd been open for a few hours now. Traffic was slow, but we'd had a few customers come in and purchase things. Since the new Jordans weren't scheduled to come out for another two weeks, I was glad to enjoy the non-chaotic day.

A few times, my mind drifted off to Antonio and how he would sometimes stop by on days like this to bring me lunch or some beautiful floral arrangement. I felt my eyes getting a little misty, but I wouldn't dare let another tear fall. During that weeklong heartbreak hiatus, I had cried enough for an entire lifetime. My tear ducts needed a break.

It's crazy how the woman is always the one sitting at home feeling bad about herself, second guessing herself, or even ridiculing herself. Questions like, *What didn't I do? Could I have done more? Was she better than me? Am I not pretty enough? Did he even really love me?* rapidly run through your mind. In some cases, even thoughts of suicide cross your mental a time or two. At least it had for me. It always seemed like I couldn't win for losing. All of my relationships in the past, including Antonio and Eli, all ended because some form of cheating happened or all of the lying they did caught up with them. It was funny too: after all of the horrible relationships I'd been in, there was still a part of me that believed I would find true love one day.

"Ummmm, hello! Earth to Audrielle. Did you hear anything that I just said? You're starting to do that zoning out thing again."

"I'm sorry, Ari. I was just thinking about something. What did you say?"

She looked at me for a minute then came and stood by my side. I couldn't look her in the eye because I knew that if I did, those tears I was trying so hard to keep at bay would come flooding over. "Look, sis." She grabbed my chin and lifted my head up. "You know I love you, and I want you to be happy in life, right?"

I slowly nodded my head.

"Don't let no weak-ass nigga take your joy away. You are a beautiful, strong, hardworking, and independent woman. You have your own house, your own money, your own business, and your own car. You basically didn't need him for shit but some dick." We shared a laugh. "Let your little sister put you up on a little secret about dick too. It's plenty of them out there, so don't beat yourself up over one that couldn't stay outta the next bitch's pussy, especially some old-ass, worn-out pussy.

"I know you're hurting right now, Audri, but you'll be okay. Antonio's and Eli's asses weren't worth any of your tears. Save those for your happy times, like when you finally give me a little niece or nephew to spoil, or on the day you marry the man who's going to love you just as much as you love him, all right?"

I wiped away the few tears that had managed to fall down my face. "Thanks, sis. I needed to hear that right now."

We hugged it out for a few seconds and then got back to stocking the shelves with the clothes I had just finished folding.

"Now that that's out the way, I could hook you up if you want me to with the fine-ass white dude. Me and his brother exchanged numbers before he left, and I'm sure I can set up some sort of double date."

"Um, Ari, I just got out of a relationship a minute ago. I'm not ready for another one this fast. On top of that, you want to hook me up with a white boy."

"Who said anything about a relationship?" she asked. "I said a date. And what's wrong with a white boy? Do you know who Alexander Mason or Robbie Gambrell is?"

I thought about it for a second then shook my head.

She playfully rolled her eyes. "Ugh! Hold on one moment." Ari ran to the counter and grabbed her cell phone. While she was walking back toward me, I could see her typing something onto the screen. By the time she reached me, she was turning her phone over to show me whatever she had pulled up.

"This, my dear sweet sister, is Alexander Mason."

I looked at her screen and saw the picture of one of the finest white men I'd ever seen. Judging by the amount of Photoshop, beautiful beach background, and the black Speedo he had on, I could tell that he was a model. Those beautiful green eyes seemed as if they were piercing my soul through the picture. Ari took her phone from out of my face and typed something in it again.

"And this right here is Robbie Gambrell." She pulled up this other sexy-ass white boy's instagram page and showed me his pictures. "So what do you think?" Ari asked, breaking me from my jungle-fevered thoughts.

"They are both quite handsome . . . for white men," I said.

"Well, that's the same thing I said about Finesse's brother. Alexander Mason is around six foot one. Finesse's brother had to be about six three or six four and kind of resembles Robbie Gambrell. He had on a T-shirt and some shorts, but I could still see his defined upper body and muscular legs. Then don't get me started on the dreads. They were neat and long, just like Mason's. Audri, I'm telling you, he was fine as shit."

I nodded my head and continued to fold the new shipment of Nike Hyperspeed camo shorts we had just received, while Ari went on and on about Finesse's fine brother again.

Around noon, business started to pick up. I had just bagged up a customer's purchase when the door to the shop opened and my best friend Rima strolled her pregnant ass in. For a moment, I just sat back and stared at her. Rima's small belly was full and round in her striped maternity dress. The glow that most pregnant women seem to have made her skin look as if the sun had just kissed it. Her chestnut-colored hair that she usually wore down was in a high, messy bun. Her chubby round face had a light coat of makeup on it. I looked at her ample breasts and wide hips. This pregnancy really did work wonders for her normally pencil-thin body.

For as long as I'd known Rima, she had always wanted to gain weight. She'd always stay a size four, regardless of how much food she ate or how many weight gaining supplements she tried to take. Nothing ever worked. I used to wish like hell I could take some of my fat and give it to her, but we all knew that was impossible. Looking at the way her body curved and filled out that dress, I knew she had to be about a size nine or ten now. She had finally gotten her weight gain; hopefully, she got to keep some after she had the baby.

"Hey, mommy to be, how are you?"

Rima was always a little feisty thing, so I didn't even pay her any mind when she put her hand on her hip and got in my face. "Ain't this 'bout a bitch? So you wanna talk to me now? Audrielle, I've been calling and coming by your house for the last week. Every time I called or dropped by, I got no answer whatsoever. How many times do I have to tell you that your pain is my pain? When you hurt, I hurt too. What kind of best friend would I be if I can't help to take some of that sadness or anger away?"

"I know, Rima. That was my bad. For some reason, I just wanted to be alone with this heartbreak."

"That's some bullshit, Audri, and you know it. How many times have I tried to shut you out when I was going through something?"

I shrugged my shoulders.

"Exactly! If you weren't with me that last time I fucked up my baby's daddy other car, I don't think I would've gotten away," she said.

I started to laugh as I remembered how I had to lift Rima up in my arms and pull her away from her baby daddy's car. We'd just busted out the windows, and I knew that someone was going to come out of the house soon. I told Rima we needed to leave, but instead of being happy with what we had already done, this heifer wanted to pour some powdered sugar in his gas tank. Before she even got the funnel in the gas opening right, I snatched her pregnant ass up and took off running.

"Yeah, I forgot to thank you for that, because I'd probably be in jail righ—"

Her statement was cut short when the door to the store swung open and four big-ass men walked in—two uniformed police officers and two men I'd never seen before. The tall white dude with dreads instantly caught my attention. Was this the white boy Ari was telling me about? If so . . . damn!

"Rima Vasquez?" the gorilla-looking officer asked.

"Yes, that's me," Rima said, raising her hand as she was staring daggers into the cute dude standing next to the Robbie Gambrell lookalike.

"Ma'am, I'm sorry to have to tell you this, but you are under arrest for vandalism and reckless behavior."

"Wait! What!" Rima screamed. "I haven't done anything!"

"Ma'am, we have you on video tape committing the offense," the other officer said as he handcuffed Rima. "Now you have the right to remain silent. Anything you say can be held and used against you in the court of law . . ."

As the officer read Rima her Miranda rights and walked her out of the store crying and slobbering, Ari walked over to the cuties who had walked in behind the police. When I looked over in their direction, a set of the most beautiful bluish green eyes were staring right at me.

"Audri!" I heard someone call my name, but I was in some sort of trance looking at this handsome and very sexy white man.

"Audrielle! What the hell is going on in here? Why is Rima being put into the back of a police car in handcuffs?" The sound of my mother's voice finally snapped me out of my daze and had me turning around to face here.

When did she get here? My head already started to hurt.

"Mom, I don't know what's going on right now, but I'll find out once I get down to the station."

"See, Audri," she said, shaking her head. "That's why I told you to stop having that girl up here. She has always been a—"

I turned back around and headed for my office, leaving my mother to fuss at the air in front of her. I didn't feel like hearing that shit today. My best friend, who happened to be very pregnant, had just been arrested in my store. I didn't give two fucks about how she felt or what the few customers who witnessed the arrest thought. Rima had always been there for me and vice versa, so why stop now? I needed to grab my purse, keys, and cell so that I could call my lawyer and meet Rima down at the station. Hopefully, they'd release her that day or let me bail her out. Either way, I knew my pit-bull-in-a-skirt lawyer would get something done today.

When I came back out to the front, my eyes scanned around for those sexy, hypnotizing eyes. To my dismay, he and his cute friend that Ariana seemed to know were gone already. I wondered why they had left so fast.

"Ari, I'll be back in an hour or two. I'm about to go check on Rima. Remember, if the lights go out again, check the breakers first. You had me panicking for nothing last time."

She just nodded her head as our mother continued to drill her about what had happened. *Better her than me,* I thought as I headed out the door. Maybe by the time I got back, she'd be gone off doing whatever she did on Mondays and my day would go back to normal.

Yeah . . . like that will happen!

10

Rima

I sat in the cold-ass interrogation room waiting for one of the officers who arrested me to come back with my hot chocolate. I knew with watching all of those criminal shows that I should've declined their offer for the warm beverage because my fingerprints and DNA would be all over that cup once I finished, but I didn't really care. My OB-GYN told me that I had anemia a month after I found out I was pregnant, and this shit was no joke. It got so bad sometimes that I had to wear a sweater and two jackets just to keep warm.

I looked at the clock on the wall above the door. I'd been down at this station for about forty-five minutes. I wondered if Audrielle was there already or if she was on her way. I had no doubt whatsoever that she wouldn't be; her coming to my aid was a given. She was truly my definition of ride or die.

When we were younger, the kids at school used to pick on her because she was a little on the chunky side, and they used to pick on me because I was real skinny. Big Tank and Noodles were the nicknames they gave us. Every day we walked into school we were teased. From the time all of the classes stood in single file lines and said the Pledge of Allegiance to the last bell that rang to release us for the day at 2:27 p.m., we were tormented. It was so bad that we didn't even eat in the cafeteria. We found a little spot behind one of the bungalows on the far side of the campus to enjoy our food and pretend that the mean kids didn't exist for about half an hour.

I remembered this one time in middle school, Audri and I were headed to our second period. We didn't have the same class, but the rooms were across the hall from each other. While we were walking, one of the popular girls, named Raquel, decided that she wanted to start the heckling that usually happened whenever we walked past her and her crew. Audri never paid them any mind because she normally heard the bashing about her weight from her mom, so to hear it from someone in her own age group didn't do too much to her; but for me, it hurt every time.

My mother was a single parent who couldn't afford to buy me new outfits every school year, so we had to share clothes. With her being bigger than me, she never bought our shared stuff in my size because it would be impossible for her to fit into. Yeah, I had some of my own outfits that I would get for Christmas or my birthday, but it wasn't enough to last me for a whole school year. I couldn't wear the same thing twice in a week; the mean kids would surely notice that and tease me even more.

On this particular day, though, I had on a pair of my mom's size ten jeans and an extra-large shirt. Now to you, those sizes probably don't sound too bad, right? Honestly, they aren't, but when you are a size four and have on a size ten pants and an extra-large top, you know that shit swallowed my little body up whole. Even with two pairs of tights on up under the jeans, they still slid down my bony hips. My mom wouldn't let me add extra holes to the belt, so I had to use a shoe string from an old pair of sneakers to keep them from falling down completely.

The name calling started as soon as we stepped in the hallway. I tried my best to ignore them, but it seemed as if they were going extra hard on that day. When Audri and I stopped in front of our classroom doors to say bye to each other, Raquel took that opportunity to pour a bowl of cooked spaghetti noodles and sardines on top of my head. The greasy and smelly concoction drenched me from head to toe. I was so embarrassed that my light skin tone was a shade of crimson red. When I tried to turn around and run, Audri grabbed my wrist and told me to stay put.

"I'm about to teach this bitch and everyone else a lesson," she said as she headed toward a laughing Raquel and her crew. Without saying one word, Audri grabbed Raquel by her ponytail and swung her so hard into the lockers that a few of them popped open. The whole hallway became quiet as Audri dragged Raquel to the pile of mess she had just dumped over my head and rolled her around in it.

When she was done, she looked out at the shocked crowd and said, "If there's anyone else who has a problem with me or Rima, speak your peace now. If not, I don't want to hear shit else about a tank or noodle when we walk into this school." She gave one more look to the hushed crowd, but when no one else said anything, she grabbed my arm and her backpack, and we headed to the principal's office.

Of course, I didn't let her take the blame for everything. I told Principal Wallace that I had a hand in the altercation too. We both ended up getting suspended for a week, with a month's worth of detention when we returned. We took our punishment with pride and came back to school a week later with some newfound respect. Even Raquel's ass would speak whenever she saw us. From that day forward, we made a pact to have each other's backs regardless of whatever we had personally going on.

The door opening and closing pulled me from my memories. An officer I'd never seen before placed a cup of hot chocolate in front of me then sat down in the chair on the other side of the table. He licked his lips and stared at me for a while before he finally decided to speak.

"Ms. Vasquez, I'm pretty sure you already know why you're here, so why don't you do us both a favor and take this pen and notepad and write in detail what happened the night you were caught vandalizing Mr. Broussard's property."

I took a sip of the hot-ass chocolate and burned my tongue in the process. I knew I wasn't imagining shit when I saw the smirk on his face as soon as I retracted my lips from the cup.

This muthafucka did that shit on purpose.

"Was that supposed to be some form of torture to get me to admit to something that I didn't do?" I asked.

"Ms. Vasquez, let's not play this little 'It wasn't me' game. We both know that you've been acting a little *out of character,* shall we say, toward the man you claim to be pregnant by."

I laughed as I looked this clown in the face. "Officer . . .?"

"It's Detective. Detective Roderick Miller."

Hmmm. I was impressed. Detective, huh? You don't see too many young black detectives nowadays, and fine ones at that. His hair and goatee looked like they were freshly tapered, and he smelled of Dior Fahrenheit aftershave. The form-fitting gray three-piece suit he had on hugged his body just right, and the expensive black oxfords on his feet set the look off. The broadness of his chest and shoulders told me that he worked out and probably had a body to die for underneath his clothes. He had an air of arrogance about him that I found desirable and would so willingly love to tame.

I bet he'd fuck the shit out of me. I knew I probably shouldn't have been thinking of sex at a time like this, but the man sitting in front of me had my pregnant ass feeling some type of way. I attempted to take another sip of my hot chocolate; maybe another burn to my tongue would take my mind out of the gutter. However, when the warm, sweet liquid flowed down my throat, I couldn't help but to wonder if his nut would go down just as smooth.

I snapped from my wicked thoughts and decided to save those for another day. Right now, I needed to focus and keep my ass from going to jail.

"Okay, Detective Miller, I've been through this type of thing before. The other officer said that there was evidence, so where is it?"

He pulled out his phone and started to play some weakly recorded video. It wasn't real clear, but you could see me and Audri busting the windows out of a car. From the angle that the video was being recorded, you could tell it was from inside someone's house. Because of the poor quality of the phone, you couldn't get a clear view of our faces, but you could tell that the smaller girl was pregnant, and her accomplice was a shapely chick with a big ass. For all they knew, that could've been anybody.

After the video stopped playing, Detective Miller sat back in his chair with that sexy smirk on his face. I, in return, sat back and did the same thing. I wasn't about to admit to anything or sit there acting all nervous and shit. If they had some concrete evidence, I would've been sitting in a cell already.

"So are you still going to sit there and act like that wasn't you on the video?" His little cocky swag kind of had me hot.

"It wasn't me."

"That's bullshit and you know it. The girl in the video is pregnant just like you, and I'm pretty sure if we dig a little bit more into your background, we can find your friend that matches the other person in the video," he said.

I was about to respond when the door swung open and in walked Sarah Blake-Hammond, attorney at law. As soon as I saw the Michelle Williams lookalike, I knew Audri was somewhere in the building.

"Rima, don't say anything else. The evidence they have is not sufficient enough or even viewable. No jury in America would convict you off of that," she said.

"Oh, we can convict her all right. The girl in the video is pregnant just like her and looks around the same height and everything. Plus, we have witnesses and sworn testimonies from Mr. Broussard and his brother. Both were inside of the home the car was sitting in front of at the time of the crime." The other detective in the room had finally decided to speak up.

"You can't be serious, right?" Sarah laughed and gestured with her head for me to get up. "How many women are pregnant in the world right now, detectives? How many pregnant women are going to fit the description of my client? Does Mr. Broussard have any other women claiming to be pregnant with his child? Have you brought any of them in?" She opened the door. "Since you don't have any hard, real, or legally obtained evidence on my client, we are about to go. Feel free to give me a call when you've found something concrete. C'mon, Rima, we're leaving."

I walked toward that door, happy as hell. I did not want to spend one single night in jail. I was so glad Sarah had come in when she did. A couple more hours of sitting in that cold-ass room and I might've told on myself just to get the shit over with.

"Ms. Vasquez?" I heard someone say. When I turned around, Detective Miller's sexy chocolate eyes were staring at me. He lifted his head. "I'll be seeing you soon."

I didn't know if I should take that as a good thing or a bad thing. The way he said it, though, had my panties getting wet. I hoped we did see each other again. Maybe next time we could use those handcuffs in a different way.

11

Cairo

I had just dropped Finesse off and was headed back to work. I couldn't believe his baby mama, who I could now match a face to, was arrested in the same store we were just in a month or so ago. I wondered what was her connection to that spot. Did she own it? Naw, she couldn't have. I remembered Ariana telling us that she and her sister owned the store. Seeing both of their faces in my head, Ariana and Rima didn't look anything alike. Now, the sexy, light-skinned thick girl who was standing next to Rima, on the other hand, could be Ariana's sister. She favored Ariana more than Rima did. When I asked Ness about her, as well as how Roderick knew where Rima would be at that exact moment, he just shrugged his shoulders and changed the subject. Shit was weird.

I didn't say anything, though, because I knew Ness didn't have those types of feelings for his baby mama, but it wouldn't surprise me if Roderick was talking to her before the restraining order even happened. Rod was a sneaky-ass bastard, a do-anything-to-close-his-case type of asshole. Even though we grew up together, I wouldn't trust him with a ten-foot pole. Dude was dirty as hell in his professional and personal life. I didn't know why the LAPD let his ass on the force, and then had the nerve to promote him to detective. If his ass was a little crooked then, I could guarantee he was really crooked now. More access and more pull. I just hoped he was smart enough to not get caught.

My mind drifted back over to the pretty chick with the kinky hair and juicy-ass lips that Rima was talking to when we walked in. Her body had my dick jumping as soon as she came into my view. I kept staring at her because I'd never seen a girl her size that pretty before. Don't get me wrong; I knew beauty came in all shapes and sizes, and I'd met a lot of different women in my lifetime, but never one that looked like her.

Because I was raised by a black woman and grew up in a black neighborhood, I stayed away from the black girls when it came to dating. I was already being picked on and clowned because I was a white boy with dreads in the hood. I didn't want to add one more thing to the list. I figured if I dated within my race, or any other race but black, that people wouldn't talk about it.

Mama Faye didn't like that logic at all. She wanted me to date black girls, especially her friends' kids, but I couldn't do it. She would give me a number to one of her church members' daughters, and I'd just pass the number to Finesse and let him talk to them. When I did bring home one of my girlfriends to meet Mama Faye, shit never went well. Either she didn't talk to them, or she'd cuss them out for being scared of being in our neighborhood after dark. I dated a few Mexican and Filipino girls too, but it was the same outcome.

When I started to bring Alex around, Mama Faye would trip. She kept saying that she'd seen her before, but she could never remember from where. She said Alex had the same sneaky eyes as this man she met many years ago, and that I shouldn't trust her. Out of all of the years Alex and I dealt with each other, I never had a problem with trusting her; it was just her crazy antics that I couldn't deal with.

I made it back to the office and worked on a few designs for the new housing development I was working on. The basketball team I coached had a game that night, so after working on the project for a few more hours, I finally packed up all of my things and headed to the gym where my team would be playing.

***

"What up, Coach Cai? Did you ever go to the shoe store I told you about?" Tyson, a member of the team, asked as I walked in the locker room.

I put my bags down on the floor and started to change out of my work clothes. "Yeah, I went by the store about a week ago."

"That shit was dope, huh?" Excitement filled his voice. "Every pair of Jordans you could ask for. Then you can get them customized on top of that."

"Yeah, it was pretty dope. I didn't get to stay long or buy anything because I got an important phone call like five minutes after I got there, but I plan on going back soon."

Especially if that plus-sized beauty is going to be there.

He nodded his head then went to warm up with the other fellas already on the court. I finished dressing then stuffed my bag inside one of the empty lockers. After making sure I had everything I would need when the game started, I walked out to the floor.

A few of the parents, as well as some of the old teammates, greeted me as I walked over to our team section. Before I could even get the attention of and talk to the refs, I heard a familiar voice calling my name. When I turned around, I came face to face with the last person I expected to see, especially in this area.

"Alex, what are you doing here? Better yet, how did you know where I'd be?" I asked as I looked around the gym. I wasn't afraid of her being there or anything; I was just uncomfortable with her ability to pop up on me unexpectedly.

"Cai, all I had to do was have my assistant Google your team's name online. After that, I had game information, wins and losses, team stats, jersey numbers, and their head coach's relationship status."

I didn't know whether to be alarmed or impressed. Whichever one it was, I still had my guard up.

"What are you doing here, Alex?" I asked again, my voice a little firmer. This time, I hoped she'd get straight to the point.

She motioned her head toward the water fountain; I guess to get a little more privacy, seeing as we were surrounded by a lot of people. It seemed as if her yelling my name at the top of her lungs and walking toward me the way she did had everyone tuned in to our little pre-game conversation.

"Have you thought anymore about what I told you?" she asked.

"You said quite a few things the last time we talked, Alexandria. Why don't you refresh my memory?"

"Alexandria? We're not friends anymore, Cai?"

See, this was the shit I be talking about. It was always games with her, and I couldn't deal with it, at least not then. I turned away from her, only to feel her hand grip my wrist and turn me back. She looked to her left then right, making sure no one was within ear range to hear what she was about to say.

"I'm talking about the inheritance money and the proposition I offered you. I know you could use the money, and so could I. It's actually a win-win if you think about it. You'd become a millionaire, and I could finally get away from my daddy."

I already knew this was what she was talking about when she first asked. I just wanted to make sure we were both on the same page. Looking at Alex and remembering some of the good times we'd had, I probably wouldn't have a problem marrying her to get the money. But for some reason, the voice that told me to run when I first met her was screaming the same thing in my head this time.

Nine years earlier

"Ay, yo Cairo, I don't know why you just don't date a sista. It ain't nothing like a woman with a fat ass, big ol' titties, and some juicy-ass lips.

Let's not forget about how wet the pussy gets either," Roderick said as we sat at our usual booth in the cafeteria with Finesse and the rest of the basketball team. Rod and Ness didn't play with us, but it was like they did, as much as they were around.

"Man, black girls aren't the only ones with nice bodies and good pussy. Case in point, the little Mexican chick I've been messing with that works in the library. She bad, isn't she, Ness?"

"Yeah, mami got a nice little body on her, and her face is right. But that pussy is dry as fuck, bro."

I laughed and threw my empty soda cup at his ass. We never shared girls, so I knew that last statement was all in fun.

"No, but on the real, Cai, I have to agree with Rod on this one. Ain't nothing like fucking with a black chick."

"Tell him, Ness, man!" Rod added, laughing. "Then his white ass always talking to those little skinny bitches. Man, you need to get you a girl with some meat on them bones. Trust me, not only is the pussy wet as hell, but it's also gushy as fuck."

I shook my head as those two idiots continued to throw jabs at my dating preference. It wasn't long before the rest of the team joined in and became interested in what they had to *say. Not wanting to hear the pros and cons of dating a girl that wasn't black anymore, I got up and made my way to the soda dispenser to get another cup of Powerade. A nice-looking Filipina girl had caught my eye while I was filling my cup. She had a pretty face, nice titties, a slim waist, and a small ass, but I didn't care about that. I was just about to approach her when someone bumped me from behind.*

"I'm so sorry. Please excuse me. I didn't see you there at all," she said.

"You good. I didn't spill or damage anything. Besides, you would have to hit me a lot harder than that to make me."

She looked up at me with her beautiful hazel eyes. Those pink, pouty lips she had went great with those beautiful white teeth. There were a few freckles on her face, but you couldn't tell unless you were really looking at her. Her skin was a shade darker than mine, so either she went tanning, or she used that fake tanning lotion shit. Her auburn-colored hair was pushed back into a slick ponytail, which made me notice how far her ears stuck out. Taking a step back to get a full look at her, I was impressed by her body and her style, but there was something about this girl that seemed kind of off. My mind was telling me to run, but my feet wouldn't move at all. I didn't know if it was the smile on her face that didn't truly reach her eyes or the small vibe I got from her that said she was trouble. Whatever it was, it had me planted right in front of her and enjoying the small conversation we were having. Against my better judgement, I exchanged numbers with her and then agreed to meet up with her for dinner after my game on Friday.

"Don't forget, my name is Alexandria, but you can call me Alex. All of my friends do," she said.

"So I'm your friend now?"

"Maybe . . . Maybe not. I guess I'll figure that out after we go to dinner this weekend." She licked her lips then turned around.

"I'll remember that when the bill comes to the table," I yelled to her back as she walked out of the student union.

"God damn, bro! Who was that?" Finesse asked as he approached me.

"Yeah, Cai, who was that?" Rod repeated as he walked up behind Ness.

I shrugged my shoulders. "She said her name was Alexandria, but her friends call her Alex."

"Well, I'd like to call her and get a piece of that," Rod said.

"Not after all that shit you and Ness was just talking about a minute ago. What could that white girl, with her white pussy, actually do for *you?" I laughed. He was always talking out the side of his neck.*

"Shit, a whole lot. I still stand by what I said about black girls and their pussy, but ain't nothing wrong with dipping in something different from time to time," Rod replied.

While he and Ness started going in on God only knows what, I went back to the table, grabbed my basketball and book bag, said my good-byes to my teammates, and then headed to my next class. Thoughts of my date with Alex invaded my mind as I was walking out. Hopefully the vibe I got that day would be different come Friday.

A loose ball hitting my leg brought me back from my thoughts. I picked it up and threw it back out to the court.

"So have you thought about the offer, Cai?" Alex asked. "I need to get started on these wedding plans if we are going to do this."

"Wedding plans? See, you never said anything about wedding plans. I don't even really know if I want the money, to be truthful. I'm not hurting for anything right now, and all my finances are in order. Life insurance policies and everything are up to date. I have a little money saved up for a rainy day, so I don't necessarily need any extra money, especially from people I don't even know," I told her.

"Are you really going to let fifty million dollars slide through your fingers like that? You can be so stubborn sometimes, Cai. You act as if you have to give a lung or a limb to get it."

"My last name is just as important as those things. When I get married, if I ever get married, I want it to be forever, not no shotgun marriage to get a hold of some money and then be divorced within a month's time. Marriage is something I want to take seriously when it happens. I also want to be in love with the woman I end up making my wife," I said.

She looked up at me with misty eyes. "You were in love with me before. I know there's still a piece of your heart that belongs to me."

In actuality, she was right. I still did have love for Alex, but not like I used to. She had changed over the years, and I didn't too much care for the woman she was now.

"Look, I have to get back out to the floor. The game is about to start, and I need to talk to the team before it does."

"How about we have lunch sometime next week to go over everything? You still have time to think this over, Cai, but not that much. Your birthday will be here before you know it."

I nodded my head, told her good night, and gave her a maybe on the lunch date. As I was walking over to my team, she called my name.

I turned around. "Yeah?"

She shook her head. "Never mind. I'll call you so we can set up that lunch."

Without another word, she turned around and left out of the side entrance.

"Yo, coach, who was that?" Tyson asked as I walked up to the team.

"An old friend."

"An old friend, huh? Not the way shorty was looking at you."

I laughed. "Shorty? I see someone's been catching up on their East Coast lingo. You ready for college in the fall?"

"I sure am. And I heard that NYU has some fine-as-snow bunnies, just like the one you were just talking to. Why don't you pass me her number so I can practice on her? If I can pull an older chick that looks like her, I wouldn't have a problem with the girls around my age," he joked.

We laughed and chatted it up for a few more moments before the game started. Two hours later, I was headed home, tired as hell and ready for bed. Dealing with Finesse and all of his drama, then Alex and all this marriage stuff had drained me dry. As soon as my head hit the pillow, I was out like a light.

12

Audrielle

After four long hours, three iced coffees, two lemon pound cake slices, and one pecan pie tart from Starbucks, Rima's ass was finally being released. When my lawyer and I got down to the police station, they gave us a bit of the run around, but once Sarah put on that Esquire hat and started to spit out all kinds of lawsuits and conjunctions being filed, they finally let her back to represent Rima.

"Okay, Ari, they're coming now. I'll call you back in an hour or two." I was on the phone with my sister, who wanted a play by play on everything that had happened since we got down to the precinct.

"Audri, don't forget to call me back. We both know Rima's crazy ass is on that video. Busting out niggas' windows is her M.O."

I couldn't do anything but laugh because she was so right.

"Wait," Ari said. "One more thing before you go. Did you see the two dudes that came in after the police officers?" As if she could see me nod my head, she continued. "Well, that was Finesse and his fine-ass brother that I was telling you about. Did you see him, girl? Wasn't he fine? Doesn't he remind you of Robbie—"

Before she could finish with her barrage of questions, I hung up in her face. I looked up just in time to see Sarah and Rima walking out of the precinct and headed toward my car.

"Hey, girlie, everything is good for now. Rima has a court date scheduled for next week sometime. I'll have my assistant call you guys with the information. Although the video evidence was inconclusive, the brick she used to bust one of the side windows came back with her fingerprints." She shook her head and giggled. "They sprung that little bit of info on us as we were walking out. Hopefully, she can talk to Mr. Broussard to see if he will drop the charges. If not, she's possibly looking at a fine and some small amount of community service, since this is her first offense."

"Damn!" I looked at Rima. "Now do you see why I keep in contact with her? Not only is she a great friend, but she's an even better lawyer." I turned back to Sarah and gave her a hug. "Thank you for everything, girl."

"No problem. Just because you and my brother didn't work out doesn't mean we still couldn't be cool. If you ask me, you were the best thing that ever happened to him." Sarah was Eli's older sister. We became good friends during the time Eli and I were together. I thought that once her brother and I broke up, we'd stop talking to each other, but to my surprise, that wasn't the case. We still talked on the phone now and then, occasionally met up for lunch, and even clowned the new woman she showed me Eli was dating.

I gave Sarah one last hug then turned my attention back to Rima. As soon as our eyes locked, we burst out laughing. This was one of the reasons why I loved her little ass. She was always in some shit.

"The brick, Rima? For real? I told you to grab everything you touched!" I said.

"And I did. At least I thought I did. The way you she-hulked me when we saw those figures running to the door, I must've dropped it."

I didn't remember grabbing her that hard, but then again, I could have. I was trying to get the hell up out of dodge while her ass was still trying to total her baby daddy's car. To be honest, I didn't understand why she was damaging his stuff. Personally, I didn't agree with doing things like that because I'd be mad as hell if someone did that to me. However, at the end of the day,

Rima needed me to ride, so I rode. She'd do it for me in a heartbeat if that were my get-down.

"So the recording they had, could you tell it was you?" I asked.

"Yep." She got into the passenger seat of my car. "And you too."

"Bitch, stop lying."

Rima started laughing again like something was funny. "It was a recording of when we were both fucking the car up. Whoever was recording it, though, had a cheap-ass phone or camcorder, because you could see two bodies beating the shit out of the car, but you couldn't see the faces clearly. You could tell that one of the girls was pregnant, so that automatically put it on me, since Finesse has that restraining order against me and I'm supposedly the only one pregnant with his baby."

Finesse. Where have I heard that name before? I wondered.

She continued. "You don't have anything to worry about. I didn't rat you out or anything. The detectives didn't even ask about my accomplice. They were more concerned with me and why I've been damaging his things. God! Can you believe that muthafucka actually filed a restraining order against me?"

"Didn't you file one against him?"

"Hell yeah. Why wouldn't I? I knew sooner or later he'd catch me, and I just wanted to have some kind of order of protection filed just in case a bitch came up missing."

We laughed for a minute, but once that died down, I took on a more serious approach in our conversation. I needed to get an understanding of why she was tripping so hard.

"Honestly, Rima, I don't know why you have one filed against him anyway. He doesn't do half of the harassing shit you do to him, let alone damage your car every chance he gets. You guys aren't even together from what you told me. Wasn't he a one-night stand?" I took my eyes off the road and looked at her. When she didn't respond, I kept going. "I'm not trying to get you upset, best friend, but I'm trying to understand your actions. In my opinion, you're mad at the wrong person. You need to be busting out your own shit for having unprotected sex with a nigga you only knew for ten minutes. Now you have to deal with this dude for the rest of your life, or at least until your baby finishes college."

I didn't know if I had hit an unknown sore spot, because when I looked back at Rima, she was staring out of the window and remained quiet for the rest of the ride back to the store.

When I pulled up next to her car, she tried to hop out without saying anything, but I stopped her by calling her name.

"Yeah, what's up?" Her tone was calm, but I could still hear a hint of irritation in it.

"Spit truth?" I asked, which was our way of getting whichever one of us was mad, bothered, or upset, to open up and let the other know what was on her mind . . . truthfully.

She looked at me for a second through the cracked window then opened the door and got back into the car. We sat in silence for about three songs on the new Jodeci CD before she finally spoke.

"How long has Ari been talking to homeboy that walked into the shop behind the cops. The one with that tall white guy?" she asked.

I thought for a second; then it hit me.

"Oh, the cute brown-skin brother who looks like that football player Devin Thomas. She just met him a few weeks ago when the two of them came into the store. I think she said his name is Ness. Finesse, or something like—" I stopped in mid-sentence. There was that name again.

Finesse. Where have I heard that name before?

I recalled my conversation with Ariana from earlier. It couldn't be. The world could not be that small, could it? My sister's new potential boo couldn't be Rima's alleged baby daddy, right?

I know I'm wrong for using the word *alleged*, but Rima was into a lot of things that I wasn't down with sexually, so you never know. Let's just say that Finesse's dick was probably just one of the ones she had that night. Don't get me wrong; Rima wasn't a ho or anything, but she liked to dabble in an exclusive kind of lifestyle from time to time.

"Please don't tell me that ol' boy who came into the shop is who you're pregnant by," I said.

She nodded her head.

"Fuck!" I thought I said it in my mind, but I actually said it out loud.

"I wasn't going to say anything at first because I just assumed he came into the store to see me get arrested for fucking his shit up, but then he was talking and looking at Ariana as if he was interested in her. You bringing up my one-night stand and not knowing anything about Finesse had me thinking about him and our situation."

I laid my head against the headrest and closed my eyes. This whole thing could potentially become a problem if my sister and this Finesse dude actually got together. Rima was already acting like the baby mama from hell without the baby even being here. Ariana and I would have to talk about this. I mean, she was my sister, and blood is thicker than mud, but Rima was also my sister, just without my father's or mother's blood running through her veins. If I was ever put in the position to pick a side, I didn't know which way I'd go. They'd both been there for me from problems at home to the ones in the world.

Maybe I was reading into this a little too much. When we had our family dinner in a few days, I would just bring it up. Luckily Rima had plans with her family, so she wouldn't be there. I would tell Ari what was going on. It hadn't been that long, so I doubted he'd put that much of an impression on her where she'd be head over heels already.

"Look, Rima, I didn't even know who your baby daddy was. It wasn't like I ever met him officially or anything. All I've ever seen was his cars." She laughed. "I don't think it's anything serious between them, and it probably won't be, especially after I tell her who he is."

She looked at me and smiled. "Are we still spitting truth?"

I nodded my head.

"She can go ahead and talk to him. He and I will never be anything but co-parents, if that. If Ari asks, tell her she doesn't have anything to worry about when it comes to me. Him, on the other hand, let's just say I wouldn't be surprised if I was baby mama number twenty."

I laughed. "Like that?"

"Just like that! Biggest man-ho I've ever seen."

I wanted to ask her how she knew that if the only time she was ever around him was the one time they had sex, but I didn't. I left that discussion for another day.

We spoke for about thirty more minutes about baby names, showers, and how her mom felt about being a grandma at an early age. When we were done chatting it up, we said our good-byes, promised to call each other before we went to bed, and then went our separate ways.

I stopped at Wendy's and got me a chicken apple salad with extra raspberry vinaigrette. When I got home and got out of my car, there was the largest bouquet of white calla lilies sitting in front of my door. Everyone knew they were my favorite, so they could have been from anyone.

There was no card or anything on the plastic stick saying who sent them, so I assumed they were another peace offering from my mother. I picked up the vase, my bag of food, and headed into my home. I'd had a long day, and all I wanted to do was get full, take a bath, then fall asleep watching reruns of *Martin*.

13

Cairo

It had been a month since I ran into Alexandria the night of my team's basketball game. All of the things she was saying sounded good, but there was something in the back of my mind that kept telling me to not trust her. The fact that a person who wasn't a part of my biological family knew more about what was going on than I did raised a few flags.

I wasn't hurting for money or anything. I made a nice living with the freelance architecture work I did, but it wasn't enough to where I could retire and not have to worry about a single bill for the rest of my life.

After that night, Alex and I met up a few times for lunch or dinner. We even double dated once with Ness and Ariana. Of course, it was by accident. Alex showed up at my home unannounced just as they were leaving to go out. Ariana must've assumed Alex and I were dating and asked if we wanted to join them. I said no, but Alex hurried and jumped on the idea. Since I wasn't doing anything and I didn't have a game the next day, I went. The night went well, especially when I asked Ariana about the pretty girl that resembled her but was a little thicker. She told me that that was her single older sister, Audrielle. I wanted to ask her more questions about her sister but never got the chance to, because Alex had returned from using the restroom.

I hadn't seen Ariana since that night we all went to the movies. When Ness brought her around again, I was most definitely going to ask her for more details.

It was a bright and beautiful Saturday morning, and I was headed over to Mama Faye's house. Every time I asked her about my other family or this supposed inheritance, she would tell me that we'd talk about it later because she wasn't feeling too good. I started to become worried because she'd been a little sick for a while now. I asked her what was wrong, but she just would ignore the question and say, "It ain't nothing a little aloe vera plant and ginger beer can't cure."

Like most of the older generation, Mama Faye stayed away from hospitals. She always relied on home remedies or natural healing to get her through anything. I remember one time she was going out to her garden and tripped over a rock. She hurt her wrist but never said anything. Finesse happened to drop by the house a few days after the fall, and her wrist had swelled to the size of a grapefruit. He sent a picture to my phone then called and told me what had happened. I didn't even give her a chance to protest when I arrived at the house. I lifted her small frame over my shoulder, put her in my car, and drove her right to the hospital. She fussed the whole way, but I didn't give a shit. After half an hour of her cussing Ness and me out in her thick Jamaican accent, we arrived to the ER. Not only had she sprained her wrist, but she had high blood pressure and a bruised hip. They kept her for a couple days until her blood pressure returned to normal. She was so mad at us for taking her to see the doctor that she didn't cook us anything for a whole month. Sad to say, we missed our home cooked meals, so whenever she wasn't feeling well, we left her home to take care of herself.

Thinking about that memory made me laugh. Mama Faye was as stubborn as a mule, just like her grandson and his father.

I pulled up to the house, said a couple of hellos to the neighbors, and then let myself in. I heard water running in the bathroom, so I stopped there first. I saw no sign of Mama, so I turned the faucet off then headed toward the kitchen.

"Hey, Fayetta!" I called out as I stared at her back. My voice and presence must've scared her because she dropped the big orange container in her hand, causing pills to go flying everywhere.

I bent down to help her pick them up, but she swatted me away and tried to get them up by herself. "What mi tell you about calling mi by my full name? I raised your tail. Call mi Mama or Mama Faye. Say my name like that again and mi bust you in da nose."

I wanted to laugh, but the way her hands were shaking grabbed my attention instead. "Mama, why are your hands shaking like that?"

When she finally looked up, I almost didn't recognize the woman before me. Her dark, smooth skin was now ashy and gray. The hair in the front of her head was thinning so bad that you could see the oil on her scalp. Even her eyes were glassy and dull, instead of full of life like they normally were.

"Mama."

She held up her hand to silence me.

"Mi blood pressure has been really high for the last few weeks, and you know mi not gonna stay in no damn hospital, so dem doctors gave mi these here pills to help control it. Instead of mi feelin' betta, mi feel worse." She shook her head. "That's why mi hate hospitals. Aloe vera plant and ginger beer is all mi need."

I looked at her appearance one last time before I helped her up. I bent down and picked up the rest of her pills then placed them inside of the orange bottle. I wanted to know what type of medicine this was, but she had already peeled off the part of the sticker that had that information. I made a mental note to talk to Ness and find out what really was going on because whatever it was, I knew it was much worse than what she was telling me.

"So what bring mi sweet boi down today?" Although her smile reached her eyes, I still couldn't help but feel some type of way about her health. "I see that head of yours is going to need to be re-twisted soon."

"Yeah, but we can worry about that when it's time. How are you, Mama?"

She coughed. "Mi fine, boi. Mi just getting older, you know. It's almost time for mi to leave here now. I sho' would be happy if I got a beautiful grandbaby before mi did."

I just laughed. She had been hinting about wanting grandbabies in all of our conversations lately. I guess since Finesse had one on the way, she wanted me to start on one too.

"We still have plenty of time for that. I have to find me a girl first."

"You need one like tha gal Ness is dating. She's a real pretty thang and very smart. I don't even recognize mi own grandson since him start to date her." She laughed. "That one der don't take none of Nessy shit."

That was true. Finesse had changed a lot since he got with Ariana. It was weird. I wasn't hating or anything; I just wasn't used to him being a one-woman man. Hell, even his baby mama hadn't been tripping. It seemed as if all was right in his world at the moment.

As much as I loved talking about my brother and his new relationship, I had to get over it. Right now, I wanted answers about my biological family and why she'd been dodging me on giving me this information.

Deciding that a direct approach would be better instead of beating around the bush, I looked at Mama Faye with a serious expression on my face and asked, "Did you know?"

She looked down at her stained apron and nodded her head.

Finally! I thought. She already knew what I was talking about, so there was no need to elaborate.

"Cairo, when I came to America many years ago, I didn't have a pot to piss in, a soul to call family, or a card to paint green. I was here like many other illegals, trying to make a better life for m'self and mi family back home. After being here and damn near homeless for two weeks, I finally started to realize that coming to this county probably wasn't the right move for mi. The day that I finally made enough money to go back home, I ran into an older white woman at the grocery store I used to panhandle in front of. She had a little boi with her that was kicking and screaming at the top of his lungs, actin' wild as I don't know what." She laughed. "Both of their faces was red as a tomato, his from being so angry and hers from being so embarrassed. Mi stood there for fifteen minutes watching her try to get the little boi to behave. After he slapped her across the face and cursed at her for the third time, mi had had enough. Being the oldest of five siblings, mi knew a thing or two about discipline. Mi walked over to that little boi, grabbed him by his ear, and told him if he ever disrespected his mama like that again, that mi would knock the donkey piss out of him."

"He didn't try to slap you?" I asked.

She smiled. "Boi, is you crazy? Mi scared his ass so bad that day that that white woman offered me a job to be her nanny. Gave mi a place to live, paid mi well, and even helped mi get mi green card. Mi raised your father to be a respectful, honest, and smart man. When he got older, I was surprised with how careless he had become. Mi guess with all the money came all of them problems.

"That girl he got married to couldn't have any more kids after she had that first baby. Your father wanted an heir bad, so he had sex with his wife's cousin and got her pregnant with twins. When she gave birth to you and your brother, your father took custody of you both because she was into them drugs heavy.

"When he brought you home to his wife and confessed, she was heartbroken. After a month or two, she came through but told him that she couldn't go the rest of her life looking in the face of two reminders of your father's betrayal. She told him to pick one baby and give the other up for adoption.

"Your father didn't want to do that, so he asked mi to take you and raise you as my own. He knew my son had just had a baby and that I was caring for him as well. He bought mi an apartment, that car out front, and gave mi enough money to take care of you and Finesse. When you turned sixteen is what we agreed upon to return you back to your family." She looked at me and tears filled her eyes.

"When I tried to contact him, he would never call me back, so I went to the house. That woman he still married to answered the door and told me that they only had one son and he was up in his room. She told mi that you were dead to them and will never be a part of their family. Mi tried to talk to your grandmother since she and I were close, but I found out that they had her drugged up in some nursing home. That woman kicked mi out of the house that day, and I never looked back. I packed up our stuff, bought this house, and moved us out here, away from those people."

"Wow," was all I could say as she finished her story. As much as I hated to admit this, I was a little crushed that my biological parents didn't want me, even after Mama Faye tried to return me to them per their agreement.

"Thaddeus."

"What? Who's Thaddeus?"

She took my hand in hers. "Your real birth name is Thaddeus Warren Wright. When you were given to me, I renamed you after my son who had just passed. Finesse's father. It was his middle name, and mi wanted you to have it.

"Your grandmother, Elinore Wright, knew of the change. She kept in contact with me up until the time that you turned eight. After that, I never heard from her again. Mi figured that's when that crazy disease she had started to take over her mind. Hearing voices, forgetting who people were, and not remembering who she was. Her and your father's wife never did get along. They hated one another; could never be in the same place together. Mi pretty sure that she devil had something to do with Ms. Elinore being put in a home.

"Once your father was of age, the family business was passed on to him, but not before your grandmother made a few changes to her will. She told mi that she was going to include you in it, but never told mi what it was."

I would have assumed that if she was close to my biological grandmother like she said, then Elinore Wright would have told Mama Faye what was left to me in the will, but since she didn't, I went ahead and told her everything that Alex had told me.

She coughed. "How does that girl know so much about you and this will? Did you ask her that?"

"Not yet, but I plan to when we meet up for lunch sometime next week."

"I never did like that child. Her eyes, they seem sneaky, just like that little boi your father used to play with that lived across the street. I can't remember his name right now, but I remember those eyes. He used to have your father in so much trouble when they were coming up. My hand would be so red from tearing up his hide behind that nasty little sneak."

I asked Mama Faye if she remembered where the house was where she went looking for my father. As she was beginning to tell me, she started to cough uncontrollably. I got her a glass of water and helped her drink it. She then had me go to her purse to retrieve the weekly pill capsule that she had in there. When I opened up the Saturday lid and turned it over, a variety of pills in different colors and shapes fell into my palm.

"What are all these for?" I knew they couldn't all be for her blood pressure. There were six pills, plus the ones she had in the orange container.

"Cairo, help mi to mi room, I need to lay down for a few minutes," she said.

I was starting to become worried. Her eyes were low, and her speech was starting to become slurred.

"Maybe I should take you to the hos—"

"No hospital. Mi told you already it's mi blood pressure. The pills I take for it make mi drowsy and sleepy. I just need to lay down for a minute and I'll be okay."

Hesitant at first, I stood in the middle of the kitchen and just stared at her. My mind was conflicted between what I was going to do and what I really wanted to do. Once she assured me again that she was fine, I took her word for it and helped her to the bedroom.

When we got to her room, I pulled her covers back and helped her into the queen size bed. After she was tucked in, I went to my old room, kicked off my shoes, got a pair of my old basketball shorts, and changed my shirt to a wife beater.

"What are you doing, Cairo?" Mama Faye asked as I got in her bed on the other side of her.

"Laying with my mama like she used to do with me when I was younger. And before you say anything, I'm not going anywhere. You g'on ahead and get some rest. When you wake up, I'll still be here. I might even have dinner or something ready."

"Dinner?"

"Yeah, dinner. Maybe a little brown stew chicken or beef roti," I said.

"Brown stew chicken, aye? Who taught a little white boi how to make that?"

"The best mother in the world," I said as I kissed her forehead and lay back. A smile graced Mama Faye's face as she finally drifted off to sleep.

I had learned a lot of stuff that day regarding my birth family. I couldn't wait until I had this lunch with Alex. It was now going to be her turn to answer a few questions. Everything Mama Faye told me was the exact same thing that Alex told me, minus the part of Mama working for the family and my stepmother not wanting me. I couldn't believe I had a brother out there somewhere, a twin brother at that. I thought maybe I should reach out to him before I did the rest of the family.

It was times like this I wished I had some pussy to dip into and beat my frustrations out on. With all the stuff going on with my real family, the deal Alex was trying to push me into, and now Mama Faye being sick, I couldn't take too much more.

The caramel-colored beauty who'd been invading my thoughts since I laid eyes on her seemed to cross my mind a lot lately. That day I saw her in the courtroom for Ness and his baby mama's hearing sealed her fate with me. I had to have her. I didn't know what it was. Maybe it was the way her big-ass titties filled that top up, or the way her booty and hips filled those jeans out. Whatever it was had my dick twitching in my shorts to this day.

I got up out of Mama Faye's bed and headed to the living room. I couldn't be laid up in her bed with a hard on; that would be some weird shit. I found the remote to the TV and flipped it to CNN, trying to see what had been going on in the world.

I watched the news for about an hour then closed my eyes, trying to think of anything but her, but there was no use. That dark, wavy hair, those full lips, and almond-shaped eyes were a force to be reckoned with. Her gaze alone had me feeling some type of way.

When she walked out of the courtroom that day, I couldn't help but to watch the way that her ass shook from left to right with a slight jiggle. Most girls her size I imagined would be loose and wiggling all over the place, but this girl was solid and curvy in all the right places.

I looked down at my dick as it began to rise higher and get stiffer.

"My nigga, can you put that damn tree branch away? That shit is gross as hell, and I don't want my girl seeing that shit. What, or shall I ask who, in the hell got your shit over there on Iron Man mode anyway?" Finesse asked as he and Ariana walked further into the living room. I hadn't even heard his ass come in. I must've really been lost in thought thinking about Audrielle.

I straightened myself up and then placed one of the throw pillows over my lap to hide my semi-erect dick. "To be honest with you, I was thinking about your girl's sister."

Ariana looked at me with a smirk on her lips and a glint of trouble in her eye. "Let me find out you on your Drake shit. I didn't know white guys liked their girls BBW."

I shrugged my shoulders. "A woman is a woman to me. Big, tall, short, skinny, fat. It's all about the way you carry yourself. Your sister is a beautiful woman, true indeed, but her confidence is sexy as fuck to me. I've never seen a woman her size exude sexiness the way she does, and it's not like she's trying to, either. It's just natural."

"Wait a minute, bro! Are you saying that you're finally interested in a sista?" Ness joked. "It's about damn time. But just a heads up: That saying, once you go black you never go back, is true as hell, so be ready."

We all laughed. "Naw, I'm ready, though, but not for that reason. I'm attracted to Audrielle, and I want to get to know her. Any ideas of how I should do that?" I turned and asked Ariana.

"If you're free next weekend, I can put you in the right place at the right time. The rest is up to you."

I nodded my head then sat back on the couch. We joked around, watched a little TV, and conversed for a bit. When I told Ness about Mama Faye and her pills, of course, he played it off like it was nothing, but I could tell that deep down he was worried about his grandmother. She was the only biological family member he had left in the States, and if she died, I didn't know what he, or I for that matter, would do.

14

Ariana

Everything in my relationship with Finesse was going great. I didn't know what it was about him, but I couldn't get enough. Maybe because he was the only real boyfriend I'd had since I was sixteen. Tonight would be the first night I introduced him to my parents. Hopefully, everything went great. I knew it had only been a couple months for us, but I felt it was time for them to meet. Plus, my mother wanted to meet the man who'd been keeping me away from the house lately.

The doorbell rang and I all but ran to get the door. When I opened it up, I was glad to see that Audrielle had arrived. I gave her a quick hug then kissed her on the cheek. We made small talk while we headed into the dining room to finish setting the table.

"Even though you have it smelling good as hell up in here, you know I'm only here because you asked me to be, right?"

"Come on, Audri, don't start that shit tonight. Mom has already promised to be on her best behavior, so you don't have to worry about her. I want to make a good impression with Ness. His grandmother made me feel so welcomed when I met her, and I want to do the same for him."

"I hear you. I promise to be good as long as your mother is good," she said as she placed the forks and knives on the linen napkins. "How is everything going with you and him anyway? Have y'all discussed the baby and how he or she may affect y'all relationship?"

See, this was the one thing that really got on my nerves when it came to Audrielle. I knew she was just looking out for me and the potential disaster that might come behind me dating her best friend's baby daddy, but as long as Rima stayed in her lane, there wouldn't be any problems.

I knew Audri asking me about the situation was her way of making sure her baby sister was okay, but on the flip side, I knew she was looking out for Rima too. Ever since we were little, she'd always included Rima in everything we did.

Vacations, parties, family reunions, church service, etc.: Rima was there. I didn't mind because they were best friends and Rima was actually cool to hang out with, but sometimes I just wanted us, me and my sister, to enjoy each other.

The doorbell ringing again caught my attention. I ran out of the kitchen to get it but saw that my father had beaten me to the door.

"Good evening, Mr. Freeman. It's a pleasure to finally meet you, sir. Is Ariana in?"

My father took Finesse's outstretched hand, shook it, then looked him up and down. Once he assessed all that he could from his look, he opened the door a little wider and let Finesse in.

"It's nice to meet you too, young man. My baby girl has told me a lot of good things about you. I hope they are all true."

Finesse nodded his head, looked at me, and smiled. "Well, depending on what your beautiful daughter has told you, I'm quite sure everything she told you is true."

I blushed at his intense stare and felt goosebumps cover my entire body. Finesse was fine as hell, there was no denying that, but his mysteriousness was what had me. Because of my mother, I normally dated the cookie-cutter type of dude, the kind who had his life planned out since the day he came out of his mother's womb, and whose idea of spontaneity was driving ten miles above the speed limit. Of course, there was nothing wrong with that type of dude, but they were boring to me. I liked to be spontaneous and enjoy life to the fullest. In a weird way, Finesse did that for me.

I looked at my boo as he laughed at something my father said. His sex appeal was beyond description. I didn't know if it was the way his light eyes twinkled when he laughed or the small curve of his lips when he smiled. Whatever it was had my panties getting moist.

"Baby girl, bring Mr. Finesse over to my study before we sit down to eat. I need to discuss a few more things with him," my father said.

"Okay, Daddy." I turned around to look at Finesse, who had the biggest smile on his face.

"Yo, your pops is cool as hell," he said.

"What were you over here talking about?" I asked as my arms circled around his neck and his arms went around my waist.

"Sports, food, and women. You know, man stuff."

"Women, huh?" He nodded. "Well, I hope the only woman you were talking about was me."

He placed a small peck on my nose then placed his lips on mine. When his tongue slipped into my mouth, I let out a low moan.

"Baby, we need to stop before we start something we can't finish," I said, breaking away first from our kiss. "Where is your brother? I thought he was coming with you too."

Okay, I kind of lied to my sister. Tonight wasn't all about my family officially meeting Finesse. I was also trying to be a matchmaker as well. I invited Cairo over in the hopes that he and Audri would click. He'd already expressed his interest in her; I just provided a platform for him to take it to the next level. Sure, she had never dated a white dude before, but what would really be the difference? Audri was claiming to be on this man break, but I knew once she got to know him, she'd change her mind.

"He should be coming in a minute. That crazy bitch Alex kept calling his phone back to back. I told him to just take the call to see what she wanted so that she wouldn't interrupt our dinner."

Alex. I didn't care too much for her, and I had only met her once when Finesse and I went on a date with her and Cairo a couple weeks earlier. Something about her seemed off. When I asked Ness what was up with her and his brother, he said that they had dated back in college and a little after, but broke up because she was low-key psycho. Hearing that made me wonder why he was on a date with her that night. Finesse said something about they had a business deal in the works and were trying to get the details together. I left it alone at that because I could tell that Cairo really didn't have any kind of interest in her. He treated her as if she were an associate, whereas she couldn't stop making googly eyes at him. Whatever it was, it wasn't too serious, or else he wouldn't have been asking about my sister.

"Ariana, honey, who do we have here?" my mother asked as she ascended the spiral staircase.

Finesse and I were still standing in the foyer, embracing one another as she decided to make her presence known. I made the introduction between the two and held my breath, anticipating what my mother would say. Finesse wasn't the type of guy she wanted me to date, so I knew she'd say something off the wall.

"It's nice to meet you, young man. My daughter seems to be very fond of you." Ness nodded his head. "What do you do for a living, if you don't mind me asking?"

Oh Lord, here we go.

"I work for Boeing."

Her perfectly arched eyebrow shot up. "Making planes?"

"No, ma'am. I work in security."

My mother's face dropped. "Oh. Well, what does a security guard make at Boeing, around thirty-five K a year?" A frown crossed her pretty face.

"Mom! Are you serious right now? Don't answer that, babe. That's none of her business," I told Ness as I grabbed his arm and started walking toward my father's study. "I can't believe you just asked him that."

"What? I don't feel I asked anything wrong. You and your sister are so sensitive. Y'all definitely get that from your father's side. I only want what's best for you, baby. If a man can't bring anything to your table but a plate and fork, why even entertain him?"

I was so glad when we made it to my father's study. I could still hear my mother talking, but I couldn't make out what she was saying. I knocked on the study door then opened it up. My father was behind his desk with a glass of some brown liquor in his hand. He was on the phone when he motioned for Finesse to have a seat and for me to leave. I gave him a kiss on the cheek and a light tap on the shoulder, assuring him that he'd be okay.

When I made it back to the foyer, my mother was no longer there; however, I could hear her voice loud and clear as I walked toward the dining room.

"Audrielle, how long are you going to hold what I did against me? I've apologized so many times. You know you and your sister mean the world to me. I just want what's best for you," she was saying.

"So hiring a man to pretend to love me for two years is what's best for me?" Audri asked.

"It was best for your self-esteem, honey, and your health. You lost a lot of weight while you and Antonio were together. You look like a different woman now. You look like the old Audrielle who caught the attention of that handsome, educated, and successful young man, Eli Blake. I hear he's dating, but it's nothing too serious. Audri, honey, I don't think you need to eat another dinner roll. You've had two since I've been in here with you."

At that moment, I decided to make my presence known. I didn't have to be in the dining room to know that Audri was about to blow her top. Her weight was a sensitive subject to her, and our mother just didn't know when to stop.

15

Audrielle

"Honey, I'm not trying to be mean or anything. I just want you to be healthy. You look like you can now use the word *teen* at the end of your size. That's a good thing. It is. But it'll be even better if you can get down to, let's say, a size twelve. You'd for sure get Eli back or find the man of your dreams then," my mother said.

I was starting to become more annoyed by the minute. If it weren't for Ari asking me to be there, I wouldn't have come. My mother was worried about me eating three dinner rolls when I could have been at Rima's, chugging down on a big-ass bowl of salted caramel pretzel ice cream with some peanut butter cookies on the side and not have to worry about anyone counting my intake. I wanted to correct her so bad and tell her that my actual size twenty did not end with *teen*. Then again, I didn't feel like dealing with her and what she would have to say about that, once she found out.

"Mom, please change the subject before I get the hell up out of here," I said.

"You aren't going anywhere!" Ariana said as she walked into the room.

I thought Finesse would be behind her, but he wasn't. I knew he was there. I had heard a little bit of their conversation as I was walking in and out to the kitchen, bringing the food platters out, but I didn't see him. Ariana still had a smile on her face, so that meant he was around there somewhere. Either he was in the bathroom or with my father in his study.

Ah, the infamous study. The one place my father went to when he was trying to tune my mother out or get ready for the shenanigans he knew she'd no doubt start. I could just see him, sitting behind his beautiful oak desk with a double shot of Johnnie Walker Red in his favorite glass tumbler, as the smooth sounds of Smokey Robinson played in the background. My father and I spent a lot of time in that room when I was growing up. Of course, I'd have a double shot of apple juice, but it had the same calming effect.

Ariana calling my name broke me from my train of thought. When I finally looked up, both her and our mother were staring at me.

"I'm sorry, sis. What did you say?" I asked.

"I said can you go get the door for me while I put the rest of the food on the table."

I nodded my head then got up and headed toward the front. As I was walking out, I couldn't help but notice the silly smile that Ari now had on her face. She was surely up to something, but I just didn't know what.

The dinner was supposed to be just for our family, or so I thought. I noticed that there were six place settings instead of five, so someone else had to be coming by. As long as the mystery guest wasn't our ho-ass auntie, everything would be all good.

I made it to the door, opened it, and gasped at the sight before me. His six foot four height easily towered over my five foot ten frame. His dreads were pulled up on the top of his head in a bun. Those piercing, bluish-green eyes had me mesmerized. I could tell by his olive-colored skin that he either tanned or was out in the sun a lot. The white V-neck shirt he had on clung to his chiseled body like a second skin. I could see some sort of colorful tattoo that started on his chest. I wondered if it extended to the beautiful sleeve artwork he had on both arms.

I was so caught up in the sight of the person that stood before me that I didn't hear my father or Finesse walk up behind me.

"What took you so long, bro? I almost called missing persons on you," Finesse said.

The visitor finally took his heated gaze off of me and looked over my shoulder. "That call took longer than expected. I'm here now, though, ready to enjoy this good food, lovely home, and"—he looked back at me—"beautiful family." I instantly blushed.

"Is everything good?" Finesse asked.

"For now," he said with his gaze still focused on me.

"Honey Bee, let the man in or close the door. I don't pay this high-ass electric bill to keep the whole neighborhood cool too," my father said.

A little embarrassed by the way I was ogling this man, I stepped aside to let this white Adonis in. I remembered getting a glimpse of him at the store and that day we went to court for Rima, but I didn't remember him looking this good.

Once he stepped in, I closed the door and had to stand with my back to them for a minute. The combination of his sexiness and whatever cologne he had on had my pussy purring and heart thumping overtime.

Never in a million years had I thought I'd be this turned on by a white guy, but something about this dude had me going delirious like Eddie Murphy. As I tried to regain my composure, Ariana and my mother made their way from the dining room.

"Hey, Cai, you finally made it!" Ari said, giving him a hug.

What kind of name is Cai? I thought as they embraced.

"Mom, Dad, this is Finesse's brother, Cairo. Cai, these two gorgeous people are my parents, Mr. and Mrs. Freeman."

"You can call me Aaron," my dad said as they shook hands.

Cairo, huh? That's different.

My mother nodded her head in his direction, not extending the same hospitality my father had. I guess he would have to call her Mrs. Freeman. She was a trip.

"Last but not least, Cairo, this is my sister that I've told you about, Audrielle. Audri, this is Cairo." She gave our introductions and stepped back with an excited expression on her face.

"It's nice to finally meet you, Audrielle," he said.

I put my hand in his. The smoothness of his skin made my heart flutter. When his soft fingertips lightly brushed against the back of my hand, I felt my nipples become hard as pebbles.

"Nice to finally meet you as well, given certain circumstances."

We stood there and stared at each other with our hands still connected, neither one of us wanting to let go first. It took my mother clearing her throat to finally pull us from the little connection we were having.

"Come on, everyone. Dinner is ready," Ari said over her shoulder as we all followed behind her.

Cairo placed his hand at the small of my back and started to walk with me.

"Mom and Dad, you sit where you normally sit, at each end of the table. Ness, you sit here next to me, and Cairo—" Ariana looked in my direction and winked. I couldn't tell if it was for me or him. "You sit right there next to Audrielle."

I wanted to slap that silly smirk off of her face, but I'd wait until after her guest left.

To my surprise, Cairo pulled out my seat and gestured for me to sit down. Once I was comfortably situated, he took his seat.

"So, Finance, will you say grace?" my mother said.

"For the last time, his name is Finesse, Mother," Ari said through clenched teeth.

I just shook my head and laughed. Tonight was going to be just like any other. I just hoped our guests didn't get too offended.

Ari looked at my father with pleading eyes. Daddy, in return, cleared his throat to get my mother's attention, then gave her the *don't start that shit tonight* look.

"What?" she exclaimed. "It was an honest mistake. I apologize for getting your name wrong." Finesse nodded his head. "Do you mind saying grace now that that's all cleared up?" A fake smile was plastered on her face.

"I don't mind at all. Everyone, please bow your heads and close your eyes," Finesse said.

Not expecting to be touched, I quickly pulled my hand back when I felt the warmness of someone's fingers on mine. I opened one eye and looked to my left. Cairo's heated gaze caught mine. As if he were willing me with his mind, I returned my hand to the spot on the table, and he grabbed it. I opened my other eye and looked around the table to make sure no one was paying attention to our little game of conquer and defeat. Everyone's head was bowed except Ari's. I made a mental note to slap her two more times for that silly little smirk.

"Dear Heavenly Father, thank you for this food we are about to receive for the nourishment of our bodies. Thank you for the hands that prepared it. We give thanks to you for allowing us to all come together and meet tonight. Continue to bless us in life with love, health, and spiritual guidance. In your blessing name, I pray. Amen."

"Amen!" everyone responded.

Before anyone could say another word, my cell phone that I thought was on silent went off.

I can be your freak in the morning, freak in the evening, just like me. I need a rough neck nigga that can satisfy me, just for me.

"Audrielle, what kind of mess is that to have coming from your cell?" my mother asked.

I ignored my mother and silenced my phone. That was the fourth time Rima had called me since I'd been here. I assumed she was only calling to see how our family dinner was going, since I'd told her that our parents were going to meet Finesse. She seemed like she was cool about it when I told her, but the constant calling was starting to make me wonder.

Turning my ringer off, I listened to my mother complain about Rima's ringtone and how today's music was nowhere near as good as the music back in her day. With that topic coming to the helm, we were finally able to have light conversation and enjoy dinner. Baby sis outdid herself with the menu: grilled salmon with lemon butter sauce, shrimp stuffed clams, mixed veggies, and honey butter yeast rolls.

Everyone was enjoying their meals, as well as the flow of dialogue going on. Dad, Finesse, and Cairo were in their own little world, talking about sports, seeing as they were seated by each other, while my mother, Ari, and I talked about the store and the expansion plans we were thinking about.

The mood did shift, however, when my mom saw me filling my plate with seconds.

"Audri, do you think you need another plate of food? Make you one to go and eat it tomorrow, honey. Leave the stuffed clams off, though. They are good, but they are very fattening, sweetie, and we all know you don't need any more fat."

"Diana!"

"Mom!" My dad and Ari screamed at the same time.

"What? I'm only trying to help. Don't no successful, well-off man want a chubby woman on his arm, Aaron. You know that."

At that moment, the water in Finesse's mouth came spraying across the table all over me, while whatever Cairo had in his mouth had him choking. Too embarrassed to look at either of them, I excused myself from the table and went to the bathroom to dry myself off.

I placed my phone on the counter and used a paper towel to dry the small droplets of scattered water on my face. I looked at my silhouette in the mirror and couldn't help but to think that maybe my mother was right. Maybe my size twenty frame was the reason I couldn't keep and/or get a man. Eli cheated on me and left me for a smaller girl, and so did Antonio. I thought I looked good in the long-sleeve denim T-shirt dress I had on. It accentuated my curves and had my tortilla flap hidden.

Am I seeing something that everyone else doesn't? A tear started to escape my eye.

Light tapping on the bathroom door caught my attention. I assumed it was Ari, so I just unlocked it and walked back in front of the mirror, examining my figure.

"Ari, I think I'ma go on a diet. Mom might be right." I turned to the side and sucked my stomach in. When she didn't respond, I continued. "And I already know what you're going to say: 'Fuck what Mom is saying, Audrielle, you are beautiful and any man who doesn't want your total package would be stupid.'"

Once I was done imagining what I would look like ten sizes smaller, I finally turned toward the door to see why Ari was so quiet. And I almost died. Those bluish-green eyes that had me hypnotized stared back at me with a look of concern and sympathy.

"I . . . I thought you were my sister."

"I'm sorry. She did get up to come check on you, but I asked her if I could do it instead," he said.

I blushed. "Oh, well, I want to apologize for everything that happened a minute ago. As you can see, my mom has no filter, especially when it comes to my weight."

His heated glare did something to my body as he searched every inch of my frame. The way he was looking at me started to make me feel a bit self-conscious, so I wrapped my arms around my midsection.

"Don't do that," he said.

"Do what?"

"Cover yourself up like that. You know, what your mom said was wrong in so many ways."

I looked up at him, interested in what he had to say. "How so?"

He stepped more into the bathroom and into my personal space. "Well, I think I'm pretty successful, and I find you very attractive. I wouldn't mind having you on my arm."

If my face wasn't red before from blushing, it most definitely was now. The gust of wind I took in from gasping so hard had my throat so dry that I started to cough.

"You okay?" he asked.

"I will be," I managed to say between pulls of breath.

"You all right, Honey Bee?" I heard my father ask from behind Cairo.

"She's okay now, sir. We were just about to come back out there," Cairo answered.

My father looked at me then back at Cairo, nodded his head, then disappeared as quickly as he came.

"Whoever was calling you with that Adina Howard ringtone earlier must really wanna talk to you," he said as he motioned his head toward my phone. "Your notification light has been going off since I got in here, not to mention your screen lighting up a few times. Seems like I have some competition."

I was speechless for a second. *Competition? With who? For who? Wait a minute! What the hell does he know about some Adina Howard?* I wanted to ask him that so bad, but I didn't.

I picked up my phone and saw that I had numerous missed calls from Rima. Instead of calling her back and feeling more awkward by talking to her about her baby daddy in front of his brother, I checked the last text message she sent.

Rima: OMW to the hospital. Tried calling you earlier. Water broke!! Your nephew is on the way!!!

"Shit!" I said as I dropped my phone and picked it back up. "I gotta go. We gotta go. Excuse me."

"What's wrong?"

I walked past Cairo without answering his question and headed back into the dining room to get my stuff. Rounding the corner, I saw my mother and father in the corner having a hushed argument, while Ari and Finesse were making googly eyes at each other and scooping dollops of whipped cream into each other's mouths.

"What's wrong, sissy? Is everything okay?" Ariana asked. Everyone's attention turned to me.

"Yeah, I'm good."

"Well, I made your favorite, strawberry short-cake," she said.

"I'll have to pass."

"Because of what Mom said?"

"Not at all. I have to get out of here."

"To go where, Honey Bee?" My father spoke up.

"To the hospital. Rima's having the baby."

I swear it got so quiet in the room that you could hear a needle drop.

"Surely you can wait to go until after we finish with dessert, Audrielle. I'm pretty sure Rima's mother and whoever the child's father is will be there," my mom said.

I didn't even see when my sister left the room, but when she came back, she had mine, hers, and Finesse's jackets in her hand.

"Come on, babe. We might as well go too. If you don't mind, Audri, I'll drive my car," Ari said.

"Sweetie, why are you going? You and Rima aren't even friends like that," my mother said.

"Well, me and the child's father are, and if I'm dealing with him, I have to accept everything that comes along with him, including this baby," Ari answered.

"So you're dating Finesse and Rima's boy-friend?" my mother asked with a disgusted look on her face.

"Finesse is the father of Rima's child," Ariana said before she grabbed Finesse's hand and headed toward the door.

I swear the look on my mother's face was priceless. Li'l sis had surely not heard the last of this. I kissed my father good-bye then left the house with Cairo right on my tail.

16

Cairo

"So what college did you go to?" I asked Audrielle.

"I went out of state for a couple of years to Hampton University but came back and finished out at Cal State Berkeley."

"Why'd you come back?"

Audrielle looked at me for a split second then turned her attention back out the window. We were headed to the hospital, trailing behind Ariana's car. I could tell that she and Finesse needed to discuss a few things before we got there, so I had offered to drive my car and have Audrielle ride with me.

For ten minutes we sat in complete silence before I turned on the radio. I didn't want her to feel uncomfortable riding with me, so I started to ask her questions. I also wanted to get to know her a little better. She seemed kind of standoffish at first, but once she realized that I wasn't going to stop probing, she began to open up.

"I let my grades slip to *C*s from partying too much. My mother felt that it was a waste of money to pay all of those out of state fees to not be bringing home *A*s. When my second year ended, she made me come back to California. You want to know what's funny?" She looked at me and waited for me to respond. I nodded my head. "I went out of state to get away from her only to have to come back two years later. She wanted me to apply to USC or UCLA, but that was out of the question. Since UC Berkeley was the farthest college to accept me, I decided to go there."

I didn't know or understand the type of relationship she and her mother had, but I could tell there was a lot of tension there.

Audrielle's long, smooth legs that had been nervously shaking since she got into the car with me seemed to stop the minute we started to talk. I wanted to reach over so bad and move the thin denim material of her dress to the side to see the rest of the thigh.

"What about you? What school did you go to?" she asked.

"I went to UCLA. I got a scholarship."

"Sports?"

I took my eyes off the road and looked at her. "Why would you think sports?"

Her leg began to shake again. "You have that athletic build like an athlete, plus you're tall."

"So that automatically tells you that I played sports?"

"Did you?" she asked.

"Well . . . yeah, I did."

"You played." She licked her lips and smiled. "I rest my case."

I shook my head and laughed. "I did play; however, my scholarship was actually for academics."

She looked at me, a bit surprised, then nodded her head. I decided to change the subject and asked her about the store she and her sister owned. Once she opened up about that, it seemed as if our conversation just started to flow from there. Audrielle told me about everything from what owning her own business was like to how she felt growing up with a mother who constantly criticized her because of her weight.

By the time we made it to the hospital, it seemed as if we'd been old friends just catching up on each other's lives. We were still in the car talking when Finesse texted me with the number of the room they were in.

"Can I ask you something?" Audrielle said as we were getting out of the car. "It's kind of personal, but I don't want you to get offended."

"As long as I can ask you something in return, go right ahead."

She squinted her eyes and cocked her head slightly to the side. "What's up with you and the dreads? Don't get me wrong, they look good on you. I just haven't seen too many white men with them."

"Well, first things first, I'm not offended, and thanks for the compliment."

She blushed.

"Second, I really don't have an answer for what's up with my locs. When I was in junior high, I wore my hair kind of long. It was just below my ears on the top and tapered in the back. The summer before the ninth grade, I let all of my hair grow and started wearing it in a slicked-back ponytail. My moms wasn't feeling my Rico Suave look, so she twisted my hair. At first, I didn't like it. I felt weird because not only was I one out of five white kids at an all-black school, but I was the only white kid with dreads, so I kind of stood out more than the others. I was already getting teased for being raised by a black woman in a black neighborhood."

"So you were picked on a lot?"

"I was, but it wasn't anything that I couldn't handle. Eventually, everyone started to like it just like I did, so it was cool."

She nodded her head as we entered the elevator. An older couple and a few other people stepped on after us.

A girl who was already on the elevator spoke to Audrielle. "Excuse me, where'd you get your dress from?"

"Oh, I got it from this little boutique in Inglewood called Pink Curves."

"It's really cute and looks nice on you. I've always wanted to find me a dress like that one but never knew where to get it. Thanks for the info."

"You're welcome, and thank you for the compliment," Audrielle said with a smile.

The girl returned the gesture then turned to her friend, who was standing in front of me and looking down at her phone. When I stepped into the elevator a few seconds ago, she had tried to catch my attention, but I diverted my eyes from her gaze. She'd also been accidentally rubbing her ass against my thigh, and I just kept moving it out of the way, bumping into the dude standing beside me in the process.

"Hey, Keesh, her dress is fly, isn't it?" the girl asked her friend.

Flipping that long burgundy hair to the side, the friend looked up from her phone, smacking her gum and side-eyeing Audrielle.

"Yeah, I guess it is cute on her, but some things they should just leave for normal-sized people, though. I understand that BBWs are the new 'it' thing, but sometimes they go too far with these outfits."

I thought I was the only one shocked by her response, but when the older woman standing next to her husband gasped too, I knew she felt the same as me. I looked at Audrielle, who had a blank look on her face. I didn't know whether to be scared of what she was going to do next or concerned that she had totally zoned out. I remembered the story she told me in the car about how she was suspended from school for a week for beating up a girl who used to tease her and Rima in high school. Her red cheeks told me that she was a little embarrassed by what the girl had said, but her balled fist told me she was also upset and ready to slap the shit out of this chick.

Looking up at the floor numbers above the door, I felt a little sweat gathering above my eyebrow. We were going to floor thirteen, but the elevator was only on floor six. Hopefully, this girl could control her mouth and whatever else may come out of it for seven more floors.

"Damn, Keesh, that wasn't right at all," her friend snapped.

"What? I'm only telling the truth. These clothing designers and niggas wasn't worried about these big bitches until Drake said that shit in his song. Now they making bikinis and backless dresses for their fat asses. Don't nobody wanna see all that meat hanging out everywhere. Shit, I know I don't, and especially not no fine-ass man." She turned around to me with a smirk on her lips. "Isn't that right?"

At that moment, Audrielle looked up at me with questioning eyes, and so did everyone else. Even the dude who was getting off on floor nine kind of took his time when the doors opened for him to get off.

Instead of responding to her question, I did the first thing that came to my mind. I grabbed Audrielle's balled-up fist into mine, pulled her in front of me, bumping little Miss Keesh out of the way, placed my other hand on the side of her face, and brought her lips to mine.

At first, I felt Audrielle go stiff, but once I forced her mouth open with my tongue, her body relaxed into mine. We stood there with our lips locked and tongues exploring each other's mouths until the older gentleman cleared his throat and told us we had reached our floor. All eyes were still on us as we disconnected our touch.

I looked over at Keesh, whose mouth was hanging wide open. Her friend, on the other hand, had the biggest smile on her face.

"To answer your question, I don't have a problem with it at all. What I do have a problem with is hating-ass females who think that they could get a second of my attention, especially with ho-ass tactics." I grabbed a still stunned Audrielle's hand and stepped off the elevator, but not before looking ol' girl up and down and leaving her with something to think about. "A word to the wise: Make sure your shit is actually together before you try to talk about someone you know nothing about."

We walked away and started down the hall before the elevator doors closed. I didn't know what the hell had come over me and had me so protective over Audrielle like that. Maybe it was the fact that this was the second time that night I'd heard someone say something to her about her weight, and I didn't like the look on her face. Or maybe I was just doing what I'd been wanting to do to her since I first laid eyes on her. Whatever it was, it felt right, and I wasn't going to stop until I could get more.

17

Audrielle

"Audri, what took you so long? Rima's been asking about you since we got here. I told her y'all were right behind us in the car, but after that, I didn't know where y'all went. Hello? Earth to Audrielle! Cairo, what the fuck did you do to my sister?"

I could hear Ariana talking, but I was still in some sort of daze. What just happened in that elevator sort of had me stuck on stupid. I'm not talking about what that ratchet-ass ghetto troll said either. I'm talking about what that fine-ass, sexy as hell Cairo did. I was not expecting that shit at all. When he took my hand, I thought it was to calm me down. Ol' girl really tried it. I was about three seconds from slapping the don-key shit out of that disrespectful bitch, but when Cairo pulled me into his arms and kissed me, I swear my whole body froze. That tingling feeling went from the top of my head to the bottom of my feet, and my whole being just melted into his. So yeah, I could hear everything Ariana was saying, but I just didn't give a fuck.

Finesse, who was now in scrubs with a cotton shower cap on his head and feet, came running down the hall. I tried to ask him which room Rima was in, but he cut me off.

"The baby's heart rate keeps getting lower, so the doctors are going to do an emergency C-section on Rima. Only one person can go in. Of course, Rima wanted it to be you, Audri, but I shot that shit down real quick. No disrespect. All differences aside with me and her, I'm not going to miss the birth of my first baby for anybody. I hope you understand."

I nodded my head.

He looked at Ari, gave her a quick kiss, then turned to Cairo and walked back down the hall with him as they talked.

"So how do you feel li'l sis? Your man is about to have a baby with my best friend." Saying that out loud got us a few stares from the other people in the waiting room, but we didn't care.

"As long as Rima stays in her lane, it's all good. Don't get me wrong; I love Rima like a sister, but I will fuck your best friend up, Audri, if she bust the windows out of my shit like she did Ness."

We shared a laughed.

"She won't." I shook my head. "We've already had a long conversation about that."

Rima and I had just sat down at Golden Phoenix to get something to eat. We'd just gotten out of court for her vandalism hearing, and her pregnant ass was craving some Chinese food.

"Hi, welcome to Golden Phoenix. Can I start you off with an appetizer platter while you look over the menu?" the waitress asked.

"No, thank you. I already know what I want," Rima said.

"Okay, what will it be?" the cute little waitress asked in her broken English as she took her notepad and pen out of her apron pocket.

"I would like the shrimp fried rice with extra shrimp, an order of orange chicken, beef and broccoli, teriyaki chicken, and a single order of fried shrimp. I'd also like some of that sweet sauce on the side, and a large Cherry Coke."

"Very good choices. I'll be back in a few with your order."

"Um, you didn't get my friend's order," Rima said.

The waitress had a weird look on her face but quickly replaced it with a smile.

"You do know our food only comes family style," she said. "They're big servings."

"I know that!" Rima snapped. "Me and this baby in my belly are a family, so what I ordered is for us. Now, if you will, please take that little notepad and pen out again so you can get my girl's order, please. Thank you."

I tried not to laugh, but I had to. Rima's ass could be so extra sometimes.

Without looking at the menu, I gave the waitress my order. "I'll take the foil-wrapped chicken, cream cheese and crab wontons, a single order of fried shrimp, and the combination chow mein."

"For your drink?"

"I'll take the watermelon saki and a glass of water. Thanks."

She bowed her head, collected our menus, then walked off toward the kitchen.

"If they substitute any of my food for dog ass or pigeon nuts, I'ma beat your ass, Rima," I joked.

"Girl, please. You already eat that shit in the combination chow mein you ordered."

We both burst out laughing, causing the whole restaurant to stare at us.

Fifteen minutes later, May Ling returned to our table with all of our food. After we said grace, I decided to see where Rima's head was at when it came to my sister and Finesse.

"Spit truth?" I asked.

She looked up at me and nodded her head with a mouth full of rice and orange chicken.

"How do you really feel about Ariana dating Finesse? Because if it's weird to me, I know it has to be weird to you."

"Honestly, Audri, it is a little weird for me, but not as much as you may think," she answered.

"I don't get it," I said.

She put her chopsticks down and wiped her mouth with her napkin. "It's weird for me in a way, because he is my child's father, and if his and Ariana's relationship is long term, my child's godmother's sister will be his or her stepmother one day. Do you see how confusing and weird that is?"

I totally understood and acknowledged that by nodding my head.

"Now, on the other hand, it won't be weird because I don't have any feelings for Finesse. We did what we did, made a baby, and that's it."

See, now I was a little confused. If she didn't have feeling for Finesse, then why fuck up his car as much as she did? I needed to know the answer to that, so I asked.

"Honestly, I don't even know. I guess because he told me some real shit and I couldn't handle it."

"Real shit like what?" I asked.

"I met Finesse at one of my freak parties. I know you don't like what I do, so I don't tell you about some of the niggas I meet, especially when it's a one-time thing. Anyways, the night I met Finesse, he had come to the party with a few of his friends. He said he was just there to observe, and you know I don't play that looky-loo shit, so instead of kicking him out, I let him sit in the security room and watch from the monitors. A couple hours had passed, and I went to check on him. When I walked in, he was sitting on the couch with his head laid back, eyes closed, and a big-ass dick in his hand. Of course, I got turned on. I mean, he was fine as hell with a big-ass dick, so who wouldn't? Anyways, he opened his eyes as soon as I stepped into the room. I had changed into my fishnet body suit, so he was eyeing the hell out of my semi-nude body. One thing led to another, and we ended up fucking without protection.

"A couple months later, I find out I'm pregnant. I get in touch with him through a mutual friend and ask him if we could meet up. He comes to the house, and I tell him about the pregnancy. I figure we could start up some sort of relation-

ship that would eventually lead us to raising our child together and possibly being a family. I stopped my parties and everything. One day I was talking about our future and what I wanted to happen. He immediately stopped me mid conversation and told me that that was not what he wanted. He told me that there would never be anything between us but co-parenting. He said that if we had to, we could go to court to let them figure out visitation schedules and whatnot. He also said that he wouldn't have a problem paying some form of child support, just as long as we get a DNA test after the baby is born.

"Of course, I wasn't trying to hear any of that. We were going to be a family whether he liked it or not. When I started to see him out with all these different women, I got into my feelings and started to damage his things. It took me getting arrested at eight months pregnant to realize that I was acting stupid and could possibly end up in jail all because a nigga told me the real deal and I couldn't handle it."

After Rima told me that story, I didn't ask her anything else pertaining to her relationship with Finesse. One thing about Rima that I'd grown to respect and love was that she meant what she said, and if she said Ariana didn't have anything to worry about when it came to her, I knew she meant it.

"Hey, Audrielle sweetie, how are you?" Rima's mother standing in front of me and waving her hand broke me from my thoughts.

"How you doing, Kenzie? You just getting here?"

She sat down next to me. "I've been here for a while, and I'm okay as okay can be. Never thought I'd be a grandmother at forty-four, but what can I do? I'm just happy Rima waited until she was older, finished with school, and had some sort of money coming in before she had one. Lord knows it was hard for me being fourteen and having a baby to take care of."

I silently agreed with her as we sat there and talked about nothing. I liked Kenzie, but sometimes I couldn't stand to be around her. She was one of those people who liked to bring up the sacrifices she had to make while raising her child. I'm all for people taking care of their responsibilities, but didn't nobody tell her to get pregnant at fourteen.

One of the reasons why Rima was always with my family was because of her. Kenzie was always at one of her three minimum wage jobs, leaving Rima to fend for herself. After she paid rent and bills, there was hardly ever any money for extra shit like school clothes or food, so I'd always invite her over to get a nice home-cooked meal and give her some of Ariana's old hand me downs.

We sat there for the next hours just talking about this and that. Every so often I'd look up and scan the waiting room for Cairo. I saw him a couple times, pacing the hall talking on the phone, but other than that, I didn't know where he was. Once, when he was passing by the waiting room window, our eyes locked, and for a brief moment, the look of desire flashed across his blueish-green eyes. He instantly averted his stare when he realized I seen it.

I wanted to ask him what that kiss was about. I mean, I appreciated what he did and how he took up for me, but I still wanted to know what had possessed him to do it.

"It's a boy!" Finesse excitedly yelled when he walked into the waiting room.

Ariana, who had been asleep, rose from her chair and gave him a hug. Kenzie had already started her way down the hall. I was just about to follow behind her when Finesse stopped me.

"If you're going to see Rima, it won't be any use. During the surgery, something happened where she lost a lot of blood and they had to do a transfusion. After that, she was complaining about being in so much pain that they basically doped her up. She's knocked out right now and will be for a minute. I told her that you were here, so she knows. Since it's after visiting hours, they're not going to let y'all back there anyway."

"So are we about to leave too? Where's the baby?" Ariana asked.

When goosebumps started to decorate my arms and butterflies danced in my belly, I didn't have to turn around to know that Cairo was right behind me. He touched the small of my back and set my body on fire.

"What's going on?" he asked. His smooth, sultry voice caused my clit to jump.

Finesse told him the news and everything that was going on. After a round of congratulations and hand claps, they finally released each other from their brotherly hug.

"The baby is in the nursery right now, and as far as going home, babe, you can just go on ahead and go. I'm going to stay here, since Rima is out of it, and bond with my son."

"If you're staying then I'm staying," Ariana said.

"Ariana . . . " He tried to protest.

"No, Ariana nothing. I'm about to go to Rally's and get us something to eat. I got a blanket and change of clothes in my trunk, so I'm good."

"How will your sister get home?" he asked.

Shit, I was thinking the same thing. I rode up there with Cairo, but I didn't want him to go out of his way to drop me off at home.

A few seconds of silence passed before Cairo spoke up and said that he would take me.

"You cool with that, sis?" Ari asked.

"Do I have any other choice?" I said.

"There's always Mom or Dad."

I didn't want to bother my dad, and I sure as hell wasn't going to ride with my mother.

"If you don't mind, Cairo, that'll be fine," I said.

He grabbed my hand. "I'm ready when you are."

Finesse led us to the nursery before we left so that we could see his and Rima's cute little bundle of joy. While everyone was ogling li'l Cassius, I managed to stop by Rima's room anyway. I congratulated her on the new baby, gave her a kiss on the cheek, and left a note on her nightstand, letting her know that I'd be there first thing in the morning.

"You ready?" Cairo asked as I rejoined the group in the hallway.

"I am now, and thanks for the ride."

"It's my pleasure," he said as the elevator doors opened.

18

Cairo

Earlier, I had sort of kept some distance between Audrielle and me because I was avoiding her. I knew that was some sucka shit, but I didn't care. I was feeling some type of way about what went down in that elevator. There were two legitimate reasons why I was avoiding her, though; one, I didn't know what to say if she were to ask me why I kissed her and two, I was afraid that I might just do it again. Her lips were so soft and inviting. The inside of her mouth tasted like whatever cherry candy she had popped into her mouth before we got out of the car. My taste buds were starting to crave that taste, and I wanted it again.

We stood in the elevator this time, quiet and in our own thoughts. Every time I glanced over at her, she would hurriedly look away from me and act as if she was impatiently waiting for the doors to open. When we finally made it to the parking garage, I took the biggest gulp of air as soon as I stepped out into the late night breeze. Audrielle, who was still inside of the elevator, waited until I started to walk toward my car before she followed behind me.

Conversation was very minimal as we got on the highway. The only time we talked was when I asked for the directions to her house. I didn't know if the silence was a good thing or a bad thing. Maybe I went too far with that kiss. Hopefully, I hadn't turned her off, because now I was even more interested in getting to know her.

"Make a left at the stop sign, then go down about half a mile. My house will be the tan-colored one on your left," she said.

I did as I was instructed and pulled in front of her two-story home and admired the beautiful landscape.

"Your home is nice."

"Thank you," she said as she nervously reached for the door handle. I thought that was the end of our night, but I was mistaken. She turned around and asked, "What was that kiss about?"

I opened my mouth to say something, then closed it shut. I didn't know how to respond to her question at that moment. After sitting mute for a second and thinking it over, I decided to just tell her the truth.

"Honestly, Audrielle, I've wanted to kiss you like that since the first time I saw you at your store. That's one of the reasons why I was staring at you like I was. I've never been attracted to any woman as fast as I was to you. That day at the courthouse, I tried to talk to you then, but you and Rima left so fast I didn't get a chance to. I debated on coming up to the store a few times, but I thought that that would look too desperate.

"When Finesse started to bring your sister around, I'd ask about you whenever I saw her. I guess she kind of figured I was interested in you, hence the invite to dinner tonight. What happened in the elevator was a combination of what I've wanted to do for the longest and teaching ol' girl a lesson."

There! I'd said it. Everything I probably should've kept to myself was now out and told to her. I'd probably lose my G card for this, but I didn't care.

I waited for her to say something, anything, but she never did.

Maybe I shouldn't have told her the truth, I thought. *I probably made her uncomfortable.*

From the look on her face, I didn't know what to think. She just continued to sit there in silence, looking at nothing in particular. With minutes slowly passing, I was starting to become a bit uncomfortable. I didn't mind spending some time with her chilling, but not in my car just listening to the radio. I looked over at Audrielle, just to see the back of her head as she stared out of the window. Not sure whether to ask her for her number now, I got ready to just take this L for the night and try again another day.

I was just about to tell her good night and that I'd see her later, but I was silenced when she grabbed my chin and crashed her lips onto mine. I was shocked by her taking complete control like that, and my dick swelled to five times its size. My shit was so hard that I'd probably drill a ten-foot hole in her pussy if she gave me the chance.

Not one to let this opportunity pass me by, I took her into my arms and pressed my lips harder into hers, while trying to pull her body against mine. Although my new Q70L was quite roomy on the inside, the middle console kept us from being as close as I wanted to be.

I broke from our lip connection and trailed small kisses along her cheek and jawline. A small moan escaped her mouth and sent a chill up my spine. When I got to her neck, she tilted her head back and provided full access as I started to massage that area with my tongue.

I was on my way to heaven until she suddenly pulled away and brought me back down.

"I'm . . . sorry, Cairo. I don't know what came over me. I don't know if we should even be doing this. We've only officially met a few hours ago." She turned away from me and started to straighten her clothes. "I don't want to regret, or even worse, have you think that—"

"Audrielle, I'm not thinking anything about you, okay?" I pulled her back into me and kissed her neck and shoulder. Her scent and taste was intoxicating, and I didn't want to stop. "Just relax. Everything is cool."

I unbuttoned the first two buttons of her dress. When she didn't stop me, I continued with the rest. I pulled down the top half of her dress over her shoulders, revealing the most perfect set of titties I'd ever seen. Kissing them softly, I heard Audrielle begin to moan louder. Before I could put her Hershey's Kiss–sized nipple in my mouth, she pushed away from me again, opened the car door, and pulled her dress back over her shoulder.

"I'm sorry. I can't. I can't do this, Cairo. This is crazy."

"It is. But it's also obvious we're attracted to each other. I know you feel whatever that connection is between us when we kiss." By this time, I was already out of my car and standing beside Audrielle on the passenger side as she silently fought with herself about what she really wanted to do. I didn't want her to shut anything down, so I decided to help her out a little.

"Look, we are both grown, so if we do decide to cross that line, it's no one's business but ours. Just know that I'm not going to try and force you to do anything you're not comfortable with, okay?" I said as I started to kiss her neck again and pull on her dress.

"Shit!" Her voice was now low and raspy. "Okay, but not out here." She broke away from me for the third time, took my hand, and led me up the walkway to her front door.

"Let me get those for you." I picked up the large vase of white calla lilies that were sitting on her porch. I didn't know why a twinge of jealousy shot through me as I lifted the beautiful and expensive arrangement. It wasn't like she was my girl or anything yet. The card that was nestled deep within the leaves was calling my name. I wanted to take it out and read it. The urge to know whose ass I would probably be kicking if they kept sending these muthafuckas after I made her mine started to take over my thoughts, and the tension must've been evident on my face, because after she looked back at me, she started to explain.

"Someone's been sending me bouquets of flowers every day for the last couple of weeks, sometimes twice a day. At first, I thought it was my mother trying to apologize for something she did, but after the second time, I knew it was too good to be true."

Not really satisfied with that explanation, I simply nodded my head and continued to follow behind her. As soon as she opened the door, the sweet fragrance that this delicate flower gave off hit my nose ten times harder. Her whole living room was cluttered with different arrangements from week old to fairly new.

"Wow, somebody's trying to get your attention," I said as I admired her living room and its botanical setup.

"Maybe, but right now I'm trying to give it to you."

When I turned around, Audrielle was standing in front of me with nothing on but her black lace bra and matching panties. Her jean dress was pooled on the floor at the bottom of her feet.

I started from the top of her head and scanned her entire body. I was in awe of her perfect hourglass shape. Her caramel skin was even and smooth. She had a couple stretch marks around her little belly, but it didn't bother me. When she noticed me looking at her stomach, she drew in a breath, trying to hold it in and moving her arms in front of it.

"You don't have to hide from me, Audrielle. I already love everything I see," I said.

I walked up to her, grabbed her wrists, and removed her arms from hiding her midsection. I got down on my knees, rested my hands on her hips, and brought her stomach to my lips, placing small kisses everywhere.

"I don't ever want to see you hide yourself from me again," I said between kisses, and she breathlessly agreed. I remembered her doing the same thing when we were in the bathroom at her parents' house. That small insecurity would be something she would need to get over if she was fucking with me. A timid sex partner would turn me off instantly.

I couldn't see her face, but from the way she was moaning and gripping my dreads, I knew that she was enjoying the way that my lips felt on her skin. I could feel the goosebumps rise on her body as I licked and embrace every inch of her.

"Are you sure you're ready for what you've started?" I asked as I kissed my way up her body and stood onto my feet.

She looked at me with those gorgeous bed-room eyes and collided her luscious frame against mine. "I'm more than ready," was Audrielle's reply as she took my mouth into hers.

19

Audrielle

Telling Cairo that I was more than ready for him was the only invitation he needed to make me feel like no other man had ever done before. The way his lips and touch made my body feel, I didn't know how much more I could take.

When he went to remove my bra and panties, I started to become a little uncomfortable again, but the stern look he gave me when I tried to cover myself up had my arms falling back down to my side in no time. I didn't know why, but standing in my living room completely naked, surrounded by bouquets of calla lilies while he took me all in, had me nervous. Although the look he had in his eyes was different from the way Antonio or even Eli used to look at me, I was still skittish about him seeing me fully nude.

Our kiss deepened the moment he took off his clothes and hungrily latched on to my lips again, causing me to forget all about my indecision. I didn't know what it was about this moment, but something in it felt so right.

He drew back from our kiss and peered into my eyes. The look of longing and desire danced in his, while the glimpse of uncertainty and timidity cha-cha'd in mine.

"Audrielle, if you want me to stop, please let me know before this goes any further. It would take a whole army to get me off of you once I get started." He pecked my lips and caressed my face.

I tried to speak, but the words got caught in my throat. His touch was electrifying and had me practically speechless. Because of my temporary selective mutism, I didn't want Cairo to assume that I wanted what we were experiencing to be over, so I grabbed his hand and led him over to my plush couch and lay down, pulling him on top of me.

My body melted the moment his fingertips started to trace every part of me. Cairo luxuriated in every single inch of my body with his kisses and embrace: my chin, the sensitive spot between my neck and shoulder, my semi-perky breasts, my navel, and my thighs. Everywhere Cairo's lips or hands touched sent that tingly feeling throughout my body.

I arched my back and screamed out his name when his tongue danced around and made figure eights on my throbbing nub. I came hard so many times that my vision became a little blurry when I tried to open my eyes. We made love in the middle of my living room with the sweet scent of calla lilies lingering in the air and the moonlight shining through the small opening in the curtain, illuminating our naked bodies.

Cairo was a skillful and attentive lover. When he entered me with slow, deep thrust, I wrapped my legs hungrily around his waist, craving the very essence of him.

"Fuck, Audri, I don't think I could ever get enough of the way you feel," he whispered in my ear as he filled me with his seed.

I didn't even care that we weren't using protection and that Cairo had just released all of his babies inside me. My euphoria had me so high in the clouds that I couldn't separate right from wrong if I wanted to. Besides, I wasn't worried about getting pregnant. The doctor had told me with my weight and my period being irregular, that the people in hell would have had two cups of ice water before I was with child. As far as a sexually transmitted disease, I knew I was clean. His status was in question. While I was at the hospital visiting Rima, I would make sure to stop by the clinic to get tested. If we did have sex again, protection would definitely be used.

Cairo followed me into the bedroom and lay down on the side of my bed that had been unoccupied for weeks. His dreads fanned out across the pillow while he had his head laid to the left with his eyes closed.

I looked down at his chest and wanted to lick the tiny droplets of sweat that seemed to form as he laid there. His pecs were huge and rock solid. The six pack in his abs was sexier than his chest. My black sheet rested below his hips, exposing that V-cut on men that turned me on. The bulge that was noticeable between his thighs had me licking my lips in anticipation of what was to come once I put my lips around it. If we happened to go another round, I was going to suck the color off of the big muthafucka.

I was so into fantasizing that I didn't feel Cairo's hand on the back of my neck until he was pulling me over to him and placing my head onto his chest.

"Having second thoughts?" His voice was low and deep. I could tell he was trying to fight the sleep that was trying to take over.

"No, not really. I'm just laying here thinking about how good I actually feel."

He turned and faced me with an eyebrow raised and one eye open. "Just good?"

I nervously nodded my head. "Yeah, good. Good is a good thing . . . right?"

"Give me about twenty minutes. Then we'll see if we can change that good to great."

I smiled on the inside and out as he shut his eye, nuzzled closer into me, and dozed off, his arm and leg possessively wrapped around my body like he didn't want to let go.

Our first session was so intense, probably the most satisfying and erotic experience I'd ever had. It seemed as if Cairo's sole objective was to satisfy me. My nub started to thump.

Looking at the time on my cable box, I saw that it was 3:15 a.m. If I didn't feel any movement out of him by 3:34, I would make sure to wake his ass up with some of the greatest head he ever had. Round two was definitely going to happen.

I woke up the next morning feeling refreshed, ready for the world, and sexy as hell. Not only did that second round go down, but a third and fourth followed soon after. I only had an hour of sleep before my internal alarm clock woke me up.

The first thing I wanted to do was go down to my kitchen and make Cairo a hearty breakfast.

With all the work he put in the night before, he deserved it. Scrambled eggs, smoked sausage links, banana pancakes, bacon, and hash browns: He deserved it all. The only problem was that I couldn't cook worth a lick. At the most, I could make him a toasted bagel with some honey cream cheese and a glass of whatever juice was in the fridge. Other than that, he would probably die from food poisoning if I attempted to cook.

I know what you're thinking: How is it that a girl my size didn't know how to cook? It's simple; I just didn't. I mean, I could make the little things like hot dogs, ramen noodles, and stuff like that, but complete meals, that was an entirely different story. With the way Cairo had me feeling, though, I figured I would probably be able to hook something up.

I looked down at that sexy man as he slept and couldn't do anything but smile and bite my lip as flashbacks of the night before ran through my mind.

"I could definitely fall in love with you," I said against his forehead as I sweetly placed a kiss there. He stirred for a second then returned to his calm pattern of sleep.

Gently easing out of bed, I went straight to my bathroom, brushed my teeth, hopped in the shower, then lotioned my body from head to toe with cocoa butter. A few light sprays of my Victoria's Secret Bombshell fragrance and I was ready to go.

I walked into my closet, looking for something to wear. Normally when I was at work, I dressed the part by wearing a pair of whatever new sneakers were out and either some jeans and a shirt, a fashionable jumpsuit, or some joggers and a tank. Today, I opted to choose an outfit from my sexy side of the closet.

I picked out my light-washed denim jeans with the slits that started at the ankle and stopped just before the pockets. Normally I wouldn't wear anything like this because I hated how big my thighs were, but with Rima pressuring me to step outside of my safety net and me loving the way the jeans fit my curves and hid my little belly pouch, I had purchased them. That was almost two years ago, and I was just now wearing them.

Not being able to decide which top I wanted to pair my jeans with, I just went to my drawers and pulled out a white wife beater. While searching for some accessories, I stumbled upon some coral-colored suspenders that Antonio's ass must've forgotten. I was about to throw them away when I remembered that they would match the new Steve Madden platform wedges I bought some time ago that had splashes of coral in them.

I pulled the shoes down from my shelf, and just as I thought, they were a perfect match. Taking everything I decided to wear back into the bathroom, I got dressed, putting everything together. I didn't feel like flat ironing my hair, so I put it up in a messy bun on the top of my head. After I applied my makeup and chunky jewelry, I stepped back and admired myself.

"Damn, you look sexy as hell," Cairo said from behind me, startling me a bit.

"Thank you." I felt my cheeks turning red.

"If I didn't have to go handle some business in a few hours, I'd make you stay home from work so we could finish where we left off."

He walked up behind me and slid his hands around my waist. When they landed on my stomach, I wanted to move them so bad, but when he started to kiss a trail down my neck, any insecurity I was having about my body slipped away.

"I'm going to hop in the shower real quick, and then we can leave. I would invite you to join me, but since you're already dressed and ready to go, I guess I'll have to take a rain check. Next time, wake me up so I can take one with you," he said as he slapped me on my ass and walked off.

Twenty minutes later, he was dressed in yesterday's clothes and we were headed out the door. Because of the early morning traffic, the ride to my parents' house was longer than usual.

Conversation in the car flowed pretty well. We talked a little more about our personal and professional lives.

When we pulled up to my parents' house, I was just expecting to say a quick good-bye then go our separate ways, but when he parked his car behind mine, shut his engine off, then got out to open my door, I knew it wouldn't be so quick.

"Audrielle, I just wanna let you know that I really enjoyed last night. I definitely want to do it again, but not before I officially take you out for a first date. Are you busy this weekend?"

I thought about it for a moment and was about to say yes when I remembered that early this morning, Kenzie had left me a voice mail asking if I could pick up Rima from the hospital since she couldn't. I didn't believe the shit for a second. According to Rima, Kenzie was only working half time now. Her new boyfriend was taking care of the majority of her bills. She only still worked for the benefits.

"I'm sorry, Cai, I can't this weekend. I'ma be with Rima."

He playfully poked out his lips and nodded his head.

"I'm free next weekend, though."

"Next weekend isn't good for me. I have a game. Maybe the following weekend?"

"Maybe," I said as I opened my car door to get in.

"We'll figure it out. Put your number in my phone and I'll call you so we can set something up," he said.

We sat there and stared at each other for I don't know how long. Cairo brought his hand up to my face and caressed my jawline with his fingertips. My eyes instantly closed and that same tingly feeling shot through my body.

He placed the sweetest and simplest kiss on my lips. "I'll call you later, okay?"

I nodded my head, still dazed, and finally got into my car. Through the rearview mirror, I watched Cairo hop into his black Infiniti Q70L. I honked the horn twice then backed out of the driveway.

The curtain moving in my parents' window caught my attention. I had known there was a chance that my mother would be home when Cairo dropped me off that morning, but I didn't really care. I was sure she'd find some kind of way to come by the store later just to bombard me with questions. I just hoped no fly shit came out of her mouth, because I was enjoying this high that I was on, and I wasn't going to let anyone bring me down.

20

Cairo

It had been almost a month since I'd seen Audrielle or anyone else for that matter. The project that I won for the city needed to be finished in an expedited time. The first few drawings I presented were rejected. My vision and what the client wanted just didn't seem to click, but once the new project manager and I had a sit down and hashed some things out, we were able to come up with some ideas that worked out well.

Alex had been calling me left and right, but I was still ignoring her. Finesse had been real busy with the baby, so I hadn't seen him in a while. Mama Faye was still hiding whatever illness she had. Although her skin was coming back around to its rich, dark color, the wig she now wore had me wondering what had happened to her real hair.

Besides Facetime, phone conversations, and text messaging, Audrielle and I hadn't seen each other since the night we had sex in her living room. Just thinking about her and her insides had my dick hard as fuck. She didn't know this, and I doubted that I would ever tell her, but a minute after her smooth, warm, tight walls wrapped around my dick, I withdrew from inside of her and came on her couch. I played it off and said that my mouth was craving a taste of her sweet nectar. I really did want to taste her, but I also needed time to recoup and get a grasp on what had just happened.

The conversation Ness, Rod, my teammates and I had in the lunchroom that day started to flood my mind. Never in a million years did I think that those fools were telling the truth when they were saying the blacker the berry, the sweeter the juice. Now that I knew the candied taste for myself and had felt it firsthand, there was no way in this world that I was turning back to my old way of thinking.

"Nigga, what the fuck are you over there thinking about that has your face looking goofy as hell?" Rod asked.

"I bet you I know," Finesse said as he took a sip of his Corona. "Only one thing can make a man's face look like that, and that, my dear friend, is some juicy black pussy."

"Whaaaaaat! You finally decided to take a dip in that sweet black berry juice?"

I shook my head. "You guys are stupid."

"Wait, is that the reason why you bought this new house? The pussy got you wanting to start a family and shit already?" Rod snapped, causing Ness to fall over, laughing.

We were sitting in the middle of my new unfurnished living room, playing poker and having drinks.

During those weeks I was working hard on that project, my realtor had called and told me that the house I had made an offer on some months ago finally came through. The couple who owned it before me wanted to get it off of the market as soon as possible, and since I was the last person to make an offer, they reached out to see if I was still interested. I was, and instead of going with the original offer, some conditions changed since they were now coming for me. As long as they were willing to lower the selling price by ten thousand and agreed to pay all of the closing costs for making me wait, I was ready to sign on the dotted line. Needless to say, after a week of contemplating on their part, they finally agreed, the necessary paperwork was signed, and the keys were placed in my hand. Because the couple was now residing in

Canada and were no longer living in the house, they didn't mind me moving in before escrow officially closed.

With the move into my new house, my condo was now up for grabs, and instead of putting it on the market like I had originally planned, I gave it to Finesse. The two-bedroom with one and a half baths was now his. The extra space I used for my office could possibly be turned into a nursery if he needed the room. I knew with him having my nephew the majority of the time, it would be a great idea.

"For your information, I was in the market to buy a house long before I met Audrielle. Just so happens that the people who owned the house I wanted finally stopped playing hard ball and accepted my offer," I explained.

"Audrielle?" Rod looked at Ness. "As in your girl's sister?"

Finesse nodded his head.

"Damn, Cai! I didn't know you were into big'ums. What do y'all do all day, eat?" He fell out laughing and so did Ness until he saw the look on my face.

"Aye yo, Rod, that's not funny. That's my future sister-in-law you're talking about," Ness said.

"I know, but bruh, is she adopted or something? Because ain't no way she can be related to your girl. I mean, they are on complete opposite sides of the Richter scale. Were their parents only feeding her and starving Ariana?" He laughed some more.

Because Rod was more of Finesse's friend, I was giving him the opportunity to check his boy about disrespecting Audrielle before I did.

"Man, Audrielle is not adopted. She and Ariana have the same parents. They look just alike. Ariana is just smaller. Audrielle is real pretty . . . for a big girl."

At that moment I had to intervene.

"What do you mean for a big girl?" I asked Ness. "You don't think big girls can be pretty?"

"No. Yes. I mean, I don't know!" He shrugged his shoulders. "I've seen some real pretty big chicks, and I've also seen some real unattractive ones."

"And you've never seen any unattractive small girls?" I challenged.

"I'm not saying that, Cai. It's just that when you're big, you have a lot more against you. An ugly small girl can get plenty of play if her body is right. You know niggas don't care too much about a girl's face when her titties are sitting pretty, the waist is slim, and the ass is sitting just right, whereas if you're overweight with rolls here and there, and your gut is sticking out more than your ass, who would be attracted to that?"

Rod nodded his head. "On some real shit, Cai, I'm surprised you're attracted to her at all. Especially if you think about all of the chicks you smashed during and after college. You had a fine stable of honeys, with Alex being your number one thoroughbred."

They gave each other dap.

"Alex ass is fine as all outdoors, but she's crazy as hell. I can't fuck with that psycho shit," Ness said.

"Speaking of psycho . . ." I decided to change the subject before some things were said and done that I would possibly later regret. "What's up with Rima?"

"She's fine!"

That answer would've been okay if it came out of Finesse's mouth, but since Roderick was the one who answered the question, I didn't know how to respond.

"Ay, Rod, how you know she fine?"

Rod was stuck for a minute after realizing his slip of the tongue, but he recovered quickly.

"I wasn't saying how she was doing, I was . . . I was saying how she looked. Rima is fine, just like Alex ass."

A smirk crossed my face as I watched Rod start to flitter around in his seat. I didn't know about Ness, but I didn't believe that bullshit for one minute. Like I said before, I wouldn't put it past him if he ran into Rima before or after he had her arrested. The nigga was dirty like that.

"Ay, Cai, I'm about to raise up out of here, bro," Finesse said, extending his hand out to me but still staring at a nervous-looking Rod. "I gotta go pick up Li'l Cass since Rima is still tripping. I hope she gets over this postpartum shit soon. I love having my son all of the time, but it's starting to affect me and Ari's relationship, especially when Rima calls during all hours of the night crying about not being able to get Li'l Cas to stop crying."

That was news to me, and maybe one of the reasons why I hadn't seen Audrielle. After she got off of work, she'd go over to Rima's. I thought it was just to spend some time with her new godson, but maybe it was more than that.

I gave Ness a brotherly hug then walked him to the door.

"I think I'm about to head out too," Rod chimed in. "I got a little party to go to." He looked down at his watch.

"Congratulations on the new house, bro," Ness said.

"Yeah, congrats, Cai," Rod said before I closed the door behind them.

With the night still being young, I decided to give Audri a call to see if we could finally go out. When she didn't answer, I decided to call it a night. The next day after I stopped by Mama Faye's, I would make a brief stop to her house. It had been too long since I saw her, and I needed to see my baby.

What was supposed to be a great morning for me ended up turning out to be one of the worst mornings in my life. After only getting a couple hours of sleep, I received a frantic call from Finesse saying that the ambulance had rushed Mama Faye to the hospital. When he stopped by her house early that morning, he had found her lying on the floor, unresponsive and barely breathing.

It took everything in me not to cause a scene at the hospital when I got there. The nurses weren't trying to give me any type of information about Mama Faye. I guess my skin color had them kind of leery of telling me anything. They all made the same *yeah, right* face when I said that I was her son. It took Finesse coming out of Mama Faye's room in ICU and cosigning for me before they gave me a visitor's pass and let me in.

I stepped into Mama Faye's room, and my heart dropped. I didn't even recognize her with all of those tubes coming out of her mouth, arms, and chest. Her skin was back to that ashy color, and all of her hair was gone, even her eyebrows. I knew it had been about a month since I'd seen her, but I didn't think she was doing that bad. A few tears started to escape my eyes as the possibility of losing the only woman I'd ever known to be my mother started to run through my mind.

"Mr. Broussard?" the doctor, who I didn't hear come into the room, called out. I looked up at the Laz Alonso replica and waited for him to continue. "Oh, I apologize. I didn't know Ms. Faye had a visitor. I thought Mr. Broussard was still in here. I'll come back later."

"No need." I looked over at Finesse, who was sound asleep on the small chair in the corner of the room. The curtain that was by the door must've shielded the doctor's sight. "My brother Finesse and I both share the same last name. Whatever you need to tell him about Mama Faye, you can just tell me."

He gave me that all too familiar look before he decided to continue with what he was originally going to say. "I have a few things that I would like to go over with Mr. Broussard . . . and yourself, if you'd like to step into my office."

I turned around and woke Ness, telling him what the doctor had just told me. After kissing Mama Faye on her forehead and whispering in her ear that I'd be back, we followed behind the doctor and entered into his spacious office that was a few floors above ICU.

"First things first, gentlemen. I'm Dr. Eli Blake, and I'll be one of the physicians keeping an eye on your mother during her stay." He stuck his hand out for each of us to shake. "I'm sorry that we had to meet under these circumstances, but I promise I am going to do everything I can to help her get better. Now, are you two aware of what's going on with Ms. Faye's health?"

Finesse and I both shook our heads no.

"The only thing I do know is that she's been taking a lot of different medications recently. I know when I asked her if anything was wrong, she would just say it was her blood pressure," I explained.

"According to the charts that were given to me for review, her blood pressure has been very high lately. Unfortunately, that isn't the only thing going on."

"Excuse me, Doc," Finesse said, "but did you just say *charts that were given to you for review*? Are you not my grandmother's primary physician?"

"As of a week ago, I am. Her previous physician, Dr. Stanton, is out of the country right now giving medical attention abroad, so I'm taking over all of his cases." He looked Finesse directly in the eye. "Do you have a problem with me attending to your grandmother?" His eyebrow rose and a challenging smirk slithered across his lips.

The look on Finesse's face told me that the doctor's authoritative demeanor and cocky personality struck a chord with him. The thing was, we didn't have any time to play "who has the biggest cock in the hen house" and so before their attitudes clashed and gauntlets were thrown, I decided to intercede.

"Neither me nor my brother have a problem with you attending to Mama Faye. We're just trying to find out what's going on, as well as what can be done to get her health back up to par," I said.

He and Ness stared each other down for a minute before he decided to continue. "As I was saying, Ms. Faye's blood pressure isn't the only thing that's going on. She does have a few medical issues that are very serious and would need a lot of medical attention. Now here at Sacred Heart, we have everything she would need to be accommodated, but it will become very expensive on her road to recovery."

"Expensive? Isn't that what her insurance is for?" I asked.

"Her insurance takes care of some of her medical needs, but not all. There is only so much that her HMO pays for. The rest will have to be out of pocket or from some other source of funding," the doctor said.

"Whoa, whoa, whoa! Out of pocket? Some other source of funding? Nigga, please! I've never heard of no shit like that. You haven't even told us what's wrong with her," Ness said with his temperature rising by the minute. "What type of treatment will cost so much that the insurance doesn't even cover it?"

Dr. Blake walked over to a table with a huge stack of files on it. He moved a few folders then pulled one out. Opening it up, he glanced over the content then sat down in his seat.

"Normally someone from the insurance department would come in and talk to you about this, but since we're here, I'll go ahead and explain what's going on. Ms. Faye has stage two uterine cancer, which means it's spreading. A year ago, she was put on radiation therapy, and we thought it worked. About four months ago, she came in complaining about some abnormal symptoms like vaginal bleeding as well as urination and pelvic pain. Because of her previous diagnosis with

UC, certain tests were done, and we discovered that the cancer had come back. This time around, we went with chemotherapy treatments, but it isn't working as effectively as we hoped, so now we have to do surgery. The thing is, while doing more testing, we discovered Ms. Faye is also suffering from neurological AVM, better known as arteriovenous malformation in the medical world. Those spells of dizziness, headaches, and tingly sensations were not from her high blood pressure."

He put some images of Mama Faye's brain on the screen behind his desk. "Because the AVM is small and located on the surface of her brain, we need to go in and remove it now to prevent any future complications. Your mother's insurance will only cover one of those surgeries. The other will have to be financed some other way."

The situation with Mama Faye was becoming more and more stressful, but something had to be done. I couldn't stand to lose her, especially if I could've prevented it in some way.

"Okay, Dr. Blake, so I know the outcome of the cancer not being treated, but what about this AVM stuff?" I asked.

"Well, if the AVM isn't removed, the most serious complication will be bleeding in the brain, resulting in a stroke, and with those, you never know what the outcome will be."

Coming out of the doctor's office, I was more confused than when I went in. Mama Faye had cancer and had had it for some time now. I wondered why she never told us. I was hurt, but Finesse was hurt even more. Not only could we lose our mother, but where were we going to get the extra money to help pay her medical costs? I had just used a big portion of my savings buying and furnishing my new house, and Finesse ran through money like there was no tomorrow. I doubted he had anything saved.

"Man, I hate to say this, but you might just have to take Alex up on her offer," Finesse said.

"Her offer?"

"Yeah, man. Marry her crazy ass for that inheritance money."

"Nigga, you trippin'! There has to be some other way we can get this money. I got about seven thousand left in my account. What about you?" I asked.

"Shit, you know I'm broke. Between taking care of my bills, Li'l Cass, Ari, and buying Rima that new car, I have about two grand in my savings."

New car? I made a mental note to ask him about that later. Right now, we had bigger problems.

"Maybe we could both try to get loans from the bank," I suggested.

"Do you hear yourself, Cai? First off, you just got a loan for that house, so I doubt you'd be able to get another one this fast, and as for me, I'm a black man with little to no credit. They ain't fucking with me, especially without any collateral."

As much as I hated to admit it, he was right. There had to be some other way besides me marrying Alex.

I scrolled down my call log and saw a few missed calls and text messages from Audri. I swear as soon as I saw her name, my heart started to beat at a rapid pace. I needed to see her beautiful smile and feel the warmth of her body wrapped around me tightly in a hug. I sent her a text letting her know what was happening. She replied with her condolences then offered to bring me something to eat since I hadn't had anything since the day before. I felt that I needed a break for a few hours, so I asked if I could just come to her house and eat whatever she cooked for me. She said yes, and I got up to leave.

"All right, bro. I'm out. I'll be back in a few hours," I said.

"Where you going?" Ness asked with bloodshot eyes and a tear-stained face.

"I'm going to get something to eat, then a few hours of sleep. You want me to bring you something back?"

He shook his head. I gave him a brotherly hug then headed for the elevator.

"Yo, Cai!" I turned around and saw Finesse walking up to me. "I know being married to Alex isn't what you want, but just think about Mama Faye for a minute. A month of you giving her your last name and putting up with her crazy antics could result in a few more years we have our mother in our lives."

"Damn!" I said as I finally got on the elevator. I might just have to bite the bullet and take this L.

21

Audrielle

"All right, girl, I'll talk to you later. Someone's at my door. What? Girl, bye. I'll call you tomorrow. Whatever it is you had to tell me could wait until then. I gotta go. Bye." I laughed as I hung up the phone with Sarah. We'd been talking about nothing for the last thirty minutes. She kept saying she had something to tell me, but every time she started to bring it up, the conversation was changed to something else.

My doorbell rang again. Man, whoever was out there was really impatient. I knew Cai was just leaving the hospital from seeing about his mom, so I knew it wasn't him. Rima was at home with the baby, and Ariana was closing down the store. Maybe it was the delivery guy with the food I had ordered from the Thai place up the street; either that or a Jehovah's Witness.

"Who is it?" I yelled as I walked toward the door, grabbing my wallet along the way, just in case it was my food. There was no response, so I asked the question again. "Who is it?"

"Audrielle, open the door please." My body froze the instant I heard her voice. I knew damn well my ho-ass auntie didn't show her face at my house. After the shit that went down with Antonio, her ass went into hiding. She knew I had an ass beating put up on the shelf with her name on it.

"What do you want, Sydney?"

She laughed. "Oh, we on a first name basis now. I'm not Aunt Syd anymore?"

I didn't respond.

"Open up the door, Audrielle, and quit being so dramatic. That's the one thing I hated about you."

I had just received some new workout gear that I ordered online. It was sitting in a box next to the door. Quickly opening it up, I took off my spaghetti-strap sundress and slipped on the Nike Pro Core shorts and crew top shirt. I slid out of my flip flops because I didn't want to take the chance of falling when I charged at her ass. My hair was already in a ponytail, so I just tightened up the scrunchie and put my hair into a ball, just in case this bitch was a hair puller.

When I opened the door, her back was turned toward me, but as soon as she turned around, I socked her dead in the face.

"Audrielle, what the fuck!" she screamed as her hand immediately went to her bloody nose.

"You thought I'd forget about what the fuck you did?" I tried to punch her in the face again, but this time, she moved, causing my fist to connect with her shoulder instead.

"Aaaaaah! Damn it, Audri, I'm not trying to fight you. I actually came over to apologize."

"Apologize my ass." I swung on her again, this time connecting to her lip. Once I was satisfied with the way her lip started to swell up, I stepped back into my house and slammed the door in her face. She banged on my door for a few moments and even threatened to call the police, but once she realized that I didn't give a fuck, she finally left.

My right hand was throbbing, so I went to the kitchen to get an ice pack. As soon as I sat down on the stool to nurse my knuckles, the house phone started to ring. One minute later, my cell phone started to go off, and then my text message alerts started to go crazy. I knew it wasn't anyone but my parents and Ariana calling about what had just happened. I would worry about talking to them tomorrow. Right now I had to clean myself up and be a little cute for when Cairo got there.

A quick shower and an even quicker change of clothes had me ready when the deliveryman arrived and looking good when Cairo finally rang my doorbell.

The minute we saw each other, our lips automatically connected. I didn't know what it was about this man's kisses, but I would probably die if I couldn't have them for the rest of my life.

Foreheads pressed together and eyes closed, we just stood in my doorway hugging as I tried to transfer all of his hurt into me. I wasn't surprised at all when I felt tears falling on my face. If my daddy was in the hospital for any kind of illness, I would probably be the same way.

"How is she?" I asked as I pulled him into my home and closed the door.

It took him a minute to get himself together, but once he did, he told me that things weren't looking too good. He explained to me the situation, and my heart went out to him even more. We were just getting to know each other and weren't in any type of relationship, but if I had the money, I would have definitely given it to him. My store was doing well, but it wasn't doing that well. I wanted to open up another location but couldn't because I didn't want to be completely broke for the first year.

"I hope you like Thai?" I asked as we went to my dining room. I had already set the table with plates and forks. All we needed was the food from the containers, and we'd be ready to dig in.

"Yeah, I'm cool with it; although I was expecting to come over to a home-cooked meal," he joked.

"Unfortunately, you'll be expecting that for a long time, or at least until I learn how to cook."

"Wait a minute. You can't cook?" he asked.

I turned around with my hands on my hips. "What, you think just because I'm a big girl that I'm Rachael Rayin' it up in here?"

"I never said that, Audri," he replied with a little bit of attitude. "I just thought since your sister knew how to cook, you did too."

"Well, I don't."

"That's cool, because I do."

We sat there and stared at each other for a few moments before we burst out into laughter.

"You know, you're really cute when you're mad. Your nose wrinkles up and your voice goes up an octave," he said.

I flipped him off then started to open the containers of deliciousness. After piling food on our plates, the conversation started to flow for the most part, and we learned some things about each other that we hadn't discussed before. I was trying to make him forget about his problems for at least a couple hours, because what he was going through was liable to make anybody go insane.

"How do you feel about marriage?" he asked.

I was kind of caught off guard by the question. Wasn't it a little too soon to be bringing up the *M* word? Nevertheless, I shrugged my shoulders and answered his question.

"It's not for everybody."

"Are you speaking from personal experience?" he asked.

I shrugged my shoulders again, not really giving him a direct answer. I continued to eat my food as the mood at the table sort of shifted. When I looked up at Cairo, he had stopped eating and was staring intently at me.

"Were you married before, Audrielle?"

I continued to eat my food as if he hadn't just asked me that.

"So you can't answer me?"

Annoyed with his line of questioning, I finally put my fork down, wiped my mouth with my napkin, and looked him directly in his eyes. "What?"

"Look, I know you don't like to talk about your previous relationships and all, but I think that knowing whether or not you've been married before is pretty important."

"Why? Would your thoughts about me change?"

He nodded his head. "So you have been married before?"

I picked up my fork and started to eat my food again. Cairo, who still had the same fork of noodles at his mouth, just sat there, watching me eat with that annoyingly sexy smirk on his face.

"No, I've never been married. Happy?"

"I am," he said as he started to eat his food again. "But why did you say it isn't for everybody?"

"Because it isn't."

"Why not?"

Just to shut him up and get this conversation over with, I elaborated on my answer. "I don't think marriage is for everybody because everyone isn't suited to be with one person for the rest of their life."

"Well, do you think marrying for money is cool?"

"It depends."

He looked at me and waited silently for me to continue.

"Take my parents, for example. They didn't have anything in common but the love of jazz music when they first met. My father came from a well-off family, but my mom didn't. When she found out who my father's family was, she was determined to have his last name. Flash forward a couple years. Something happened where my father took some money from his family and friends and invested it in this bogus-ass company one of his so-called friends put him up on. The company disappeared into thin air, causing my father to lose everything he put into it. He didn't want to tell my grandparents, or anyone else for that matter, what happened, so he tried to figure out a way to get all of their money back.

"Just so happens around that time, my mother's aunt died, but before she did, she took out this huge life insurance policy and had my mom as her only beneficiary. Long story short, my mother offered my father the money to pay back the loss, but only if he married her in return and let her help him start his own company. Six months after the ink dried on that check, they were married, and my father took the money that she gave him and quadrupled it. To this day, the stock brokerage firm they started makes money."

"Okay, that is a great story. What's so wrong with that?" he asked.

I wasn't hungry anymore after telling that story, so I pushed my plate to the side. "My parents have been together all of these years, and the only three things that they have in common are their love of jazz music and my sister and I. I know they love each other, but it's not the type of love people who've been married for over twenty-five years are supposed to have. Do you know they have that big master suite in their home, but the majority of the time, my father sleeps on that couch in his study? My mom tries to put on this front like they're the happiest couple whenever others are around, but in actuality, they're not."

"Why don't they get a divorce?"

I shrugged my shoulders. "Simply put, it's cheaper to keep her and all the bullshit that follows."

The expression on his face was unreadable, and I didn't want to get into whatever he was thinking about. This whole conversation about marriage and my parents had kind of ruined the night for me. He'd have to do something that really turned me on if he wanted to get some sex before he left.

"Come here." His low, raspy voice summoned me over to his side of the table. He licked his lips, and without so much as a single thought, I rose from my seat and walked over to him. All that shit talking I just did, and it only took him licking his lips to really turn me on.

He scooted back from the table, hiked up my maxi skirt, and pulled me into his lap. As soon as the dick print that was poking through his pants rubbed against the thin fabric of my panties, I knew he had a wet spot on his jeans.

"You know your juices just seeped through my pants and are now on my thigh," he said.

"I'm sorry," I breathlessly replied.

"Naw, don't be sorry. I might never wash these things again, just so I can smell your sweet scent whenever I want to. That is unless you want to give me those panties you have on to keep instead. As a matter of fact, take those muthafuckas off, and this skirt. I haven't felt the inside of you in over a month, and I can't wait any longer."

I did as I was told and removed each article of clothing. When I turned back around to Cairo, he'd already unbuckled his pants and pulled his dick out.

"Mmmm," I said just looking at that sexy muthafucka.

"Don't just mmmm. Get up on this dick and make me remember why I haven't thought about anyone else's pussy but yours since the last time we fucked."

That was all I needed to hear as I straddled his lap again and slid down on this white chocolate goodness.

"Damn, Cai. I fucking missed your ass."

"I missed you too, baby. I've been going crazy thinking about this pussy." He grabbed my ass and started to squeeze so hard that I could feel his nails sinking into my skin.

"Fuck, Audri. I'll never get tired of the way you feel."

I started to rock my hips a little faster, moving to the beat of Raheem DeVaughn's "Temperature Rising" song I was singing in my head. I could feel the puddle of cum I was making in his lap. The gushy noise my pussy made when it was being dicked down properly was getting louder and louder as I bounced up and down.

Cai looked me in my eyes then took my lips into his. My pussy got wetter the minute his tongue touched mine. I grabbed a hold of his dreads, which were now hanging loose, and tried to pull him into me.

He smiled against my lips. "I think I'm already inside of you as far as I can go, baby."

"I know. I just wish . . . you . . . could be . . . further . . . aaahhhhhhh!" I released again.

"I want you to be mine, Audri. I know we haven't known each other that long, but I really feel that you're it for me. Can I have you, baby?"

Of course, I nodded my head, which made him grab onto my hips again and start to thrust upward into me harder.

"Ca . . . Ca . . . Cai! Damn it, baby."

"That's right. This my pussy now. No one else's."

I nodded my head. I was so high at that moment that I was going to agree to anything he said.

"Your pussy belongs to me, Audri? Huh? I can't hear you!"

"Yeeeeesss, baby."

"I can get it anytime I want it."

I nodded my head.

"I don't understand head nods. Can"—*thrust*—"I have"—*thrust*—"my pussy"—*thrust*—"anytime I want it?" *Super thrust.*

I came undone when he did that. Cum was squirting everywhere and so much that I thought I had peed on myself.

"Yes! Fuck yes, Cai! Anytime you want it, baby!"

He got quiet for a minute, like he was thinking about whether he wanted to say whatever was on his mind. Still beating my shit up as I lazily hung onto his neck for dear life, he started to whisper in my ear.

"Will you marry me, Audri?"

My eyes popped open, but I couldn't say shit. I think I was suffering from dehydration at the moment because I had cum so much. However, me not answering that question must've done something to him, because next thing I knew, I was laid across my table as he stood between my legs and pushed into me again. I didn't know why, but this position was really doing something to me as he drilled deeper and deeper into my pussy.

"I'm going to ask you this one more time before I cum." He started to push into me faster and faster. "Will you marry me, Audri?"

A million *no*s were swimming through my mind, but what came out of my mouth next as we both climaxed at the same time shocked the hell out of both of us.

"Yes, Cairo, yes, I will fucking marry you!"

22

Cairo

I was laying in Audrielle's bed, staring at the ceiling, thinking about everything that had happened earlier. Twenty-four hours ago, I would never have imagined that I'd be at the hospital trying to figure out ways to pay for Mama Faye's extra medical bills and then becoming engaged to a woman I felt like I'd known all my life but really didn't. The light sounds of her snoring could be heard throughout the room, which caused me to glance down at her. Audrielle was so beautiful—even with the little bit of drool she had falling from the corner of her mouth.

I wanted to flip her onto her back and fuck the shit out of her again, but I knew I drained her dry with that last round of unbelievable sex we'd just had. Quietly getting out of the bed, I grabbed my phone off of the dresser and went downstairs into the kitchen for a late night snack. With not too much of a selection to pick from, I decided to make a BLT sandwich. I took the lettuce and tomatoes, which were nice and fresh, out of the fridge, then snatched the potato bread from the pantry. This microwavable bacon was going to be new to me, but as long as it tasted like the real thing, it was okay.

My phone vibrated on the countertop, but I didn't pick it up because Alex's name was flashing across the screen. She'd been calling me all night, but I ignored each and every one of her calls. I wouldn't need to speak with her anymore, especially since I didn't need her anymore to get this inheritance money. I already had a bride, one I really wouldn't mind being married to and spending the rest of my life with.

When Audrielle had told me the story about how her parents got married, I was kind of taken aback. Looking at them, I would've never thought that they weren't in love. Although Mrs. Freeman was a real bitch to Audri, I could tell that she really loved her husband from the way she looked at him.

"Ay, Ness, what's up? Mama Faye good?" Finesse had just called my phone, and I was hoping he wasn't bearing any bad news.

"Yeah, she good, bro. They still keeping an eye on her, though. Ay, thanks for the food earlier. I wasn't expecting that delivery."

"You good. I knew you probably hadn't put anything in your belly since this morning, and I knew you weren't going to be leaving Mama Faye's side anytime soon. It was the least I could do since I won't be back until tomorrow."

"That was real good looking out," he said.

We chopped it up for a few more minutes before I heard Ariana enter the room with Ness. He told me that he'd see me in the morning and then asked me to bring him some breakfast from somewhere, then we ended the call.

The microwavable bacon wasn't all that bad, so I made another sandwich and ate it before I went back up to the room.

"What were you doing down there?" Audri asked as soon as I walked into the room. She was sitting up in the bed with her back against the headboard and the sheet pulled up over her body.

"What I tell you about covering yourself up when you're in my presence?"

"I thought that rule didn't apply when I was cold," she answered.

"I got something that will warm you up if you're up for it. I can actually go a few more rounds after that hearty snack I just had."

She sat there and stared at me for a minute, bottom lip tucked in her mouth, her curly black hair shielding half of her face, while the other side was sticking up in the air. It was dark in the room, but the glow of her skin gave off enough of a shine that I could clearly see her. She looked so beautiful to me in that moment. I couldn't help but to lean in and kiss her sexy lips. Our mouths stayed entwined for a minute before she released my bottom lip and pulled her head back.

"Why did you ask me to marry you, Cairo? And when are you trying to marry me?" she asked.

Right then would've been the perfect opportunity for me to put everything on the table and tell her the other reason why I asked her to marry me. I knew that if she ever found out later on down the line what this really was about, I would regret it. On the flip side, though, I would have my whole life to make it up to her if she'd let me.

"I wanna marry you because this connection that we have is so strong, and I don't think I would be able to spend a day without you in my life. If it were up to me, I would marry you today, but as long as we do it before I become an old man and turn thirty, that would be perfect."

"When do you turn thirty?" she asked.

I smiled because I knew she was going to trip a little bit when I told her this. "I turn thirty in two months."

"Two months! Are you serious?"

I nodded my head.

"Two months, as in sixty days from now?"

I nodded my head again. She just stared at me with wide eyes and an open mouth. I didn't know what she was thinking about. I just hoped she didn't change her mind.

"This is all going so fast."

"It is," I said, "but I've heard of people who got married a week after they met, and they are still together. Their connection was just that strong."

"I've heard of those people too. It's just kind of hard to believe it's happening for me and you, because you've never even told me that you love me, yet you can ask me to marry you?"

"I did tell you," I said.

"When?"

"The first night we made love. I told you that I was in love with you."

"You said that you could fall in love with me."

"Well, I did. The first time I saw you, I think I fell in love."

She blushed then cupped my cheek into her hand. "I don't know what it is, but there's something in my heart that keeps telling me that this"—she pointed between us—"is real. This connection we have is real. This love we share is real. I just hope you're ready to be with me for the rest of your life. You can call that little chick that's been blowing up your phone all night and tell her that you are officially off the market. Either that or she could get her ass beat to have the message conveyed for her."

"There won't be no need for that," I said as I laughed and climbed in between her thighs. "She's already a distant memory. Now how about you close those pretty eyes, pucker those gorgeous lips, and open up these juicy thighs for your soon-to-be husband? I need some more of my pussy, and I will not be denied."

"And you never will," she said as I took her mouth into mine and made love to her again.

23

Audrielle

I woke up the next morning refreshed and happy about life. Not only was I still on that euphoric high Cairo had me on every time we made love, but I was excited that I would be Mrs. Audrielle Broussard in a month.

I was sitting at the island in the middle of my kitchen, ogling over a half-naked Cairo and how sexy he looked making me some breakfast when the doorbell rang.

"I'll be right back, babe. It's probably my gardener. He's the only one that would be ringing my bell this early."

"Okay, but hurry back. Breakfast is almost ready, and I want another helping of the lethalness you have between your legs before I go up to the hospital." He turned away from the oven, pulling me into his warm body, and kissed me with so much passion my knees almost went out.

I wrapped my arms around his neck and pulled our bodies closer. He moaned then pulled back from our kiss.

"Babe, go answer the door before you fuck around and have me burning your house down," he joked, swatting me on my ass then stealing one last kiss.

I turned away from Cairo and headed in the direction of my front door. Whoever was there was knocking now.

"This better not be Sydney's ass again," I said to myself as I stepped in front of the door. "Then again, I could go a few more rounds, making sure she learned her lesson."

I didn't even look out the peephole when I finally reached the door. I just placed my hand on the knob and swung it open, ready for whomever was standing on the other side.

My whole body stiffened when my eyes connected with a pair of amber irises that I knew all too well. A light mist of perspiration kissed his smooth, walnut-colored skin, and black, curly hair was plastered to his head. His chiseled Indian features were intense with concentration. I looked at the gray sleeveless T-shirt, black basketball shorts, and gray Dual Fusion running shoes.

I see his ass is still with the morning workouts, I thought as I took in his tall, muscular frame. So into my daze, I never noticed the bouquet of calla lilies in his hands until he pushed them toward my face.

"What . . . How . . . ?"

"I know I'm probably the last person you want to see right now, Audrielle, but just let me explain."

I took the beautiful floral arrangement as he handed it to me. "So it was you who's been sending me the flowers all this time?"

He bit his lip and nodded his head. "Calla lilies, pina coladas, *Law & Order SVU*, Tyrese, and the color pink. How could I ever forget Audrielle's five favorite things?"

I didn't know whether to be impressed or pissed off. When we were together, he acted as if he didn't know that or just didn't care. There were many holidays, birthdays, and special occasions where I either got nothing or he'd bring me a gift that he picked up from a Mexican store while exiting the freeway.

"I . . . don't know what to say." I turned my head and looked back toward the kitchen. I could still hear the sizzling sound of bacon, so I knew Cairo was still handling his business.

"That's because you don't have to say anything. I'm the one who should be doing all of the talking." He licked his lips, and I almost died when a flashback of what those things did in the bedroom invaded my thoughts.

"First off, Audrielle, I just want to apologize for how we ended. I know that we solemnly promised a lot of things to each other, a lot of things that I reneged on. I just want you to know that it was never my intention to hurt you in any way. You were the best thing that ever happened to me. That's why I asked you to be—"

I held up my hand, silencing him instantly. "Please don't go there right now. You've had over five years to rectify some of the damage that you've caused me."

"I didn't know how to get in contact with you, Audri. You changed all of your numbers, deleted me from your social media, and even moved from the home that we shared."

"Yet you show up on my doorstep today," I said sarcastically.

"I had to practically promise my sister everything, including my first born, to get your address. Anytime I would ask her for your contact information, she'd never give it to me."

My girl. I still made a mental note to call Sarah up and cuss her ass out. She knew I was with Cairo now.

Hmmm, Cairo. Just thinking about him has me . . . Shit! Just that fast I forgot my sexy, white, dread-headed king was in the kitchen cooking us up a meal. I needed to wrap up this little impromptu conversation and get this unwanted guest the hell up out of there. Then again, since I did plan on marrying Cai within the next two months, I needed to get the situation I had with this man taken care of.

"Look, Audrielle, I know I have a lot of apologizing to do before you can ever forgive me. Just let me take you out to dinner tonight so we can start somewhere. I know you've been missing me as much as I've missed you. That's why when I was offered that position at Sacred Heart, I jumped on the first thing smoking back to Los Angeles. My sister didn't even know that I was coming back. I wanted it to be a surprise."

The hopeful look in his eyes probably would've had me if I still had feelings for this man, but since I didn't, that look didn't do shit.

"Eli, first off, just let me say thank you for the flowers. I really appreciated them. They made me smile when I was going through a little rough patch. Each and every arrangement you sent was beautiful, and I loved them all. However, whatever it was that we had all them years ago, I don't feel it anymore. Not only did you lie to me about a lot of things, but you broke my heart. We made a promise . . . " I didn't know why, but I started to tear up. "You made a promise to love me for the rest of your life, and you broke it. Left me for that skinny-ass nurse bitch who you swore nothing was going on with."

He shook his head. "That's not even what happened, Audri. If you let me explain, I'll tell you every—"

"No need. I'm over whatever it was that we had. All you can do now is make me happy and give me a—"

"Baby, our food is ready. What's taking you so long at the door?" I heard Cairo say as he walked up behind me. "Oh, hey, Dr. Blake! What. are you doing—Wait! Is something wrong with Mama Faye? Is she okay?"

A look of recognition and confusion was now on Eli's face. "Uh, Ms. Faye is still doing okay. The nurses and the other attending physician are keeping an eye on her."

"That's cool. I'ma head on up that way once me and this beautiful lady here enjoy the breakfast I just made us."

"Breakfast, huh?" Eli asked, nodding his head. "How do you and Audrielle know each other? I wasn't expecting to see you when I rang her doorbell this morning."

Cairo snaked his arm around my waist and kissed me on my neck as if he was marking his territory. Both men never broke eye contact as Cai possessively pulled me into his body.

"Well, as of last night, Audrielle is my fiancée."

"Fiancée?" His eyes immediately went to my ring finger. I tried to hide the fact that it was bare, but the smirk that was now on Eli's face told me that he noticed. "I would say congratulations, but then again, it wouldn't be any use."

I felt Cairo's body tense up as he released me and pushed me behind him a bit to get into Eli's face. "Now why would you say some shit like that?"

Eli's eyebrow lifted, and that cocky demeanor he tended to get was now on display. "Should I, Audrielle, or would you like to do the honors?"

I shut my eyes for a minute and prayed like hell that this was a dream. Unfortunately, once I said Amen and opened my eyes, the man who was my past and the man who was my future were both staring straight at me.

"Audri, what is it that I need to know?" Cairo asked as he turned me fully around to him, the look of concern etched across his face.

"I . . . I . . . I—" The words got caught in my throat, and I couldn't seem to speak English intelligible for anything.

"Well, since Audri here is having technical difficulties, let me be the one to tell you for her. Audrielle can't marry you anytime soon because she's still married to me. What will it be, six years tomorrow, baby?"

My eyes bugged out of my head as this asshole told the one secret I'd never told anyone. Not even my parents knew that we got married. We were supposed to live in wedded bliss for a year, then announce our marriage and have a big reception following. Instead of us celebrating our union at our one-year mark, I was at home crying my eyes out because my husband left me for another woman and moved to a different state.

I looked up at Cairo, and my heart sank to my feet. The look of hurt and anger was all I could see as I looked into those bluish-green eyes.

He had removed me from his embrace, so I reached for his hand. "Cai, let me explain."

"Don't even," he said, raising his arm out of my grasp. "You lied to my face and told me that you've never been married. What were you going to do when we got to the altar? Pretend like you got cold feet and run away?"

"Cai, please!" I begged, tears streaming down my face. "Can we talk about this in private?"

"For what? You had all the time in the world to talk to me in private. I'm good. Audrielle, I didn't just need to marry you; I wanted to."

Need? Why would he need to marry me?

"Cai wait!"

He didn't give me the chance to explain. After throwing his shirt over his head and slipping his feet into his shoes, he grabbed his keys off of the coffee table and stormed out the door.

I couldn't stop sobbing. I fell down to my knees and tried to catch my breath. I felt as if the wind had been knocked from me. I looked up at Eli, who was still standing in my doorway with that ugly-ass smirk on his face.

"Ahhh, baby, don't cry over that white mutha-fucka. It wouldn't have worked anyway. He wouldn't know how to handle a girl like you. Me, on the other hand, you already know how I get down. Cheer up, baby, and stop all that crying. Your husband's home now!"

24

Alexandria

"Good morning, Ms.Tate. You received a few calls from some potential clients, as well as a couple from Amir Reid at Reid Moore and Associates. All of your morning meetings have been scheduled, and the afternoon meeting's rescheduled per your request, so you're clear after twelve thirty."

I looked at my assistant and massaged my temples as she rattled on about shit I didn't really care too much about. The only person I wanted to hear from was not calling me back at all, and I couldn't understand that for the life of me.

When I had called Cairo some time ago and told him about the inheritance money his grandmother left him in her will, I just knew he'd start to call me asking for information, but to my surprise, he never did. I mean, he wasn't hard up for money, but still, $50 million, who in their right mind would possibly pass that up?

I sat back in my plush and comfy leather chair as my father's last little fling, Lisa, Leah, Lauren, or whatever the hell her name was, kept talking. I thought about the first time my father and I talked about the reason behind me meeting Cairo.

"Daddy, I don't understand why I have to continue on with this charade. It's been two years, and I still haven't run into this Thaddeus boy you told me about. I hate going to this ghetto-ass school."

My father looked at me over the rim of his glasses, which were nestled at the tip of his nose. "Alex, darling, I know you had your heart set on attending Princeton with Tiffany and Megan, but as I've already told you, the young man I need you to become friends with didn't get a scholarship to any Ivy League colleges. Only from the ones local to him."

"Well, why couldn't I just try to find him after I graduated from Princeton? It isn't like you wouldn't be able to locate him then," I said, rolling my eyes. "I don't see why I have to meet him right now anyway if he has until he's thirty to be married so that he could inherit the money."

My father finally folded the newspaper in his hand, ate his last piece of toast, then drank the last sip of his now lukewarm coffee. Henrietta, our maid, hurried to the kitchen table and cleaned up my father's mess before placing a plate of scrambled eggs and turkey bacon in front of him. She offered me a plate, but I declined.

"Thank you, Henrietta," he said as she refilled his coffee mug. He turned a stern eye to me as he stuffed a forkful of food in his mouth.

"Princess, I probably could've found him some years after you graduated, but by then, he might've already had a wife, girlfriend, or fiancée. I need you to meet him now so that you guys can form some sort of relationship and attraction to each other. That way you can be in the running for one of those titles, if not all three."

"But Daddy!" I whined. "I can't make someone fall in love with me. Besides, what about Matthew? I mean, he is my boyfriend right now, and he says we're going to get married right after we graduate." I sat on my stool with the biggest smile on my face. Just talking about Matthew and our future always did that to me. However, my smile immediately turned into a frown when my father started to speak again.

"*Alexandria, you need to get your head up out of those clouds and keep your eyes on the prize. It's not hard to make a man fall in love with you. How do you think your mother snagged me?*" He laughed at his own corny joke. "*And as far as Matthew goes, you might as well cut that relationship off. He and Tiffany have been seeing each other since they left for Princeton.*"

I sat there shocked for a moment as I processed everything my father had said. As soon as my mind replayed the news he had told me, my breath left my body. I felt my eyes start to water up and my heart instantly break. I didn't need to ask my father if what he said was true either. He always made it a point to know everything about the people around me or himself, especially when it came to making money.

"*Princess, I didn't mean to hurt your feelings with that little bit of information, but it's better you know now rather than to know later.*" He ate the last bit of food on his plate before he continued. "*Now that I'm assuming he's out of the way, you can now focus on being the perfect girlfriend and potential wife for Thaddeus. Well, as soon as you meet him.*"

I didn't know what caused me to nod my head, but I did. I was still sitting on the stool *when my father walked over to me, gave me a small hug, and kissed me on my cheek.*

"I have to go to work now, sweetie. Get the black card from your mother and go buy yourself something nice to cheer yourself up, okay?"

I nodded my head again then wiped my eyes. "Before you go, Dad . . ."

He turned around and gave me his undivided attention.

"With UCLA having over fifty thousand students walking around and being such a big campus and all, it would be nice if you could get a class schedule for him or a list of the type of activities he likes to participate in. I'll more than likely run into him faster that way if I know where he actually hangs out."

He smiled at me. "See, that's the type of thinking that'll have you taking over the family business in no time. Hell, maybe even help you start up your own company. I'll get that information for you sometime this week. Have fun shopping, princess," he said over his back as he walked out the door.

"Um, Ms. Tate. Did you hear what I just said?"

I looked up at Lisa and shook my head. I must've been out for a minute, because when I looked down at my desk, she had already placed my bagel and hot tea in front of me.

"No, I'm sorry, Lisa. I didn't hear you. What did you say?"

"If I wasn't fucking your father. . . ." I heard her mumble as she shook her head. She cut her eyes at me then placed another stack of papers on my desk. "First things first, my name is Laurie, and you might want to remember that. Secondly, you have a phone call from your father on line one and another call—"

"Shit," I cursed to myself. I knew my father was calling to see how my progress was going with Cairo. It was him who told me to keep the inheritance thing a secret, marry him, then divorce him so that I could take half of the $50 million. If I was any normal gold-digging chick, that's exactly what I would've done, but because I had actually fallen in love with Cai, I couldn't hurt him like that. Plus, I really wouldn't mind being his wife. That was why I told him about the money and offered him that five percent deal. It would be a win-win situation on both ends. He'd become rich, and I'd become his wife.

I redirected my attention back to Laurie and asked her to repeat the last thing she'd said.

"You also have a second call on line two. A Mr. Broussard, he said."

"Cairo?"

"I think that was the name."

"Well, tell my father that I will call him back in a couple of hours, after I get off the phone with this potential client."

She nodded her head then turned around and walked out of my office.

I didn't know why I became so nervous that Cairo was on the phone. It wasn't like this was going to be our first time talking.

I opened my desk and located the little file that I was looking for. If Cairo had any thoughts about marrying this big bitch that I could tell he was falling hard for, I was about to seriously burst that bubble with the information I had found. There were only two months until his birthday, and I needed to be the one saying I do.

As if he would be able to see me, I looked in the little mirror on my desk and made sure my makeup was on point.

"Alexandria Tate speaking," I said into the receiver like I didn't know it was him.

"Hey, Alex, this is Cairo." He sounded so sad. I wondered what had happened. Then again, I really didn't.

"Oh, hey, Cai. How's everything going? How's Mama Faye?"

He blew out a breath. "Look, Alex, meet me at your house in an hour so we can discuss the deal you told me about."

Before I got too excited, I had to ask, "Uh, Cai, what deal are you referring to?"

"Look, just meet me at your house so we can go over some things."

Shit, he didn't have to tell me twice. After I got off of the phone with him, I had Laurie cancel all of my meetings for the day.

"Wait, Ms. Tate, what about your father?" Laurie asked. "When I told him that you would call him back, he said that he was on his way up here."

"Just tell him to call me on my cell!" I yelled as I walked out of the office. It wasn't like his ass was really coming to see me anyway. Now they could have the whole office to themselves.

25

Audrielle

"Yo, you know who you've reached. Leave a message after the tone, and I'll get back to you at my earliest convenience. Beep!"

"Hey, Cai, it's me again, Audri. I was just calling to check up on you and see how everything's going. I know this is probably like the hundredth message I've left, but we need to talk. If you could give me a call back, I'd really appreciate it. Okay, talk to you later. Bye. Oh, and before I go, Cairo, please know that I love you."

It had been a little over a month and a half since I'd last heard from, talked to, or even seen Cairo. What happened that morning when Eli showed up at my door and opened his big-ass mouth was what caused everything to go from sugar to shit. All of my calls were being unanswered, and even my text messages were being ignored. I got so desperate for Cai to at least look at me that I popped up at Mama Faye's house for his birthday, thinking that someone would at least be there, but there was no answer.

I left his gift on the front porch. It was a candid picture of us one morning when we woke up in my bed. The rays from the morning sun were hitting our faces just right, so that the selfie looked like it could've been professionally taken. Hopefully, he got it or someone gave it to him.

Whenever I would ask Ariana if she'd seen him, she would either change the subject or ignore my questions altogether. I guess she was still salty from me being the same way when she would ask me things pertaining to Rima. Oh, well. Maybe I would try my hand with Finesse. We'd always gotten along for the most part. I would hope he'd keep it real with me when I asked him about his brother's whereabouts. Then again . . .

The door chime going off alerted me that a customer had entered the store. I really didn't want to be there, but it wasn't like I had anything else to do.

"Hello, welcome to Kick Biz. Feel free to look around. If you need anything, just let me know."

The young man that entered nodded his head and went straight to the Nike Air Foamposite display. The young girl he was with followed right behind him, reading the store flyer she had picked up when they came in.

"Yoooo, I swear this store has the sickest shoes ever. I can't wait until my birthday. My pops said as a going away to college present he'd hook me up with a couple pair of kicks, customized and everything."

"Fo' real?" His girlfriend exclaimed excitedly. "That's super dope. Maybe I can get you a few of these T-shirts and shorts to match. We can't have you going all the way to NYU looking broke and dusty."

They shared a laugh that soon died down when his phone started going off. Whoever he was talking to must've really wanted to know where he was, because I heard him say more than once "I'm at the store I was telling you about." After a few more uh-huhs and okays, he finally ended the call.

I watched the cute little couple walk over to the other side of the store while I continued to stock the shelves. A few more customers came in, purchasing shoes and things that took my attention away from them. Since I was the only one in the store that day, it did become a little busy, but I handled it like the true professional that I was.

I had just bagged up the last customer's purchase when the door chimed again. My back was turned to the entrance because I was trying to find some more of my store bags, so I didn't have a chance to see who walked in. Nevertheless, I gave my greeting and continued to handle business.

"Hey, Mr. B, you should've seen Tyson the whole time you've been gone. He almost had a heart attack when he thought his precious Coach Cai would miss his going away party next week," someone said.

Coach Cai? No, it couldn't be.

I became nervous all of a sudden. That flipping feeling I'd get in the pit of my stomach whenever he was around started to go crazy. I felt his eyes on me before my body sensed his presence. When I turned around, our eyes collided, and the breath I'd been holding was still caught in my throat.

Cairo looked so good. Wherever he'd been had really done him well. His skin was beautifully tanned, causing his bluish-green eyes to stand out even more. His dreads were French braided and pulled to a ponytail in the back. The ripped, stone washed jeans that shielded his legs gave him that sexy, relaxed look, while the graphic V-neck T-shirt from Hollister gave a sneak peek of his rock hard chest and extremely toned arms.

Because I knew what every tattoo on his arm looked like by memory, I instantly recognized the newest artwork he had done around his wrist. I couldn't make out what it said, but I knew that it was new.

I was so caught up in his appearance that I didn't even see him walk up.

"Audrielle, you look . . . beautiful as always," he said, startling me.

I looked down at the black skater skirt and lace racerback tank I had on. Not the usual type of outfit I would wear to work, but ever since that first night with Cairo, I'vd been stepping out of my comfort zone a little more. The outfit went well with the new Nike wedges I had on.

"You don't look so bad yourself," I said.

He gave me that sexy smirk that he knew drove me crazy. "Thanks. You know I try."

I nodded my head. We stared at each other in silence for a moment before someone cleared their throat.

"Uh, Coach, are you good?" the young boy I now knew as Tyson asked as he and his girlfriend walked up to us.

Cairo finally broke from his trance. "Yeah, um . . . yeah, I'm good. Pardon my manners. Guys, this is Audrielle. Audrielle, this is Tyson and his best friend, Karla. Tyson plays for the basketball team I coach from time to time."

"Nice to meet you," Karla said as she shook my hand.

So the little KeKe Palmer lookalike was only his friend. Seeing her up close now, she was prettier than I thought. I guessed their relationship status would change soon.

"So this is the mystery lady that I've heard so much about?" Tyson shook my hand. "And to think it took you two getting married for me to finally meet the lady of my favorite coach's life."

"Since when did I become your favorite Coach, Ty?" Cairo asked, totally ignoring Tyson's last statement, which I knew he had heard. His eyes damn near popped out of the sockets when he said it.

"Ever since you showed me that white men really can jump, as well as pull one of the finest sistas I've ever seen," Tyson answered.

Karla socked Tyson in the gut, causing him to fold over. "What the fuck was that for? I'm sorry, but you can't deny that she's pretty. Plus, she owns one of the freshest shoe stores in L.A."

Best friends, my ass.

I blushed. When I looked up at Cairo, his gaze was very intense. The look in his eyes was something I'd never seen before with him. Was it regret? Was it shame? I wanted to ask him what he was thinking about but decided to wait until we were alone again.

"Thank you so much for the compliment, Tyson, and just a little FYI, Cairo and I are not married," I said.

"Really? Then why did Ness tell me that you were on your honeymoon when I ran into him at the gym a few weeks ago?" Tyson asked his coach.

Honeymoon? Why would Cai be on a honeymoon?

I looked up at Cairo again, but this time, his eyes were cast down to the floor. I was taken aback for a moment because he'd never retracted his gaze from mine. Something was definitely going on, and Tyson had just taken the lock off of Pandora's box.

Karla must've sensed it too because she made up an excuse about needing to go study and practically dragged Tyson out behind her.

"What was he talking about, Cai? A honeymoon? You went and got married to someone else?" I laughed. When he didn't say anything or respond to any of my questions, my heart started to beat a little faster. "Cai, what was he talking about?"

He still wouldn't look at me. He tucked his hand into his pocket and started shifting his legs from left to right. Since he wouldn't answer any questions in regard to what Tyson had said, I decided to go at it from a different angle.

"Cai, where have you been for the last month or so? I've been calling you like crazy. I know what happened the morning after you asked me to marry you was crazy, but you didn't even give me a chance to explain."

He opened his mouth to say something but shut it when the door chime went off.

"Welcome to Kick Biz. Feel free to look around. If you have any questions, I'm here to assist you." I never took my eyes off of Cairo as I greeted whoever had just walked into the store.

"Oh, sweetie, there's no need for that. I don't wear these types of shoes anyway. I came in here to locate my husband and to see what was taking him so long."

I directed my attention toward the sweet yet pernicious voice that seemed to resonate the closer she got. A gorgeous, average height brunette with a body that most people would kill for and a face as pretty as Megan Fox strolled arrogantly into the store. She had that certain air about her, the one that screamed, "I came from money and will continue to stay with money." Yeah, she was one of those types of bitches. The little cut-off denim shorts she had on were cute, but the V-neck Hollister graphic tee she had tied up in a ball, showing off her flat tummy, was what caught my attention because it matched the one Cairo had on.

"Oh, there you are, babe!" she said, and I looked behind me, but there was no one in sight. I looked to my left then my right and got the same results. In fact, after Tyson and Karla left, I think Cai and I were the only ones there.

Wait a minute. I know she's not talking to—

"Cai, baby, let's go. You said you came up here to meet with the little boy on your team, not hold conversations with the employees," she said.

"Alex, please?" He was obviously irritated by her presence, but she didn't want or care to see that.

"Please what? I'm ready to go now, Cai. I need to go home and change before we meet up with your brother and his little girlfriend. Are you done here?"

I swear my heart tore into a thousand pieces when I finally noticed the matching band sets on their ring fingers. I wanted to cry so badly, but I didn't want to give this muthafucka the satisfaction.

Here we go with this shit again. I can't win for losing.

Maybe Eli was right. Maybe Cairo only did want me for his little black girl fantasy. All that bullshit he'd been feeding to me was nothing but lies. He knew all along that being in a committed, long-term relationship with me was never going to happen. He basically just strung me along until his Cover Girl came to her senses.

I watched their interaction. She hung on to him lovingly, like this was the happiest time of her life. I couldn't really decipher what Cairo was feeling because his face was now blank.

"Look, Audrielle, I'm sorry, and I didn't want things to go down like this, but I had to do what was best—"

I held my hand up. "It was nice seeing you again, Cairo. Congratulations on your recent and unexpected marriage."

"Oh, thank you!" the bitch had the nerve to gush as she flashed her ring in my face.

Cairo looked at me one last time before he turned around and walked out of the store.

"Oh, and Audrielle, sweetie, please stop calling and texting my husband at all times of the night. We would really appreciate it if you would." She held up her ring finger again. "You know this could've been yours if you would have handled your business and gotten a divorce when your ex left you."

I was confused. "How do you know anything about me?"

"Oh, honey, believe me, I know a lot more than you think. Like for instance, I knew the minute that Cairo told me about you that he was in love with you. And I must admit, it kind of made me jealous. The way his whole face lights up whenever your name is mentioned told me that. I knew then that my plan to get my hands on him and that money was going to go down the drain if some sort of miracle didn't happen. When I found out about your marital status, I didn't think that little bit of info would come in so handy. Imagine my surprise when it did. I'm so glad California frowns on bigamy. Now I can finally have my happily ever after with Cai like it's supposed to be."

"Hold up. What money are you talking about? And again, how do you know anything about me?" I asked.

When she got to the door, she stopped. "Cai didn't tell you about the inheritance money, huh? Guess he didn't care as much as I thought he did. Oh, and as a little parting gift, I'm going to leave you with this: Did you ever wonder how Dr. Blake wound up at your home the morning after Cairo proposed to you?"

I was a little curious about that, but I had just figured that Sarah told him.

"It wasn't his sister, if that's what you're thinking. Let's just say that your little secret marriage wasn't as secret as you thought to someone really close to you."

26

Cairo

The look on Audrielle's face when Alex flashed her wedding ring literally broke my heart. Yeah, I was mad at her lying about being married, but that didn't change the way I felt about her. If I really didn't need the money for Mama Faye's surgery, Alex's ass would not have been carrying my last name. On some real shit, as much as I loved Mama Faye, I thought about just letting her go on home to the Lord a couple of times before I even said I do, but every time I went up to that hospital and saw her lying there, barely speaking and staring at whatever was on television, I knew what I had to do. Even if it wasn't what my heart truly wanted.

"Cai, why the hell did you come up here anyway?" Alex asked, snapping me from my thoughts. I glanced at her as she flipped the visor down and looked at herself in the mirror. There wasn't a hair out of place or an area on her face that wasn't perfectly covered by makeup, so I had no idea what she was looking at. Her slim lips looked full and pouty with the plum-colored lipstick she had on. The dark, smoky makeup around her eyes made her hazel irises pop. Her auburn hair flowed past her shoulders, shining and smelling like coconuts. I watched as she inspected her flawlessness then slowly licked her lips. My dick twitched at the sight of her wet, pink tongue but went right back to limp when she cut her eyes at me and smiled.

I blew out a frustrated breath and wiped my hand down my face. I didn't know how I would be able to put up with this charade for the next couple of minutes, let alone a month. Ever since the minute we stepped out of the courtroom as man and wife, we'd been arguing nonstop. Even on our fake-ass honeymoon to Hawaii. I spent half of our trip on the beach and in the water, while she stayed in the spas and shopping. When it was time for us to go to bed, she slept on one side, and I slept on the other, with pillows stacked high in between. Throughout the night, she'd catch me off guard by knocking my make-shift wall down and cuddling next to me. For about two minutes, I'd hold her back and play with her hair, just like I use to do to Audri, but when my body would get that unfamiliar touch, I instantly woke up and scooted away from her as fast as I could.

"I know you hear me talking to you, Thaddeus!" she said.

"Don't fucking call me that! That is not my name."

"One, it is your name whether you like or not, and two, it's the only way I can get you to pay attention to me for longer than five seconds," Alex said as she looked at me with heated eyes. "Did you at least hear what I said?"

My head fell back against the headrest while I stared at the black fabric on the ceiling of the car. "No, Alex, I didn't hear you. What did you say?"

I could see the smirk forming on her lips from the corner of my eye. "Still thinking about your little fat friend back there, huh? You worried she won't talk to you anymore now that she knows you've moved on to bigger—wait, maybe bigger isn't the right word to use since I'm obviously way smaller than her." She laughed. "Oh, I know, how about sizable? You've moved on to sizable and better things. How does that sound?" She waved me off when I didn't give her a response. "It doesn't matter what you think anyway. At the end of the day, bigger or smaller, I'm still Mrs. Broussard to her and the rest of the world."

I shook my head. Maybe this wasn't such a good idea, I thought, as I put the key in the ignition to start the car. I wanted to drown out her nagging voice any way that I could, so I started scrolling through my phone, trying to find a playlist that would have me on one and tuning her ass out. While I was going through my library, the silence that I prayed for was nowhere to be heard, because Alex continued to talk and annoy the fuck out of my soul.

"Cairo, if we want people to believe this marriage is real, we got to at least have some form of communication that doesn't look forced or as if you're annoyed every time I talk to you," she said.

As much as I hated to admit this, she was right for once. There did need to be some form of communication between us. It was just that the way my fucks were given regarding this arrangement, Alex had another think coming. The communication she wanted was far from the type of conversation I was about to give her.

"You wanna talk, Alexandria, then let's talk! What the fuck was up with all that in the shop? You didn't have to run your mouth like you did. We both know damn well that if I wasn't out enjoying the water in Hawaii by myself, I was asleep, and it wasn't with you."

She turned in her seat to face me. If this were back in the day, I probably would've been turned on by the little bit of thigh action she was giving me. Alex's body had always been in great shape, and any man could see that. This man, however, already knew the craziness that dwelled inside of that perfect figure, and I didn't want any parts of it.

"Look, Cai, I hope you don't think you're going to make me look stupid in front of that fat black bitch, or anyone else, for that matter."

I was about to get on her for that foul dig on Audri, but she rose her hand and cut me off.

"You better start acting like a husband, or I'll annul this little marriage arrangement and stop any chances of you getting your hands on that money." She crossed her arms over her chest. "You know Daddy already took care of all of Mama Faye's expenses, and we ain't talking about a couple thousand dollars either. Try more like hundreds of thousands to make sure she has the best care before, during, and after her surgery. If you want out, just let me know now, and I'll make that call, but I doubt you wanna spend the rest of your life paying my father back every last cent."

She had a point there. I didn't want to spend the rest of my life paying her old man. Just thinking about the big-ass smile he had on his face as we said our vows had me feeling some type of way. I probably would've believed that the upward curve of his lips was genuine if I hadn't seen the dollar signs in his eyes flashing bigger and brighter.

I finally pulled out of Audrielle's store parking lot still feeling like shit. I couldn't get that look on her face out of my mind. I would try to reach out to her and apologize for that little episode in a few days. Maybe I could get Ariana to soften her up a little too.

Naw, who am I kidding? She probably feels the same way I did when that bitch Dr. Blake told me that they were married.

It had taken me a few weeks to get over that bit of news. I went to her house once I finally got over the shock of finding out she was already married. Her car was in the driveway and everything; however, when I rang the doorbell, Eli answered that muthafucka like he lived there. Asshole had the nerve to answer the door with his shirt off and everything. I didn't stay to ask any questions or anything. I just turned around and got in my car and left. The one chance I took to see if marrying Alex was a mistake didn't pan out like I thought it would have, causing me to make what was probably the biggest mistake of my life.

***

"What's going on, bruh?" Finesse asked as he opened the door and allowed us to walk in. We gave each other a half hug then headed to the living room.

"Hello to you too, Finesse," Alex said snidely as she eyed all the baby toys in the living room. "I see you're still sloppy as ever, even with a kid."

Finesse ignored her dumb ass and went to the kitchen, returning with two ice cold beers, one for me and the other for him.

"Damn, Ness, you hate me that much that I can't get anything cold to drink too?" Alex complained.

"Sure you can get something cold to drink," he replied, tipping the bottle of beer to his lips and taking a sip. "You just can't get it from my house."

"Your house?" Alex laughed. "If I remember correctly, isn't my husband still listed as the owner of this little condominium?" She walked over to the fireplace mantle and picked up the family pictures of Ness, Ari, and my nephew. "With me being the Mrs. now, technically I have the power to put you, your bastard love child, and your little girlfriend out on the streets, move another family in, and maybe then get treated with some decent hospitality."

Finesse slammed his empty beer bottle down on the coffee table so hard that it shattered. He stood up and charged at Alex so fast that I didn't have time to react. I watched as Finesse wrapped his hand around Alex's throat and forcefully slammed her against the wall, causing a few of the hanging pictures to fall.

"Bitch, you threatening me and my family? Huh? You sure are playing this role pretty serious just for it to be all an act, aren't you? Yo' ass may have Cairo fooled, but you don't fool me. You've been foul since the day he met you, and I doubt that you've changed any since then. You better think twice about what you say to me when you're in *my* house from now on, because the next time, I'm not even gonna touch you. I'ma just let my *little girlfriend,* as you say, handle your ass."

I knew I should've followed my first mind and dropped Alex's ass off at home and come here by myself, but I didn't feel like driving all the way across town just to turn around and come back. This little situation could've totally been avoided had she just kept her mouth shut and stayed thirsty. Then again, it was only a matter of time before these two would've bumped heads anyway.

When Alex and I dated in college, she and Finesse got along well for the most part, but toward the end of our relationship, something happened, and they became enemies real fast. They would argue and say slick shit like this to each other all the time. Neither one would tell me what happened when I asked. They'd just say fuck the other one and keep their distance.

"Ay, Ness, man, let her go. She's not worth the ass whipping Ari is sure to give you if you go to jail behind her," I said.

It took him a minute, but once he finally released the hold he had on Alex's neck, he backed up and walked over to the couch and sat down.

Alex was still standing against the wall, holding her neck and coughing like she couldn't breathe. Instead of checking on her, I went back to my seat, grabbed my beer, and continued our conversation.

"So where's Ari and my nephew?" I asked.

He cut his eyes at Alex, who was now standing up and examining herself in the mirror, then looked back at me. "She left a few minutes ago. Her phone rang, and she ran up out of here. I asked her where she was going, and she told me to mind my business, but she had the nerve to take Cassius with her." He shook his head and smiled. "I swear, that girl drives me crazy sometimes, but I wouldn't trade her ass in for nothing."

I nodded my head. "That's what's up. You do have a good one there. She's had your back since day one, and I respect that a lot about her."

"You have a good one too. You just gotta get rid of this current situation," Ness said as he nodded his head toward Alex, who was sitting in the dining room with her phone in her hand. I thought she was going to have something smart to say because of the evil smirk she had on her face, but nothing never came. She was so into the text conversation she was having on her phone that she wasn't paying attention to us or that cold drink anymore.

"Even when I do get this marriage thing over with, I don't think Audri will want to have anything to do with me. You should've seen the look on her face when Alex followed me into the store today, flashing her ring and our marriage all over the place."

"Word?"

"I could literally see her heart breaking into a million pieces, man. She tried to cover it up and save face in front of the customers and Alex, but when you have the type of connection that she and I have, I knew it was all a front. I wanted to just grab her and hold her, but I didn't want to make the scene worse than what it was, you know," I said.

"Man, y'all be okay. All you gotta do is tell her what's up, and if she loves you as much as she says she does, she'll understand that choice you had to make in order to make sure Moms was taken care of."

Speaking of Mama Faye, I needed to go check on her soon and tell her about everything that had been going on before someone else did. I hadn't been up to the hospital to see her since she had the surgery a few weeks ago.

The timer in the kitchen went off, alerting Finesse that the dinner in the oven was done. While he went to go take care of that, I looked around my old condo and noticed some of the changes that had been made. With the exception of my nephew's toys all over the floor, the big screen TV being mounted to the wall now, the large area rug that covered most of the carpet in the living room, and the outlets and cabinets being baby proofed, I still got that bachelor feel with the place. Everything was black or had some type of black trim, which went well with the white walls and carpet. Every now and then, you'd get a splash of red, whether it was some vases, picture frames, or the throw pillows that were on the sofa. I figured with Ari practically living here now that she would've added her touches here and there, but nope, it was still decorated the way I had it.

I looked over at Alex, who was still into her texting. Whoever she was talking to wasn't telling her what she wanted to hear, because the smirk on her face was replaced by a scowl that I could see from a mile away.

"Yo, Cai, dinner's ready. I just got off the phone with Ari. Her and the baby will be here in about ten minutes. She said we can eat, though. She'll just warm up her food when she gets here," Ness said.

"That's what's up. What we having for dinner anyway? It smells good as hell," I asked, getting off of the couch and heading toward the dining area.

"It smells fattening if you ask me," Alex added.

"Well, no one asked your ass anything. It wasn't like you were going to get some anyway. Just continue being quiet and texting on your phone or you can get the hell out. Either one is fine with me," Ness shot back.

"So you just gonna let him continue to disrespect me like that, Thaddeus? It's bad enough you didn't come to my rescue when he damn near choked me to death," she complained.

"First things first, what the fuck I tell you about calling me that? Cairo is the only name I'm going to answer to, so you need to get that through your head. Secondly, you can miss me with all that bullshit. You always running your mouth, thinking people aren't going to react because of who you are. Him putting his hands on you was wrong, but your slick-ass statement was out of line too. Everything that happened today could've easily been avoided had you kept your mouth shut or just stayed your ass at home," I said.

She looked back and forth between Ness and me, trying to figure out her next move. I could tell she wanted to leave, but at the same time, she didn't want to let me out of her sight. I guess she figured if there was any chance of me going back up to Audri's store to try to make things right between us, she'd be there to block.

We stood in complete silence for a couple of minutes before the jingling of keys unlocking the door caught our attention, causing us to turn our line of vision when it opened.

The first thing I saw was my nephew's sleeping face as Ari walked in carrying him on her hip. After she had picked up the diaper bag and some other purse, she closed the door softly and turned toward us. She took in the scene before her and didn't say a word as she walked down the hallway to Cassius's room to tuck him in for the night. When she returned to the living room, she completely ignored Alex, rolled her eyes at me, and then went to kiss Finesse.

"Baby, I'ma take my plate and go eat in the room. I don't feel like entertaining company right now. Especially after coming back from making sure my sister didn't have another breakdown because of them." She pointed to me and Alex. "We had to close the store early because Audri was so upset. I expect you to have your brother and that bitch out of the house by the time I come back down to get dessert, all right?"

I knew that I'd regret asking this as soon as it came out of my mouth, but I didn't care. "Is she okay?"

Ari cut her eyes at me so fast I didn't even see her do it. "Why the fuck do you care? You wasn't worried about how she was doing when you left for two months then came back married to someone who wasn't her. I had high hopes for you guys, Cai, and I thought you were one of the good guys, but now I see you're just like any other man." She looked over at Alex, who was enjoying this little banter with a smirk on her face. "On second thought, baby, I don't even want them eating my food or anything off of the plates and forks I bought you. You guys can go. Maybe when you make things right with my sister, Cai, we'll be back on good terms. Until then, you and your little porch monkey are dead to me."

"You people kill me," Alex said.

"You people!" Both Finesse and Ari yelled.

I shook my head. Hadn't I just told her about her mouth? Before anything could get out of hand this time, I snatched her by her arm and headed toward the door.

Ari made sure to give me some parting words. "You stay away from my sister, Cairo, since you so easily moved on. Give her the same respect to do the same as well."

I nodded my head in agreement, but I wasn't agreeing to shit. I was going to see Audri every chance I got and plead my case until she couldn't take it anymore.

27

Audrielle

Sitting in the corner of my master suite with the blinds closed and a few candles lit, I felt a little at peace. With everything that had gone on within the last two weeks, I was just happy to feel some kind of contentment. Shit, who the hell was I kidding? Let me stop lying. I was still in my feelings about the whole Cairo situation. That was why I was sitting there listening to one of my favorite George Tandy Jr. songs for the hundredth time and sipping on my fourth glass of sweet peach wine.

You and I . . . You and me belong . . . You and me belong together.

George was singing to my soul as I laid my head back on my comfortable lounge chair and looked up at my ceiling. A single tear ran down the side of my face as I closed my eyes and wished I could just get away from everyone, including myself. I knew I had a business to run and other things that I was trying to do, but for a second, I just wanted to not feel an inkling of pain in my everyday life.

I looked down at my vibrating phone on the nightstand next to me and saw that Cairo was calling me again. He'd been nonstop with the calling ever since that little dinner thing they were supposed to have at Finesse's house that Ari had told me she shut down real quick. After she had gone home from seeing how distraught and upset I was over the whole situation, she wasn't going to pretend like everything was all good between her and Cai.

Our relationship had become a little distant because of whatever she and Rima were going through. Ari felt that I needed to pick a side in the situation and have her back, but at the end of the day, we were sisters and couldn't nothing trump that. Besides, there wasn't any side to have to pick, if you asked me. Rima told me that she and Finesse co-parented, and that was all. There was nothing going on between them other than raising my godson, Cassius. Whatever Ari thought was happening between them was solely her imagination or a guilty conscience speaking. Hopefully, she'd get it together before she drove a wedge in the middle of her and Finesse's relationship and ended up losing him over nothing.

My phone ringing again brought me back to the present and had me groaning in annoyance. I knew that I would have to block Cairo from calling or having any form of communication with me if I wanted to try to get over him. It was going to be hard, but I needed to do it and do it fast. He was now married to his ex, a beautiful Megan Fox lookalike. How could I possibly compete with that?

My TV, which was on mute, was starting to give off a little more light than I wanted, so I picked up the remote and turned it off. I even got up and blew out a few candles, only leaving the last two on my dresser lit. After pouring another glass of wine and taking a few gulps, I stood in the middle of my room, looking into the darkness. Mario's soulful voice was now serenading me about somebody crying out for him, and I couldn't help the flow of continuous tears that started to stream down my face.

A little tipsy now, I swayed back and forth as if I were dancing to the song. My glass of wine, which I had finished a few seconds before, fell onto the floor and shattered into a million pieces.

"Shit!" I didn't feel like leaving the safe confines of my room, but I needed to get this glass up before I forgot that it was there and stepped on it later.

I walked down to my kitchen in search of the broom, dustpan, and a rag when my doorbell chimed. I was going to ignore it at first, but the constant ringing would surely get on my nerves if the visitor decided to be a pest and continue. Not wanting to deal with any added pressure to the headache I could already feel coming on, I went to answer the door.

"Bitch, this is the second time I had to come hunt you down after a breakup. First it was with that loser Antonio, and now with this fool Cairo. How many times do I have to tell you that you don't have to go through this shit alone?" Rima asked as she barged into my home uninvited.

My eyes followed her little ass as she strolled toward my dining room table with a white plastic bag in one hand and a black one in the other. For a short moment, a surge of jealousy shot through my body as I took in my best friend. The glow she had surrounding her seemed to enhance her beauty. Some of the pregnancy weight she had picked up stayed and had her body filling out like she had always dreamed of. Her hair was dyed jet black now and flowed flawlessly down her back. The makeup on her face highlighted her high cheekbones and brought out her amber-colored eyes. Even her attitude seemed a little different, in a good way. If having a baby gave a person this kind of change, then maybe I needed to have one as soon as possible.

I shook my head after I had that thought. I'd need to find a man first if I wanted that to happen anytime soon.

Rima walked into the kitchen, took something out of my fridge, and then walked back out. I glanced down at the bags in her hand. I could see two Styrofoam to-go plates in the white one, but the contents of the black bag were a mystery.

"I do appreciate you coming over here, Rima. I did want to call you for a pow-wow session, but I figured you'd be busy taking care of my godson." My words were a little slurred, but I didn't care. If she had a problem with me having one . . . two . . . hell, let me keep it real, three bottles of wine to myself, she could leave the same way she came in.

"Girl, bye. His little ass been with his daddy and Ari for the last week. You know we alternate. It wouldn't matter anyway, though. You know I'm here for you whenever you need me. Cassius isn't going to stop that for one second. His little ass will just be here with us, crying and shitting."

I laughed, something I hadn't done in a minute. "See, girl, that's why you're my best friend. Ride or die, down for whatever."

She nodded her head and placed the items in her hand on the table, then turned back around to me with a more serious expression on her face.

"Spit truth?"

I really didn't want to have any deep conversations right now, but I figured I should get this shit out of the way right now rather than later on when I was ready for her to leave so that I could sulk by myself again.

"Yeah, spit truth," I said. "What's up?"

"Why didn't you ever tell me that you and Eli got married? On some real shit, my feelings were hurt when I found out through Finesse about that little bit of information. I argued him down when he told me that. Called him all kinds of lying bastards and everything, only to have to apologize a few seconds later when I heard him and Cairo having some sort of heated conversation over the phone."

See, this was what I was trying to avoid. I knew everyone, especially my parents, would be down my throat about me getting married and not telling anyone, but I just wanted to discuss that topic when I felt ready to.

"Rima, I really don't—"

"Don't do that, Audri. Don't try to close me out or say something to try to justify us not having this conversation. It's obvious you need to get this shit off of your chest and talk to somebody.

You've been locked away from the public again for the last two weeks and haven't been keeping yourself up at all."

I looked down at my oversized sweat pants and black tank top. My hand subconsciously went to my hair and felt what could only be described as a bird's nest on top of my head. I looked at my reflection through the glass in my china cabinet and had to do a double-take. My eyes had bags under them and were bloodshot red. I lifted my arm up a bit and put my nose toward my armpit and sniffed. I was a little tart, but not to the point where I could smell myself.

"I don't look or smell that bad," I said.

"If you say so. Anyway, I brought some food from Tito's Tacos, and a few of those Hostess Honey Buns you eat, and this new Blue Moscato wine I've been wanting to try." She removed her liquor store bounty from the black bag. "I know you haven't eaten any real food, so I won't take no for an answer, and while we're sitting here digging in, I need you to fill me in on everything you obviously forgot to tell me about back then and up to two weeks ago."

We sat at the table and talked about the situation with Cairo, as well as my marriage and how it happened. Rima did express again that she was hurt by me not including her in on my nuptials, but she understood my reasoning.

After we filled both of our bellies to the max with some good Mexican food, then topped it off with another glass of wine, she caught me up on everything that had been going on in her life, including the new man she'd been seeing. When I asked her if and when I was going to meet this mystery man, she told me in due time.

"Now ain't this about a bitch! Wasn't you just getting on my ass about us keeping things from one another?" I teased.

She laughed. "Yeah, I was, but this situation with ol' boy is kind of new, and I'm just testing the waters. If, and I mean if, it becomes something more serious, you will be the first one to check him out."

I just nodded my head as I sipped on my wine.

"Audri, can I ask you something?"

"Anything."

"Who do you think told that crazy bitch Alex about you and Eli being married? I mean, I don't see who could've told her if no one but you and Eli knew about it. You don't think she went down to the Hall of Records, do you?"

"Even if she did, she wouldn't have found out anything, because our marriage wasn't public information," I said.

She put her wine glass down and looked at me with a confused expression on her face. "Then how did she find out?"

I had thought long and hard about this same question, too, until I remembered the one thing I totally forgot, which was us needing a witness at our ceremony. Since we didn't want to use some unknown Joe Schmoe from off the streets, we ended up using someone we both trusted.

"A witness?" I could see the hurt building back up in Rima's eyes. "You really didn't feel that you could trust me with that information?"

"I did, but you know you and Eli didn't really get along."

"And for good reason. He was such an asshole. I don't know who was worse with the fat girl comments, him or your mother." She took another sip of wine then continued. "Who did you guys end up using as a witness?"

"His sister . . . Sarah."

28

Cairo

"Thank you, sir, and have a wonderful day."

"You as well." I thanked the young cashier in the hospital gift shop and headed toward the elevator. This had been my daily routine for the last week coming to see Mama Faye. A nice bouquet of flowers, a newspaper so that she could do the Sudoku and crossword puzzles, and a can of her beloved Ting. What she saw in this grapefruit-flavored soda, I couldn't tell you. What I did know is that it cost me an arm and a leg to get it sent from some online site every month. I tried to get her a few cases of Squirt one time, seeing as how it was a grapefruit-fla-vored beverage too and cost way less than Ting, but Mama Faye was not having it. She opened each can in the three twelve-packs and poured the contents down the drain to show me how she didn't appreciate me bringing home an impostor, and I quickly learned my lesson.

"Good evening, Mr. Broussard. Up here again, huh?" the cute hospital receptionist asked me as I strolled past her desk. Alex wasn't lying when she said her father spared no expense to pay for Mama Faye's accommodations. After she had her surgeries, she was moved into a part of the hospital I didn't even know existed. There were about twenty rooms on this floor, and each of them looked like an expensively furnished studio apartment.

"You know that beautiful woman in room seven would kill me if I didn't bring her daily gifts," I informed the receptionist, motioning to all the things I had in my hands. She smiled and continued to watch me as I walked by, then went back to doing whatever it was she was doing on the computer.

My phone vibrated in my pocket. When I looked down and saw Alex's number flash across my screen, I ignored the call. She'd been calling me for the last few hours, wanting to know my whereabouts, and it was really starting to irk my nerves. After reiterating to her that this agreement we had did not entitle her to question me like this was a real relationship, she started crying and going off again about annulling the marriage. I was so tired of her empty threats that I told her to go ahead and do it. The money was due to be wired into my account any day now, so I wasn't tripping. That shut her ass up real quick and had her changing her approach. Instead of nagging and acting crazy, she was now trying to be the supportive and understanding wife. It didn't matter one way or the other. She knew our days as a married couple were coming to an end.

Not paying attention to where I was walking because I was reading the text Alex sent, I bumped into someone hard, causing them to drop all of the papers in their hand onto the shiny hospital floor. I was just about to bend down and help pick up the mess I caused until I saw that it was Dr. Blake who I had collided with.

"So you just gon' act like you didn't cause me to drop all my paperwork?" he asked as he squatted down and started sweeping the papers together with his hands.

"My bad. Didn't see you."

"Yeah, I bet."

When he finally got up, we stood there in an awkward silence, each assessing the other—probably each trying to figure out what Audri saw in the other.

"Well, if you will excuse me, duty calls." He held up his stack of paper. "Plus, I have to call the wifey and see how she's doing. She's slowly but surely getting over the last loser she was with that broke her heart. I'm just happy I came back in time to pick up the pieces. Now we can work on our marriage and start to live happily in wedded bliss like I assume you are." He gave me a once-over then smirked and started to walk away.

If looks could kill, the one I gave him would've had him laid out in the middle of this hall. I started to say something but was cut off by a Code Blue being called over the speaker system. My heart started to beat fast when I saw Dr. Blake and some of the nurses running toward Mama Faye's room, but when they headed farther down the hall, a sigh of relief escaped my lips.

After that small interruption, I continued my stroll to her room. I was just about to walk in but stopped when a man I had never seen before came walking out. When we looked at each other, I instantly knew who he was, even though I'd never met him before. His face was a complete replica of mine, just the older version. He had a dark skin tone, probably from tanning on some tropical island during one of his many family vacations without me. His low-cut dirty blond hair had strands of white trying to come into the mix. His facial hair was neatly trimmed and lined up. His eyes were low and tight. He kind of reminded me of that McSteamy dude from *Grey's Anatomy*—again, just older. The thing that really caught my attention, though, were his eyes. While one was a bluish-color with specks of green like mine, the other was a shade of green with specks of blue that reminded me of the ocean.

The look of regret, shock, and happiness could be seen all over his face, and at that moment, I knew he wanted to say something to me but didn't know how. We stood there for a minute, looking at each other as if the last thirty years were replaying in both of our minds. I was trying to figure out what life would've been like if I had grown up in my biological parents' household, while he was probably trying to see how different my life was because I hadn't.

"Thaddeus . . ." His voice was deep and raspy voice.

"Cairo."

He nodded his head at my correction.

"I don't know. . . . I just want—"

I held up my hand to stop him from talking. It was not the time for us to have this discussion. Not in a hospital, and not when our time would more than likely be cut short for some unknown reason. I had a lot of questions that I wanted to ask, and I didn't want any of them to go unanswered. Naw, if we were going to do this little reunion, it would most definitely be on some other day and in a different setting.

"Cai!" I heard Mama Faye yell strenuously. I turned my attention toward her and walked into the room to make sure she was okay.

"Boi, if ya don't bring mi Tings in here right now, we gon' have serious problems. What ya just standing in da do'way for anyway?"

"I was just talking to—" When I turned around to address the man I undoubtedly knew was my father, he was nowhere in sight. I turned back around with squinted eyes, looking at Mama Faye. "What was he doing here?"

She stretched her head to the side to look around me. "He who? Mi no have the slightest idea of what'chu talkin' 'bout, boi."

"How long has he been coming to visit you? When were you going to tell me?"

Mama Faye waved me off, completely ignoring my questions like she didn't know what I was talking about, but I knew better. This was her M.O. She would keep her mouth closed and just act like I was imagining whatever I was questioning, so she didn't have to say anything about it. That was her way to get out of lying, but I wasn't having it.

"So you really gonna sit here and act like you don't know what I'm talking about? Like I just didn't see the man that walked out of this room who looked exactly like me? The same man you told me you haven't talked to since I was young."

She coughed. "A lot of questions ya want de answers to, yet ya still keeping tings from mi."

"Things from you like what?" I asked.

"Like ya being married to that gal with the sneaky eyes mi don't like. Mi warned ya about her then, and mi warned ya about her not too long ago. Mi knew she was up to no good when she came back sniffing around ya."

I stood there speechless for a minute because I didn't know how she found out about me and Alex being married. Finesse and I thought it would be best to keep that bit of information from her while she was in the hospital healing. We didn't want to cause any more added stress to what she already had.

I blew out a frustrated breath and walked over to the side of Mama Faye's bed, kissed her on the forehead, and handed her the things I had bought for her. I could see now that the questions I had in regards to my biological father were not going to be answered anytime that day, so I just left it alone for now.

Pulling up a chair from the corner of the room, I sat down next to her and watched as she took a sip from her soda then unfolded the newspaper and started on the crossword puzzle. The flowers I bought lay on top of her cover, resting against her legs. In about thirty minutes, when the nurse came in to check her vitals, she would ask her to empty out the water from the old pitcher and replace it with some fresh water so that she could stick the flowers in there.

"Mi need a nine-letter word for . . . a request for a congratulatory slap?" She looked over at me, and I shrugged my shoulders. "Ya no help, boi."

I nodded my head then took out my phone to go through my messages. This was what we did every day. After I had finished up some drawing for work, I'd come and spend a few peaceful hours with her, then return to the house in Palos Verde that Alex and I were sharing for the time being.

I had a few e-mails from some clients, as well as a couple from some of the parents of the basketball team, asking about the banquet we had coming up for the season we had just finished. After responding to the majority of the e-mails, I went through my text messages. There were none new, but that didn't stop me from checking my inbox. I was hoping Audri would respond to the *I miss you* text I had sent her the week before, but just like every day since I'd started sending them, there was nothing. Maybe Dr. Blake wasn't lying about them working things out. Maybe they were trying to make their marriage work. If so, I was going to try my hardest to fall back. I mean, who was I to try to break up what they were trying to do when I had my own situation? Audri wasn't side chick material, and I wouldn't knowingly approach her in that manner either.

A feeling of nostalgia came over me, causing me to tense up a little and bite my bottom lip as I reminisced about the last night Audri and I had together.

"She still loves ya, ya know."

I looked at Mama Faye. For a minute I forgot she was in the room because she'd been so quiet. Looking at her with the pen in her hand, reading glasses sitting low on her nose and concentrating on her puzzle, had me smiling for a second. This was one of those times where I didn't regret doing what I did. To see her doing what she loved and on the road to recovery did something to and for me. I was finally getting my Mama Faye back. Her skin wasn't ashy anymore, and her hair was slowly getting thick again. She was even gaining some weight, thanks to that sugary drink I was giving her and the Jamaican food that Finesse was smuggling in for her. Soon she would be well enough to go home and everything would be back to normal.

"Ma, I really don't care if Alex still loves me or not. We only got married so that I could get my hands on that inheritance money, so that I could pay for your surgery and medical bills. It was only for a month anyway. In a few weeks, I'll be a single man, and she'll be a single woman with five million dollars in her bank account."

She shook her head. "I'm not talking about that gold-digging gal ya married to. Mi talking about the gal whose heart ya broke. The one ya should have married."

"Audri is already marr—"

She held up her hand, cutting me off.

"I already know everyting about de situation, so no need to go over dem again. I just hope by de time ya divorce that sneaky-eye gal, it's not too late for a chance with mi real daughter-in-law. That one right there is going to give me plenty of grandbabies. I can feel it."

We shared a laugh as I silently prayed that everything worked out in that way.

"Cairo."

"Yeah, Ma."

She looked at me with misty eyes. "Thank ya. Thank ya for putting your happiness on hold just to make sure mi could live to see anotha day. Ya may not be mine by blood, but you're mine in every sense of de word, and don't ya forget it. Soon ya will be reunited with your real family, and mi just want ya to know that mi door will always be open to ya."

I wiped away the few tears that fell down her cheek with my thumb, then gently wrapped my arms around her and gave her a hug.

"You and Ness will always and forever be my family, regardless of who comes into my life. No one can ever take your place."

"Or make your favorite Jamaican dishes," she added.

I laughed. "You better believe it."

29

Audrielle

I had just left from seeing a few new store location, with my real estate agent and was headed to my parents' house. I really didn't want to go over there, but it had been a minute since I saw my father. If anyone could give me some good advice on the things going on in my life, it would be him.

Pulling up into my parents' circular driveway, I noticed a car I'd never seen before parked behind my mother's. It wasn't anything fancy, but it was a new car nonetheless.

Must be one of her sorority sisters visiting, I thought as I let myself in.

I walked into the home I grew up in and couldn't help but to smile. Although my mother could be a bitch sometimes, it didn't take away from the good times I did have when we were all getting along.

I heard muffled voices coming from the sitting room, so I decided to head that way. I didn't want to be rude and not speak to whoever was in there, even if I had to hear something slick come out of my mother's mouth. As I got closer, the hushed conversation they were trying to have was starting to become clearer. I also recognized who the second voice belonged to.

"Wait, so tell me again what happened to your face?" my mother asked my auntie.

"I told you I got into a little fight with a few of these young girls who were being disrespectful and pushing up on Antonio while we were out."

"And that's the story you're selling?"

"It's the truth, Diana. Why would I have to lie to you?"

"Oh, I don't know," my mother said. "Maybe because you don't want to admit that your niece is the one who really kicked your ass." She snorted her nose then laughed. "Ariana already told me what happened, so you can save that lie for someone else."

"Whatever. Audri just caught me off guard."

"What were you doing at her house anyway? The last time I checked, you two weren't on speaking terms behind that whole Antonio situation."

"We weren't, but I was going over there to apologize," my aunt said. "Audri didn't give me a chance to say anything before she hauled off and slapped the shit out of me."

"Well, that's what you get for messing with my baby."

Baby? I don't think I'd ever heard my mother use that term of endearment toward me. Maybe there was some hope for us after all.

"Di, knock it off. That girl is far from being your baby. You and I both know that. That's why you stay on her about all that extra weight she's been carrying around."

"Her weight doesn't change the fact that I gave birth to her. I just should've been a little more careful when it came to allowing her seconds and thirds after meals. Maybe if I would've told her no then, she would not excessively eat now."

And there it went. The hope I'd had for my mother and I having a relationship was gone that fast. Not wanting to hear anything else they were going to say, I silently turned around and headed toward my father's study. I knew he had to be in one of his moods because I could hear the soulful sounds of the Average White Band's "A Love of Your Own" floating through the air.

Without knocking, I walked into my father's study and closed the door. The music, which was a little loud, must've drowned out my entrance, because my father never stopped what he was doing to acknowledge me. He was sitting in his chair with his back turned to the door, looking out of the large-pane window. I could see a glass of some brown liquid, which was more than likely a shot of Johnnie Walker Red, in his left hand and what looked like an old piece of paper in his right.

I took a moment to take in the room that I had the privilege of spending a lot of stressful nights and cheerful days in. The decorative ceilings were always one of my favorite things to look at; that and my father's favorite inspirational sayings that were stenciled along the wall. The dark, hand-carved wooden desk he had made in Italy was another focal point. The plush furniture, family pictures strategically placed throughout the room, and the way his Cuban cigars would lightly scent the air whenever he left the box open were added bonuses. I loved this room more than my own bedroom.

"Honey Bee, how long have you been here?" my father asked, jogging me back from my memories.

"I just got here. I wanted to drop by and speak to my old man."

"Old man? There isn't anything old on me, Honey Bee," he joked. "What did you need to talk about?"

"Well, I just came back from looking at a few properties for a new store, and I think I finally found a location that I like. The only thing is, the problem I'm having with the bank. After presenting them with the revenue of the current store and showing them how good we're doing, they still don't want to approve the loan for the amount I need."

"Why do you need more money?" he asked.

"Because this new store is going to be twice as big as the last one."

"Do you think that's a smart move?" he asked as he poured me a shot of whatever he was drinking and put the picture he had in his other hand under a pile of papers. I wanted to ask him who the lady was in the in the picture. It obviously wasn't my mother, because this woman was a little darker.

"I believe it is. It's a few blocks from UCLA in that shopping center where the kids go to purchase used books. I went over that way today, and there was a lot of foot traffic in the area with it being the summer semester. Just imagine when school starts back up in the fall. Not to mention football and basketball season soon after," I said.

My father nodded his head in approval. I took a sip of the whiskey and felt the burn slowly go down my chest. I wished there was some apple juice in there that I could have chased this shot with, but my father threw that out the minute I became old enough to drink alcohol.

"Well, if this is what you really want, I'll go ahead and give you whatever amount the bank won't loan you," he said.

As much as I wanted to accept my father's help, I had to put on my big girl panties and decline his offer. I was still paying him back for the loan he gave me for the first store, even though he didn't want my money at first, but after I had explained to him how I wanted to be an independent business owner and not a parent-dependent business owner, he started to accept my payments. Plus, I didn't want my mom to feel as if she had a say in the way I ran my store like she did with my first store.

My father and I sat in his office for the next couple of hours, listening to his oldies and sipping on our drinks. We talked about everything and anything, including the woman in the picture he had tried to hide.

"So who was that lady, Dad?"

He took the picture from under the stack of papers and handed it to me.

"That is the woman I should've married."

Kind of stunned by his bluntness, I sat there and continued to listen to him as I stared at the Garcelle Beauvais lookalike.

"A few years before I met your mother, I dated and fell in love with my childhood friend, Erika Little. She literally took my breath away whenever she was in my presence. That's how beautiful she was. We had plans of attending the same college, graduating, then getting married, having a bunch of kids, and living happily ever after. We ended up getting accepted to two different colleges, me USC and her NYU.

"The night before she was supposed to leave, we met up at this little secret spot we had at the Redondo Beach Pier. One thing led to another, and she ended up giving me a woman's most prized possession. After I had turned her into a woman, I made promise after promise after promise that we would be together forever, and I would do right by her during our long-distance relationship.

"For the first year, we were good, but the following year, I messed around and joined my frat and ended up breaking all of the promises I had made to Erika. Unbeknownst to me, she came home early one semester to surprise me and ended up finding me knocked out in my bedroom with two women in my bed. I tried for weeks to get her to talk to me, but she wouldn't.

"After a few months of me pleading and begging, she finally broke down and used the plane ticket I had bought her to come see me. I was happy as all outdoors. When I picked her up from the airport, I noticed there was something a little different about her. Her body was spreading out a little more, and her face was getting a little chunky. The first thought that ran through my mind was that she was pregnant, but then I remembered we hadn't had sex in almost nine months.

"The whole weekend she was at my house, she was sick as a dog. When she kept refusing to take any of the medicine I was buying her, she finally broke down and told me that she had been seeing some cat from New Jersey and was now four months pregnant by him. To say I was devastated would be an understatement. I was so mad that I dropped her off at her parents' house and never called her again.

"Over the years, she reached out to me, but I would just ignore her. Then once I started messing with your mother, she hurried up and nipped that situation in the bud real quick and real fast." He laughed.

"For years I wondered what would've happened if I would've never cheated on her and kept my promises. Would we be married right now and would she be you and Ari's mother?"

I saw the far-off look in his eyes as a light mist glossed over them.

"Honey Bee, you know I don't normally get into you or your sister's love lives or anything like that, but I told you this story to tell you this: don't let one mistake ruin a beautiful thing. The reality of this is that people mess up, we are human, and it's in our design to be flawed. Mistakes are forgivable, especially if one has the courage to admit them. I don't know all of the details that happened in you and Cairo's relationship, but I do know that you need to hear him out about his reasoning behind what he did."

"How do you even know—"

He cut me off.

"That night he came to our home for the family dinner, I heard everything he said to you in the bathroom after your mother embarrassed you, and although I hate to admit this, I'm man enough to tell you that I almost got choked up a little after hearing him. Then you can't deny the look he had in his eyes when you opened the door and he saw your face." He shook his head. "I know that look all too well. It was of a man in love, the same way I looked at Erika when her family first moved into the neighborhood and the same way your mother wishes I looked at her."

I slowly nodded my head as my fourth shot of whiskey started to take effect. A light knock on the door had us both turning our heads in its direction.

"Honey, I'm about—Audrielle, what are you doing in here? When did you get here?" my mother asked.

"Oh, hey, Mom. I've been here for a couple—a few hours." My words were a little slurred, but I knew she understood what I said, especially after she turned up her nose and shook her head.

"Shouldn't you be at the store running things instead of sitting here with your father getting drunk? It's not even cocktail hour yet. And what's wrong with your hair? Should I make an appointment for you to get it done today?"

"Mother, my hair is fine. I'm just doing the natural thing today."

"Well, the natural thing doesn't look good on you at all. You have to have the right size face, and yours is a little too round. Maybe if you—"

"Diana, that's enough!" My father's voice cut through the stale air. "Audri can wear her hair any way she wants. You don't hear me talking about that dead poodle you've been wearing on top of your head lately, do you?"

My mother gasped loudly and grabbed her chest. She could be so dramatic at times. Not wanting to deal with any of her shenanigans or slick comments, I instantly sobered up and got ready to leave.

"I'll see you later, Daddy. I'm going to go check on the store, then head on over to the gym," I said.

"The gym?" both of my parents said. My father had a normal look on his face, while my mother's lit up like the fourth of July.

"Yeah, Eli kind of finagled me into working out with him. One day he came over to check on me and ended up calling me out on all the junk food and sweets I was eating to help me deal with this Cairo situation. We started last week, and I can honestly say that I enjoy it."

"Well, that's good, Honey Bee. Keep up the good work. Even with that nice dress you have on, I can tell you've been slimming down a bit," my father said.

I looked down at the pink floral-print maxi dress I was wearing. While the bottom flared out and hung loosely, the top fit snug in my breast area. When I had bought it a month before, I couldn't even zip it up all the way, so I guess my new workout regimen was working.

"It's funny you say that, because I actually lost ten pounds already," I said.

"Which hardly isn't enough," I heard my mother say under her breath.

Choosing to ignore her, I kept my attention focused on my father.

"I can see it. Go on and get out of here, Audri. I have to talk to your mother about a few things anyway."

I gave my father a kiss then headed for the door before he called my name.

"Yeah, Dad."

"Don't forget what I told you, Honey Bee. At least hear him out."

I nodded my head and left. My father was really sipping on that brown liquor a little too much if he thought that I was really going to talk to Cairo anytime soon. He chose who he wanted to be with when he disappeared for two months then came back married to that bitch Alex. I would hear him out all right; the minute hell froze over. Until then, my main focus was my body, finances, and businesses. Once those were all squared away, then maybe I just might respond to one of Cairo's texts or answer one of his phone calls.

30

Cairo

I swear I had ninety-nine problems, and a nagging, fake wife was one. Alex was on my back tough about any and everything, from still having the house I bought not even a few months ago to not attending any of her after-hour business dinners, pretending to be the loving and supporting husband she wanted me to be. She was even starting to complain about me not having any form of physical contact with her. Alex knew sex was out of the question, so I didn't even know why she was tripping. I couldn't see myself putting on this act too much longer. That was why I was so happy that I would be having another meeting with my grandmother's lawyer in a few weeks. It had already been over our one-month agreement by a week, and I needed this marriage to be over as quickly as it happened.

My phone ringing through the speakers in my car jolted me from my thoughts.

"Call from . . . Do Not Answer."

I lightly chuckled at the name I had pro-
grammed in my phone for Alex. She even complained about that. I didn't know how she knew
that was the name I had her registered under,
but she did.

As always, I ignored the call, grabbed my
workout bag, and hopped out of my car. I'd been
spending a lot of time in the gym lately, trying
to work some of this stress out and to get away
from Alex for a few hours. At first going to the
gym was working out in my favor. I was able to
be stress-free, even if it was only for a few hours;
that is, until she started to show up and try to
have couple's sessions. That's why I was at the
new Equinox gym on the other side of town. She
wouldn't be able to accidentally bump into me
there.

The odor of sweat, chlorine, and rubber hit
my nose as soon as I walked through the door.
I looked to the left and saw men and women of
different shape and sizes on the treadmills, leg
lifts, bicycles, and Stairmasters. I looked to my
right and could see the other gym rats in their
swimwear about to go for a swim.

Walking over to the front to check in, I couldn't
help to notice the googly eyes the girl behind the
desk was giving me.

"Hi, I'm Laurie. Welcome to Equinox. May I see your membership card and ID?"

I handed her my information and signed in.

"Cairo Broussard." She looked up at me and studied my face lustfully. "This has to be your first time coming here."

"How do you know that?"

She blushed. "Let me rephrase that. I know this has to be your first time coming here in the last four months since I've been at the front desk. I would never forget a face like yours."

I smiled at her compliment then decided to humor her a little. "Am I that ugly?"

Her cheeks went up two more shades of red. "You're far from ugly, and any woman can see that whether they're gay or straight." She handed me back my things. "Your eyes and hair would be my weakness for sure."

"Been told that about my eyes, but never my hair. Why is that?"

She shrugged her shoulders. "I just have a thing for dreads. Never seen them on a white boy before, but I must say they are sexy as hell on you. Twisted all neat and stuff. I normally like them when they are hanging loose and free, but all in one ponytail like you have it is sexy too."

I knew that if I didn't stop her anytime soon, Laurie would continue to throw herself at me. So after promising to say bye before I left, I was finally able to get my workout going.

I had been on the weights for about an hour before I decided to go and do some leg lifts. After wiping down the seat that was just occupied, I sat down, adjusted the weights, and then started to lift. I was just about to put my headphones on when I heard a moan that sounded rather familiar.

"Naw, it can't be," I said to myself as I shook my head. There was only one person whose moans would make my dick jump up the way it did, but as I quickly looked around, I didn't see her anywhere. I really was starting to hear things.

I guess when you're missing someone so much, it starts to happen that way, especially when you're horny as fuck and craving to feel their walls sucking the life out of you. I shook the thought off and adjusted my shorts. Having a hard-on in the middle of the gym would get me a lot of questioning glares, so I decided to focus on my workout and get out of there. Before I could put my headphones on to get the sound out of my head, that sweet noise happened again, this time causing my dick to shoot straight up.

When my eyes scanned the area again, they landed on a pair of thighs I had been dreaming about being between for the last few months. There was someone blocking my view of her face, but I would know her body and the noises she made anywhere.

I knew interrupting her session was going to be rude, but if this was the only way that I could talk to her, so be it. I stood up from the equipment I was occupying, leaving my towel, water bottle, and iPod behind. I was not worried about anyone stealing my things at the moment. I eyed the way the trainer was touching her legs and started to become pissed off. Why was he touching her as if it was something he'd done before?

Her laughter filled the air, which led me to believe that she was enjoying whatever corny joke he must've told her, but I was about to break up that joyful moment. I was just about to tap ol' boy on the shoulder when he stood up from his squatting position as if he sensed me walking up. He turned around.

"Dr. Blake?" He had that smug smirk on his face.

"Cairo?" Audri said with wide eyes as she stood up next to him.

I took in her appearance. She looked good, even with sweat dripping down her face and perspiration spots all over her grey Nike Pro shirt and shorts. I couldn't help but notice the way her body was slimming down. Those sexy curves were still defined and intact, just a little smaller. The shorts showed off her smooth legs, while the shirt displayed a nice amount of cleavage. Her hair was up in one of those messy buns, and her face was makeup free. The glow she seemed to have made me smile as my eyes connected to hers.

"How have you been, Audri? I've been calling and texting you—"

"I know. I've just been real busy with trying to open this new store location, then working out whenever I can. Plus, I still spend a majority of my time at the store in Fairfax, even though I hired a store manager and a couple staff members."

"So you finally found a location?" I remembered during a few of our late-night conversations on the phone, she had talked about opening a few more stores. She said she just didn't want to have to ask her parents for the money.

"Yeah, I found one that I really like, but the bank won't loan me the amount I need to open it."

I heard everything she had just said, and I wasn't trying to be inconsiderate, but I needed to get what I'd been holding off my chest, just in case I never got the opportunity to talk to her again.

"Look, Audri, I just want to apologize for everything and how it went down. It was never my intention to hurt you in any way. What I felt for you was real, is real, and will always be real. Just let me explain everything to you. How about we go out—"

I was cut off by wack-ass Dr. Blake angrily calling her name. "Audri!"

We both turned our attention to him. I hadn't noticed until that moment that he had left our conversation and was now standing by a Stairmaster, adjusting something on the screen.

"*We* need to get back to our leg day workout if *we* want to get out of here in time to catch that movie you wanted *us* to see."

She furrowed her eyebrows and pursed her lips. Either she was a great actress for my sake, or she was totally surprised by what he had said. She shook her head then looked back at me. A lustful gleam danced through her eyes as she looked at me from head to toe. When her eyes reached my lips, I inadvertently licked them, causing her to let a small gasp escape hers.

"I . . . I would . . ." she started to say to me, but she was interrupted.

"Oh, there you go, baby. I've been trying to reach you for the last couple hours," Alex said as she walked over to us.

How the fuck did she find me way over at this gym? I need to go through the apps on my phone, I thought. Knowing her, she had probably put a Family Locator app on it. I looked at her and shook my head in annoyance. She was dressed in a black low-cut cocktail dress with some black strappy heels. Her hair was braided on one side, with loose curls falling on the other. Her makeup was flawless as always, and the weird-smelling expensive perfume she liked to wear was lingering in the air.

"Cai, I hope you're finished. I hope you didn't forget that we were having dinner at my parents' house tonight," she said.

I didn't forget. I just didn't want to go. Dealing with her family was something I tried to keep at a minimum. I had already paid her father back for Mama Faye's expenses, so there was no reason for me to be in his presence anymore—except that I still had questions about my biological father, which Mama Faye didn't have the answers to.

My eyes were still trained on Audri's, whose eyes were now on Alex. Every time Alex would use her hand with her wedding ring on it to pick at the imaginary lint on her dress, I could see the hurt I was just trying to apologize about on her face.

"Thanks for the apology, Cairo, but it wasn't necessary. I was over whatever we had the minute you walked into my store a married man." Her gaze returned to me. "Have a nice life, Cai, and I wish you many wonderful years of wedded bliss." With that, she grabbed her towel off of the floor, threw it over her shoulder, and headed toward a pissed off Dr. Blake. They argued in hushed tones for a minute before she threw the towel over her shoulder in his face and stormed out of the gym altogether.

"I still don't understand what you saw in her. She doesn't seem like your type at all," Alex said, reminding me that she was standing beside me.

"See."

She had a confused look on her face. "See what?"

"It's not what I saw, it's what I see in her, which is something you'll never understand because you don't possess what it is that she has." And with that, I headed toward the showers to get changed and mentally prepare myself for what was about to go down that night.

***

"So, Thad—I mean, Cairo—how does it feel being a millionaire now? I know you're happy you don't have to live in that low poverty neighborhood anymore. Right, son?" Alex's father said.

See, this was the reason why I hated coming around this bullshit. If he wasn't talking about the neighborhood I grew up in, he was trying to pressure me about starting a family with Alex. Whenever that topic came up, I didn't even dignify him with a response. The only person I wanted to carry my seed was somewhere with her husband, probably making up at that moment.

"Cai, I know you hear my father talking to you. Show a little bit of respect to your father-in-law," Alex whispered in my ear.

I didn't respond to her either as I played with the pork chop and apple slice dish their maid had just placed in front of me. Man, what I wouldn't give for some jerk chicken, steamed cabbage and carrots, rice and peas, and sweet plantains. I hadn't had any good food since Mama Faye had been in the hospital; just a lot of takeout, TV dinners, or sandwiches and chips. Every now and then when Ness and Ariana would invite me over for dinner, I'd have a decent meal, and I was thankful for that.

"Cairo, dear, what is the first thing you're going to do now that you got your inheritance money?" her mother asked. For some strange reason, I liked her and always had. She was always so sweet and friendly. I didn't know if it was just in her nature to be that way or if the alcohol that radiated from her pores had anything to do with it. Whatever it was, I liked it.

She flicked her blond bangs and took a sip of whatever was mixed with the red drink she had in her wine glass. Closing her eyes, she savored the taste before she put it down and turned her attention toward me, I guess expecting my answer.

I looked around the table, and all eyes were on me, including Alex's older brother Matt and his best friend, Oliver, who I could tell was his lover. He just hadn't come out of the closet yet. The way they looked at each other reminded me of the way Audri and I would look at each other after we had sex. It was that longing look, where you just knew that you wouldn't mind being with that person for the rest of your life. I was not sure how his parents or Alex hadn't caught on yet, but I noticed it the first time I saw them together.

I coughed and cleared my throat. "Well, after I pay off certain debts"—I looked at Alex—"I want to buy my mom a house and maybe improve a few areas in the neighborhood I grew up in."

"Such as?" Oliver asked. He pushed his glasses up on his face and looked over at me with genuine interest.

"Fixing some of the basketball courts at the parks and getting some new equipment for the after-school programs mainly. After that, I just want to live my life and be happy."

"Nothing makes a man happier than witnessing the birth of his first child," her father said. "Something about that moment does something to you." He looked at Alex's mom who just nodded her head and guzzled down her drink.

When she asked the maid to refill her cup, I took that as an opportunity to get a drink as well. I needed something strong to mellow me out if I was going to be dealing with these types of statements.

Two hours later, it was safe to say that I was completely wasted. My words were slurring and everything. It was the only way that I could get through the rest of that dinner and not blow a gasket. I'd asked a few questions about my father, which seemed to be like pulling teeth. Eventually, Alex's dad gave me the address to his home in Calabasas that I'd be visiting sooner rather than later. I just hoped it wouldn't be a problem when I showed up on the doorstep unannounced. I mean, you would've thought that after the run-in at the hospital and meeting their lawyer, we would've met by now, but nothing.

When we retired to the family room, Alex's mom and I had us a good ol' time doing shots at the bar and reminiscing about things we did in our college years. Matt and Oliver, who had started drinking before me, left about an hour earlier to go to his house to do only God knows what, while Alex and her dad sat on the couches across the room, having a hushed conversation.

"Okay, Ms. Lydia, I think it's about time that I head on home. I've reached my limit for the night," I said.

She poked out her lips, looking upset. "All right, Cairo, you be safe out there. Make sure you call and let us know you made it home okay."

I nodded my head and stood up, just to be pushed back down into my stool with a firm hand.

"He's not driving home until he sleeps off some of that alcohol," Alex's dad said as he handed me another shot. "Matter of fact, there's plenty of rooms in this house. You two can take one of the guest rooms on the left side of the property. I'll have Francesca put some fresh linen and things in there for you."

"And where would Alex sleep?" I asked. She knew we didn't sleep in the same room at her home, so we weren't going to do it at her parents' house.

"In the room with you, of course," her father said. "You two are married, so we don't have a problem with that."

I was just about to protest when Alex gave me another shot and waved her father off. "Daddy, don't mind him right now. He's just drunk. Let's go get you settled, Cai."

Against my better judgment, I slowly stood from my stool, swaying back and forth before Alex grabbed my hand and led me to the guest room I'd be sleeping in until the alcohol wore off.

"Alex, I'm not that drunk. All I need is a few hours. You need to sleep in another room. I'm not sharing a bed with you," I said as I plopped down on the bed, fully dressed. "And when are you going to tell your father about the divorce?"

She started to say something, but I couldn't hear anything because my head started to spin like crazy. I felt her lift my legs and pull off my shoes, then my pants, leaving me in my boxer briefs and T-shirt. After my head had calmed down a bit, I stood up and pulled the covers back to get comfortable. Alex, who was sitting on a stool at the foot of the bed, just sat there and watched me.

"You can go now." My words came out sluggish, but I knew she understood what I had said. Without a word, she stood up and headed for the door.

"Please turn off the lights."

She did as she was told and left out of the room.

The sun shining brightly through the curtains woke me up the next morning. To say that I had one of the worse hangovers in the world would be an understatement. The only good thing that came from it was the dream I'd had about Audri.

She looked so beautiful in the black lace bra and panty set she was modeling for me. Her smooth caramel skin looked ridiculous in it. She would still try to cover up her stomach whenever I looked her body over, but as I told her before, I didn't care about that at all, especially not in that moment. I needed to feel her. I needed to be inside her.

After teasing me for a minute or two, she finally crawled on the bed and straddled my lap. We were going at it something crazy, trying to out-kiss each other. She would grip my dreads and pull my head back, assaulting my neck, and I would fist handfuls of her hair and kiss every inch of her chest, shoulder, neck, and face. My dick was so hard. I couldn't wait until her wetness was dripping all over my stomach and balls.

The thing that kind of tripped me out was the way she felt around me. It wasn't that snug, tight, wet, and warm fit that I was used to. Something was different; something was off. However, it didn't stop me from thrusting inside of her with so much force and enjoying the moment. She rode me until neither one of us could take it anymore and we climaxed together.

With both of our bodies drenched in sweat, we sat there for a minute and just relished in the high we got from the intense lovemaking session.

I couldn't have asked for a better series of images to occupy my mind as I slept this hangover away.

I went to get out of the bed but stopped when I realized that another pair of legs was tangled in mine. Throwing the covers off of my body, I almost shitted on myself when I saw Alex sleeping soundly behind me. A black silk robe covered her body as her hair lay fanned out on the pillow. There was a small smile on her lips as she moaned and shifted her position.

"What the fuck, Alex!" I yelled, causing her to jump and sit up straight.

When her robe fell off of her shoulder and revealed the exact same black lace bra Audri had on in my dream, I vehemently started to shake my head.

"Naw . . . Naw . . . Hell naw. Please tell me we didn't—" I stood up from the bed and noticed that my shirt was off, but my briefs were still on. "Tell me we didn't have sex last night. And don't lie."

She rolled her eyes then turned back over in the bed and started to doze off.

"Well?" I asked, kicking the bed. "Did we?"

Without even turning around to face me, she spoke. "You said not to lie." And with that, I could hear her light snores as she nestled deeper into the covers with a satisfied smile on her face.

31

Ariana

"No, Rima, I got it. I'll come pick him up in about an hour. . . . Okay. . . . Gone."

I stood behind the closed door of the bathroom in Finesse's master suite and listened to his quick conversation with Rima.

At first, I had said that I was cool with the situation, being that I practically grew up with Rima and she assured me that she wouldn't disrespect the relationship that Ness and I had going on, but something seemed up to me.

In the beginning, Finesse would ask me to ride with him to pick up Cassius and everything. I would even talk to Rima when he couldn't and go pick up the baby myself. But over the last couple of months, he hadn't included me in anything—the pickups, the phone calls, hell, even the doctor appointment. Nothing.

Rima had also started calling more frequently, even at all times of the night. Finesse and I had countless conversations and arguments about this, but every time, he just hit me with that, "If it pertains to my son, I don't have to explain shit. I'ma go get him." Now, don't get me wrong, I totally agreed with that, but when you are being called at one, two, or sometimes three in the morning about your son, some foul shit has to be going on.

"Baby!" Finesse said as he knocked on the bathroom door, breaking me from my thoughts. I looked at myself in the mirror. At five foot nine, I was a little above average in height, but I never had a problem meeting men taller than I was. My brown skin was smooth and flawless, thanks to my MAC Mineralize Timecheck moisturizer. Body wise, I was a ten straight across the board. With a small waist, flat stomach, wide hips, melon-sized breasts and a nice amount of ass, I was always turning heads. However, the only person's head I wanted to turn my way right now was Finesse's, and for some reason, I had a feeling he was starting to look the other way.

"Ari, are you okay in there? You've been in the bathroom for an hour. Aren't you supposed to open the store this morning?"

I didn't respond to his questions as I opened the door and walked past him with a slight attitude. Yeah, I didn't have anything to really be mad at him about, but the fact that he was on his way to Rima's for the third time this week was swirling around my mind heavy. It wasn't even his week to keep Cassius, so why was he going over there to pick him up again?

Sitting down on the bed, I grabbed my Victoria's Secret Sheer Love trio set and began to spray and lotion my body.

"So you just gon' ignore my question, huh?"

I shrugged my shoulders and continued to moisturize my skin.

"Yo, Ari, what the fuck is up with you? I'm really starting to get tired of your attitude."

Still in my own world, I walked over to his huge walk-in closet and dug through a few of the drawers Finesse had given me for my things. I didn't have to turn around to know he was now standing in the doorway. I felt his presence before I opened the first drawer.

I turned for a quick second and looked at him, but quickly averted my line of vision. I would be lying if I said Finesse's ass wasn't fine as hell, because he most definitely was. Everything about him screamed sex appeal, from the low-cut Caesar fade at the top of his six foot three frame to the soft and well taken care of bottoms of his feet. His smooth and blemish-free mocha skin was immaculate. Those dark, coffee-brown eyes would pierce you to your soul. His beautiful smile and teeth could make the strongest woman drop her panties in 1.2 seconds, and let's not even get on his body. All those years he spent playing football and drinking his milk definitely did his body good.

"This must be something big. You can't even look at me for more than two seconds." His deep voice boomed as he stepped farther into the closet. He blew out a frustrated breath and swayed his head side to side, cracking his neck. "Ariana, we can't fix the problem if you don't talk to me. Albeit, I'm not sure what you're mad at, but whatever it is, can we please just talk about it? You know I don't like all this confusion and drama."

After finally pulling my outfits and accessories out and placing them on the small bench in the middle of the closet, I looked up at him.

"Ness, I'm not mad at anything. I'm just a little unsure about why you keep having to run to Rima's house to pick your son up when it's not your week to have him."

"Man, here we go with this bullshit." He shook his head and laughed. "How many times do I have to tell you—"

I held my hand up to cut him off. I already knew what he was about to say, and I didn't want to hear it.

"So are you saying that if the tables were turned, you'd be okay with me calling my baby daddy at all times of the night and having him come over to spend time with our child like we're some big happy family when it's not even his week to parent?"

"You really gotta be kidding me," he said.

"Just answer the question . . . hypothetically, of course," I said as I dropped the towel that was around me and stood in all my naked glory.

I watched as Finesse bit his bottom lip and lustfully looked my body up and down. When his eyes crossed my hairless pleasure spot, he licked his lips and smirked.

"If I wasn't trying to figure out why you're always tripping on the way that Rima and I co-parent our son, I'd bend your ass over that bench and knock the lining out of my pussy."

I stood there speechless as my bud started to thump. Just thinking about the way his lips always gave me that suck-you-to-the-last-drop treatment had her going crazy. I sat back on the bench and tightly crossed my legs, trying to stop the insane throbbing that was going on. Finesse thought his ass was slick by trying to change the subject to sex. He knew how my body responded to his heated gazes alone, but as turned on as I was, I wasn't going to fall for it today. He really had another think coming if he thought he would just fuck my concerns away for another day. I wasn't going to be giving up any of my goods until I got to the bottom of this "Rima calls and I go running" situation.

"Unfortunately, baby, I don't have any time for a quickie. I'm running late," I said, slipping into my panties and shorts. "Besides, don't you have somewhere to be?"

"I mean, yeah, I do, but that can wait." He started walking toward me with that sexy predatory look in his eyes.

I hurriedly clasped my bra together and threw on my shirt. Just when he was about to reach out for me, I sidestepped him and headed toward the bedroom.

"What the fuck, Ari? Why you playing with a nigga? I know you see my dick trying to bust out of my basketball shorts."

"Yeah, I do," I replied as I hungrily looked at the big bulge between his legs. "But I'm not in the mood right now."

"Not in the mood?" He looked at me with a screwed up face. "Since when?"

I picked up the hobo bag I'd been carrying for the last couple of days off of the dresser and emptied its contents out on the bed. My back was still turned to Finesse as I transferred everything into my Coach backpack.

"I haven't been in the mood since right now." I chuckled because I knew he was pissed. "Besides, didn't you just tell me how late I was running a few seconds ago?"

When I turned back around to Finesse, he was just standing there and looking at me as if he were trying to read my mind or figure something out.

"Are you fucking somebody else, Ariana?"

"I should be asking you that." I thought I said it under my breath, but I was wrong.

"Who am I supposed to be fucking, Ari?" he asked with slight irritation in his voice.

"I don't know. You tell me."

"Ahh, shit." He laughed. "I get it now. This is all going back to that Rima bullshit you always talking about, right? You were ear hustling the conversation I just had with her while you were in the bathroom again, huh?"

I said nothing as I began to comb my fingers through my wild and curly hair.

"Maybe your mother was right about this relationship," he said, pointing between us. "Maybe we jumped into it too fast."

My eyes started to water up at his admission. I wasn't going to cry, though. At least I was going to try not to.

"Is that how you really feel?" I asked.

"If you can't trust me when I tell you that Rima and I are only co-parenting, can you blame me?"

That was a good question, and honestly, it had me questioning myself. Did I really have cause to not trust him, or could this be some form of insecurity? I mean, I'd never been jealous of Rima. She was like a distant sister to me, and I knew she'd never do anything to hurt me. Then again, what does being *like* a sister really mean when there are actually sisters born from the same parents who will fuck each other's man in a minute? I didn't really have any concrete evidence that Finesse was cheating on me, so I didn't know why I was tripping.

"I trust you, Ness," I said as I walked over to him and tried to put my arms around his waist. He moved back before I could even touch him.

"No, you don't, Ari. You trust me just about as much as you trust Audri, right?"

I snapped my head back to look at him. "What the hell does that mean?"

He shook his head then started to put on the clothes he had already laid out on his bed: some slim straight-leg jeans from American Eagle

Outfitters, a red-black-and-white button-down, and some all-red Supra Skytops. A few sprays of Tom Ford Noir Extreme and he was ready to go. That same thumping between my thighs I'd had a few minutes earlier started right up again. My baby was looking and smelling real good, and I was just about to change my mind about that quickie until he started to speak again.

"When you and I first started messing around, you and Audri were just as close as Cai and I. Somewhere down the line, and I think when Rima had Cassius, shit started to change. I can't pinpoint when it was, but it happened. So much so that you didn't even tell Audri about Cairo marrying Alex's crazy ass and why he did it."

Damn. Maybe he was right. I knew it was wrong for me to not tell Audri about the whole marriage thing. I will admit that I was in my feelings about some shit, which was the reason why I didn't tell her, but he wouldn't ever know that.

"I didn't tell her because I felt that that was Cairo's responsibility." I knew it wasn't the best excuse, but it was something.

"Don't give me that bullshit, Ari. Somewhere in that beautiful mind of yours, you think Audri is keeping something from you about me and Rima; hence, you keeping something from her.

But I'm here to tell you, baby, that there is nothing to worry about. I see and go to Rima's strictly for our son, and that's it. We slept together once and ended up creating a beautiful little boy. That does not and will never change the way I feel about you. I respect you, us, and this relationship. If it ever came to me wanting to fuck someone else, baby mama included, I'd break up with you first before it ever happens."

After looking in the mirror against the door and brushing the top of his head with his hands, Finesse turned around, kissed me on the forehead, and then cupped my face in his hands. I tried to pull away from his grasp, but he just held on a little tighter and lifted my face until I was staring directly into his eyes. He gently kissed my lips then pulled back a bit to make sure I was giving him my undivided attention.

"I don't know where this insecurity shit came from, but you need to lose it. I want the confident and together Ariana I met all those months ago. The one who stood up to her mother about our relationship when she found out that I was Rima's baby daddy."

I didn't know why I became so emotional. I didn't even know I was crying until a lone tear fell from my eye and he kissed it away.

"If we're going to work, baby, I need you to trust in me and in what we have, okay?"

It took me a second, but I nodded my head.

"You sure you can do it? Because if you can't, I would prefer we go our separate ways now and remain friends, rather than to stay in a relationship we both will regret in the long run."

I nodded my head again as he pressed his forehead against mine and closed his eyes. For a minute, we just sat there in silence, having our own little intimate moment, neither of us opening our eyes as we breathed in each other's breath. He lightly pressed his soft lips against mine again, and goosebumps tickled all over my body.

Even though the kiss was simple and sweet, the soft touch of his mouth against mine had me hungry for more. I kissed his lips this time and drew his bottom lip into my mouth. A low, guttural moan escaped his throat as I pulled his face and body against me.

"Now this is the Ari I missed, the take-charge-and-get-it-how-she-wants-it Ari," Ness said against my lips before I slipped my tongue into his mouth.

"Hmmm, baby. Why don't we go back into the closet so that you can bend me over the bench like you said earlier?"

"As much" —*Peck*— "as I want to"—*Peck*—"I can't." *Peck*.

I drew my head back and looked into his handsome face. "Why not?" I knew I had shut down having sex earlier, but now I was ready.

Finesse kissed me one last time before he smacked my ass and went to grab his red Phillies hat out of the bathroom. "Well, for one, you're already thirty minutes late for opening the store. Then two, I'm about to go pick up Cai and Cas then head up to the hospital to see Mama Faye."

Damn, I didn't know I was that late. I looked at the time on my phone. I knew Audri was going to be talking mad shit if I called and asked her to go and open up until I got there. It would take me another hour to make it there with traffic. She only lived like ten minutes away. It shouldn't be a problem like that. Besides, it would give us a chance to talk for a few. I shot her a text then grabbed my things and headed for the door.

"Tell Mama Faye I'll be up to see her sometime next week, okay? And tell Cai he's still on my shit list until he gets his act together."

"I will, baby," Finesse said as he laughed and grabbed me into his embrace. "We're going to go eat and have a drink after we leave the hospital. Cai said he needed to talk to me about something. After that, I'ma go drop Cassius back off at Rima's then come home, okay?"

I nodded my head, gave him one more kiss, and then headed to my car with a fake smile plastered on my face. Yeah, I had heard everything he said earlier about not disrespecting our relationship, but something just wasn't sitting right in my soul with him and this Rima situation.

I looked down at my ringing phone and saw that Audri had text me back.

SMH!!! You could've said something earlier or just said no to opening today!!!

I didn't even respond to her message as I pulled out into traffic and away from the condo. Maybe it was time that Audri and I had this talk. I needed to get to the bottom of some shit, and I knew she'd more than likely have the answers that I was looking for.

32

Rima

"Hey, Ness, just give me a few minutes to pack the rest of his things, and he'll be good to go," I said over my shoulder after opening the door for Finesse.

"Come on, Rima. You knew I was coming over an hour ago. You should have had all of his things packed up and ready."

As always, Finesse was fussing as he walked into my new three-bedroom, two-bathroom townhouse in Culver City. My old place was becoming a little too cramped with all of my things and my baby boy's new stuff. Plus, I had my mother move in with me to help with watching my baby at night when I hosted my parties.

Walking over to my burgundy fabric sectional, I picked up the trail of baby toys that were scattered in the walkway and placed them in the toy bin. Cassius was in his playpen, laughing at the monkey dancing on the screen, while I took a seat on my couch and finished putting things into the baby bag.

"I don't know why you insist on packing so much stuff. He has a gang of shit at my house already, and whatever he does not have, either Ari or myself will go out to get."

"I know that, Finesse," I snapped. I was getting so tired of him chastising me about making sure my baby had everything he needed whenever he went off with him. "I guess it's just the mother in me. I'd rather send him with too much rather than too little and give you or Mama Faye something to talk about."

Completely ignoring my last comment, Finesse walked over to our son and lifted him up out of the playpen. I swear his smile grew ten times wider whenever his daddy was near.

"Ay, little man. Daddy missed you." He tickled Cassius's chubby neck and kissed his cute little cheek. "Yo, what's these bumps on his face?"

"That's from everybody kissing on him all the time."

"Whose dirty-ass mouth do you have kissing on my son, Rima?"

"Shit, between you, Ariana, my mom, Audri, and myself, there's no one else," I answered.

"Well, the only people who need to kiss on him is me and you. Everyone else needs to kiss a hand or something," he snapped as he examined the rest of Cassius's little body.

This was one of the things that killed me about Finesse. He was so overprotective about Cassius. I think that was one of the reasons why he'd come and pick him up with no questions asked whenever I called.

In the beginning, it wasn't like this at all, and that was fully on my part. I had a hard time letting Cassius out of my sight. Wherever he went, I went, and that was causing a bit of a problem. Even on the weeks when it was Finesse's turn to keep him, I'd bug the hell out of him, asking him to send pictures or little videos of Cass just laying down doing absolutely nothing.

We used to argue a lot about Cassius's living arrangements too. After the first couple of months, however, things started to change. Not only did I have to go back to work, but I started dating someone new. I wasn't lying to Audri or Ariana when I told them both that I did not want Finesse in any kind of way. Although he was fine as hell, and if my memory served me correctly, great in bed, that ship had sailed a long time ago. That talk we had about us just being co-parents a few months before Cassius was born sealed that deal.

"So, I'll have him back later on this evening, okay?"

I got up from the couch and handed Finesse the baby bag. "I was hoping you could keep him for the night if possible. I kinda have something to do."

He looked at me with a questioning glare. "Something like what, Rima? I was planning on taking Ari out to ease some of the tension in our household."

"I get that, and I do apologize for the last-minute request, but I really wanna go to this party," I said.

"Party? Ah, hell naw, Rima. Where's Kenzie? Isn't that why she moved in with you? I'm not about to stop my plans with Ari just so you can go and hump around for the rest of the night. On some real shit, Rima, I really thought after you had Cassius that you'd chill out on that shit."

"It wasn't a problem when I met you, though, right?"

He stood there with a dumb expression on his face. "I'm saying, though . . ."

"Saying, though, my ass. Do I ask you for anything when it comes to Cassius?"

"No, but—"

"No, nothing. How I make a living to provide for me and my child shouldn't even be a concern of yours. Just as long as he's taken care of and wanting for nothing, you shouldn't have a problem."

He laid a now sleeping Cassius back down in the playpen and set the diaper bag down on my glass coffee table. I walked over to my little man and admired his handsome face. He had a lot of Finesse's features, but those pouty lips, small button nose, and caramel-colored skin were all me.

"Look, Rima, I just don't feel that as a mother you should still be out there like that," he said.

"Out there like what? You act as if I'm out here dealing with all kinds of people. You know as well as I do that I only deal with high-end clientele." I raised my hands up and circled around my home. "How do you think I can afford all of this? It sure isn't on no nine-to-five salary."

I lived in the high-end part of Culver City, where the cheapest car you'd see driving around was an Infiniti G35. Everything else rolling through these parts was your standard luxury car or SUV.

My townhome was furnished with some of the most expensive handmade Italian furniture. African art and statues adorned my walls and certain corners of each room. My rugs were all designed to go with the African theme of my home and were very expensive. That was why I didn't allow anyone to wear shoes in my house. Hell, even Cassius's things cost a pretty penny, all courtesy of me and the people that I dealt with, so fuck what he was talking about.

"Look, Ness, I don't feel like arguing with you right now. Just bring him back around five this evening. My mom should be home by then, so I'll just have her watch him."

He looked me up and down before he grabbed the diaper bag again and picked up my baby.

"Naw, don't even trip. I'll keep him tonight. I'll just have Ari drop him off in the morning on her way to work," he said as he headed for the door.

"Thanks, Ness. I really appreciate it, and not that it's any of your business, but I'm not hosting a party tonight. I'm actually going to the BPLA auction with Audri."

"BPLA?"

"Yeah, Black Professionals of Los Angeles. It's a charity auction event that they have every year."

"Oh, yeah. Rod mentioned something about that the other day when we went to have a few drinks. I think he's one of the professionals being auctioned off."

A small smirk crossed my face. Roderick's sexy ass being a part of the auction was one of the reasons why I was most definitely going to be in attendance. Although we'd only been messing around for a couple months, I wasn't about to let another female get an ounce of intimate time with him.

"He is? I didn't know that. Then again, I do think I remember seeing his profile in the little booklet they sent out for the bachelor lineup."

Ness just nodded his head as he walked to the door. I walked him and our son out to his car. After buckling Cassius in, I kissed his forehead then came back into my house. I needed to take a shower then go out and run a few errands before I went to the mall, nail shop, and salon. I had to look extra cute for my new boo, as well as for some of the new potential clients I was more than likely going to be pulling in.

33

Cairo

I was at my house chilling and working on this new project for the city when I received a text from a number I'd seen before but couldn't remember. It was a picture message of some kind of charity auction that was happening that night. I almost ignored it, until another message came in telling me that Audri was being added to the list of eligible bachelorettes being auctioned off. I went to my computer in my home office and logged onto the Web site I had seen on the flyer. Sure enough, there was a profile of Audrielle, along with a selection of other beautiful women. The picture they used was the same picture I had for her contact photo in my phone. It was a candid shot of her laughing, with her head slightly thrown back, with strands of her crazy wild hair crossing her face. She was absolutely breathtaking. The sun was shining at the right angle, which highlighted all of the beautiful features of her face.

A small ping shot through my heart. I didn't know if I could keep going days, weeks, and even months without seeing her smiling face every morning or hearing her voice before I fell asleep each night. I needed to get her back, and if this auction was a slight chance of that happening, well, I would be in attendance with my checkbook ready and open.

Getting up from my desk, I went back over to my workspace and finished what I had been working on. I looked at the time and noticed it was already going on nine in the morning. I'd been up since five working on this project, and although I was tired as hell, I still had plans to meet Ness at the hospital in an hour or two to see Mama Faye then go grab a bite to eat. We hadn't really been around each other and needed to catch up on a few things. With my new work schedule and his, along with him taking care of Cassius and trying to keep Ari happy, we hadn't really had a chance to hang out like we used to.

I heard my phone ringing as I walked to my master bedroom. I didn't turn around to get it because I already knew who it was by the ringtone. Ever since I left Alex at her parents' house the morning after we had sex a few weeks ago,

I'd been staying at my own home, away from her crazy ass. One of the provisions in the will was that we cohabitated while we were married, but I couldn't stand being around her ass anymore. For some reason, though, she'd been blowing me up and leaving these crazy-ass messages like we were really in a relationship or something. I didn't have time for her or any of her drama, so I ignored the call like all the other ones before.

After grabbing some clothes to throw on, I went to the bathroom to handle my hygiene, wash my hair, and get ready to head out to see Mama Faye.

"Ay, bro, what's good? It seems like I haven't seen you in forever," Ness said as he gave me dap then a half hug. We were in the parking lot of the hospital, getting ready to go up for our visit. I took my nephew out of his arms and tickled his little tummy after giving him a quick kiss on the forehead.

"Man, you know me. I'm just working as always."

"I don't understand how or why you wanna continue to work after you came up on all of that money. That is definitely some white boy shit." Ness laughed as we walked through the lot. We got on the elevator and proceeded into the hospital.

"Honestly, I don't know what to say besides the fact that I love what I do." I shrugged my shoulders. "I'd probably go crazy sitting at home all day just twiddling my thumbs."

"Shiiiiiit. Well, why don't you transfer your bank account balance to mine and I'll show you how it's done."

We shared a laugh. "Anyways, man, where did you get them shoes from and where can I get a pair? Those are hot," I said as I eyed the all-red Supra Skytops he had on.

"Dude, you already know I got 'em from Kick Biz. I lucked up falling in love with a girl who owns a sneaker store. I swear my shoe collection has tripled since Ari and I started dating. If I'm not buying my own, she's surprising me with some."

Out of everything Ness had just said, there was only one thing that stood out to me.

"So you're finally going to admit that you're in love with Ariana, huh?"

He blushed. "Man, Ari is my baby. She just doesn't know it yet."

"What do you mean?"

Ness went on to tell me how he and Ari had been fighting a lot lately because she thought that he and Rima were still messing around. When I asked him if they were, he simply told me no and I believed him. Ness was the type of dude who didn't mind telling you if he was smashing this girl or that girl. He'd always had a healthy appetite for the opposite sex, but it seemed that after he met Ariana, all of that changed. Even Mama Faye noticed it. Hopefully, Ari would too before she pushed him away and into the arms of another who wasn't Rima.

We got off the elevator on Mama Faye's floor and began walking to her room. As always, the little receptionist at the front desk flirted with Ness and me while giving us our visitor passes. We stopped at the gift shop and purchased a few bouquets of flowers then went to see our favorite girl.

"Is that mi great gran looking so handsome in his big boi outfit?" Mama Faye said as soon as we entered the room. The smile on her face brought one to mine. I didn't think I'd seen her lips curl up that much since she'd been there.

"Hey, Mama!" I said as I gently placed Cassius on her lap and kissed her cheek. "How you feeling today?"

"Oh, boi, mi feelin fine. Stop fussing ova me now. Ya think mi smile would be this big if mi wasn't feeling okay?"

"Yeah, you're right," I said as I took a seat in the chair next to her bed.

"Mi always right, and ya betta not forget it."

I nodded my head as I watched her and Cassius interact with one another.

"Ness, him look just like your daddy when him was born. Spittin' image, I tell ya."

"Yeah, I remember the pictures you showed me. I went by the house and picked some of them up to show Ari, and she said the same thing."

"Oh, yeah. How is mi future daughter doing nowadays? Is she following dem recipes mi told ya to give her?"

"She's fine, and yes she's been trying to do the recipes you gave her. Some turned out good, while others . . ." Ness trailed off, and we laughed.

"What'chu talkin' 'bout, boi?" Mama Faye asked, still laughing.

"Let's just say the other night she wanted to surprise me with some goat curry stew. When I say that mess looked like a pile of shit over rice, I mean it. It even smelled weird. Of course, I ate a few bites to make her feel good, but my body paid for it the next day at work. It's weird how she can throw down on anything in the kitchen, but she can't get this Jamaican food down for shit."

I sat back in my chair and laughed as I thought back to that morning Ness called me, crying about how bad his stomach was hurting after Ari messed up one of his favorite dishes.

"What'chu laughing at, Cai. At least Ness got him a woman who is trying to make him a decent Jamaican meal. That wicked gayl ya up and married probably can't make a bowl of rice, let alone a curry gravy."

"Maybe I should take some of the recipes that I gave to Ari and give 'em to Alex," Ness said as he picked up Cassius and checked his diaper. Little man had gotten so quiet laying on Mama Faye's chest that I forgot he was there.

"Ya will do no such ting. That gayl isn't a part of this family, so she doesn't need to see any of mi family recipes."

The air in the room shifted a little as it always did whenever Alex's name was brought up. I looked over at Ness, who looked away from me and tended to a shitty-ass Cassius. Trying to avoid Mama Faye's glare myself, I picked up the TV remote and started to flip through different channels.

"Cai, turn that TV off," Mama Faye said. Her Jamaican accent was becoming thicker by the second.

"Don't you want to watch your—"

She cut me off. "Mi don't wanna watch shit. Now turn the damn ting off."

I did as I was told but still kept my eyes trained on the blank screen. Something in the tone of her voice told me that this was going to be a serious conversation, and I had to get my mind right.

"Ay, I left Cass's milk in the car. I'll be right back," Ness said as he and my nephew walked out of the room. I wanted to scream for him to stay, but before I could, he had already disappeared.

I shifted uncomfortably in my chair. I could feel Mama Faye's eyes on me, but I refused to look her way.

"When ya getting a divorce from that gayl? It's been way over a month, yea?"

"It has," I said, blowing out a frustrated breath and wiping my hands down my face. "But I just found out some shit that Alex neglected to tell me when we had a meeting with our lawyers a few days ago."

"Tings like what, Cai?"

I shook my head then rubbed my now throbbing temples. Taking the hair tie from around my dreads, I let them fall loosely all over my head, covering a little of my face. What I was about to tell Mama Faye was sure to have a few of her monitors going crazy. Finding out some of the shit I did when Alex, our lawyers, and I met for what should have been an annulment of our fake marriage was sure to give anyone a heart attack. Not wanting to beat around the bush anymore, I dove right in and told her what went down.

My lawyer, Chase Brinks, and I arrived at the law offices of Levy, Stone, and Hammond to meet up with Alex and her lawyer. Of course, I stuck with my end of the bargain and gave her the five percent she was asking for, plus an extra million to cover any and all expenses her dad paid for Mama Faye's surgery and everything.

We were about to sign the papers when all of a sudden there was a knock on the office door. I should've known something was going on from the way Alex kept winking her eye and smirking at me, but I was so focused on getting this paperwork signed and getting out of there that I didn't pay it too much attention. We went back to signing shit when there was another knock.

This time, someone got up to answer it, and when they did, an older white gentleman who looked to be in his early sixties walked in with a briefcase in hand. By his demeanor, I could tell that he was a lawyer—whose, I just didn't know. He took a seat at the other end of the table and placed his briefcase in front of him. Because anyone had yet to acknowledge him, I figured he was just one of the firm's owners sitting in on our session. Needless to say, we continued to ignore him and got back to what we were doing.

Chase had just finished going over the annulment agreement and handed it over to me to sign. Before I could even pick up the pen, the older gentleman opened his briefcase and cleared his throat. He said there were a few things pertaining to my grandmother's will that we had to go over before I could sign the paper.

"And just who might you be?" Chase asked, already going into lawyer mode.

"I am William Reumont III from the law firm Reumont and Liebowitz. I had the distinguished pleasure of being your"—he pointed at me—"grandmother's lawyer for years before she died."

"Okay, and now that we've been informed of who you are and where you're from, what does that have to do with my client and what's going on right now?"

"Oh, it has to do with a lot," William said, taking a stack of papers out of his briefcase and passing them to everyone in the room. *"I have a feeling that my presence here is somewhat of a surprise to yourself and Mr. Wright?"* he asked Chase while still looking at me.

"My client and I were not told that we would have counsel from another firm joining the meeting today. We came here under the assumption that we'd be meeting with Mrs. Broussard and her representation to sign these annulment papers then be on our way. She has already been given the monetary compensation she and my client verbally agreed on, so yes, your presence here is somewhat of a surprise to Mr. Broussard and me," Chase said as he slouched back in his chair and swirled his pen between his fingers.

I laughed at the confused expression on Williams's wrinkled face. I was pretty sure that where he was from, it was not every day he saw a six-foot-two, 230-pound, Armani suit–wearing, Morris Chestnut–looking brother talking to him the way Chase was. Although Chase had graduated from Yale law school, the hood swag he grew up with was still evident in his tone and body language.

"If you can please turn to page ten of the paperwork I just handed to you and read over

the highlighted section, you will see why I am in attendance at this meeting today," Reumont said.

I looked over at Alex, who still had the silly smirk on her face with her eyes dead set on me. There was something different about her, but I couldn't put my finger on it. As I sat across from her and took in her undeniable beauty, I noticed how round her face had become. Not only that, but it seemed as if she was glowing. At that moment, a weird feeling washed over me, and my heart started to beat a little bit faster.

"This is some bullshit!" I heard Chase yell, breaking me from my wandering thoughts.

"I assure you, Mr. Brinks, bullshit is nowhere in this will."

"What's going on, man?" I asked, now looking over the highlighted paragraphs in the paper-work before me.

"Do you guys mind if I have a word with my client outside?" Chase asked. When no one objected, we both rose from our seats and headed out of the room.

There were a few people in the hallway, but none of them paid attention to us. I sat down on the bench across the walkway and watched Chase pace back and forth in front of the door.

His black fitted jacket was now open and being pushed back by his arms because his hands were rested on his waist. For a long time, we sat out there in silence, and I couldn't take it anymore.

"Man, what's going on? I was about to read what the paper said, but you asked to speak to me in private. We get out here, and you're not saying anything."

"Bruh, when you went to sign the paperwork for that inheritance money, did you read the stipulations like I told you?"

I shook my head. "Not really. I just skimmed over it then signed. Why?"

"Dude, how many times do I have to tell you that you never sign a piece of paper without reading it?"

"Look, Chase, to keep it real, all I was worried about was getting my hands on that money to help Mama Faye out. Anything else, I figured I'd just deal with it as it came."

He stopped pacing the floor and faced me. "Even if that means Alex will be entitled to half of your inheritance on top of the five percent you've already given her?"

It was now my turn to pace the floor. "What are you talking about, Mr. Brinks?"

"Your grandmother had a few stipulations in her will. Yes, you'd inherit fifty million if you

were married by your thirtieth birthday, but that wasn't all. In order for you to get the rest—"

I cut him off. "The rest? What the hell are you talking about, Chase?"

"Cai, from what I've read, your actual inheritance amount isn't just fifty mil. It's actually a hundred. You get the first fifty after you're married. The additional fifty comes only if you have an heir within the first year that you're married."

I stopped pacing the floor and looked at Chase like he was crazy. "Well, I guess I can kiss that other fifty good-bye because I'm not about to stay married to Alex any longer than I have to, let alone get her pregnant."

"Are you sure about that?"

"What the fuck is that—" I started to say but stopped when I saw the law firm's receptionist rushing into the room we had just left with a few bottles of water and a handful of paper towels.

The stench of vomit hit my nose before I even stepped back into the room. I looked around and noticed everyone standing up in a semi-panic on their phones as Alex sat on her knees in front of a trash can, throwing up and heaving.

"What's going on?" I asked no one in particular and got no response.

After drinking a few gulps of water from the water bottle the receptionist had given her, Alex slowly got up from the floor and weakly wobbled over to the chair. She took a napkin from the table and wiped her mouth, then ran her fingers through her hair and tied it into a knot. Her blouse was wet and sticking to her skin, while her makeup was now smeared and running everywhere on her face.

"I didn't want you to find out like this, but since we're here, might as well let the cat out of the bag," she said.

The young receptionist walked up to me with a blue envelope in her hand and handed it to me. "Mr. Broussard, you've been served."

"Served for what?" Chase snatched the paper out of my hand and read it over.

"Shit," was all I heard as he wiped his hand over his face and took a seat.

Snatching the paperback, I skimmed over it and stopped when I saw that Alex was suing me for fifty million dollars.

"Alex, what the fuck is this? You know damn well after paying your dad back and giving you your cut that I don't have fifty million dollars still."

"Oh, but you will in eight more months."

"How is that? For one, I'm about to be single again as soon as we sign these papers, and

two, I don't have a baby on the way," I said as I remembered the info Chase had told me about the will.

"So you forgot about that morning we made love at my parents' house?" she asked.

I smacked my lips. "You mean the morning you tricked me. You know damn well that I didn't intentionally sleep with your ass. The combination of me being drunk and missing Audri had me thinking I was fucking her in my dreams, and you took that as an opportunity to hop on my dick and pretend that you were her." Everyone in the room gasped loudly as I checked Alex on the lie she was trying to put out there.

She laughed. "Cairo, come on now. Your precious Audri clearly has at least two hundred pounds on me, so I'm pretty sure you could feel the difference of me being on top of you as opposed to her."

"You jealous of Audri, Alex? Huh? You mad that the girl who is, in your words, two hundred pounds heavier than you, has my heart and attention? I bet it's just burning you up that I can't wait to divorce your ass to run back to her, huh?"

Tears started to well up in her eyes, but I didn't give a fuck. I was getting so tired of *playing this game with Alex. She knew what it was before we even agreed to this marriage shit. I told her all about Audri and how much I was in love with her. I even told her that if Audri weren't married already, she would be the one with my last name instead of Alex. But I should've known she had different motives for wanting to marry me so bad.*

"Truthfully, Cai, your cow can have you. Unlike her, I'm all about money, and since I have the golden goose growing inside of me courtesy of you, I want what's rightfully mine, or should I say ours?" She patted her stomach. "Now, either we can continue to live in this fake wedded bliss for the next eight months until we have this baby and split that money, or we can sign these papers to get annulled, and I hit you for all the money you have left from that money in your account right now."

I didn't respond to anything she said or to her calling my name as I grabbed my things from the table and left. Pissed off was not the word I would necessarily use to describe how I was feeling at that moment. Livid was more like it. Audri definitely wouldn't want anything to do with me after she found out I was having a baby by my fake wife.

***

"Ouch!" I yelled after Mama Faye hit me hard in the back of my head

"Boi, how could ya be so stupid? Mi raised ya betta than that. I told ya that gayl was up to something. Mi never liked her. Eyes sneaky just like her snake father."

I was going to say something, but she held one hand up, silencing me, as the other picked up the phone sitting next to her bed. She dialed a number then waited for an answer.

Her voice had softened a little before she spoke. "Mi tink it's time ya talk to your boi. Him here now, so ya come." She hung up the phone and focused her heated glare back on me.

"Who—"

"Don't chu ask me no ting, Cairo. Ya just sit yo' ass there and hold tight."

I didn't say anything else as I sat back in my chair and flipped the TV back on. As long as whoever she called came within the hour, we would be good. Anything over that, they'd have to catch me at a different time because I was going to the BPLA that night regardless of who this mystery visitor was going to be.

34

Rima

"Damn, girl, what the hell is wrong with you?" I asked Audri as she slipped into the passenger seat of my 2015 BMW X6.

"Today was not my day at all. Not only did Ari and I have this big blow-up at the store this morning, but my mom just called and told me that because of the big turnout the BPLA was expecting, they added a women's auction on the program."

"Oooookaaaaaay," I slowly dragged out. "What does that have to do with you?"

"According to my mother, she pulled a few strings and had me put into the auction. Something about me being more desirable to Eli if he sees other men vying for my time."

"Wait! Are you and Eli back together or something?"

"Hell naw!" she snapped as she pulled the visor down and applied another layer of the nude lipstick as she looked at herself in the mirror. "We're just cool. He's been a listening ear and a real sweetheart with all of the drama that I've been going through. I mean, we've always been cool communication wise. I could always talk to him when I was feeling down about my weight or stressing about the heavy load of work I had in school." She closed the visor and turned her attention toward me. "Besides, I don't even look at Eli like that anymore."

"Like what?"

"Like in a relationship sort of way. Even though he's hinted at wanting to explore us being a couple again, I just can't go there with him. Besides, my heart—"

I cut her off and finished the sentence for her. "Is still with Cairo."

She sat in her seat, quiet for a minute, looking out of the window before she spoke again.

"You know what's funny? It's been a few months of him being in wedded bliss, and I can't seem to get him out of my head. I actually ran into him a few weeks ago at the gym. I promise I wanted to jump on that weight bench and fuck the shit out of him he was looking so good. I

almost fell into his trap again, until I remembered what he did, and once that happened, I
lashed out at him. Then to make things worse,
Eli told Cai something, I guess trying to make it
seem like he and I were back together; then we
started arguing. Girl, that day was just crazy,"
she said, shaking her head.

I didn't do anything but nod my head as I
continued to listen to Audri vent. Hell, maybe
her mom entering her in this auction was a good
thing. She needed a break from the heartache of
losing Cairo.

We finally arrived at the venue, and I was
in complete awe of everything before me. The
BPLA auction was being held at the Langham
Huntington Hotel in Pasadena, and the place
was beautiful. I could already tell by the stunning
decoration on the outside that this was going to
be a swanky affair for the Los Angeles elite. I was
so glad that my girl and I had come dressed to
impress and ready to party.

Audri's long-sleeve red lace romper looked
good on her now size twenty frame. Her legs
were looking long and toned in the six-inch gold
strappy gladiator heels. Her makeup, which you
could hardly tell she had on, was beat to the
gawds. I even loved the way she was wearing her
hair. A bone-straight, slicked-up high ponytail

that hung to the side with huge spiral curls. My girl was looking good. I just needed her insides to match the outside.

As soon as the valet attendant opened my car doors, Audri and I stepped out of my ride looking and smelling like a million bucks.

My short green evening dress hugged my curves just right. The heart-shaped neckline showed off just enough of my cleavage, while the satin material under my breasts that tied into a bow in the front highlighted my small waist and accentuated my now thick hips.

The Gianvito Rossi kace and suede knee boots, compliments of a certain somebody, went perfectly with my dress and manicured toes. My hair, which I had half up and half down, complimented my round face.

"Damn, do you see all of these sexy black professionals?" Audri asked as I stood in awe of everything that was going on around me.

"Girl, yeah. Why didn't you tell me this was how this thing was? Do you know how much money I could have been making had you dragged me here years ago?"

Audri laughed. "I don't think any of these people would be interested in your freak fest parties."

"Honey, please! Married couples and professional people like this are my normal clients. Of course, they want discretion, and that's cool with me."

While we stood in the line for Audri to check in for the auction, I gazed around the lobby. As if there were some kind of magnetic pull on me, my eyes darted to the entrance of the hotel. The sexiest brown eyes connected with mine, and I couldn't help the way my panties started to soak. His chocolate skin looked smooth and rich. The fresh lineup of his hair and face made him even sexier. My eyes traveled down to his black fitted Armani suit. I licked my lips in admiration. His muscled body could easily be seen through his clothes. Never had I seen a man look so good tailored.

I saw the way that his eyes assessed my body, and by the slight nod of his head, I could tell that he approved of what I was wearing and how I looked.

He started to walk toward me but was stopped by a herd of cackling admirers, who I had no doubt would be spending their hard-earned money to win a date with him. However, they were going to be in for a rude awakening when that time came around.

I took out my phone and shot him a quick text.

Me: Having fun talking to your groupies?

RM: You mean one of my potential dates!

Me: LOL. You're funny

RM: I hope you bought more than a little change cuz they're not playing about winning a night with me.

Me: Don't worry about my coins. You just make sure you tell your fans they better have their money up because I'm playing and playing for keeps.

RM: Oh yeah?

Me: Oh yeah!

RM: Well may the best groupie win. You included. LOL

I smiled as I put my phone back into my clutch. It was that cocky attitude right there that had me ready to cash out on this man in the first place.

"Oh, shit. Why the hell is he here?" Audri said from behind me. "He can't possibly be a part of the auction."

"Who? Roderick? You already knew he was in it."

"No, not Roderick," she said as she pulled me toward the women's restroom, slightly ducking her head as if she were hiding from someone.

"Then who are you talking about?"

She nodded her head in Roderick's direction. Because his back was turned, giving someone a brotherly hug, I couldn't make out who she was referring to. When Roderick pulled back and stepped to the side, though, my mouth dropped, and a warm, tingling sensation zipped through my body, causing my pearl to thump. Out of respect for my girl, I would never act on that little feeling of wanting to strip this sexy man down and jump all over his dick. However, I couldn't hide my lust-filled eyes if I wanted to. I never knew a white boy could look that damn good in a slim-fitted suit.

I looked back at Audri, who was still trying to find somewhere to hide, and laughed. *So much for getting over that broken heart with someone new, especially when you have a Greek God hot on your trail.*

35

Audrielle

I didn't know why I became so nervous the second my eyes landed on Cairo. All the hate I'd been trying to conjure up against him seemed not to exist for the moment. As I blew out the breath I didn't even know I was holding, my hands instinctively went to my stomach to try to calm the butterflies that seemed to be fluttering wildly.

"You good, girl?" Rima leaned over and asked me after noticing the shocked look on my face.

"Yeah, I . . . think . . . I think I'ma sit down for a minute or two before everything starts."

Without waiting for a response, I turned in the opposite direction of Cairo and high-tailed it out of the hotel lobby. I wanted to go to the bathroom and hide out until the function started, but the line I saw forming on the outside quickly nixed that idea.

Instead, I weaved my way in and out of the crowded hallway and ushered myself and Rima through a pair of open double doors. Entering into what I learned was the main ballroom where the charity auction was going to be held, I looked around in complete amazement. Whoever decorated the night's festivities really outdid themselves and spent a pretty penny on transforming the room.

The high ceiling had individual strings of tiny lights hanging down, giving off the effect that stars were twinkling in the sky. Eight-foot-tall black organza curtains covered each wall in the room. Ten-person tables dressed with black silk tablecloths and silver glitter runners were strategically placed around the huge space, covering up almost every square inch of the floor. The pop of color came from the tall red-and-ivory floral pieces in the middle of the tables. Strands of Swarovski crystals hung from each centerpiece to add a bit more glitz to the already glamorous atmosphere. Although everything I described would have the tackiest person in awe, the focal point of this room had to be the runway that took up a small portion of the dance floor. In about an hour, I would be strutting down that bad boy with my best Naomi Campbell–inspired walk. I just prayed that I didn't miss a step and fall flat on my ass.

My mind was still so gone on how beautiful everything was that I didn't hear my father calling my name until he walked up to me. Looking ever so dapper in his Canali classic fit suit, I couldn't help the smile that formed on my face after noticing how a few of the women who were standing up or already in their seats were checking out my father.

"Hey, Daddy!"

"Honey Bee, you look beautiful," my father said as he embraced me in a hug and kissed my forehead. His favorite Clive Christian No. 1 cologne lingered in the air. "You're going to cause a bidding war in here tonight."

I blushed. "Thank you, Daddy. You look quite handsome yourself."

"You know I try to do a little something whenever I come to these kinds of events. I have to look the part."

I nodded my head as I looked over his shoulder, looking for his wife. I knew she had to be somewhere in the vicinity. Diana Freeman was not about to let my daddy be by himself for too long, especially with all these single women floating around.

"Where's Mom?" I finally asked.

"Your mother is in the bathroom with your aunt." He paused then smiled. "And Nana."

"Nana's here!" Rima and I said at the same time. I didn't know who was more excited, me or her. "I thought she wouldn't be here until next week."

"She came in a week early. I was going to call and tell you, but she wanted to surprise you."

"How long is she going to be here?" I asked.

"I think she said for a couple of months. She's having some work done to her house and doesn't want to be there with all of the noise that will be going on."

I smiled. "Yeah, it's either that or she's out here visiting one of her little play toys."

My father rolled his eyes and grumbled something under his breath. He didn't like the fact that his mother was a cougar. At seventy-five years old, the woman got more action than me and him combined. She was always somewhere on vacation with one of her young counterparts. Hawaii, Barbados, the Florida Keys: you name it. This woman had a better social and traveling life than me.

"I just don't understand what she sees in these little toddlers she likes to date. Why can't she find someone her own age and settle down?" my father asked.

"Because an old stiff can't keep up with everything I like to do, let alone what I have to offer,"

Nana said, motioning her hands up and down the length of her flawless body.

"Nana!" I screamed as I jumped into her arms. "Why didn't you tell me you were coming in early? I would've had your room at my house ready."

She shook her head. "That's why I didn't tell you. I wanted to spend a few days here with my knuckleheaded son. I'll be staying at your place starting next weekend, so make sure you have everything set up by then, okay?"

I nodded my head excitedly, still holding on to Nana's small frame. For a woman her age, you'd be surprised at how fit and in shape she was. Her five foot seven frame was slim, with a few dips in her hips and back area. She never had too much in the breast department, but a few years ago, Nana had found a surgeon who agreed to perform a breast augmentation for her, so now her small A-cup titties were a full and very perky C-cup. Because of the continuous workout and diet regimen she stuck to, her skin was toned, tight, and blemish free. I didn't think I could remember ever seeing a wrinkle grace her beautiful face or any part of her body. Nana was seventy-five years old but didn't look a day over forty-five. I think that was another reason why she preferred to date younger men. There weren't too many senior citizens her age that looked as young as her.

My mother and aunt joined us shortly but didn't have too much to say, and that was all in thanks to Nana, more than likely. Ms. Sandra Lunell Freeman didn't tolerate anyone talking real slick about her grandbaby, and that included my mom and her sister. That's one of the reasons why I always loved when she came to visit. For a short amount of time, I didn't have to hear any remarks about my weight or what I could be doing better to improve my life.

As we continued to make small talk, the MC came to the mic and announced that all auction participants were needed in the gathering room before the show could get started. After hugging my Nana one last time, kissing my father on the cheek, and saying bye to Rima, I made my way out to the main ballroom and back into the lobby. There was still a nice amount of people standing around and engaging in what I can assume were interesting conversations. A few heads turned and looked my way, but no one said anything other than "Good evening."

My eyes searched the small crowd for those piercing blue eyes, but when I saw that they were nowhere in sight, a small sigh escaped my lips.

"Get it together, Audri." I quietly coached myself as I started walking down a narrow hallway. "You need to forget all about his ass." As much as I wanted to make myself believe that that would happen tonight, I knew it wasn't going to transpire anytime soon. I mean, it had been some months since he and I had been together, and I still couldn't get him out of my head.

Trying to put my love dilemma on hold and focus on the task at hand, I continued walking through the lobby in search of where I needed to be. As organized as they were, you would think the BPLA would have some sort of signs pointing participants in the right direction, but unfortunately, there were none.

"Excuse me, sir," I asked one of the hotel employees who I was passing for the second time. "Do you know where I can find the gathering room?"

He looked me up and down with an appreciative gaze then pointed down the hallway to another pair of dark mahogany double doors that had a small piece of paper attached to it.

"Thank you," I said with a small smile.

I was almost to the doors when a large arm wrapped around my waist and pulled me back.

His scent and touch were familiar, so I had a pretty good idea of who it was. The minute my body nestled against his hard chest, my thoughts were confirmed.

"What I tell you about touching me like this, Eli?"

He put his nose to my neck and inhaled my scent before kissing my ear and letting me go. "How can I not touch you when you're looking like this? Audri, you look amazing this evening."

I stepped away from his embrace and turned around to face him. For a quick second, my knees buckled a little. Eli had always been a very handsome man, but tonight, that handsomeness was shining brightly.

I nodded my head. "You don't look so bad yourself."

He smirked and winked his eye. I had to clench my thighs this time. Eli's ass almost did a little something with that small gesture he just did.

"I wasn't expecting to see you here," I said.

"Why not? I'm black, and I'm a professional. Plus, I live in L.A.—again. Why wouldn't I be here?"

"Because this isn't your type of thing. How long have the BPLA charity auctions been going on? I remember when we were younger, your mother had to drag you in here kicking and screaming to do volunteer work. Then once we got older and you had a choice, they couldn't pay you enough to step foot at an event."

"Well, let's just say I had a little incentive this time around," he said, stepping into my personal space again. "It's the only way I could think of to get you to go out with me since you won't do it willingly."

I shook my head and sighed. "That's because I don't want to go out with you, Eli. Like I keep telling you, whatever it was that we had doesn't exist anymore, at least for me. The divorce papers I had drawn up should have been a clear sign of that." I stepped away from him. "I'm going to always love you because you were my first in a lot of things; however, my heart isn't with you anymore."

He wiped his hands over his face then started massaging the back of his neck. "But it's with that confused white boy who thinks he's black just because his adoptive mother is and he has dreadlocks? What is it with you black women and dating outside of your race? That white fucker will treat you the same way any other man would. Hell, maybe even worse than I did. His real family will never accept you, and because of that, all you will ever be to him is a big black girl with some of the best pussy on the planet. That white man will never be able to give you the type of life you deserve. If you gain back all of the weight that you've lost, please believe that he will drop you for the next skinny white chick. Shit, he's already done it once."

I looked around the hallway, completely embarrassed. A couple of the auction participants and some of the hotel staff were standing around us, listening to our whole argument. Eli's sudden outburst had obviously grabbed their attention, and they couldn't look away.

"Wow," I said on the verge of tears.

"Audri, please. I'm so sorry. I didn't—" He tried to apologize as he looked around at all the unfamiliar faces.

I held up my hand to cut him off. Somehow I gathered up all of the strength I had to not let one single tear fall. Eli wasn't worth seeing me upset, and neither were the people standing around us.

"Naw, you're not sorry about it. You meant everything you just said."

"That's not true, Audri. I didn't mean—" He tried to interrupt me again, but I kept going.

"No, no, you did, and the funny thing is, I never thought I'd hear that coming from your mouth, seeing as your sister is married to a white man.

It's cool, though. Like I said a few moments ago, our time has passed. I appreciate everything you've done for me for the last couple of weeks, but I think it's about time you let whatever you think we can have go. It's not going to happen today or any time in the future."

"Audrielle, please don't do this. I'm sorry. Let me make it up to you?"

I turned away from him and headed toward the gathering room. "Audri, please. What can I do to make this right?" he asked, his tone now laced with a hint of regret.

"Sign those divorce papers," I replied over my shoulder as I disappeared behind the big mahogany doors.

36

Eli

"So what was that all about?" my sister asked.

I blew out a frustrated breath. "Not now, Sarah."

"Not now, Sarah." My sister mocked me. "If I didn't know any better, I would've thought you started to have feelings for her again."

"And if I am? We are married, for Christ's sake."

"You wasn't worried about that marriage when you were fucking all of those whores, now were you? I could've easily ratted you out the hundreds of times Audri came around asking questions, but I didn't, so you owe me."

"How do I owe you, Sarah? I've been gone for seven years. Telling Audri right now about all of those women will go in one ear and right out the other."

"True, but will she forgive you for her credit history right now? You are the reason why she can't get a loan for that second store, and she doesn't even know it."

"You wouldn't." I turned my heated glare toward her.

"But oh, dear brother, I would. And with me being a lawyer, you know I could dig up all the evidence she would need to see. Being a true friend and all," she said sarcastically. "So if I were you, I'd just stick to the plan, and don't you even think about going back into hiding."

I laughed. "What, like you? You've been ducking and dodging Audri's calls for the longest. How long did you think it would take her to figure out that you were the one who told your friend about us being married?"

She shrugged her shoulders. "I'm not hiding from shit. I knew she'd figure it out sooner or later. I just need a little time to get some shit together before she confronts me with it."

"You are something else," I said as I shook my head and walked away. I needed to get some distance from this bitch before I slapped the shit out of her.

Ever since we were little, she'd been a pain in my ass. One of the main reasons why I left Audri the first time was because of her. Somehow she found out about the extracurricular activities I was having with a few nurses at the hospital I was interning at, as well as the pharmacist I was fucking to get my hands on all kinds of drugs, and she tried to blackmail me with it. Instead of letting her hold that shit over my head, I applied for an internship at another hospital and moved out of state two days after I was accepted. I knew I was wrong for not coming clean with Audri and telling her about everything that was going on, but it was the only way I could leave without seeing the same look she had on her face a few seconds ago.

For seven years, I stayed away from Sarah's manipulative ass, my family, and Audrielle, with no intentions of coming back. I moved on with my life and was doing quite well. That was, until a few months ago, when my sister and her friend called me with a proposition that I should have, but couldn't, refuse. They offered me one million dollars just to come back and break up whatever Audri and ol' boy had going on. It seemed like easy money to me. I was single and didn't have anything tying me down out there. Plus, I had started gambling again and owed a few more people some money, so I took them up on the offer.

The fact that Audri and I were already married was icing on the cake for my sister's friend, so she threw in an extra half mil because of it. Why our marital status mattered to her kind of threw me for a loop, but it didn't stop me from applying for a transfer to Sacred Heart Hospital and moving back out to Cali.

I wasn't expecting the feelings I used to have for Audri to resurface as strong and as much as they did. I mean, being gone for seven years with no communication whatsoever with your ex should have kicked any inkling of love I had for her away right? I don't know what it was, but when she opened her door the morning I dropped by her house unannounced and told her little boyfriend that we were married, sparked something in me that I thought I'd buried deep. I wanted what we used to have, and if disrupting her little relationship was what got me that, then the $1.5 million I was being paid wasn't even necessary. I'd willingly wiggle myself back into her life and bed for free.

37

Cairo

My breath caught in my throat when I laid eyes on Audrielle. Out of everyone in the room, it seemed as if my sight zoned in on her the minute I walked through the double doors of the lobby.

I stood next to Roderick as he entertained a group of women that looked like his type. On a few occasions, he tried to include me in their conversation, but I was so mesmerized by the honey-kissed beauty standing a few feet away from me that I continuously kept tuning him out.

"Man, if you don't stop staring, she might think you're crazy," Roderick said, leaning into me. "Look, she already trying to get away from you."

"This coming from the same man who keeps looking at Rima on the low."

"What? Nigga, ain't nobody checking for her freaky ass. You see the group of girls that just left from over here. Every single one of them slipped me her number, and I didn't even ask for shit," he bragged.

I nodded my head and kept on half listening to him trying to throw me off of whatever he and Rima had going on. The only reason I noticed those two trying to secretly eye each other was that they were doing a piss-poor job of trying to hide it, especially when they were texting each other. It was like a game of ping pong going on with all the back and forth messaging. He'd send a text then look at her. She'd send a text back then look at him, both wearing silly smirks on their faces.

I shook my head as I walked farther into the room, leaving Roderick in the same spot I'd found him in. We had about thirty minutes until the auction started, and I needed to register for a paddle. After paying the small entrance fee and signing a few papers, I finally had everything I needed to get this plan of mine started.

Looking around at my possible competition, I saw that there was a lot of money standing in the room. I could tell by some of the people who were in attendance that the BPLA would raise a nice chunk of change. There were doctors, lawyers, politicians, firefighters, and even some of Los Angeles' finest socializing in their suits and ties or Sunday best. I wasn't worried, though. I was willing to pay top dollar for just five minutes of Audri's time if that what was it took. Luckily for me, all of the people being auctioned off had to agree to go on a date in the next couple of days with whoever bid the highest for them, so if I played my cards right, I'd have Audri all to myself for a few hours.

My eyes scanned the crowd, looking for Audri, but I couldn't see her anywhere. Somehow she had slipped from my line of sight when I was signing up for the night's festivities, and I hadn't been able to spot her again.

I made it to my assigned seat and greeted the few people already sitting down. I was just about to take my seat when a firm hand grabbed my shoulder.

"Cairo, my boy, it's good to see you made it out tonight," Mr. Freeman said as he shook my hand. "I almost thought that you'd be a no show."

I didn't know why he thought that. "No, sir, I wouldn't miss tonight for anything in the world."

He nodded his head. "That's my boy. Sometimes you have to do crazy stuff to get these women's attention, especially after you mess up." He looked at me sternly, as if he were trying to relay a message, then down at my black Dolce and Gabbana three-piece shawl collar suit, then back up to my dreads, which were neatly braided to the back, thanks to Mama Faye. "You clean up real good there, Cai. You're almost giving me a run for my money."

"Well, they say you learn from the best, sir."

He laughed. "Indeed they do, son, and what did I tell you about that sir stuff? Aaron is just fine."

"My bad, sir—I mean Aaron."

We laughed and sat down at my table for about five minutes, talking about a little business before the lights started to dim in the room. The MC's announcement that the show was about to start was Mr. Freeman's cue to go back to his table with the rest of his family. He invited me to sit with them, but I graciously declined when I saw the way Audri's mom had her nose turned up at me. After agreeing to meet up sometime later in the week to talk about some other things he and I had been working on, he shook my hand once more and left.

The eligible bachelors were up first, and they had the women going crazy, bidding back and forth for a chance to spend the evening with them. For a while, I played around on my phone, reading e-mails and playing a games, until it was time for Roderick to come out. The women he was talking to earlier were front and center with their paddles ready to be raised. Bidding started at five hundred dollars and quickly climbed up to five thousand. I thought the beautiful older black woman sitting next to Audri's father was going to come out the victor in this one, but when Rima came from the back wearing a trench coat, a fedora sitting low on her face, and a big silver briefcase hanging from each hand, I knew some shit was about to pop off.

"Ten thousand!" she yelled as she placed the first briefcase on the table in front of her.

"We have ten K from the sexy mystery lady in the front. Can I get eleven?"

"Twelve!" someone shouted, followed by a high-pitched, "Thirteen!"

The bidding war started again and got all the way up to twenty-five thousand before I noticed Rima getting bored with waiting for it to die down.

"I have twenty-five K from the young lady in pink all the way in the back. Can I get twenty-six? Anyone willing to pay twenty-six?" The announcer looked around and waited for a response but never got one. "Okay, so we have twentuy-five thousand going once, twenty-five thousand going twice." He raised his gavel, ready to end Roderick's bidding war, but stopped when Rima slammed the second briefcase onto the table.

"Fifty thousand!"

Sharp intakes of breath could be heard all around me, followed by a thunderous amount of applause after the auctioneer excitedly yelled, "Sold, to the trench coat–wearing mystery girl in the front for fifty thousand dollars!"

The crowd rolled over laughing as Roderick hopped off of the stage and scooped Rima up into his arms, bride style, and ran out of the nearest exit.

"I would've done the same thing if that was me," the MC said, still laughing. "For fifty thousand dollars, she wouldn't be able to get rid of me for shit. Did you see her sexy ass? Forget a date for one night. We'd probably be married before the sun came up tomorrow morning."

After telling a few more jokes and informing us of a fifteen-minute intermission, the lights were turned back up, and everyone was free to use the bathroom and do whatever they wanted to do before the next auction started. Instead of getting up and walking around again, I sat in my seat and waited for the next round to start. Because the participants weren't being called out in the order they were listed in the booklet, I didn't want to miss the chance of being the first to place my bid for Audri and shutting down what could have possibly been her own little bidding war.

The nice little waitress had just left the table from taking my drink order when Audri's mom came and sat down next to me.

"How are you doing this evening, Cairo?" she asked.

"I'm fine, Diana. How are you?"

"It's Mrs. Freeman, and I'm fine, thanks."

I nodded my head and turned my attention back to the stage. She wasn't about to ruin my night with her uppity attitude. I hoped me ignoring her presence gave her enough sense to go back to her table.

An awkward silence lingered in the air for about two minutes before she spoke again.

"Look, I really don't have anything against you, Cairo. I just know that my daughter deserves to be happy, and with you, that's not going to happen. All she's gotten since you came into her life was a broken heart and about fifteen extra pounds after you left. Now, her ex-boyfriend, *Dr*. Eli Blake is all the man she needs. Since he's been around, she's been shedding all of that breakup weight you left her with and has been smiling every day. It's because of him I was able to put her in the auction tonight. Some of my sorority sisters noticed her change and wanted her to participate now that she's looking a little more desirable to these men. Of course, none of that matters because Eli's going to outbid anyone who tries to raise their little paddles." She looked down at the one sitting in front of me. "Do yourself a favor and bid on one of these girls who don't mind being a mistress to a married man."

"With all due respect, *Diana*, I'm going to ask you to get out of my face and go back to your seat before I say something that I might not regret. Although you and Audri don't have the best relationship, I know she loves you, so I will never disrespect you; however, if you push me too far, I won't be liable for what may come out of my mouth next."

She grabbed at the pearl necklace around her neck and started to twirl it around her fingers. Her amber-colored eyes stayed focused on mine as she thought about what I'd just said. When the room lights started to dim again, she finally stood up from the chair she was occupying and walked away.

"Wow, man, what a bitch," the dude sitting next to me said.

I just nodded my head and turned my attention back to the MC.

"All right, all right, all right. Let's get this party started. For those of you that haven't been paying attention so far, it is now time for the fellas to be in here going crazy. Ladies, you had your chance to pay for one of our eligible bachelors, and if you won one, congratulations. If not, start saving your money now, because this time next year, there will be a whole new batch of handsome men to salivate over. Now, fellas, I just had the privilege of being backstage with the women who are about to be out in a minute, and all I can say is um, um, um. Short, tall, slim, thick, we have a plethora of sexiness about to come to the stage. So without further ado, bachelorette number one, bring your sexy self on out here."

The minute I saw Audri's face appear from behind the curtain and then her sexy frame in that red lace get-up she had on, my heart rate started to speed up, and my dick became hard as a brick.

"Five hundred thousand!" I had shouted before the auctioneer had a chance to start the bidding off at the normal five hundred dollars.

The look on Audri's face was priceless. Her eyes were as big as saucers, while her mouth hung open in shock.

"Well, damn," the MC said. "You ain't letting nobody else have a chance to try to win a date with her, huh? That's what I'm talking about, bruh. I wouldn't give 'em a chance either. Not with her sexy ass."

I looked over at Audri's family table and got a thumbs up from her father. Her mother, on the other hand, was trying to get the attention of someone in the back of the room. When I turned around to see who she was looking at, I wasn't surprised in the least to see Eli back there, standing next to a woman who looked a lot like him. They were arguing about something that he obviously wasn't trying to agree to. I could see her grabbing his hand with the paddle and trying to raise it up, but he kept snatching it away from her.

"So that's five hundred thousand going once, five hundred thousand going twice . . . Sold, to the handsome gentleman at table four!" the auctioneer announced.

I rose from my chair and headed straight to the cashier. I'd had a long day and was ready to go home and go to bed. Once I wrote this check, I was out of there. I needed some rest before Audri and I went on our date the next night.

38

Audrielle

After rescheduling our date to the following weekend, Cairo was finally on his way to pick me up. I was a ball of nerves, and I didn't know why. If I didn't pull myself together soon, I'd be a nervous wreck by the time he got there.

"So did my future grandson-in-law tell you where he was taking you tonight?" Nana asked as she cracked a few eggs into the large mixing bowl. She was trying to show me how to make her famous white chocolate double layer cake, but I only got as far as sifting the flour before she kicked me out of my own kitchen.

"How many times do I have to tell you that Cairo and I are not getting married, Nana? We tried the relationship thing. It didn't work; he's moved on, and so have I."

"You haven't moved on, and you know it. If you did, you wouldn't be sitting here nervously waiting for him to pick you up for a date you keep labeling as a charitable one."

"But it is."

"Audrielle, please stop with all of the bullshit. It's me you're talking to, not your judgmental-ass mama or messy-ass auntie. You know as well as I do that you're still in love with that man, married or not. And his ass is gone just as deep. What man do you know will pay a half a million dollars to spend a few hours with a girl he's supposedly moved on from?"

I shrugged my shoulders.

"Exactly. I've been on this earth a long time, and I've never seen anything like that before. You better stop pushing him away and fighting how you feel before you lose him for good," Nana said as she divided her cake batter into two round pans.

I didn't say anything else as I sat at the island in the middle of my kitchen and thought about what she'd said. Would I be okay if I pushed Cairo permanently out of my life? Could I really move on with the understanding that I would never be able to feel his kisses or touch anymore? As much as I didn't want to, I knew I had to get over the idea of Cairo and I ever being together again. I just had to make sure I told him how I felt during our date that night.

"Audri, are you pregnant?" Nana asked, bringing me from my thoughts and damn near causing me to choke on my spit.

Once I stopped coughing, I had to ask, "Umm, Nana, where the hell did that come from?"

She shrugged her shoulders. "I'm just asking because I had a dream about fish a few weeks ago. The last time that happened, your mother was pregnant with you, then Ari a few years later."

"If anybody is pregnant around here, more than likely it's Ariana. She's the one with in-house dick. I haven't had sex for a while."

"You sure?"

"Yes, Nana, I'm sure. I'm losing weight, not gaining," I replied as the doorbell rang.

Saved by the bell, I thought, hopping off of the stool and checking myself one last time in the mirror. I loved my Nana to death, but sometimes she would say and or ask some of the craziest things. Me, pregnant? Yeah, right. That would be impossible, especially since the doctor nixed that idea a long time ago. He told me I would need to lose over a hundred pounds before I even thought about conceiving a child. He said because of all the weight that I was carrying, my chances of having a baby were less than 25 percent. Imagine the way I felt when

I found out that I was too fat to give Eli any offspring after we got married. My heart and my soul were crushed.

"All right now, baby. Don't keep that fine man waiting," Nana said, ushering me toward the door. "You make sure you have fun tonight and don't try to rush home. Let him get his five hundred thousand dollars' worth."

"Nana!"

"Don't *Nana* me. That man is gorgeous and just my type. You better be glad he wasn't one of those bachelors being auctioned off. I would've given up every last penny in all of my accounts for him."

See what I'm talking about? Seventy-five years old and still hot in the pants.

By the time we left the kitchen and were walking through the living room to the foyer, the doorbell was being pushed again. Royal Mayfair cologne by Creed was what greeted our senses as soon as I opened the door. The back and forth banter between Nana and I came to a screeching halt the minute the soft but very masculine fragrance ascended into our nostrils.

As if having my nose under complete control wasn't enough, Cairo had the nerve to capture my eyes and breath too. I scanned his whole being from head to toe, not leaving one inch of his sexy frame unseen. The crisp white denim jeans and V-neck T-shirt he was wearing went great with his tan skin, while the teal suede Tom Ford bomber jacket and spiked Louboutin sneakers made his eyes pop. His hair was freshly twisted and braided up into one of those sexy man buns on the top of his head.

I tried to speak, but nothing came out as my eyes remained locked on his. Then, as if the sight before us couldn't get any better, he parted his mouth and turned his lips up, showing off those beautiful teeth and that gorgeous smile of his.

"Damn!" The word slipped from both mine and Nana's mouths as we took in a casually dressed Cairo and all of his sexiness.

Sitting on the passenger's side of Cairo's car had my mind going back to the first night we had sex. Wait, let me take that back. The phrase I should have used was *the first night we made love*. The way he handled, touched, and kissed my body that night was most definitely not a quick and meaningless act of pleasure. His heart and soul were into it, and for the life of me, I wished for one second we could go back to the moment. Things would probably be so different now.

Instead of Alex having his last name, it probably would be me. Instead of sleeping in my bed alone every night, I'd have him to hold. And rather than my B.O.B. bringing me spontaneous moments of pleasure when needed, I'd have that skillful mouth and long, thick stallion of a dick between his legs making my body shake and my eyes roll to the back of my head. Who would've thought that a ride home from the hospital would end up with me falling in love with someone I'd only known for a short while?

I brought my mind out of the gutter for a minute and looked out the window. I had no idea where we were headed, but I knew it was somewhere outside of L.A. *WELCOME TO THE BEAUTIFUL CITY OF CALABASAS* was on the sign we had passed about ten minutes earlier. I wanted to ask Cairo where we were going but decided to hold off on that. During the whole ride up there, he hadn't uttered one single word to me, and I found that kind of odd, seeing as he'd been trying to talk to me for the last four months. These past two hours would've been the perfect time for him to get whatever he wanted to say to me off of his chest, but he chose to remain quiet.

I turned my attention toward Cairo. Some sort of dialogue needed to start between us right now or this night was going to get worse by the minute. Not sure of where to start, I said the first thing that popped into my head.

"How's the married life treating you?"

He cut his eyes at me then looked back at the road. "If you don't mind, that's a topic I would rather not discuss right now."

"Ooookay. Well, how is business going? You still doing that freelance work for the city?"

He nodded his head and still remained quiet. I was slowly becoming pissed off. Cairo and this aloof attitude that he was giving me had me feeling some type of way, and he was about to hear my mouth.

"What the fuck, Cai? You spend five hundred thousand for a date with me, and you're giving me the silent treatment. What was the point of you dishing out that kind of money if you were going to completely ignore me? And by the way, where did you get that type of money? If you ask me, we could have continued this zip-lip game from a distance, like we've been doing for free."

He ran his free hand down his smooth face then looked at me. "I'm sorry." He paused for a minute. "I just have a lot of things going through my mind right now, and that has my head all gone."

For the first time since I'd been in the car, I really looked at his face. He must've been putting on for my Nana when he came to the door because he had looked like he was happy as hell. Now, he looked as if he was ready to break down at any minute.

"What's wrong, Cai? You know you can tell me. We may not be how we used to be, but you know you can always talk to me. Is something wrong with Mama Faye?" My heart started to race. That woman was his heart, and I knew if something else were to happen to her, he'd probably go crazy. "I just went to see her a couple weeks ago, and she seemed fine."

He shook his head. "Nah, she good."

"Then what is it?"

Pulling the car over to the side of the road, he finally turned all his attention toward me. When he drew his bottom lip into his mouth and bit down on it, my panties were instantly saturated with my juices. I closed my eyes and took a deep breath, trying to focus on the task at hand. I could not and would not get caught up in Cairo and one of his rousing sex faces.

"I need you, Audri," he said, grabbing my hand.

That tingly feeling I always got whenever he touched any part of me shot through my body and right to my heart.

Ah, shit. I need to stop this before things get out of hand.

"Cai—"

He shook his head, cutting me off, and shifted his body so that he was leaning over the middle console. His face was so close to mine that I could literally taste the cherry candy he was eating. If I messed around and sucked in a breath, I was sure his tongue would be down my throat.

When I tried to put a little distance between us, the back of my head hit the window.

Cairo looked from my eyes to my lips. "I swear I wanna kiss you so bad right now," he said as he pressed his forehead against mine. "I miss you, Audri. I miss us. You just don't know what I've been going through these last few months without you."

I was speechless. "Cai . . . I . . ."

"Shhhh. Let me finish." He lightly brushed his wet, soft lips across mine.

My mind tried to stop the reaction I was having to his kiss, but my body had other plans.

"I apologize for walking out on you the morning Eli showed up at the door. I should've given you the opportunity to explain what was going on instead of pushing you away. Believe me when I say that me marrying Alex wasn't done intentionally to hurt you. I haven't had feelings for her in a long time.

"When Mama Faye's insurance company told us that they could only cover one part of her surgery, I didn't know what to do. It just so happens that before you and I got together, Alex told me about an inheritance my biological grandmother left me in her will. I was to inherit fifty million dollars if I was married by my thirtieth birthday. With time winding down and Mama Faye's health on the line, I did what I thought was a good decision at the time. I married Alex for the money and ended up driving you back into the arms of your husband."

"Eli and I are not back together, Cai, and we haven't been since the morning you left my house." I didn't know why I chose to clarify that little piece of information after all of the things he had just told me.

I slowly blew out the breath I'd been holding and sighed. My mind was still in overdrive, processing everything he said as we stared into each other's eyes. I don't remember how or when it happened, but somehow I ended up straddled across Cairo's legs, trying to relay how much I'd been missing him through the kiss we were now locked in. My yellow Roya high-low dress by Monif C was pulled up around my waist, and the crotch of my black lace panties was pushed to the side. I knew that what we were getting ready to do was wrong, but I needed to feel Cairo deep inside of me. Too much time had passed since my insides were filled to the brim by him.

The minute I slid down on his dick, I welcomed the loud moan that started from the bottom of my stomach and worked its way out of my mouth.

"Fuck!" we both hissed at the same time.

His eyes remained closed as he guided my hips up and down on his lap.

"I've fucking missed this, Audri. I fucking miss you."

"I know your windows are tinted and everything, but do you think this is a good idea to be on the side of the road having sex? What if someone pulls over?" I asked.

"Well, you better hurry up and make me come so we can get out of here," he moaned. "We're going to be late for dinner."

Obliging his request, I closed my eyes and started to roll my hips in a back and forth motion. Cairo's grip tightened on my hips as he sucked all over my neck. I wanted to lift my head up so that he could get better access to the other side, but the tight space that we were in only allowed me to move around so much. Before long, Cairo's hips started to work a little and meet mine, thrust for thrust. After I came all over his dick for the third time, he finally released his love in liquid form all over my contracting walls as he pulled me into his chest and held me tight.

We sat still for a few minutes, trapped in each other's embrace before he tapped me on my ass to get up. I rolled back over to the passenger's side of the car and melted into the cool seat. Neither of us spoke a word as we straightened ourselves up. I flipped the car visor toward me and smoothed down every out-of-place piece of hair. I didn't have on a lot of makeup, so all I did was apply a fresh coat of my lip gloss and was back to looking good as new.

A lethargic feeling took over my body as I buckled myself back into the seat belt just as Cairo pulled back into traffic. Hopefully, we were headed to one of these nice hotels out this way. I needed to hop in the shower real quick and then take a long nap.

"Would it be all right if we just skipped dinner? Thanks to you, I don't feel like going out to eat anymore," I said as I looked at the scenery outside of the window. I knew Calabasas was where a lot of wealthy people lived, but I didn't know it was like this. I could tell that you had to be making racks on racks on racks on racks to even consider living out there.

I scrunched my eyebrows together as I noticed us turning onto a residential street instead of the freeway. "Cai, where are we going?"

We pulled up to a gated estate on top of a hill that I was sure could've housed a small nation. The landscaping looked like something out of the Disneyland picture book, with animals and everything floating around. The beautiful water fountain in the middle of the circular driveway was for sure the selling point for this home. I couldn't take my eyes off of the marble cherubs and exotic goldfish that danced around. If that wasn't enough, the dazzling panoramic mountain and city would make anyone sign on the dotted line.

I looked over at Cai, who had that blank look on his face again. Something was up, and he was going to tell me right now. Before I could even form my lips to ask the question, he was opening his mouth to speak.

"We are about to have dinner with my biological parents," he said, literally shocking the hell out of me. Since when had he been in contact with them? For as long as I'd known Cairo, he'd never expressed an interest in meeting his biological parents. Man, I'd missed a lot since I'd been gone.

"Wait. Your what? Wait. What did you just say?"

He grabbed my hand and faced me. "The reason I rescheduled our date to today is because I wanted you to be here with me when I met my biological parents. Last week, Mama Faye called and tried to have my father and I officially meet at the hospital, but something came up and he couldn't make it. He invited me to join him for dinner instead, so here we are. I spent half a million dollars to have you by my side, and I wouldn't want anyone else in the world with me at this moment, Audri."

Cairo kissed the back of my hand then got out of the car. I didn't know how to feel except for honored. He trusted me to be there for him with this important event in his life.

Maybe I should think about giving him another chance—of course, after he divorces that bitch first.

39

Alexandria

"So you're sure he's on his way to the Wright Estate sometime today?" I asked.

"I'm sure. Unless things have changed within the week, but I haven't heard anything different."

"Do you know if he went alone?"

There was a brief pause. "From what I was told, he has someone with him."

"Someone with him? Is it Finesse?" I asked the caller.

There was another brief pause. "He took her."

"Her who?" I was so tired of this beat-around-the-bush game. Honestly, that was why I liked to do my dirt by myself, but when you're going on three months pregnant, things tend to slow down some.

"He took Audrielle."

I tightened my grip on the phone when I heard that. Why couldn't Cairo leave this girl alone? It was like he was just as obsessed with her as I was with him. Even after my father and I drugged him the night we had sex, he was still thinking about her, moaning her name and shit while it was me grinding on his dick.

I had gotten so mad that I left the room in tears. If it weren't for my father telling me that we had to at least make Cairo think that we had unprotected sex in order for our plan to work, I wouldn't have returned to the room and slipped back into his bed at all. I couldn't go to sleep for shit that night, thinking about how much he was really in love with that fat bitch.

The next morning, when Cairo woke up freaking out about me being in his bed, I was pretending to be in a deep sleep when he started to go off. I wanted to laugh so bad at his dumb ass, but I didn't want to blow my cover.

Now he was on his way to his parents' house to meet them for the first time. I'd been blowing up his phone for the last few weeks since he left my house, and he hadn't answered one of my calls. That was why I hired someone to follow Cairo, so that I could know his whereabouts at all times. If he didn't want to have any communication with me, I'd just have to keep tabs on him my way.

"I thought your brother was supposed to be on top of that bitch," I said. "I didn't pay his ass over a million dollars to just stand on the sidelines and watch. Where was he at? Shouldn't he have worked his way back into her bed and life already?"

"It's a little more complicated than that, Alex. Not only does Audri ignore his flirting and shit, she finally served him with divorce papers. Every time he tears them up, she has another set drawn up and delivered to him."

"Aren't you her lawyer? Why do you keep drawing up the paperwork?" I shook my head. *What a fucking idiot.*

"Audrielle doesn't use my services anymore. Ever since she put two and two together and figured out that it had to be me that told you about her and Eli's marriage, she hasn't been reaching out to me for legal matters at all. I thought when she was approved for the new store that she'd send the contracts over for me to look at, but when my assistant called to follow up with her, Audri advised that my services were no longer needed."

"New store? What new store?" I asked.

"She's opening up a second shoe store over by the UCLA campus. Way bigger than the first one, but still the same concept as the one she already has. It almost didn't happen, though, because the bank kept denying her for the amount she needed to have the whole place remodeled, staffed, and stocked."

"So what? She went to Mommy and Daddy with her hand out?"

"Nah. Some anonymous person financed the whole thing. Went to the bank on her behalf and paid for everything up front."

Anonymous, my ass. That shit has Cairo's name all over it. So he bought her a store, huh? I wonder what else this asshole has been paying for with our money.

"Look, Sarah, I got to make a few more calls, so I'll have to holla at you later. You make sure you have that brother of yours on standby because I'm pretty sure Audri's going to hear some news today that will make her upset, and I'm sure she's going to need a strong shoulder to cry on."

"Look," Sarah said, "I'll call my brother and give him a heads up, but after that, I'm done. I don't want to be a part of you and your father's sick, twisted game to rob this man out of all his money anymore. Audri is a great friend to me—well, she was, and she doesn't deserve this. That's why I never told her about all the shit my brother was doing. I wanted her to move on because she deserved better."

This bitch. Wants to get all sentimental and self-righteous after she was the one who got this whole little plan rolling.

"If you don't want your husband or his partners to find out about all of those client trust accounts that you deliberately mismanaged, then you better get with the program before you're divorced and disbarred and possibly thrown in jail." I knew I was wrong for blackmailing her ass, but oh well. I had to do what I had to do to get what I wanted. She was a pawn in this game and could easily be disposed of with one phone call.

"One day you're going to get yours, Alex, and when that happens, I'm going to be the first one laughing at your ass," she said.

"Yep, you and the other people in my life that I don't care about. I gotta go now. I'll call you if I need anything."

I hung up the phone and rubbed my belly. I was hungry and craving something spicy. Good thing my father went ahead and ordered our lunch while I was on the phone. This little fella was ready for some good ol' Thai food.

"I ordered the cashew chicken, BBQ pork ribs, chicken panang, and yellow curry. They don't have any of that tea you like, so I just got you a water with some lemon slices in it," he said.

My eyes danced with pure delight as I eyed each family-style plate. I piled my plate high and dug in.

"What was that phone call all about?" my father asked as he ate a rib.

"Nothing that I can't handle. Just got some unexpected news. Have you talked to Grayson and Marjorie lately?"

"Not really. I've been real busy at the office—and other things."

I rolled my eyes. The other things he was talking about were the women he was cheating on my mom with. They were the reason why we were almost in bankruptcy now.

"Why do you ask?" he said.

I swallowed a mouthful of food then took a sip of the cold water. My mouth was on fire, but I liked it. "There's something I need to take care of. Let me see your cell."

He eyed me for a minute before he reached over and tried to give me his business phone.

I shook my head. "No, I need your personal line."

His eyebrows hunched up, and his face went blank. I hated when he did that shit because he always reminded me of the actor who played Wyatt Earp on that movie *Tombstone,* especially with him growing that ugly-ass mustache now.

He reached down to his belt and unclipped the phone. Once he handed it to me, I scrolled down his contacts until I found Marjorie's name. Why he had her number in this phone and not her husband, who was his best friend, already told me what I needed to know about their relationship. However, that was neither here nor there for the moment. I needed to plant this bug in Marjorie's ear right quick before Cairo and his mistress got there. I was pretty sure she was going to be high as always, and with this little information about a cheater, she was going to most definitely show her ass tonight at that dinner.

"Hey, handsome, didn't expect to hear from you today," she cooed into the phone when the call connected. "I can't see you today. Grayson invited his bastard son to dinner tonight."

"And that bastard is the exact reason for this call," I said, catching her off guard.

She started to stutter. "Al–Al–Alex, I didn't know—I mean—"

I cut her off. "No need to explain anything. It's none of my business. However, if you would like for me to forget what I just heard and everything that I know, I need you to do something for me."

She paused for a minute, which allowed me to stuff some more of that cashew chicken into my mouth.

"Where's your father?"

"Oh, he's sitting right here eating lunch, but that's neither here nor there. I need you to do something for me when my so-called husband comes to your house tonight. As you can see, I wasn't invited to the festivities. His little mistress was."

She cleared her throat. I knew I had her attention then. As much as she hated to admit it, her ass was still salty about her husband fucking her sister and having babies with her. I knew once I mentioned the word *mistress* she would be game.

"Okay, I'm listening. What do you need me to do?" she asked.

I broke down everything I wanted her to say and how to say it. Five minutes later, I had her sympathizing with me and more than ready to cause some ruckus at that dinner.

"You're not going to tell your mother about that, are you?" my dad asked when I handed him his phone.

"As long as you don't renege on our deal, you good."

40

Cairo

After I helped Audri out of the car and closing the passenger's side door, we walked up to the front door. I watched Audri nervously fidget with her dress and play with her hair. She was always so sexy when she was jumpy like that. It reminded me of the first time I kissed her in the elevator at the hospital. Just the thought alone had my dick getting hard again. Trying to adjust myself as we walked up the steps, I lost my footing and almost fell.

"Are you okay, Cai?" Audri asked, looking back at me. The look in her eyes was as intense as it was a few minutes ago when she was riding the shit out of my dick on the side of the road.

Shit! I need to stop thinking about her intoxicating kisses and that golden creaminess between her thighs if I want to get through this night without my dick sticking straight up.

I nodded my head that I was fine, and we continued on our way.

We made it to the top of the steps and just stood there for a minute. I wanted to knock, but for some reason I stalled. Was I really ready to formally meet my parents? Was I ready to be in their presence? What if they didn't like me? What if I didn't like them? So many scenarios were swirling around in my head that I almost turned around and went back to the car. The only thing that stopped me in my tracks was the door swinging open and Audri nudging me in my side.

I had expected a maid or a butler to answer the door, but it was neither. Looking into the eyes of the woman I was assuming should've been my mother didn't have me feeling any type of way. All of that nervous energy that had been inside of me was gone. The connection I shared with Mama Faye was way stronger than the one I thought I'd have with my own blood, so I had nothing to worry about.

I took in her facial features, trying to find any resemblance to mine, but the obvious work she'd had done to her face wouldn't allow me to do that. Taking in her appearance again, she kind of reminded me of Dina Lohan, just with lighter skin, a tighter face, a pointier nose, and bigger

Botox-injected lips. I watched her brown eyes look me up and down then shift over to Audri. A look of annoyance flashed across her face, but it snapped back to its stern look when the man I know now as my father walked up behind her.

"Thad—I mean . . . Cairo." He put his hand out to shake. "I'm glad you could make it tonight. Why don't you and your lovely guest come on in and make yourselves at home." He moved to the side to allow Audri and me to walk in. "Welcome to the Wright Estate. Dinner will be ready in a minute. I hope you like rack of lamb."

"Never had it before," I said as I looked around the mansion in amazement. I heard Dina Jr. grunt, but I didn't pay her any mind. As my eyes wandered around the immaculately decorated front part of the mansion, my mind could only imagine what the rest of the place looked like. The first time I went over to the Freemans' home, I thought that their house was nice, but this one right here put theirs to shame.

"You have a beautiful home, Mr. and Mrs. Wright," I heard Audri say as she walked up to me and grabbed my hand.

I looked down at her beautiful face and our entwined fingers then nodded my head. Her putting aside whatever it was that we were going through for the moment and just being there for me made me fall in love with her even more. I had missed the opportunity to express the way I really felt during the ride there, but I planned on doing that and a lot more on the way back.

While my father nodded his head in appreciation to the compliment he'd just received, my so-called mother looked at Audri with her nose turned up and her lips twisted.

"I hope you're not here to case the place," she said.

"Marjorie!" my father yelled, face turning red from embarrassment. "Apologize this instant. That's no way to treat our son and his guest."

She rubbed her already red nose and snorted again. I could tell by the way her eyes were dilated and glossy that she was high off of something. "Don't you mean *your* son, Grayson? If I remember correctly, it was you and my sister who brought this bastard into the world, not us. I'm getting so sick of you trying to push your mistakes on me. Wasn't it enough that I helped you raise one already? Now you wanna bring the second back to try and be one big happy family." She laughed. "You can never leave well enough alone, can you? Always wanna make the shit that should stay wrong right."

"Please, Marjorie, now is not the time to discuss this. You already knew Thaddeus was going to be joining us and the rest of the family this evening, so stop making a scene. Maybe you need to go lay down or get you a little something to drink until Toby and Mel get here."

"Toby and Mel?" I asked. To my understanding, it was just going to be them and us. I didn't want to meet anyone else until I got some of the questions I had floating around in my mind answered.

"Yes, your brother Tobias and his girlfriend ShaNiece are coming, as well as your sister Melanie and her"—he shook his head—"friend. I hope that's okay," his deep voice replied as he turned his attention back to me.

I opened my mouth then closed it. Was I really ready to meet my siblings? Did I want to meet my siblings? Audri nudging my side again brought me from my thoughts.

"Nah, it's fine. I just thought it was going to be us tonight. Figured I'd get to ask you a few questions and get to know you a little better before I met everyone else."

He reached into the pocket of his dark denim jeans and pulled out his phone. "I can call and tell them not to come if you like."

I shook my head. "It's all good. The more the merrier, right?"

"Well, now that that's settled, how about a tour of our home before dinner starts?"

Audri and I followed behind him, still hand in hand, as he guided us over 21,000 square feet of luxury. Of course, he didn't walk us around every inch. Some things were pointed out from a distance, but we still got to see just about everything. In addition to the two guest homes in the back, the eight-bedroom, eleven-bath-room masterpiece had a theater, game room, wine cellar, gym, spa, gourmet kitchen with two islands, family room, two offices, a bonus room, and even staff quarters. Growing up there would've been a hell of a lot different than the three-bedroom, one-bathroom home I was raised in by Mama Faye.

After showing us the classic car collection in one of the four garages on the property, he took us back into the main house for dinner. As we walked through the sun room and got closer to the dining area, I could hear a few unfamiliar voices having a heated conversation.

"I don't know why I even came here tonight. Me staying away was for good reason." The voice slightly resembled mine.

"Really, Toby? You aren't the least bit curious to see how your brother looks? Twin brother, at that. I'd be pretty stoked if I were you," a feminine yet deep voice returned.

"Well, didn't nobody ask you now, did they, Rochelle."

"Please refrain from calling me by my full name, Tobias. It's either Roc or Ro. Either one is fine with me."

Toby started to say something else but stopped dead in his tracks when we entered the room. Marjorie, who was seated at one end of the table, looked as if she were about to black out at any moment, totally oblivious to the argument going on right in front of her. I guess it was safe to say that she chose to get her feelings under control by getting a little bit higher in our absence rather than lying down.

A prettier and younger version of Marjorie shot up from her chair and embraced me with a hug.

"Oh my God! You look just like Toby." She turned to face the table. "Toby, doesn't he look exactly like you? The only difference is his eyes. His are blue with specks of green, and yours are green with specks of blue. Oh my God! The mystery of Dad's two different eye colors is revealed. One side represents Toby, and the other represents you!"

As soon as I looked up at her, my eyes connected with a face and body identical to mine leaning against the wall. His arms were folded across his chest as he gave me the same inquisitive glance I was giving him. Although this was our first time seeing each other, it wasn't hard to notice the matching traits we shared: a tall, muscular frame; tan skin; dirty blond hair; broad shoulders; strong jawlines; and full lips. The only things that set us apart were our eyes and the fact that I had dreads. He, on the other hand, had his hair styled the same way Ryan Seacrest wore his.

"We couldn't deny each other if we tried," he said, extending his hand out to break the awkward silence. "What up, man? I'm Tobias, but everyone calls me Toby. From what my dad tells me, I'm your older brother by two minutes."

I laughed. "Oh, yeah? That's what up." I looked around at all the expectant eyes that were now back on me. "Well, It's nice to meet you, and continuing on with the introductions, I'm Cairo, and this"—I pulled Audri forward—"this is my . . . Audrielle."

I knew as soon as the words left my mouth that Audri was going to squeeze the hell out of my hand and low-key grill me from the side. But I meant what I'd said. She was mine and the only woman I would willingly claim in front of them or anyone else. If she didn't want me to let our relationship slip out that way, then she should've never given me the goods again. I was going to do anything in my power to make sure she became mine again.

Toby smirked at me then gave Audri an approving once over. "Well, it's finally nice to meet you and your beautiful lady. I'm sure when my Niecey gets here, you'll see that we have a lot more in common than just our looks."

I didn't know what he meant by that, but I couldn't wait to see what he was talking about.

We finally sat down for dinner, and, for the most part, had a good time. Thirty minutes after we began eating, Niecey showed up, and I understood what Toby meant. We both had a hankering for that sexy dark meat. He just liked his a little leaner than I now preferred mine.

"So, Audri, what do you do?" Niecey asked as we got ready to eat dessert.

She gently wiped her mouth then placed the napkin back in her lap. I swear I wanted to lean over and capture her ripe lips into mine, but I calmed myself down. "I own a shoe store named Kick Biz."

"Kick Biz? I think I've been there before. You sell and make customized sneakers there, right?"

Audri nodded her head. "Yeah, we also sell regular sneakers, sports apparel, and some designer labels. What do you do?"

"I'm the head of Human Resources at Sacred Heart Hospital."

"Are you guys hiring?" my sister Mel inter-jected. "Because Ro here needs a job. I'm tired of taking care of her and everything else. My little trust fund money will be gone in no time if I keep on financing her lifestyle and mine." She laughed.

"Well, you could always be like your big brother over there and marry somebody to get your hands on the real money. Or resort to selling drugs like the other one used to," Marjorie sluggishly said. The drinks she had started guzzling not too long ago were already taking effect. "Personally, I think you should marry for money and then make an overweight shoe store worker your mistress. You'll be broke again in no time if you do that, though." She laughed then turned her attention toward me. "Tell me something, Cairo. Would your wife care to know you're here parading that cow around, while she's at home going out of her mind, wondering where you are?"

My phone, which had been going off all night, started to vibrate in my pocket again as a devilish grin crossed over Marjorie's face. Because my hand was sitting comfortably on top of Audri's thigh under the table, the second her body tensed up, I felt it.

"Marjorie!" my father yelled. "Go up to the room. You've had enough for tonight. I'll be there in a minute."

"Don't *Marjorie* me, Grayson, and don't try to ship me off. You know as well as I do that I'm only speaking the truth right now. I called it last time Toby brought that other hood rat he was dating to dinner, and I'm calling it now. These two black bitches only want you dummies for your money, and y'all too pussy whipped to see."

"Toby, you better get your mama. I know this is only our first time meeting, but I'm not going to be too many more hoes, hood rats, or black bitches," Niecey said, moving her empty plate out of the way and scooting her chair back from the table. "You know how I get down."

"First off, she's not my mom, so let's get that straight. Secondly, she was right about the last chick I dated. Her ass was a gold digger, but I found that out for myself. Third, if she disrespects you again, by all means, babe, pounce on her ass. You wanted to know the reason why I don't come around; now you see why."

"No, Toby, the reason you don't come around is because you know we don't allow them drugs anywhere near our home. You would think after embarrassing your father and I the way you did when you were in college that you'd learn to show us some kind of respect," Marjorie said.

"Respect? I'll respect you when you start to lay off of those Mandrexes you're still buying from my boy Pablo. Yeah, I may not be in the game anymore, but I still know who's buying what and from whom," Toby said, smirking at the shocked look on Marjorie's face.

Everything seemed to happen in a matter of seconds as things started to get real tense. Melanie, who had been quiet during the whole exchange, was in her seat crying, while her girl-friend, Ro, was trying to console her. Grayson, or my father, was up pacing the floor as he fin-ger-combed his hair, mumbling profane words to himself. Niecey was on her phone, texting, looking like she was ready to go off at any min-ute, and Audri sat next to me with little to no emotion on her face.

"I think we should leave. Maybe this wasn't such a good idea," I said to her as I started to stand from my seat.

"This is all your fault! I knew this shit would happen when Grayson told me he invited you to dinner. Why did you invite him, Grayson?" Marjorie stood up and turned to my father. "You didn't want to be in his life for the last thirty years. Why try to start now? Is it because of your bitch of a mother, Elinore?" She laughed. "Even from her grave that crazy witch still haunts me."

"Now you wait a minute, Marjorie—"

"No, you wait a minute! I've put up with your shit for long enough, and I'm tired. I'm tired of everything, Grayson. So much so that I take a little something-something every now and then to help me cope with your betrayal, me having to raise my sister's kid, my husband being gone all the time, and last but not least, my daughter being confused about her sexuality. Never have any of you done a damn thing for me. All I do is give, give, and give, while you muthafuckas just take, take, and take. Then to add insult to injury, you wanna bring the little bastard we got rid of back into our lives. For what? To make this family seem whole again? Or is it to right your wrong? If anything, you need to be teaching him how to be the opposite of you before he gets this one pregnant too," she said, pointing at Audri.

"Pregnant too? What is she talking about, Toby?" Audri asked.

"Oh, shit!" Marjorie laughed, walking around the table and close to Audri. She leaned over her shoulder and got in her face. "You don't know this married man has a baby on the way with his wife?"

Audri turned her heated glare to me. "She's pregnant, Cairo?"

"Audri, look. Let me explain," I said.

"What was all of that shit you were saying to me in the car? I thought you only married her

for the money. You were sleeping with her too?"
she screamed, getting up from the table. I tried
to grab her wrist, but she pulled away.

"Audri, please."

"Every time I find a man to fall in love with, he
always breaks my heart with this bullshit!" She
started to cry. "Not you, Cai. I thought you were
different. I thought we really had something."

"We do, babe. Please, just calm down so we
can talk this over in private."

"There's nothing to talk about anymore. And
to think I was going to forgive you and wait for
you to handle all of the shit you had going on
with her, and then welcome you back with open
arms once you got everything squared away."

I was now standing next to her and trying
to get her to look me in the face, but she kept
turning her head. "Audri, please. I still want you
to wait for me. Alex and I will be divorced soon,
and I'll be all yours."

"Until the baby comes, right? Then you'll have
my head so fucked up like Ness has Ari's. Except,
in this case, you'll probably still be fucking
your baby mama. Maybe for some more money,
right?"

"Audri, just—"

Smack! She slapped the shit out of me before I
could even beg for her forgiveness again.

"You stay away from me, Mr. Thaddeus Wright. You keep your ass right over here with the rest of these crazy assholes you wanted to meet so bad." She turned away from me, still crying. "I need to get out of here. Where's the door?"

"Straight down the hallway and to your left, and please don't steal anything on your way out," Marjorie said, pointing to the front of the mansion.

Audri looked into the faces of everyone in the room, nodding her head at each of them, and then she turned to me. Her bottom lip trembled before she pulled it into her mouth and headed back the way we had come in.

"Audri, wait!" I tried to go after her, but a pair of strong hands grabbed my shoulders.

"Let her cool down for a minute, bruh, She'll be okay after she gets some fresh air," Toby said to me. "Niecey, can you go make sure she's all right? We don't want the neighbors calling the sheriff and shit."

Niecey nodded her head and excused herself from the table. I watched as she swiftly walked down the same hallway Audri had just disappeared down.

"Why don't we go have a drink while we wait for them to come back, twin? I've heard some things about your fake wife that you may want to hear."

41

Rima

"If you don't quiet down, you're going to cause my receptionist to come in here," I told Roderick as I uncuffed his wrists.

"Well, how do you expect me to be quiet when you have a naughty mouth such as yours?" He smirked then flashed that devilishly handsome smile at me. This man could literally cause my death if I wasn't careful.

It was a cool Saturday evening as we lay tangled up in my office. Cassius was at home with my mom, so I had a little free time to get some work done that day. Sometimes when I wasn't busy, I would do private weekend sessions for some of my clients, which was why I was there that day. Jamiko Kato was a new case referred to me by an associate of ours. I had an idea of what was going to help her out. I just hoped she was open to my invitation.

I got up off of the floor and walked to my office bathroom. I needed a towel to clean up the mess I had just made all over my leather couch.

"Hey, Ree, your phone is ringing again." Roderick laughed.

I rolled my eyes. For the past hour, someone had been blowing up my phone. I didn't want to answer it because I thought it was my mother calling. I was supposed to be back home almost an hour earlier to resume my motherly duties, but I was there being a little freaky.

"Can you get it out of my top drawer and see who's calling while I clean myself off some?"

"And how am I supposed to do that with my legs still tied in these crazy-ass knots you got them in?" he asked.

I busted out laughing at that. Roderick knew I was into some kinky shit. He just didn't know the extent until now. Ever since the auction, we had been spending every night together, and he'd been begging to see that side of me, so that day, I granted his wish when he popped up on me a few minutes after my session with Jamiko ended.

When I emerged from the bathroom a few minutes later, I found the spot where Roderick had been laying vacant. I heard a drawer close and turned my attention to my desk. There he was, standing with my ringing phone in his hand, looking like a chocolate God. My eyes scanned his body from head to toe, and I couldn't help but lick my lips, thinking about all of the nasty things I still wanted to do to him. I noticed he had slipped his briefs back on, and that made me frown. If I was still standing there naked, then he needed to be as well. I wanted to go for another round before we left or before he got called in for another case.

He held my phone up. "It didn't have a name on the screen, just some 310 number calling."

I shrugged my shoulders. That number could belong to one of the many people I consoled. If it was important, they'd leave a message or call the front desk to schedule an appointment.

"Why you standing all the way over there?" Roderick asked as he lustfully eyed my body up and down. Thanks to Cassius, my figure was finally the way I wanted it to be: thick thighs, slim waist, fat ass, and perky breasts. I wasn't that little stick figure anymore, and men were starting to really take notice. "I can remember telling you that I wanted to taste you while you laid across this beautiful desk of yours."

My nipples instantly started to swell. I loved being talked dirty to. I gestured my head toward his briefs. "I thought you tapped out on me. You already started getting dressed, I see."

He looked down at his dick, which caused my
eyes to look down there too. I promise I almost
came all over myself at the sight of that thick rod
poking straight out, trying to be freed.

"Does it look like I'm ready to go anywhere
anytime soon? Now get your little sexy ass over
here and give me what I want," he said.

See, this was the reason why Roderick and
I were a perfect match. His freak meter was
as high as mine. Relationship wise, we were
a great match too. Our signs were compatible
and everything. The only problem we had was
how everybody would feel once they found out
that we were messing around. Well, maybe not
everybody, per se; it was more like how Finesse
would feel. He and I were nothing but co-parents to Cassius, but you know how some niggas
get when they find out that their best friend or
homie is fucking their baby mama. They say that
they're cool with it, but deep down inside, it's
the total opposite.

I didn't feel like what we were doing was
wrong, but Roderick did have some concerns.
That was why there were only three people who
knew about us: my mama, Audri, and now my
receptionist.

I tilted my head and bit my bottom lip. I
was trying to play coy for a minute, but the

hungry look in Roderick's eyes had me walking straight over to my desk, assuming the position. I lay back on the cool cherry wood desk and spread my legs wide. Roderick didn't need any further invitation as he dug in head first. His long, skilled tongue licked me from the back to the front and in between. Before long, my legs were shaking and my thighs were locked around his head. I was in mid moan when the door to my office flew open.

Now, I just told y'all a minute ago that both Roderick and I were some freaky muthafuckas, right? So you know he didn't stop feasting on my shit, and I didn't stop cumming when my receptionist walked in unannounced.

Our eyes connected as I came again, and she just shook her head.

"What . . . what is it, Dahlia? Can't you see that I'm busy?" I moaned.

"Clearly I can." Her voice was dripping with attitude, but she'd get over it.

I felt Roderick moving his head up my body, placing soft kisses along the way.

"Hey, Dahlia," I heard him say. I didn't even need to see his face to know that he was smiling. I could hear it in his tone.

She smacked her lips and rolled her eyes. "Rima, you have a call on line one."

"Tell whoever it is I've gone for the day and won't be back in until Tuesday." Cassius had a doctor's appointment on Monday, so I had decided to take the whole day off. "Either they can schedule an appointment or call back later on in the week."

Roderick kissed my lips, and I could taste the sweetness of my nectar all over his mouth. I wrapped my legs around his waist and pulled him closer to me. I wanted some dick, and I was about to get some regardless of Dahlia being in there.

"I did, but she said it's an emergency. She was crying so hard I couldn't really make out her name. I know it's something that starts with an A, though."

"Audri?" I said, pushing Roderick off of me. My pussy was missing his touch, but my best friend came before any nut.

"Yeah, I think that's it. She seemed really—"

"Thank you, Dahlia," I said, cutting her off. "I'll take the call right now, and next time, knock before you come in." I gave her a knowing glare as she rolled her eyes and walked out.

"Is there something I should know about the two of you?" Roderick asked as he sat back in my chair.

"Nothing that concerns you." *Yet.*

I turned my naked ass around on my desk and picked up my office phone and pressed line one.

"Audri, what's wrong?"

"Rima!" she cried. "I fucking hate him!"

"Hate who, bestie?" I asked as I sat up on my desk. I'd never heard Audri this distraught.

"Fucking Cairo. She's pregnant, Rima. The bitch is pregnant! Not only did he marry her ass, but he also got her pregnant and had the nerve to ask me to give him another chance."

"Wait. Cairo asked you to give him another chance? And who's pregnant?" I heard an unfamiliar voice in the background trying to calm Audri down. "Audri, who is that you're talking to?"

I could hear her trying to control her breathing, but it wasn't working. She started to sob again but stopped a few minutes later. "I'm in the car with Niecey. She's Toby's girlfriend."

"Who is Toby?"

"Cairo's twin brother."

"Wait. What? Cairo has a twin brother?" I looked at Roderick for confirmation, but he just shrugged his shoulders. "Audri, where are you? Do you wanna come to my house so we can talk? I'll head that way right now and meet you there."

I heard Roderick smack his lips, but he had another think coming if he thought I'd leave my best friend hanging over some dick.

"I'm on my way to my house. Can you just meet me there?" she asked.

"You sure you wanna go home? He might try to come there to get you."

"You act like he doesn't know where you live. You do have a baby with his brother." Her attitude was on ten right now, so I just let that little smart remark slide. I knew she didn't mean it in a nasty way. She was just in her feelings at the moment.

"Okay, Audri, I'm about to leave the office now. I'll call you when I'm close."

"I'm calling you from Niecey's phone because mine is dead, so write this number down."

I grabbed a pen and paper and wrote down the number I could hear Niecey calling out in the background. When I got off of the phone, I started to get dressed.

"So you just gonna leave my mans sitting here like this?"

I looked down at Roderick's dick. He was now just as naked as I had been a few seconds earlier, and his dick was looking rather delicious, but as much as I wanted to hop on that thing and ride him out, I'd have to pass.

I gathered my purse and the rest of my belongings then went to my office phone and told Dahlia her presence was needed. When she walked in, I watched her eyes keep going from me to Roderick then to his dick.

"I'm about to go handle something right quick. Can you please take care of Mr. Miller for me before he gets blue balls?"

"Wait. What?" I heard Roderick say, but I cut him off with a few kisses to his lips.

"I'll call you after I get Audri together, okay?" I kissed him one last time then ran out of the office. Yeah, Roderick's and my freak meters were on the same level, but I was pretty sure there were some things he could learn from me.

42

Audrielle

"It's the house to your left," I told Niecey as she turned on my street then pulled into my driveway. "Thank you so much for the ride. I don't know how I would've gotten home if it weren't for you."

"Girl, don't even trip. It wasn't a problem at all." She grabbed my hand. "For what it's worth, Audri, I know exactly what you're going through. Although our situations are a little different, I still know how you're feeling right now. I'm not the best at giving advice, but I will say that you might want to give Cairo the opportunity to explain what's going on. The look on his face when you ran out of there was of a man that was crushed. Maybe what some of that bitch said was true, but then again, you know how bitter hoes are when they mad that you have a relationship they only wish they could have."

I nodded my head.

"Program my number into your phone when you charge it, and call me sometimes. I'm in L.A., and you're in L.A. I'm dating a hot white guy; you're dating a hot white . . ." Her words trailed off. "See, I told you I wasn't the best."

I laughed. "Naw, you're good, and for what it's worth, Toby is hot."

"He is, isn't he?" I could tell by the look in her eyes that her mind was going to the gutter. If Toby was packing anything like Cairo was, I knew her thoughts were nothing but good ones.

We chatted for a few more moments before I got out of her car and headed to my front door. As soon as I reached the porch, I noticed the big bouquet of white calla lilies sitting on my mat.

"Eli," I said, shaking my head as I picked up the arrangement. I looked up and down my street to see if I could spot his car, but when I didn't see it anywhere, I unlocked my door and entered my house.

The first thing I did after I placed the flowers on my table was plug my phone up to the charger and turn it on. As soon as my home screen came on, Cairo's face appeared. I ignored his calls and sent Rima a quick text, telling her that I was at home and she could just use her key when she got there. I was on my way up to my room to take a shower and lie down for a bit. I knew I wasn't going to feel like coming down to unlock the door for her when she finally arrived.

I decided to go check on Nana and see if she was okay while I retired to my room for the rest of the night. "Nana!" I called out as I walked toward her room. When I didn't hear the TV on, I knew she had to be somewhere else. "Nana!" I called her name again, and there was still no answer. I checked the bathroom, the backyard, the den, and the reading room and still came up empty handed. The last place I looked was in the kitchen, which was also empty. What I did find, though, was the double layer white chocolate cake she had made earlier in my crystal cake stand with a note taped to it.

Nana's fast ass was out on a date with one of her cubs, and she had the nerve to tell me to not wait up for her. Boy, my life really did suck if my 75-year-old grandmother was getting more play than me.

I'd just submerged myself underneath the warm water coming from my rainforest shower head when I heard my doorbell go off. Rima had another think coming if she thought I was about to stop what I was doing just to let her in;

especially when I'd already texted her and told her to use her key. I continued to bathe myself and wash any traces of Cairo's scent off of me. If I wanted to make it through the night without crying again, I needed to have any memory of him gone.

My doorbell going off again brought me from my thoughts and had me pulling on my plush pink bathrobe without drying off. With wet hair and a wet body, I stomped my way down the stairs to the front door. Swinging it open, I was ready to go off on Rima's ass, but my voice got caught in my throat when I finally focused on who was standing on my porch.

"Eli? What are you doing here?"

"I came to see if I could take my soon-to-be ex-wife out to dinner one last time before we finally part ways." He held up a manila envelope, which I was guessing had the last set of divorce papers inside. Hopefully, he remembered to sign those, unlike he did the last ones he sent back. "Did I catch you at a bad time?" he asked, looking over my shoulder.

"No, you didn't. I just thought you were Rima. She's on her way over here."

"Are you guys going out tonight or something?"

I shook my head and tried to look everywhere but his face. Eli was looking so good to me right now for some reason that I felt a little tingle down below. Even though he only had on some basketball shorts, a tight-fitted V-neck T-shirt, and an Anaheim Angels' hat low on his face, that didn't take away from his handsome dark features or that sculpted and toned body.

We stood in my doorway with an awkward silence as time seemed to move slowly. Every time a car passed by or pulled up, I was praying it was Rima, but I had no such luck. I didn't know how Eli and I got like this. We were always able to joke and be around each other even after being in our feelings for a while, but the way that he showed his ass at the BPLA that night was an Eli I didn't know. Those seven years away had changed him, and it wasn't a good look.

"Soooo, Rima will be pulling up any second now. I'll just take those papers from you, and you can be on your way. I'm sure you have a hot date or something planned for tonight," I said, ready for him to leave.

"Nope. No date. Just me, Jack Daniel's, some Panda Express, and Netflix tonight." He wiped his hand down his face. "Look, Audri, if it's any consolation to you, I just wanna apologize again for my behavior a week ago and for leaving you the way I did after we got married."

"I can forgive you for what happened last week, but as far as the way you did me after we got married, it doesn't even matter anymore. You obviously moved on, and so have I, Eli." As soon as the words left my mouth, a pang of hurt shot through my heart and settled in my chest. I was pretty sure he had forgotten all about me and enjoyed all the women coming his way. Where he probably moved on and kept the title of heartbreaker, I was still on the other side of love, trying to find the right one and continuing to get my heart broken. My eyes started to water, and I could feel a fresh set of tears threatening to fall, but I was not about to cry in front of him.

"Thanks for stopping by, Eli. It was good seeing you again, but I think it's about time for you to go," I said.

He handed me the envelope with a sad but sexy expression on his face. "If you ever need anything or anyone to talk to, Audri, please know that I'm only a phone call away, okay?"

I nodded my head. His words were sincere, and I'd probably take them into consideration one day, but not anytime soon. He kissed me on my cheek, looked at me one last time, then turned and walked away.

I was on my way to close the door when I spotted the calla lilies I had picked up off of my porch earlier. I stuck my head back out the door before he got into his car.

"The flowers were beautiful, Eli. Thank you."

He stopped in his tracks then turned to face me. "Flowers? I haven't sent you any flowers in a few months."

I looked at him then back at the arrangement sitting on my dining room table. *If he didn't send these things, then who did?*

I walked over to the flowers and plucked the envelope I hadn't noticed before. I opened it. A sonogram picture was glued to one side, while the other had a handwritten message for me.

> *Audrielle,*
> *Thought I'd be the first to announce to you that we're expecting. In a few months, Cairo and I will be the proud parents of a precious bundle of joy. I hope by that time you're over this little schoolgirl crush you have on my husband, realize that he and I were destined to be together, and finally leave us alone. We will be registering at Babies R Us, so if you want to send a parting gift, you know where to go.*
>
> *Sincerely,*
> *Mrs. Alexandria Broussard*

I didn't even know I was crying until I saw a few of my teardrops fall on the sonogram.

Everything that I was trying to forget about earlier all came rushing back to me at once. I was starting to get so upset that my hands began to shake. I tried to sit down but didn't make it when my legs gave out on me. Before I hit the floor, a strong pair of arms wrapped around my waist and pulled me back up.

"Audri, are you all right?" I heard Eli's husky voice whisper against my ear. I didn't know why goosebumps started to cover my body, but they did.

"She's pregnant," I said so low that I hardly heard myself. "They're going to have a baby and live happily ever after."

"Who are you talking about, Audri? Who's having a baby?"

"Cairo. Cairo and his . . . his wife." I started to sob again. Where the hell was Rima at? She should be the one comforting me, not my soon-to-be ex.

Eli turned me around to face him and wiped my tears away with his thumbs. After kissing both of my closed eyelids, he grabbed my chin and pulled my face close to his.

"You are Audrielle Freeman, one of the sexiest and baddest business owners I know. Your smile can light up any room, while your body . . . your body will make the gayest man take a second look."

I laughed a little as I slowly opened my eyes and looked into his.

"The one thing I always admired about you is your ability to just let shit roll off of your back and move on. Yeah, it would hurt you for a second, but eventually you'd bounce back stronger and more determined than ever. I know you love that cat Cairo, but he's not the man for you, baby. He never has been, and he never will be."

"Then who is, Eli? You left me, Antonio fucked my auntie, and Cairo married his ex. So far my track record with men isn't making my odds of finding the one look any clearer for me."

"That's because you already had him. He just needed some time to get his shit together and come back a stronger and better man for you," he said.

I looked down at the floor, biting my bottom lip, and then looked back up into Eli's eyes. "Who are you talking about, E?"

"I'm talking about me," he said as he grabbed my face and pressed his lips against mine.

I tried to resist his kiss at first but shortly gave in after he sucked my bottom lip between his and snaked his tongue into my mouth.

"Let me make you forget all about him, Audri. Let me make you feel good," Eli whispered as he loosened the tie on my robe and removed it from my body. I stood in the middle of my living room completely naked as he skillfully moved his hands over every inch of me.

"I don't think we should do this, Eli," I said breathlessly.

He was doing this thing with his tongue on my neck that had me in a trance. I could feel my juices start to spread around my thighs as he laid down his assault.

"All I'm asking for is one night, Audri, and after that, I will leave you alone if you want me to. Please." He kissed my shoulder. "Just one night." He kissed my neck. "And I promise." He kissed my jawline. "You won't regret it." He gently kissed me on my lips then stepped back and looked me in my face.

"Just one night?"

He nodded his head. "All I need is one, baby, unless you want me for more. In case you don't, you already have the signed papers. Turn them over to the hall of records and I'll leave you alone for good, but if you just give me this one night, I promise I'll make you forget about Cairo, the baby, the money, and everything else."

I was so drunk in love with the intoxicating way he had me feeling that I didn't bat an eye when he mentioned me forgetting about the money. It didn't click in my head until later that I had never mentioned that part of Cairo's marriage to him. Needless to say, I let him have his way and take me to heights unknown for three hours straight. Although his touch felt foreign to me and he wasn't the one I wished was caressing my skin, I still allowed him to make me feel wanted, loved, and needed; so much so that when Rima finally decided to show up an hour later for our little pow wow, I never stopped what we were doing to answer the door. I knew I'd have about a hundred messages on my voice mail with her cussing me out in the morning, but at that moment, I didn't care. Eli was giving me an out from this pain I was feeling, and I welcomed it with open arms, even if it was only for this one night.

"Sis, I need a cup of whatever wine you're over there drinking. I'm really feeling this glow thing you have going on," I said.

"Yeah, I meant to say something about that a few weeks ago at lunch, but it slipped my mind after I got that freaky text from Roderick," Rima answered.

"I still can't believe you're messing with him out of all the fine brothers on the planet. I mean,

Roderick does have it going on, don't get me wrong, the brother is fine. Plus, he has a good job and his own home—major plusses in my book. But you don't feel a little weird humping on your baby daddy's best friend? Isn't that like going against the code or something?" Niecey asked, which caused everyone around the table to laugh. Although she'd only been hanging around our circle for the last couple of months, you couldn't tell she was the newbie of the group. She'd really gotten to know quite a bit about our personal lives, and we'd gotten to know hers in return

"You guys need to leave my Rima alone. If she wants to move on with one of her ex's friends, then so be it. Just like the heart wants what it wants, the pussy does too, so don't feel bad about whatever you and this Roderick fella have going on, baby. Have fun and live your life the way you want to, because you don't wanna live to be my age and find yourself seeking out these younger men just to get your rocks off," Nana said.

"Oh my God, Nana! Not while I'm eating." Ari frowned. "The thought of you getting freaky with anyone at your age just made me lose my appetite completely," she said, pushing her plate away.

"If anything, you better hope you live long enough to be like me at this age. Thanks to the low-carb diet and Pilates classes I've been taking, this old lady will give you a run for your money on any day. Just give me a few hours with that sexy-ass grandson-in-law of mine. You'd never hear from Finesse again. He'd be with me in some foreign country, enjoying everything your sweet little Nana has to offer him, my dear."

The whole table erupted in laughter at the look on Ari's face. If I were her, I'd stop testing Nana because I believed every single word she said. The way she had her young suitors following her around like some lovesick puppy dogs, I was pretty sure Finesse would have no problem falling in line.

I took a sip of the sweet red moscato wine and smiled. We were on one of the private patios at Shanghai Red's, having a good time at Sunday brunch. Not only were we catching up on each other's hectic weeks, but we were also celebrating the successful grand opening of Kick Biz 2. After stressing and slaving over every tiny detail the last sixty days, my second store was finally open. That night we were having this big blowout party, and I wanted to spend a little personal time with the people that were the most important in my life before all of the craziness started later on. With all of the media

Ari had scheduled to be there—the mayor of Los Angeles, fashion bloggers, sneaker heads, and some of the coaches and players from UCLA and USC—I would be entertaining more than a few people at the night's festivities.

"So, Nana, have you been dreaming of fish lately?" Rima asked. "I just noticed Audri here is polishing off her third plate. I haven't seen her eat that much in a long time."

I rolled my eyes and took another sip of my wine as she smirked and took a sip of hers. I should've never told Rima's ass what Nana said the night I went out on that date with Cairo, because she'd been asking me if I was pregnant ever since.

"No shade, Audri, but you have been eating like crazy. Just before we all met here, we were at Johnnie Pastrami's getting you a sandwich and slice of cheesecake from there. Now you're in here going in on this buffet." Niecey snickered. "Plus, I've also noticed that little glow everyone else has been talking about."

"A girl can't glow just because she's enjoying life? I can't have this certain aura surround me because for once in my life I'm finally man and drama free? Why does me being in a good mood have to equate to me being pregnant? Ari's been in a good mood lately," I said, looking at my sister. "Are you pregnant?"

All eyes turned to Ari, and a blush decorated her light face. I knew I was not the only one who noticed she hadn't had a mimosa or one single glass of wine. I, on the other hand, had been drinking since I sat my ass down.

"Well, I wasn't going to tell anybody, since I haven't told my parents yet, but there is a slight possibility that I am pregnant. I haven't had my period this month, and both Finesse and I have our fingers crossed."

I looked at Rima from the corner of my eye to see if she had any type of reaction to the news Ari dropped. It was one thing to be okay with your baby daddy moving on, but a whole different set of problems could occur when he moved on and had a baby with the next one. Although I knew my girl was happy with Roderick and what they had going, you never knew what would set her off about Finesse, even though she claimed to have no type of feelings for him.

"See, while y'all are all focused on me and my glow, you guys completely overlooked Ari's. Besides, like I said before, I would have to be having sex if to be pregnant," I said.

"And you don't call what you and Eli have been doing sex?" I heard my Nana say under her breath. I was sure if I heard it at this small table, everyone else did as well. I should've sent her ass home or back to my parents' house a long time ago. I shook my head. Unbeknownst to Nana, she had just opened a can of worms that I knew my best friend was not about to let slide.

Rima's head snapped in my direction. "So you're still sleeping with Eli? Audri, I can't believe you! You said it was only that one time and that was it. So you lied to me. Is that where we're at now, Audri?"

"Rima, it's not even like that."

"Spit truth."

I couldn't believe she was doing this in front of everybody. Nana and Ari were okay, but Niecey and the few other people we had with us really didn't need to know my business.

"Rima, why don't we—"

She cut me off.

"No. Spit truth. If you really don't want me to be in my feelings right now, I suggest you agree."

I thought about it for a moment then nodded my head. I kind of trusted everybody at this table, or else I wouldn't have considered them friends. "Okay, Rima. Spit truth."

"Are you thinking about getting back with Eli, Audri? Because I know you, and you don't have sex to just be having sex, so there has to be some sort of feelings there," she said.

"Believe me when I say there aren't no feelings there. Certainly not on my end. Eli and I are just having fun. That's it, and that's all," I responded.

If these were normal circumstances, my best friend would be right. She did know me, and she knew that I didn't mess around like that, but in this case, I just needed a release whenever Eli and I did hook up. As much as I wanted to pretend that what happened between Cairo and me wasn't affecting me anymore, it still was, especially when Alex kept sending me sonogram pictures of their growing baby.

I'm not going to lie; I did miss him, especially on those nights when I lay in bed all alone and images of what we did on the side of the road in the front seat of his car flashed through my mind. Even when Eli and I were having sex, it would be Cairo's face, touch, kiss, and feel I would imagine.

A few times I thought about answering one of his phone calls and giving him the chance to explain things to possibly make us right again, but I didn't. This was the second time that he'd broken my heart, and I wasn't so sure that I had enough love left in me to forgive him this time. It would take a true act from God to make me even think about reconsidering giving Cairo another chance. Until then, I would just do me, enjoy the things happening for me in my life, and wish him and his family the best.

43

Cairo

Mama Faye was getting discharged from the hospital, and I couldn't be any happier. Not only had she made a full recovery from her surgery, but she was no longer in the fight for her life with cancer. The doctors said they had never seen anyone heal as fast as she had. Let Mama Faye tell it, it was the good ol' Jamaican food she would have smuggled in and her beloved Ting, but we all knew it was just her will to live and to be here to see me give her a second grandbaby.

I'd just turned into the hospital entrance when my phone rang. The number was private, and I almost didn't answer it because I thought it was Alex again. Ever since I'd officially moved back into my home, she'd been calling me every day, trying to get me to move back in with her. She said something about wanting our family to be under the same roof, even if we weren't sleeping in the same room, and the baby getting used to hearing my voice every day. She even had her father calling and trying to persuade me to move back in, but like I told him, I just didn't see the logic in Alex and I cohabitating together anymore. I wasn't putting on this marriage front for anyone else, especially since it caused me to lose the one person who mattered the most to me.

"Yeah, hello," I answered my phone.

"What's up, bruh? What are you getting into today?"

I smiled hearing Toby's voice. Since we had reunited a couple months ago, it was if we were never split up at birth.

"Shit, nothing, man. About to pick Moms up and then head to the house for the little get together. You still coming, right?"

"Yeah, we'll be there," he said, referring to him and Niecey. "I just have to stop by my club real quick and talk to my boy Jerome."

"Whatever happened with that situation? You never got around to telling me the last time we met up what went down."

He blew out a frustrated breath. "Man, for a while now, I've been noticing some of our liquor inventory coming up short. And I'm not just talking one or two bottles. I'm talking more like seven or eight. Whole fifths of our top shelf liquor are just disappearing, and no one knew where it was at. I started asking the bartenders and waitresses if they were dropping them, at least then they would be accounted for, but when everybody kept assuring me that that wasn't the case, my mind started to wonder.

"I don't know why, but something told me to view the security footage at the club, and when I did, not only did I find out that Jerome was the one stealing the alcohol for himself, but he was taking cash from our accounts as well. For what, I don't know, but I will be addressing that shit at our little meeting we are about to have."

"Damn, bruh, I know that messed you up. And he's like your boy, right?"

"Since college, man. We clicked the first time we met and had been friends ever since. The only reason why I invested in the Lotus Bomb was because we were real tight and I thought that it was a good investment. The business plan he drew up was enough to impress me and have me hopping right on board."

"So where does this leave you guys?" I asked, watching one of the candy stripers roll Mama Faye out in a wheelchair. I couldn't do anything but copy the smile on her face when she looked up and our eyes connected. My eyes got a little

misty seeing my number one lady back and
looking like her old self again. Her skin was its
normal smooth coffee color. Her hair was real
low because of the chemo, but it was growing
back nice and thick up under the wig she had
on. She even had the nerve to have on a little
makeup, obviously something Ari had talked her
into doing when she went to get her dressed and
ready to go.

I listened to Toby tell me what he had in store
for his friend as I stepped out of my cool car and
went to open the passenger's side.

"All right, bruh. I got my moms now. I'll see
you and your girl tonight, okay?"

"Okay, Cai, man. Holla at you later," he said
then released the call.

After thanking the flirty candy striper for
bringing Mama Faye down, I kissed her on the
cheek, helped her into the car, then got in on my
side. For a good part of the ride, both of us sat in
our seats, clearly in our own thoughts, but that
didn't last long once I reached my hand out to
turn up the radio.

"Don't chu dare turn that radio up louda. Ya
and mi need to talk before we get to dis party ya
havin' at mi house."

I put my free hand back on the gear shift and
continued to drive. I could feel Mama Faye's

dark brown eyes drilling a hole in the side of my head, but I wouldn't take my eyes off the road to look at her.

"Ya hair looks good. Who ya let do it since ya not come to mi?"

I'd gone to a little twist shop I found not too far from Audri's new store one day while I was riding past, trying to see if she was there. I didn't want to go, but I needed my dreads re-twisted badly. The last two times I went up to the hospital to let Mama Faye do it, she was so weak from the chemo that I wasn't going to allow her to pass out because of me. My stylist, Anita, was good, but I would never tell Mama Faye that.

"I let some lady at this shop hook me up." I shrugged my shoulders. "She did okay."

Mama Faye nodded her head as she looked at my hair then back to the side of my face. "So who did ya all invite to dis party? I hope it's people mi like."

I knew she was taking that dig at Alex, but she didn't have to worry about her. I had already told her to stay the fuck away because this was a family function, and she and I were not family. At least not yet.

"Ari, Ness, and the baby will be there. Roderick said he and his date were going to come after his shift. Then we have a few of the neighbors coming, as well as the people who own that restaurant you say reminds you of home."

Her face lit up. "Oh, yeah? Mi hope ya got them to bring de food for de party, because if that gayl Ness is with cooked, ya might's well put me back in de hospital."

I laughed. "Come on, Mama Faye. I know Ariana's food doesn't look, let alone taste like yours, but at least she tries."

"She tries to kill mi grands with her cooking. That gayl is good for Ness heart, but not for his stomach. I hope Ness don't let her feed me great grands with that. Mi don't know why ya all say de gayl can cook and clearly she can nawt. Ness brought me some fish tea soup that gayl made, and mi almost died. De fish was not cleaned properly, de yams were not tender, and the taste was bland. Not enough jerk seasoning, thyme, or garlic. Fish tea 'pose to be spicy, yeah, but her soup was nawt."

I couldn't do anything but laugh because Ness said the same thing whenever Ari tried to make Jamaican food. He didn't want to hurt her feelings, so he never told her. "Well, you won't have to worry about Ari's cooking this time around. We actually had the restaurant cater."

She nodded her head. "Did ya invite mi soon-to-be daughter-in-law?"

I looked her way, but she turned her head to look out of the window.

"Mama Faye, how many times do I have to tell you that Audri and I are not together anymore? And we probably won't be, especially after how she was embarrassed at that dinner."

"That gayl is still in love with ya, boi. I can see it in her eyes. She just in her feeling right now. Don't know how to separate her heart from her head. But once she give me my grandbaby, she will see where it belongs."

I didn't know why Mama Faye kept bringing up Audri being pregnant. If she was with child, I doubted it was mine, especially after I heard she'd been spending a lot of time with Eli. Since the dinner, Audri had been up to the hospital to visit Mama Faye a couple of times, always when I was either at work or had just left. She would call Mama Faye's room to make sure I wasn't there; then she would spend a few hours with her. Whatever they talked about, Mama Faye would never say. She'd just tell me to mind my own business and to not give up on her future daughter-in-law yet.

When we made it to the house, I almost had a hard time finding somewhere to park because cars were lined up and down the street. Some belonged to people I recognized, while others didn't. I sent Ness a quick text to let him know that we were on our way in. Even though Mama Faye new about the party, we still wanted everyone to scream when she walked into her home.

As soon as we entered the door, Cassius was the first one to wobble up to Mama Faye in the darkened living room, running smack dab into her leg. His little baby talk was so cute as he reached his hands up and called out to his "Ganny." Mama Faye didn't get a chance to pick him up all the way before the lights were turned back on and everyone screamed, "Surprise!"

I looked around the room at all of the familiar faces then back to Mama Faye's. Tears were springing from her eyes, which caused me to turn my head and clear my throat. I became a little choked up seeing her so happy, but I didn't need everyone else seeing me cry.

"Welcome home, Fayetta," Ari said as she took Cassius from Mama Faye's arms and gave her a hug. "I was praying for you every day. Me and this little man right here," she said, tickling Cassius on his tummy, causing him to giggle and reach for his daddy. Ness walked up and kissed Mama Faye on her cheek then grabbed hold of Cassius.

"How you feelin, Ma? You think you're up to partying a little bit, or do you want to go lay down?"

She waved Ness off. "Boi, if ya don't get out of mi face wit' all that crazy talk. Mi been cooped up in that hospital bed fo' months. I want to talk to mi friends, eat some *good* Jamaican food, and drink some of that rum punch ya got ova there."

"I don't think—" Ness started to say but stopped when Mama Faye headed farther into the house, ignoring him completely.

"Man, just let her do her for a minute. I'm sure in a couple hours she'll be tired and ready to go to bed," I said.

Ness nodded his head. "Just make sure you keep an eye on her. If it looks like she's overdoing it, I'm going to shut this party down. I told you this was a bad idea anyway. We should've just waited until a few weeks from now. You know she's still a little weak."

I walked away from Ness and went to get a drink. He could be so worrisome sometimes, but I understood where he was coming from. Besides me, Mama Faye was the only living family member he had left in the States. Once she passed on, it would just be him.

"Hey, Cai man, how's it going?" Kong asked me, breaking me from my thoughts. "The last time I was here, I was towing your car to my shop. I guess since Ness isn't out there being Mr. Lover Man, y'all haven't had any car damage, huh?"

We shared a laugh. "Naw, everything's been good. Once he had Cassius and Ariana came into his life, he's been doing all right with himself," I said as we watched Finesse and Ari kiss each other then kiss Cassius.

Kong took a sip of his Kingston Lager then looked back at me. "Having a kid will do that to some people, change them for the better. What do you think it's going to do to you?"

I wasn't offended by his question because Kong knew about everything that had happened to me in the past six months. Because we grew up together in the neighborhood and were such good friends, I invested in his auto shop when I got my money. He gave it an upgrade and everything. All I wanted in return was for him to keep on giving back to the community and hooking up some of the young dudes with summer jobs to try to help keep them off of the streets.

"I don't even know what it will do to me. Other than stopping me from wanting to kill Alex's ass, I think that's about it," I answered.

My beer bottle was empty, so he reached into the ice bucket on top of the table and handed me another.

"Do you think the kid is really yours? And I'm only asking because you know how some of these bitches can be, especially when it's money involved. She already low-key tricked you once. You don't think she would do it again with more money on the line?"

I nodded my head. Kong wasn't the first person I'd had this conversation with. Ness and I talked about it the day after I came from the lawyer's office, when I found out that Alex was pregnant. We all knew she was a little on the crazy side, so I wouldn't put anything past her. That's why as soon as the baby was born, we were going to have a DNA test taken, just to make sure it was mine.

Kong and I stood by the alcohol table for a few more moments, just shooting the shit before I walked over to the buffet station and made me a plate. With so much to choose from, I didn't know where to start at first. There was escovitch fish and dough bread, jerk chicken, jerk beef ribs, Jamaican stew chicken, tuna cakes, ackee and saltfish, rice and peas, roasted lemon potatoes, beef patties, pork patties, and fried plantains. Once I got to the end of the table, I figured I wouldn't have enough room for dessert, but with choices like sweet potato pone, blue drawers, toto, and rum cake, I was most definitely coming back for samples.

As I ate my food and made small talk with family and friends, the front door opened and in walked Roderick, holding hands with a smiling Rima. When the door stayed open for a minute after they entered, I was hoping and praying that Audri would walk through. I had made sure to invite her via text and also sent word through Ari and Ness, but when Toby and Niecey came in and closed the door, my hopes of seeing Audri were thrown down the drain.

Surprisingly, Niecey and Toby fit right in with everyone, and this little party was going full swing. Mama Faye was having a good time and didn't seem to be the least bit sleepy. I scanned the crowded living room for Ness so that we could bring out the cake, but when my eyes connected with his, something else that kept causing his jaw to flex had his attention. When my eyes followed his line of sight, I wasn't the least bit shocked that he was looking at Rima and Roderick. They were so into filling up on each other that they didn't feel his heated gaze.

I was about to go check him before Ari did, but my phone vibrating in my pocket stalled me for a minute. It was a text message alert from the last person I expected to get one from. My heart felt like it was about to beat out of my chest.

MyLove: After having some time to think about the situation, Cai, I think it's best that we leave each other alone. You and I are so broken right now that I don't think we can ever be fixed. I'm sorry I couldn't make it to the party, and I hope Mama Faye isn't mad at me. Tell her I will talk to her soon and give her a welcome home gift before I go on my trip. Know that I will always love you, but we can never be. Please respect my decision and do not call or text me anymore. Love you always.

Totally forgetting about the disaster that was sure to happen between Ness, Rima, and Ari, I went to my old room and lay down on my bed. My stomach started to become queasy, and my head started to spin. It felt like my whole world had just come crashing down, and I didn't know if I was going to be able to come back from that.

I woke up from my nap to the sound of laughter. One voice I recognized, the other I didn't. After finding my phone and checking the time, I noticed I had been out for almost three hours. I had a text from Toby saying that he and Niecey had left to attend another party, a missed video chat from Finesse, and a gang of missed phone calls and voice mails from Alex. Not concerning myself with anything other than the two voices I kept hearing, I got up from the bed and headed toward the living room. Other than a few people from the Jamaican restaurant cleaning up their catering things, there was no sign of anyone from the party.

When I made it to the front, Mama Faye was on the couch, talking to a beautiful older woman whose face looked familiar. I tried to place where I'd seen her before, but I kept getting a blank. She looked to be in her early forties, much too young to be one of Mama Faye's bingo friends, but as they talked and sipped on their tea, I couldn't help but notice the way she seemed so familiar around Moms.

"Fayetta, these young people today don't know anything about love. You try to give them a little advice and they act as if you don't know what you're talking about."

Mama Faye nodded her head. "Mi tell Cairo and Finesse that all de time. Now, Ness, he listened and got himself a nice young gayl. Can't cook Jamaican food worth a damn, but her heart is strong. Not too many gayls would accept a baby like that. She's good for both my grands and great grands."

The beautiful mystery woman took a sip of her tea then placed her cup back on the table. She swiped her small hand across her forehead to move the bangs falling over her eye. I couldn't stop looking at her because some of her features reminded me of—

"Audrielle and Ariana are both phenomenal women, and it would take an extraordinary man to lead them down greater paths," she said, looking directly at me. "I think Finesse is the perfect match for Ariana, just like I think you are the perfect match for Audrielle." She stood up and walked over to me. Her arms stretched out, inviting me into a hug. "It's so nice to formally meet you, Cairo. I'm Sandra Freeman, Audrielle's grandmother, but everyone calls me Nana."

Nana. This was the same woman sitting at their family table at the auction and the same one who answered the door with Audrielle when I picked her up for our date. I embraced her in a hug and almost got turned on when her Flowerbomb perfume by Viktor & Rolf invaded my nostrils. She was so much more breathtaking up close. Her gaze was almost hypnotizing. This woman's presence and aura were commanding, sorta like Audri's when she walked into a room.

"I know you're probably wondering why I'm here, and I'm going to tell you why. But first things first, young man. What are your true intentions with my grandbaby?"

"Well, I . . ." Her directness kind of threw me off, causing me to stumble on my words.

"Speak up, boi. Mi taught ya betta than that."

I looked at Mama Faye and nodded my head then looked back into Nana's face. Her questioning gaze gave me the courage I needed to answer her question with conviction.

"Nana, to keep it all the way real with you, I'm in love with your granddaughter and want to be with her for the rest of my life. In order to take care of my family, I did something I should've thought about long and hard before acting on impulse. That morning I left Audri at her house after Dr. Blake showed up was the worst decision of my life. I've tried on numerous occasions to get us back on track, but every time it seemed like we would be in sync again, something or someone would come along and push us further apart."

Nana looked at me for a minute before she returned to her seat on the couch next to Mama Faye. Both women gave each other a knowing glance before they turned their eyes toward me.

"Cairo, I normally don't get into my grandbabies' love lives because I believe that we all need to experience love in the way that it's presented to us. If you choose to accept a love that hurts you, I only wish that you realize your mistake before it's too late, and if you choose to accept a love that stands by your side through good, bad, and confusing times, I hope you learn how to hold on to that love, to nourish it, and to never let it go. You and Audri have that type of love. I can see it in the way you look at her, and in the way she looks at you. She and I had a conversation last night where it seemed like she was ready to give up on that love. She's really hurt behind what went down between you two, but I believe that you still have a chance."

"But she sent me a text earlier—"

She raised her hand to cut me off.

"I know all about that shit. I told her stubborn ass not to send it, but I guess she did anyway. A text is the coward's way of trying to end things when you're trying to make yourself believe that something's not true."

One of the ladies from the restaurant came out with slices of rum cake. When she offered me one, I declined. Mama Faye and Nana, on the other hand, accepted their pieces and dug right in. A slight chill ran through my body because of the air conditioning that was on full blast. Goosebumps decorated my tattooed skin. I wanted to go back to the room and get my T-shirt, but my mind was on other things.

I stretched my body against the wall and crossed my arms over my chest in deep thought. Maybe I was giving up on this thing with Audri, and I had too easily. I knew it would be a long shot, but if Ari was willing to accept Finesse and Rima's baby and still be with him, then maybe Audri could do the same thing with me.

I needed to find a way to talk to her so that I could see for myself if she meant what she said in that message. Nana was right about one thing: Breaking up through text was the coward's way to do it. Audri knew if she told me that mess face to face, I would've seen right through that shit, even with her being mad at me. I turned around, still in my thoughts, and walked back to my old bedroom. After straightening the bed, putting my shirt back on, and grabbing my keys and jacket, I was headed to the door. Since Audri wasn't answering any of my calls, she'd have no choice but to answer her door because I planned to stay out there all night until she did.

"If you're looking for Audri, you might want to head on over to the new store. Tonight is the opening party, and she's been there all day trying to get things in order," Nana said before I was about to leave. "I was there earlier but came here to talk some sense into your cute little head and to meet your mother. Seems like she and I have a lot in common when it comes to you two."

I looked at Mama Faye, who smirked then took a sip of her tea. "Ya go on now and get my future daughter-in-law back. Mi told ya she and I have to discuss baby names."

Mrs. Freeman looked at Nana, and they both burst out laughing as if they knew something I didn't. Maybe Nana was on Audri's head about us having a baby, just like Mama Faye was on mine. I wasn't worried about anything that night, though, other than getting Audri back. If all went well, they might get that grandbaby sooner than later.

44

Audrielle

"Audrielle, do you mind if we get a picture for the upcoming feature in next week's issue?" Marcos, the sexy magazine editor of *Sneaker Freaker* asked. "We just need a few shots for the printed ad, as well as the spotlight we will have online."

I shook my head in agreement and went and stood by one of the Michael Jordan replica statues in the middle of the store. These things cost me a pretty penny, so I was going to show them off any chance that I got.

"All right now, Ms. Freeman, I'm going to take a few shots now. Try to give me a couple of pretty poses while I'm snapping, okay?" the photographer asked.

"That won't be hard for her to do at all," Marcos added, causing me to blush.

I looked down at the red off-the-shoulder crop top I had on. It was a pretty bold choice for me, being as my stomach wasn't all the way flat, but nonetheless, it looked good on me, especially after pairing it with my low-rise black skinny jeans and the custom black python Air Jordan 4s I had made specifically for this night.

My mother almost shitted on herself when she walked into the opening and saw me in this outfit. "Business owners need to look the part, Audri, and right now you're giving off employee instead of boss. Plus, you still need to work on those abs before you try to show them off to everyone. You've lost some weight, which is good, but you need to work on toning now," she had said.

After kissing my dad on the cheek and giving him a hug, I excused myself from where they were to mingle with my guests. I'd be damned if I was about to let her ruin that night for me, especially when I didn't need her help to open it.

After taking a few photos and dodging the flirtatious conversation I was sure Marcos was getting ready to start, I walked to the other side of the store and sat on one of the wooden benches, taking everything in. A lot of the shoes I'd ordered earlier in the week were on display against the wall and ready for purchase if anyone was interested. Instead of aisles to walk down, I had sneakers covering every wall in the store. I wanted my customers to walk in and be able to do a three sixty to see every pair of shoes we had to offer. Other merchandise like sports apparel, designer clothes, and accessories were stationed around the cash registers, which I strategically placed in the middle of the store. When the customer was ready to check out, I wanted them to be able to grab a pair of socks or a matching shirt with their purchase.

A waiter carrying a tray of champagne passed by, and I happily grabbed a glass. Taking my phone out of my pocket, I blew out a frustrated breath when I noticed my notification light wasn't blinking. I'd sent Cairo that message about us not seeing each other almost three hours earlier, and he had yet to respond. Not that I blamed him. I should've listened to Nana when she told me not to send it in the first place. But the damage had already been done, and I probably just made his decision to stay with Alex for the sake of their baby much easier.

As I sipped on the bubbly drink with a smile on my face, trying to mask my hurt, I watched as some of my guests mingled with one another in casual conversation, while others stood around looking at shoes or ogling the few pro basketball and football players that were in attendance.

UCLA and USC alums like Matt Barnes, Nick Young, King Harris, and Reggie Bush came out to support, and I really appreciated it. They even posed with me for the press when I cut the red ribbon.

I was just about to go check on things in the back of the store when there was a light tap on my shoulder. I turned around and came face to face with the last person I expected to see that night. My stomach, which was already feeling kind of queasy, started to do flips.

"Audri, I know that I'm like the last person you wanna see right now, but I couldn't let this night and accomplishment go by without stopping by and saying congratulations."

I looked Sarah up and down before I returned my glare to her face. I had to admit, she was looking fierce in her navy blue pantsuit and matching pumps. The big emerald studs hanging from her ears matched the necklace and bracelet she had on, as well as the scarf hanging from her neck. A few shades darker than Eli, her skin was as smooth as silk, adding to her undeniable beauty. The work she had done on her nose, eyelids, ears, lips, and cheeks added to her beauty, and I would never deny her that.

"Eli sends his congrats as well. He wanted to come too, but I thought it wouldn't be a good idea seeing as you finally filed for that divorce. I wasn't sure if you would want to celebrate with him in attendance."

I was still on mute as I sipped on the rest of my champagne and listened to her babble. Just like my mother, I wasn't about to allow her to ruin this night for me, so if she didn't hurry up and get to her point of being there, I'd have to get security involved.

"I get it, Audri. I get that you're mad at me, but at least say something, please. I never meant to hurt you or your relationship with Cairo. I was just asked a question, and I answered."

I didn't know why, but something clicked in my head at that moment, a question I'd been meaning to ask Sarah but never got the chance to because she kept ducking and dodging my calls.

"I only have one question for you, Sarah, and your answer to this question will determine where we stand in the friendship."

She nodded her head, telling me to go on.

"How do you even know Alex?"

She opened her mouth to say something, closed it, and then opened it again. "Her family does business with our firm. My husband and her father are good friends."

"And me and my marriage to your brother just happened to come up in casual conversation? Out of all of the things you two can talk about?"

Sarah blew out a frustrated breath. "Look, Audri, just be careful, okay? Alex is real sneaky and will do *anything* she has to do to get what she wants, including blackmail."

The way she said that last line seemed as if she was speaking from experience.

"I need to head home now if I don't want to start getting calls from the hubby and all." She laughed; I didn't. "Again, Audri, congratulations on the opening, and remember what I said." She turned to walk away but turned right back around. "You look hot tonight, by the way. I'm really feeling your new look and body. Whatever Cairo is doing or has done that has you glowing like you are is really working." And with that, she turned and disappeared into the crowd.

"Was that Sarah's big-mouth ass?" Rima asked as she and the rest of the crew came up behind me.

I'd been so busy with entertaining the bloggers, the media, celebrity guests, and customers, that I didn't have time to greet my family and friends when they arrived. Ness, Ari, Rima, Roderick, Toby, and Niecey had been there for almost two hours now, and this was my first time talking to them. I hugged everyone that surrounded me to give me love. As I looked around at all of their faces, I couldn't help but to feel the pang that shot through my heart when I thought about the only person who wasn't here to help me celebrate. Cairo.

As if on cue, the funny fluttery feeling I'd been getting in my stomach for the last few weeks started to go crazy, so much so that I started rubbing my hand up and down my belly.

"Audri, are you okay?" Ari asked as she stepped into my space.

I nodded my head. "Yeah, I'm good. My stomach is just doing that little thing I told y'all about."

"You need to stop being scared and go get that shit checked out. Since you're so sure that you're not pregnant, it might be something else. Something that needs to be looked at ASAP, especially since you've been sleeping with Eli's dog ass."

I rolled my eyes at Ari and shook my head. She could be so extra sometimes. But she was right, though. I needed to go to the doctor for a checkup. I'd been throwing up a little and having diarrhea for the last couple days. I was pretty sure it wasn't a sexually transmitted disease. It just might be a small case of food poisoning. At least that's what it was the last time I felt that way.

I'd just left clowning with Rima and them and was headed to the back of the store when a set of strong arms grabbed my waist from behind and pulled me through the side door and into the hallway that led to my office and security room.

"What the—"

"Shhh," Cairo said as he turned me around and pinned me against the wall. "I've been waiting for the perfect time to get you alone since I got here. Please just listen and let me talk."

I was speechless as I looked into those beautiful blue eyes. All I could do was move my head up and down and try to control my hormones and breathing. It had been weeks since I last saw him, and although I was mad at him, my body still reacted to his touch, presence, and scent.

Cairo released my arms and laced his fingers with mine. Blowing out a slow breath, he lowered his head to the side of my face and began to whisper in my ear.

"I don't know how many times we are going to end up in this space that we're in right now, but I promise I'm going to keep on chasing you until I make everything right. I wasn't lying to you when I told you that I loved you and wanted to spend the rest of my life with you. You are it for me, Audri, and I want you to know that once I take care of all this shit going on with Alex and everything, I'm coming for you. I'm coming for your heart, your soul, your love, and even your last name." He placed his hands on my belly, and the fluttering started up again. "I'm even coming for this womb. By the time I'm finished filling you up with babies, we will have a small tribe running around the house that I'm going to buy you and grow old with you in."

He grabbed both sides of my face and looked me in the eye. "All I need is for you to wait and give me the chance to make everything right. I swear I will live the rest of my life making up for all the pain I've caused you within the last year. I love you, Audrielle, and I will never stop coming for you."

I closed my eyes as he placed the sweetest kiss on my lips. I was sure the heat radiating through my body could be felt through his fingertips.

"Will you give me one more chance to make everything right, Audri? Will you wait and give me the opportunity to prove to you how much I love you?"

I bit down on my bottom lip and placed my forehead on his. As much as my heart, body, and mind wanted to scream yes, the pain of what happened the last time we were together and what Sarah said to me earlier kept popping up in my head.

"Be careful. Alex is real sneaky and will do anything she has to do to get what she wants."

I didn't think I could ever forgive Cairo if anything happened to me or anyone that I loved behind a crazy bitch that didn't know how to let go. I grabbed Cairo's hands, removed them from my face, and gently pushed him back.

"As much as I want to believe you, Cai, I can't. Especially with Alex having your baby now." I started to cry because the look on his face was one I'd never seen. He was disappointed in me. "You're going to have a little person who's going to need you way more than me, and maybe it's best if you try to make it work with the mother of your child."

"But, Audri . . ." he said with sad eyes.

"I meant everything I said in the text I sent you earlier, Cai." I lied, but he didn't have to know that. "Now please leave before I have to ask security to escort you out." I turned my face away from his piercing gaze and looked down at the ground.

He tried to grab my chin and turn me back to him, but I snatched away.

"Please go, Cai. Don't ruin this night for me by causing a scene, please."

Since he couldn't grab my face, he grabbed my hand. "I'ma leave, but you just be ready when the time comes. Like I said, I'm coming back for you and everything that already belongs to me. Including this." He pointed at my heart. "This." He pointed at my head. "And this." He pointed at my pussy.

When he finally let go of my hand and disappeared behind the door, I fell to the floor. The queasiness I had tried to ignore earlier came back and had me releasing everything I had in my stomach onto the floor.

"First thing Monday morning I'm headed to the doctor," I told myself.

The doctor came back into the room with a manila folder in her hand, as well as with a nurse who was pushing this big-ass monitor thing in behind her. My heart literally dropped down to the pit of my stomach.

Oh God, there's something wrong with me, I thought as my stomach started to do those flips again. Damn Rima and all that Chinese food she couldn't seem to get enough of. I knew when a restaurant went from having an A rating to a C there had to be some crazy things seriously going on. Now that my body was finally down to a size that I was comfortable with, I wasn't going to live long enough to flaunt it.

"So Ms. Freeman, we did some tests, and it's safe to say that anything that has to do with any type of food poisoning, STDs, or incurable diseases is not the issue. However, we did do one test that we didn't mention, which came back with some positive results."

My eyes started to water up, but I didn't want to have a major breakdown in front of the doctor or her nurse. I needed something to occupy the part of my brain that controlled my tear ducts, so I started looking around the small space, focusing my eyes on any and everything, like how many cotton balls were in the glass jar. I looked at the small, medium, and large boxes of latex gloves against the wall and tried to remind myself to grab a handful of them before I left. I even went so far as to look at the poster on the wall of the Mexican family playing on the grass at the park. I had no idea what the words on the board meant, but that didn't stop me from trying to figure it out.

"Uh, Ms. Freeman, did you hear me?" The doctor was waving her hands in my face.

"I'm sorry, Dr. Jacques, what did you say?"

She stared at me with a concerned look on her face before she opened her mouth again. "I asked, do you remember when your last menstrual period was?"

"Um, I actually just had it about a week ago. Why?"

Dr. Jacques looked back at the nurse and whispered something to her, causing her to leave the room for a minute.

"Are you sure it was a full-blown menstrual period, or was it just spotting?"

"It was full-blown like it usually is. Light bleeding the first day, then real heavy on the second and third day, back to light the last two days."

At that moment, the nurse returned with a long, light gray stick covered in plastic. She removed the device from its wrapping then connected it to the big screen thing she had pushed in earlier.

"Do you mind if I call you Audri?" the doctor asked, and I shook my head no. "Well, Audri, when all of the tests we took according to your symptoms came back negative, I was kind of confused, until I ordered the nurse to run one more test just for the hell of it."

"And what test was that?"

"A pregnancy test."

"Oooookay," I let out slowly. "That should've come back negative too, seeing as I've had my period every month since the last time I had sex."

"And when was the last time you had sex?"

"About a month ago," I answered, thinking about the time Eli and I had sex the night he came over to my house unexpectedly. I was in my feeling again about Cairo and ended up letting him ease away the pain like the few times before. I had promised myself that night would be the last time I ever used Eli for an escape. He was beginning to become too comfortable with our arrangement, and that wasn't what I wanted, especially when I had finally turned in the signed divorce papers to my lawyer a few days prior.

"Did you guys use protection?" I guess from my silence and my eyes rolling to the back of my head, she had figured out what I just happened to remember.

We didn't use protection at all. Damn it.

"Are you trying to tell me that I'm pregnant right now?"

She nodded her head. "I am. The pregnancy test we did came back positive. The blood work we took earlier confirmed it as well. I was going to do an ultrasound on your belly at first, but after you told me that you've been having your period regularly, I decided to do a vaginal ultrasound, so we can get a better view of how far along you are."

As I sat up and prepped myself to be poked and prodded vaginally, I couldn't do anything but laugh. Every time I thought I was finally getting rid of having Eli in my life, he popped up someway or somehow and turned it upside down.

I watched as the doctor rolled the condom on the long stick then pushed my legs apart. When she eased the instrument into me, my walls immediately clamped down on it and started to release some juices. I became a bit embarrassed at the way my shit was reacting and tried to shut my legs and move up on my seat a little.

"Just relax and don't worry about that. It's a normal reaction when something is being inserted into your vagina," the doctor said as if she were reading my thoughts again.

I could feel her go a little deeper as she pushed some buttons on the monitor's keyboard and scrunched her face at whatever she was looking at.

"Is something wrong, Doc?"

"Uhhhh, when was the last time you said you had sex, Audri?"

"About a month ago. Why?"

She removed the instrument from me and gave it to the nurse, removed her gloves, then walked over to the sink and washed her hands.

She returned to my side and pushed the monitor over to where I could see the screen fully.

"The reason why I asked you that is because according to the pictures I just took of the baby, there's no way you're only a few weeks pregnant." She pointed to a few shots on the screen to show me. "According to the measurements I just took of your little girl, you're about thirty-seven weeks."

"Thirty-seven weeks?" I had to do the math in my head quickly.

There are four weeks in a month. Four times five would be twenty weeks. Six . . . twenty-four. Seven . . . twenty-eight. Eight . . . thirty. . . .

"Nine months! Are you telling me that I'm nine months pregnant?" I didn't mean to yell at her, but I was in shock.

"You're actually a little over nine months. You're at the time of pregnancy where we would want first-time mothers to be delivering their child. Anything over thirty-eight weeks could be a health risk to the baby."

"You . . . you have to be wrong. There's no way I can be pregnant, let alone ready to deliver. I didn't have any symptoms, and my period came every month like clockwork. And not only that, but I've actually been losing weight instead of gaining." I grabbed my stomach. "And look at my belly. Does this look like the stomach of a nine-month pregnant woman?" Because of the way I had been eating, I wasn't alarmed when I had seen my small pouch start to form again. I just figured when I got back from my vacation I'd start to do my everyday workouts like before.

"It's normal for some women to have their menstrual cycle every month during pregnancy. It actually happens a lot. The fact that you didn't have any symptoms like morning sickness or food cravings is also normal. That little flutter you thought was your stomach flipping was actually the baby moving. And as far as the weight loss, that actually is a good thing, being as you are still slightly overweight. We do normally recommend that patients who are already overweight when they get pregnant go on a healthy diet anyway. The possibility of getting diabetes and preeclampsia is way higher when you have all that extra weight on you," she explained as she put some stick on my stomach that was attached to another device she held in her hand. "You hear that? That's your baby's heartbeat, and it's pretty strong."

I sat there and listened to what sounded like the sweetest noise I'd ever heard, and I cried. I, Audrielle Marie Freeman, was about to be a mother. I couldn't wait to get out of there so that I could call Rima, Ariana . . . hell, even—

"Oh, shit!" I screamed.

"What's wrong? Did your water just break? Are you feeling any pain, Audri?" Doctor Jacques asked as she hurried back to my side. She had just gotten off her cell phone, talking to God knows who.

"I gotta go." Not caring that she and the nurse were in there, I pulled the hospital gown off and put my clothes back on, grabbed the rest of my belongings, and headed toward the door.

"Wait, Audri!" the doctor screamed after me. "I just got off of the phone with Labor and Delivery at St. Mary's. I already explained to them how far along you are. We need to get you and the baby hooked up to the monitors to keep an eye on the stress level. More than likely, you will have to be induced, so get ready to become a mother either tonight or tomorrow."

I just waved her off as I hurried out of the back room and into the full lobby. A million things were going through my mind, and having a baby right now was not one of them. St. Mary's would just have to wait until my water broke before they would see me. I needed a few days to wrap my mind around everything I had just found out anyway. And I needed to figure out whose baby I was actually carrying.

Not paying attention to what was in front of me, I ran smack dab into the back of something hard and soft at the same time. Before I could fall flat on my ass, a pair of familiar arms stretched out and grabbed me.

"Cai? What are you doing here?" I nervously asked as I finally looked up into the bluish-green eyes that I couldn't seem to get out of my mind.

He looked me up and down before he pulled me into a hug. I swear my body melted into his the minute he engulfed me in his embrace. His dreads, which were loosely hanging all around his head, brushed against my shoulders, causing me to shudder a little. I closed my eyes and inhaled his deep masculine scent and drifted off to a whole different world, one where only he and I existed, and nobody or nothing else mattered except our love and now our family.

Thinking about the baby I would be delivering any day now had my brief little dream come to an end. A smile spread across my face as I imagined the proud look that would be on his face once I told him the good news.

"Cai, we need to talk. Do you have a minute?"

The look he had in his eyes was nothing but pure love for me, and I was hoping that he could see the same look in mine; however, our moment was instantly broken up when the most annoying voice I ever heard started to screech at the top of her lungs.

"Really, Cairo? Really? I can't leave you alone for two minutes to go relieve the bladder that your son won't stop pushing up against before you're hugging up on the next bitch?"

I shook my head. I was so caught up in the fairytale ending Cairo and I should've had that I forgot that quickly he already had a baby on the way with her ass.

Ignoring her, Cairo looked down at me and grabbed my chin in his hand and wiped away the lonely tear that I didn't even feel escape.

"I can't talk right now, but please believe me when I say everything isn't how it seems. Just call me in about an hour or two and we can meet up somewhere, okay?" he said.

"Audri!" Alex laughed. "Wow, girl, I almost didn't recognize you from behind. You lost a little weight. It looks good on you, don't get me wrong, but if you ever want to catch another man close to my husband, you need to lose about twenty more pounds. That way, when you get lucky enough to carry his baby, you can still look good like me," she bragged as she stood there in her strapless white maxi dress, rubbing her perfectly round belly. Even with the big-ass dodge ball under her dress, I couldn't deny her beauty. The glow she had warmed her skin and brought out her gorgeous brown eyes, while the little weight she had gained actually complimented her small frame. With her hair in a loose ponytail and hardly any makeup on, she could've easily been ready to grace the cover of any magazine.

I had just opened my mouth to respond when the most horrific pain shot through my body. My mouth hung open as my high-pitched scream seemed to make everything around us freeze. Not even two seconds later, a warm liquid that made me feel like I'd just peed on myself shot down my legs.

"Audri, baby, what's wrong? Are you hurt?" Cai asked frantically.

I tried to shake my head, but another sharp pain ripping through my body had all of my bodily reactions at a standstill.

"Someone get a doctor! Call 911!" I heard a few bystanders yell as I doubled over for the third time and fell to the floor.

"Audri, honey, I need you to breathe," Dr. Jacques said. I didn't even see where she came from. "I knew I should've sent you over to St. Mary's by ambulance. I had a feeling this would happen."

"What's wrong with her?" Cairo asked, holding my hand as he knelt by my side.

Being the one who wanted to break the news to him, I held my hand up to stop Dr. Jacques from answering his question.

"I'm apparently pregnant and about to have this baby any second."

He looked down at my tummy, which did not show any signs of pregnancy, then looked back up at me. His beautiful eyes became misty, and the hurt look in them damn near broke my heart. "You're having his baby, Audri?"

"No, Cai—" Another contraction was about to hit, and I groaned. "I'm having yours."

To Be Continued in

Black Love, White Lies 2

Coming in 2017